CARL HUBERMAN

In those days, the town was brand new and the heaters smelt like nothing on earth.

CARL HUBERMAN

EMINENT DOMAIN

PAN BOOKS

First published 1996 by Macmillan

This edition published 1997 by Pan Books
an imprint of Macmillan Publishers Ltd
25 Eccleston Place, London SW1W 9NF
and Basingstoke

Associated companies throughout the world

ISBN 0 330 34718 7

1 3 5 7 9 8 6 4 2

A CIP catalogue record for this book is available from the British Library

Photoset by Parker Typesetting Service, Leicester
Printed and bound in Great Britain by
Mackays of Chatham PLC, Chatham, Kent

To my wife Anne for her enthusiasm

He who pays the piper calls the tune

PROVERB

HOT

The great questions of our day cannot be solved by speeches and majority votes . . . but by iron and blood.

BISMARCK

1

Kent Hollis sat up and stretched. Morning. Good sleep. He'd needed it. He clambered out of his black satin sheets and walked to the toilet and peed. Looking around the black tiled floor, he was glad to see they had finally cleaned up the mess from a couple of evenings before. The girl had bled like a pig.

Stepping into a pair of boxer shorts, he made his way through the Winnebago Elante to the kitchen area. While he fried some Canadian bacon and duck eggs on the black hob and perked some coffee, he used his Braun electric shaver on his thin stubble. Finished, he flipped on the TV and swigged from a carton of freshly-squeezed grapefruit juice, savouring the pith as it caught between his perfect teeth. News was much the same as it had been for weeks.

There was another war brewing in Africa, the place looking like it was ripe for another carve-up and a field day for mercenaries. Was a time he'd have given serious thought to playing a part – he was still an avid reader of *Soldier of Fortune* – but he had his duties to perform. Not that he gave a flying fuck about duty, but the perks were unmatchable anywhere, even in some wasted baboon backwater where the only rule is there ain't no rules as long as the news cameras aren't around.

Some cartoons came on, and he finished wolfing his food watching Little Beenie and Jambo beating the shit out of each other. Why, he wondered, if computer animation was so damn good these days, didn't the little fuckers bleed now and again? Give it some realism.

Breakfast over, he returned to his black bedroom and dressed in his Nike jogging gear. The red phone had been quiet for eight days now and he was getting a little bored. He put in his Walkman ears, tuned in to a disco revival station, clipped the player to his waistband and left his trailer.

The weather outside was perfect. Always was, in the Solardome. He looked around the tiered ranks of empty seats. Thousands of them, in blue and red and yellow and white plastic, all folded up as if on sentry duty, stared down at him. Seventy-four thousand in all, and not one had been home to a sports or rock fan's butt in months. He'd asked for the Clinger Solardome as a joke, and they'd given him it anyway. Just like that – no arguments. They gave the owners some bull about a super *legionella* outbreak and had the place closed. Public-health hazard; tests still being conducted. Cheaper to lose some weeks' revenue than fight lawsuits from any ass-wipe who so much as got a cold after seeing the Clinger Coyotes or U2. Then they'd hauled in his forty-foot RV, parked it on the thirty-yard line and posted guards around the outside of the giant building to make sure the only people who got in were people Hollis wanted to see. Some of them he even let leave. Some.

Three months he'd been here. Hadn't felt lonely once. When he wanted company, he got it: whoever he wanted, whenever he wanted. Perks. Went with his job. In fact he could do just about any damn thing he pleased as long as he carried out his work and didn't ask too many questions. Like were there any others like him? He still didn't know. Maybe there were none, maybe a hundred; he was curious but not so curious as to jeopardize all this just for a peek at any competition.

He started running the perimeter of the field, the smell of the fresh grass as wonderful as ever. As a kid he'd lived in the country and he'd always liked that early summer morning smell. The grass had been another of his off-the-cuff demands. Tear up the plastic shit, put down real grass, he'd said. Zip, three days later it was done. They'd even brought in some shrubs in tubs and real birds, to make it more homey. Madness. When he had shot the last of the birds, they'd installed tapes instead. That was better; he could always switch the damn twittering off when it got too much.

He cut across the field, faked a few passes. Maybe he'd let them play a game again some time. Maybe he'd even let in a few spectators.

The Bee Gees were playing in his ears. Good. He liked the Bee Gees. 'Tragedy'. An oldie but goldie. Loved that high-pitched voice. Was it Barry or Robin? He pulled out one of his ear speakers and started singing along, enjoying the sound of his own voice in the vast emptiness of the building. Hey, what the hell, let's get some *real* sound in here. He stopped and shouted up at the closed roof, his voice small and distant.

'Get me the Bee Gees on the speakers. Now.'

Twenty seconds later and the Solardome was reverberating to a segue from 'Tragedy' into 'Jive Talking'. Ace. Music for the feet. He started off, running again, trying to time his steps to the beat, but found the song's stutter threw him, so he gave up.

After a couple of laps he took a rest, checked his respiration. Good as ever. Thirty-three years old, hundred and eighty pounds, and as good as anyone fifteen years younger, even if he'd have to start dyeing his greying hair the blond it had always been previously. Thinning, too, but he had one of those faces that could take a receding hairline without looking like a buffoon. Still, who'd laugh at him now?

He leaned back against the guard-rail near the players' entrance in the southeast corner, and hawked a wad of spit onto the grass. That'd be gone as soon as he left the 'Dome. Ha. They'd wipe his ass if he asked. Look at that little Swedish girl he'd asked for – and got, naturally. She'd *licked* his ass clean. Pretended to like it, too. Asked for more. Silly bitch. She couldn't pretend to like the pain though, could she?

He started running again, smiling at the memory. She'd had cute tits when he'd first stripped her. He wondered how bad the scars would be now. Maybe he'd ask for her back, for a repeat performance. He could just imagine the look on her face . . .

What a fucking life!

Third circuit complete, he heard the urgent beeping of the red telephone. Shit. Another lap and he'd answer it. They couldn't complain. As long as he answered it eventually, they would be as nice as pie.

Two laps later – fuck 'em – he jogged back into the black Winnebago. Inside and out, it had been painted black at his request. He knew they called it the Black Hole behind his back but he didn't mind. It all added to his rep. It had been another of his little tests, but even he found it a bit oppressive. Maybe he'd get them to change it. Change the whole mobile home. Maybe something bigger, with a jacuzzi. Yeah, a jacuzzi.

He picked up the intercom to the Solardome control room.

'Rain. I want rain.'

No one answered. They didn't waste their breath.

He stripped naked and stepped outside. The beeping had stopped: they knew he'd heard it and that he would be pissed if they annoyed him too much. Two minutes later it rained. God knows what it had cost them to install the sprinklers up there. Still, didn't he earn it all?

As the boss man had said, that one time he had deigned to speak to Hollis face to face, the people he sent him to love were a threat to the integrity of the USA, and his talents were 'virtually priceless'. Well, he'd certainly held the fucker to *that* description, what with the 'Dome and the Winnebago and all, but even Hollis knew there had to be a limit – or someone cheaper – so he was wary not to overstep the mark; but, as it still looked like a sellers' market, he reckoned he had the edge. For now.

Thoroughly refreshed by the artificial downpour, he grabbed a towel and, as he dried himself to K.C. and the Sunshine Band's 'That's the Way I Like It', he finally condescended to answer the phone.

'Good morning, Mr Hollis,' said the familiar soft male voice. 'I trust you slept well?'

'Uh-huh, uh-huh,' he grunted in time to the music. 'Stick it. What is it?

'Town called Riva. West of the state. She's a waitress in a diner.'

'A waitress? What are you handing me?'

'I'm handing you another mission, Mr Hollis. As per your contract.'

'Okay, okay. The diner's name?'

'The Stop Inn. It's the only one in town. She'll be there all day.'

'A waitress? Sounds like she's a *real* threat.'

'You know the deal, Mr Hollis. Your transport's outside in the north parking lot. Do what you like, but make sure you . . . love her.'

Hollis slammed the phone down. Shit. He might enjoy his work, but it sure as hell looked like they were beginning to take him for granted. Treating him like some fucking soldier. A *waitress*, for Chrissakes?

Still, shouldn't grumble. Get to it, Kent. Quickest started, soonest finished. Momma had said that, and momma had always been right. Always. After all, hadn't she helped him get this job in a million? Besides, when he came back, he could ask to see some catalogues on mobile homes. Maybe even the American Eagles . . .

Ten minutes later Hollis was strapped into a helicopter flying southwest, Earth Wind and Fire boogieing through his Walkman.

2

The chopper dropped Hollis a mile out of town, after a ninety-minute flight, and waited for him to return.

A fifteen-minute walk in a hotter than usual October sun brought him into Riva, where the Stop Inn turned out to be a real crappy diner – but it was right at home in crappy Riva. The town couldn't have offered more than two thousand people and, judging by the specimens Hollis saw on his walk in, most of them looked to be over sixty. It was like a retirement colony for people who couldn't afford retirement.

He passed the sheriff's office, two general stores – both, quaintly, called 'Jack's' – and a garage with two prehistoric pumps cowering under the narrow canopy. The sun was up, and it was hot. Texas hot. Ain't none hotter, ain't none finer, as long as you got cold beer, a warm woman and something to do. Riva looked like it missed on all three counts, and then some. He crossed the dusty main street to the diner, stopping in the middle of the road to survey the scene.

It was like an abandoned movie set. Any minute the James Gang could come shootin' and shoutin' up the street, or Warren Oates would storm into town in a raggedy old Jeep, swigging on a bottle of cheap tequila, with the hots for some señorita from south of the border who'd give him more than a paper donkey to remember her by. Those were the days, if ever those days were like that, but Hollis couldn't help thinking that, whatever attractions the old anarchic past could offer, nothing could match what he had now. He was one lucky sonofabitch. Good old momma, if only she'd known what she had really been doing all those years . . .

He stepped back as an ancient Dodge pick-up rattled by, a scruffy hound in the back yarfing at him halfheartedly as it pulled into the gas station. Not surprisingly, an old guy got out of the truck, and another old guy started shugging gas into its rusted tank. The dog hobbled down and took a leak against one of the pumps. Shit, even the dogs were old in Riva. He looked back at the diner. Funnily enough, he was hungry. Loving always gave him an appetite.

It was a single-storey affair about fifty feet long, its central glass and screen doors flanked by four large windows, two on each side, that rose from knee height up to a sloping pitch roof and its antique neon logo. He could see that the establishment had now been reduced to the STO NN. Somehow he knew that this place was not going to be a centre of culinary excellence.

He walked through the door and into a bastard child of Rockwell and Hopper: mid-century Middle America with tooth decay. A world passed by – and the world grateful for it. Everything was wood, including the counter, tables and chairs. Food would probably taste the same too. Chances were the old Grammo jukebox was there just to drown out the sound of roaches screaming as they got fried up with the burgers and hash.

The place was empty apart from a waitress and some guy singing tunelessly out back in the kitchen. He walked up to the counter, parked himself on a stool and dropped his pack on the floor. A little cloud of dust rose up, motes sparkling in the harsh streams of light that managed to cut through the grimed windows. The place, oddly enough, didn't smell of food or grease, but of damp. No, not damp – rot. Yes, the place must be riddled with dry rot. And termites too, most likely. Wonder it hadn't been shut down, but then who'd bother coming out here to check?

The waitress, dressed in a light blue dress with a yellow striped apron and scuffed brown flats, walked over to him chewing gum, a pencil pushed behind her ear like it had grown there. She was somewhere in her thirties, skinny, her hair dyed blonde, with brunette roots showing. She had a sharp face, like all the corners had been chipped off. The harsh light and deep shadows in the diner did nothing to flatter her.

'Waddyawant?' she said, her voice deep and hoarse, her accent pure Lone Star.

'Some of that coffee,' he said, nodding at the Kona. 'Make sure it's black and strong.'

'Ain't none stronger,' she said without interest, pouring him a cupful. 'Food?'

He checked the menu. If they couldn't spell their food right – chilly, bluebery pie, shaikes – chances were they couldn't cook it right either. Best to play safe.

'Scrambled eggs, toast.'

'Coming up. Jack! Chicken brains and burnt sheets!' The woman noticed Hollis's surprised expression.

'Little joke. Keeps us happy.'

'Little things . . .'

'What?'

'Little thin. This coffee's a little thin.'

It wasn't. It tasted like stain remover.

'All we got, bud. Anything else?'

'Got a paper?'

'You think this is a newsstand?'

'Have you got one? Please?'

She passed him a two-day-old *Dallas Times*. Hollis flipped to the shares and checked his stock. It didn't really matter whether they had gone up or not, he'd never be poor, but he liked to think he had a knack for the market.

He hadn't. They'd dropped over thirteen points between them. He slapped the paper down in anger and spun on his stool to look through the window at the dusty street outside. It wasn't worth the effort.

Christ, he could have sat at this seat and seen the same empty street and the same empty faces, if and when they walked by, any day for the last – what? hundred years. More. What do people do out here for fun? Do they know what fun is? Well, in a few minutes from now he'd be showing them. Maybe that'd perk up their lives a tad.

An old man with a grey beard so grizzled it looked like he'd rented it on the cheap came in, nodded in Hollis's direction, settled his obviously weary legs in a window seat and scanned the menu.

'Hi, old timer, how's it hanging?' said Hollis with his most ingratiating smile.

'It's just hanging, dammit.'

Hollis laughed. Rare for him. 'Any action?'

'Two dogs fucking up by the grocery store. Guy selling washing machines got a flat; he's changing it. You'd almost think it was Saturday.'

'That exciting, huh?'

The woman dumped his plate of food in front of him, for

all the world as if customers were an inconvenience. They probably were in this backwater. Hollis gave it a glance. It looked as bad as he'd thought it would be. He turned back to the old man. He reminded him of his pop before he got killed in the plane crash.

'You lived here long?' said Hollis.

'All my life, if'n you can call it living.'

'So why stay?'

'Why leave?'

'See the sights, check out the cities, travel the country.'

'Dust looks the same anywhere you go, son. Where you from?'

'Clinger.'

'Went to Clinger once.'

'And?'

'Got robbed. Didn't see no reason to go back.'

'Fair enough.'

The woman brought a plate of apple pie and ice cream and a cup of tea over to the old man, then sat down with him. Neither of them spoke while the old man ate his food slowly and methodically, as if unsure whether his few teeth would hold out.

Hollis reluctantly returned to his own food. Clearly eating and talking at the same time were considered a waste of valuable energy in Riva.

He pushed his scrambled eggs around with his fork. They looked like they'd come out of a carton. Mind you, in this heat, any chicken was likely to end up fried before it set to laying. Hollis laughed again. A fly buzzed past his ear on its way to the insectocutor. One harsh *phutz* and it joined a hundred others, scattered in the hungry pan of the electric trap. That could well have been the highlight of the day for any Riva resident quick enough to catch it.

Hollis looked up into the narrow mirror behind the counter. He could see the woman eyeing him. He wondered if she knew. They never did, never suspected. Made his job all that much easier and this sullen bitch would be a pleasure to off.

He cracked a piece of toast and dipped half of it into his eggs, then licked it clean. He enjoyed his work best when there was an audience, but in this one-horse town you wouldn't draw a crowd if Jesus Christ was coming back and he'd given thirty days' notice. Looking at the old man gumming his way through his pie, he suddenly felt sorry for the old coot, if sorry was the right word. He *did* remind him of his father, though Hollis's memories were based on a smell of whisky and trips in the backs of cars at night and photographs his momma had shown him, warning him of the many bad things men do. He doubted very much that his father had ever done anything as bad as he himself did, but he also doubted he'd ever had as much fun, especially not with his momma.

He found the old memories flooding back, just as they always did when he was asked to love. Of course, he had done it without bidding at first. Lots of times, nearly thirty in fact, until they'd caught him. Then they'd made him the deal, after they got him out of the execution chamber. He'd have agreed to ream out the President for all eternity if it meant he could keep on breathing. Then, when they'd spelled out the deal and he'd tested their veracity by icing that doctor, well, heaven had just come right down here to earth. That was four years since, and things had just kept on getting better and better.

He pushed the plate away and played idly with his coffee.

He wondered how he'd do it. Quick or slow? Would he take his clothes off? He honestly didn't know. Whatever he did, he'd have to do it in the diner. He wondered if he'd let the cook go.

He'd heard him singing, but hadn't seen him, so he stood up and edged his way along the counter until he could see into the kitchen at the back. Surprise, surprise, the guy must have been sixty if he was a day. Black too, and busy scraping away at a griddle as dark as himself.

A nigger. Hollis had no reason to like niggers, but then he had no reason to hate them. He neither loved nor hated anyone, except his mother of course. Fuck it, he'd push the old coon out just as he started. Simpler that way. And he'd make it quick. This place was getting on his nerves. Yeah, ice her quick, get in the chopper, and in a couple of hours he'd be back in Clinger doing anything he wanted. He'd been getting hard-ons lately watching a chick who reported sports on Channel 8. A Chink. He wondered if he could meet her. No harm in asking . . .

He noticed the old guy was finished, and was fishing in his pocket for change.

'S'okay, old timer,' offered Hollis. 'I'll take care of it. Least one of us will have enjoyed the food. You have yourself a good day.'

'Well, thanks, son. I ain't about to be all polite and say no. Money's tight, best of times. Maybe I'll see you around tomorrow. You can buy me lunch.'

'Maybe, maybe. You take care, y'hear.'

The old man waved vaguely as he left, and let the door crash shut behind him.

The woman let out a big sigh and cleared up his crockery and walked back round the counter.

'That'll be $3.80.'

'The food may be shit but at least your prices are funny.'

'Wise guy. And that'll be $3.50 for *your* stuff.'

'Stuff's about the word for it.'

The woman took his near-full plate and emptied the contents into a large bin by the door into the kitchen. Hollis could hear the buzzing of happy flies from where he sat. Hygiene was obviously a low priority in these parts. The waitress handed the plates through to the black cook, then came out, perched herself on a stool by the end of the counter, and started reading *today's* newspaper.

That decided it for Hollis. She had deliberately given him an old paper, the bitch. Just like momma: no matter how polite you asked, you didn't get nothing unless she wanted you to have it.

Hollis stood up, stretched, and slowly surveyed what was to hand. The woman deserved something inventive, but what? There were lots of knives, glasses, bottles, even the spikes for holding orders. Ah, now there was something he hadn't tried in a while . . .

He slipped off his thin white cotton jacket and opened his shirt a couple of buttons. He liked to be able to move when he loved. He walked over to the door, flipped the CLOSED sign so it faced the outside, and pulled down the shade. The four large windows remained open to the noon sun, but it was the gesture that counted. And it worked.

'Hey, boy, what are you doing?'

'Boy? I like it. Keep it up, momma.'

The waitress was suddenly scared. Hollis could smell it. A

mixture of sweat and piss and warm blood, just oozing out of her armpits and cunt and asshole. Already the bubbles would be starting in her stomach juices, and her bowels would be twisting, knowing something was wrong. He walked slowly towards her flexing his back, aware his muscles would be looking beautiful in his short-sleeved shirt.

He was only a couple of steps from the counter, smiling. Her mouth would now be dry and her head would be tight.

'What . . . what . . . ?' she managed to croak.

Her tongue would be sticking to her teeth and her eyes would be blurring. She'd have to start blinking – and there she went, like she had dust in her eyes – and then there'd be the shaking, of course, starting in the hands and the knees, and then her breathing rate would increase as real *fear* took hold and adrenalin was let loose to run round her body, desperately pleading with her to do something, *anything*, to release the unwanted tension. And then she'd *change*. In this case, she'd put on twenty pounds, her hair would grey, her face lose all make-up. And there – *yes!* – it had happened.

Magic.

'Jack, come here quick,' she managed to say, her voice an octave higher and sounding solid Nebraska, never taking her eyes off Hollis, who was now standing by the counter.

He watched the kitchen door as the old guy hobbled into view, looking first at the woman, then over at Hollis. His frown was almost comical.

'I don't want no trouble here,' said the black man in a high-pitched voice. 'This is a respectable—'

'This dump wouldn't be respectable if you exorcised it, Mr

Jack. Now, I'm gonna give you one chance, and one chance only, old man. Go. Now.'

The cook looked over at the woman and his hand started to stray towards a rack of knives. Hollis saw the movement, but simply stared at the man without changing his expression.

Realizing the futility of opposition, the old man mumbled, 'Sorry, Ida,' then stumbled through the narrow kitchen and out the back door, letting it slap shut like a rifle shot.

'Now we're all alone. And your name ain't Ida, is it? It's Helen, ain't it? My momma's name was Helen, and you sure look like a Helen to me. Now, momma, tell me what we should do,' Hollis said.

'You come near me, boy, and I'll cut you.'

From somewhere the woman had picked up a knife. Ten inches long, it glinted in the dusty sunlight like a sword in the rain.

Hollis pulled a Colt .38 out of his pocket and shot the woman in the hand. The knife spun away over her head in an arc of blood. She didn't scream. Momma never did.

'On your knees, momma – on your knees. Your boy wants to show how much he loves you.'

The woman started to protest, so Hollis shot her in the wrist of the same hand. Hugging her wounded arm to her stomach and biting her bottom lip to stop from crying out, she sank off the stool and squatted down on her knees.

'Lie down on your back, arms above your head, momma. Let your Kent see you all laid out nice and simple so he can love you his best.'

The woman did as she was told, her eyes wide with shock.

Swiftly Hollis extracted two ice picks from his pack and

slammed them down, one after the other, into her outstretched hands, effectively pinning her to the floor.

'You're gonna die, momma, and it's gonna hurt, just like you hurt me all those times, and then you'll know just how much your boy really loves you.'

'But I'm . . . I'm not your . . . mother . . .'

'Oh yes, you are. You can't hide from me. I love you, momma. I love you so much it *hurts*. Just like you taught me all those times.'

He slapped her face, then hopped over the counter to the wall-mounted water-heater. There he drew off a jugful of steaming water and walked back round to her. Without speaking he pulled down her lower jaw, inserted the spout of the metal jug into her mouth and slowly poured two pints of near-boiling water down her throat.

She tried to scream, but soon her throat was a bubbling bloody froth and speech was out of the question.

He then filled the jug with cold water and poured it over her face to revive her.

'Enjoy your drink, momma?'

The woman couldn't hear him now. She was coughing and hacking blood over her face and chest, desperately trying to draw breath through a throat that was slowly dissolving into mush. She didn't see or care that Hollis had grabbed a large carving knife.

He knelt down beside her and slowly slicing open her dress exposed her stretch-marked white belly. Then he simply sliced it open as easily as he would an envelope and pulled the skin, viscera and intestines up and out to one side.

He leaned over the woman and looked her in the face as she started retching and jerking.

'Bye bye, momma. I love you – you know that, don't you? You must do by now. No matter how many times I kill you, I'll never tire of it, and neither will you. That's what you taught me, momma: love and pain are the same thing. It hurts to love, and to love you have to hurt, and I love you so, momma. I love you so . . .'

He leaned closer and kissed her bloody, pulped lips, then thrust his thumbs into the orbits of her skull until he felt her pupils rupture and warm liquid smear his skin.

He leaned down again to her ear. 'You still in there, momma? Hello, hello, can anyone hear me?'

A deep moaning came from somewhere inside the woman, and her thrashing legs beat a tremulous drum solo on the dusty wooden floor. Hollis started laughing.

'That's it, momma. Get into it. Enjoy it. *Enjoy* it.'

The woman suddenly stopped twitching, but then started hissing. The sound irritated Hollis, so he grabbed her hair and pulled her sightless head back up and thrust the blade up into her jaw and felt it slide in real easy for four or five inches and then meet resistance. He pulled harder on her hair and put his shoulder into the upward thrust of the blade, and was rewarded with the sight of steel coursing through the bloody pulp of her empty right eye socket and on up into her frontal lobe. And then she died. His momma died. And it felt so good. He felt it, her life force zapping out of her and its exit turning her cold and loveless.

Hollis ejaculated in his pants and laid her down gently, kissing her scarred lips one last time.

'That's how much I love you, momma. Sorry I couldn't make it last any longer. I hope you liked it.'

Hollis slid back on his buttocks, until he could feel the

warm wood of the counter against his back, and caught his breath. She'd put up some fight. Momma usually didn't. She always seemed sort of – what? – surprised, even astonished, that her Kent could get up the nerve to love her all the way. Well, she only had herself to thank. She had been one hell of a teacher. One *hell* of a mother too.

Hollis checked his watch. He'd been in the diner just over twelve minutes. Time to go. Even the shitkickers round here should have heard the shots. He snagged his pack and slung it over his shoulder, but as he started for the door it slammed open and a sweaty fat man in a grey sheriff's uniform ran in, pointing something at him. Hollis guessed immediately what the bulky object was.

'You, boy!' screamed the sheriff, terror shielded by reflective polaroids and the bluster that a handful of gun gives a man with a badge. 'Don't move a fucking inch!'

Hollis froze, then slowly raised his arms above his head.

'It's okay, sheriff, I'm not going to do anything rash. If you'll look in—'

'Shut your goddamn mouth. Ida! Ida! She dead, boy?'

'Well if she ain't she's damn good at faking it.'

'Don't smart mouth me, boy! What you done to her?'

'Lots.'

The sheriff, fat and fifty and red enough to have been running across half the state, took a step closer to what remained of Ida. The bloody pools of her eyes stared up at him, weeping scarlet tears onto the floor, staining the boards diarrhoea brown.

'Ida! Son-of-a-bitch,' said the sheriff, still unable to fully comprehend what he had discovered.

'In my top pocket, sheriff, there's—'

The sheriff stood up straight, dragged out a second gun, levelled it at Hollis's chest and pulled the trigger.

'Motherfucker!' were the last words Hollis heard.

An accurate assessment if ever there was one.

3

The black Lincoln Continental stretch limousine with darkened windows drifted through the mid-afternoon Seattle traffic like an oil tanker amid a flotilla of lesser craft, the boomerang-shaped antenna on its trunk like a rudder. It turned off the busy street and descended the ramp to the underground parking lot of the Fothergill Building.

Rolling down the circular entranceway it reached sub-level 5, where it cruised the ranks of parked automobiles until it berthed in a service area designated Bay 10A.

Halting with a sharp squeal of its tyres, a noise generated by the slick road surface rather than the speed of its stopping, a black-suited chauffeur in sunglasses got out, walked to the back of the car and opened the door. Two men stepped out of the driver's side, one dressed again in a tight dark suit and dark sunglasses, the other, taller man dressed in a white Armani suit, peach T-shirt and Ray-Bans.

Together they walked three abreast to a service elevator. One of the men in the dark suits – the two were interchangeable such was the anonymity of their clothing, sunglasses, square-framed shoulders and square-set jaws – pressed the button next to the elevator. They waited in silence until the doors scraped open and, once the inside was seen to be empty, the man in the white double-breasted suit entered on his own and pressed the topmost of the two buttons set in the wall. The doors slid shut and the elevator began its rise to the top floor. The man removed his sunglasses and looked at his brush-chromed reflection in the elevator door.

He saw a six-foot-four frame that managed to fill out his twelve-hundred-dollar suit without spoiling its lines. He admired a full head of dark hair, trimmed that very morning by Davidovitch, the most exclusive cutter in town – the tip alone more than some hard-working barbers might pull down in a week out in the boonies.

He brushed his long manicured fingers through his hair and tilted his head to one side, then to the other. He was handsome and he knew it. Ethnic, true, but not so much that the words *greaseball*, *kike*, or *wop* would immediately spring into a prejudiced mind. He forced his smile – always an effort – and immaculate tombstones glinted back in the light from the single bulb over his head.

He adjusted the silk handkerchief in his top pocket that echoed his peach-coloured Gianni Versace T-shirt, then grabbed both his lapels and adjusted his stance. Perfect. But then he noticed his shoes. Beige Polo Ralph Lauren loafers with a triangular pattern, the right one had a small scratch near the tip. This upset him. He prided himself on his taste, and if anything was amiss it was likely to throw his concentration out. Image was all; he couldn't afford to let his guard down. He debated whether to try a spit and a rub, but he felt the elevator finishing its ride; he'd have to live with it.

The elevator came to a halt. He winched up the corners of his mouth into his hello-I-acknowledge-your-presence-but-please-don't-waste-my-time smile and waited for the doors to open onto the twenty-eighth-floor offices of Stratton, Blakeboro & Henshaw Advertising.

He turned left, nodded at the attractive brunette on reception – Deborah something – and walked the length of the building, nodding and occasionally waving at people he recognized through open office doors or as they passed him in the corridor. The agency was as busy as ever, and so he soon tired of his forced bonhomie and instead turned his attention to the gallery of framed advertisements and packaging designs that lined the route to his corner office.

Trucks, pharmaceuticals, defence equipment, baby products, textiles, ice cream, soft drinks, frozen foods, office furniture, plastics . . . it was a wide-ranging portfolio of accounts that had produced a steady growth for the agency of over twelve per cent per year for the last five years. Billing was topping two hundred million dollars and SB&H was beginning to win awards and national recognition.

The man reached his office – and found his secretary's desk unattended and a note informing him that she had a dental appointment. Her absence annoyed him – she was the breakwater to the tide that was about to come washing over him as his presence in the agency became known – but she was so damned efficient at her job he allowed her to take the occasional liberty. But even as her absence registered, so did someone else's presence: a man even taller than himself blocked his office door.

Dressed in what could best be described as lumberjack casual – heavy brown cord trousers, red and black check shirt, Timberland boots and rimless spectacles – Jeff Beam was the creative director. Thirty, prematurely grey, extremely talented, and so hyper he downed Pepto-Bismol the way most creatives sipped Evian.

'Hi, Karel,' he said, his Brooklyn accent thick enough to qualify as a handicap. 'Good weekend?'

Karel Siemens, owner of Stratton, Blakeboro & Henshaw – despite its name – pushed past the pushy Beam and entered his wide office with its immaculate grey and chrome furniture, cream carpets and low, wide sofas backed by a breathtaking vista of the harbour area. Rain was trundling in from the west and giving the sky, through the tinted glass, a fifty-fifty split between dark blue and grey.

'Do I detect a hint of sarcasm there?' said Siemens as he walked round to the window side of his vast, uncluttered desk and checked the telephone messages on his blotting pad.

'How d'you mean?'

'It is Wednesday.'

'Oh. No, didn't mean that. It's Hoffnung's. Problems. Need your insight.'

'Cut the bull, Jeff. You want my approval. What is it?'

Beam smiled and shut the door. He had his audience.

'Old Hoffnung wants a black girl. Wants to be radical. See his point. Like his thinking, but . . .'

He pulled out two A4 black boards he had behind his back and held them out, side by side. The left one showed a beautiful black girl in white lacey underwear sitting at a kitchen table licking syrup off a spoon as it dripped over some waffles. The other shot had a blonde girl in the same underwear in an identical pose. Both headlines read: HOFFNUNG'S SYRUPS. IT'S OBVIOUS.

'That's—'

'Yes,' said Beam, nodding at the blonde on the board to his right. 'Anna Cam. Free for now. The photographer did us a favour; she's his girlfriend.'

'Far from free if we use her.'

'Worth it. But Hoffnung still insists on the black girl. Now, I got nothing against her. Great bazzooms, ass you could serve dinner on to your mom, but it's the demographics. Hoffnung's is A/B. Predominantly Mid-West and here; they haven't shipped to either coast yet. Black girl, white bread product. I don't give a shit but—'

'— the customers might. Is she a professional?'

'What makes you—'

'Tits. Too big. Is old Hoffnung—?'

'She's his – what did he call her? – "research assistant".'

'Researching into what gets his pants tenting out no doubt. What do *you* want to do?' Siemens was already losing interest in the conversation. He had switched on his PC and called up the memo board. There were a couple of dozen messages, none important, except one timed barely five minutes before, from their Fort Worth office, about the 'Ice Cream' account, which he knew had to mean trouble.

'Go with Anna,' said Beam. 'She's known. She's right for the market. She's—'

'—not licking Hoffnung's syrup off Hoffnung's nuts. Go with the black girl. Call it radical. Daring. Different.'

'Or stupid? Sucking up? A disaster?'

'Hey, since when did you give a shit about creativity on Hoffnung's account? Christ, two years ago it was a guy dressed up as a bee cursing because "Hoffnung's Beats Honey Three Times Out of Four". Go with the black girl, but try and retouch the tits; give the product a fighting chance of being noticed. Now, if you don't mind . . .'

Beam nodded and walked to the door.

'Don't thank me,' said Siemens, picking up the phone.

'Thanks,' said Beam without looking back.

As the door shut, Siemens fired the remote that locked it, then punched for an outside line, dialled a number and switched on the scrambler. Standard gear in these days of industrial and creative espionage but at that moment the least of his worries was a rival agency hearing about their latest homage to Hoffnung's Syrups.

He sat down and pulled open a drawer and shucked a fresh-breath mint into his mouth from the box sitting next to his Colt Diamond Back .38. As he waited for the telephone to ring at the other end, he rattled the mint around his teeth and thanked the Lord he had Beam as his creative director.

Thc guy was intelligent, dedicated and worth every penny of the hundred and fifty thousand dollars and Ferrari they paid him – to say nothing of the health plan, pension and stock options – but he was also paranoid about treading on Siemens's toes when it came to dealing with clients who had a special relationship with the man. In these cases he always liked Siemens to have the final say. Chances were he would have chosen the black girl anyway, out of deference to Hoffnung – there's creative and then there's making sure you have accounts to be creative on – but now the mantle of responsibility for fucking up had been removed. What Beam didn't know, however, was that they could have run advertisements that screamed DON'T BUY HOFFNUNG'S SHITTY SYRUPS and the account would have remained. That was one of the advantages of working at SB&H: the majority of the accounts were simply never going to leave. Not that anyone except Siemens knew that, but then Siemens knew a lot more than his staff at SB&H could ever dream of.

The phone rang three times and a man answered.

'Castallano's Ice Cream,' he announced blandly.

'It's Siemens. Give me Baxter.'

There was a crackling, then another man's voice came on. High-pitched, Californian, worried: 'We have a problem.'

'Get to it, Baxter.'

'Seems one of our salesmen got himself locked up.'

'After a sale?'

'Yes. The customer was the girlfriend of the local sheriff, and he found our man just as the sale was completed. He's saying he's going to take it all the way.'

'Well, we can't allow that. Which territory was it?'

'Clinger.'

This was *not* good. 'We need to send someone down there to talk to the sheriff.'

'Eminent Domain?'

'Exactly.'

'Clinger used this number as instructed, and I called back. The sheriff is not interested in co-operating.'

'For his sake he'd better change his mind. Looks like Eminent Domain all right. Any recommendations who to send?'

'Options limited. We have a lot of men out in the field because of the Washington business. Atlanta and Buffalo have stretched us, too. Looks like it'll have to be home office.'

'A clerk?'

'I can't go. You can't go. Who else could you trust?'

'Fuck. Best make it a Rip Up then, just in case.'

There was a long pause. 'A Rip Up? Yes, sir.'

'And keep me posted. Zero the file to me as soon as you've decided.'

'Half an hour max.'

The phone went dead and Siemens replaced the receiver, then stretched out in his revolving white leather chair. Things had been going so well, too.

As he rubbed his hand over his face, he became aware of the smell of his crotch. He must have been rubbing it as he talked to Baxter. One of his bad habits when things got tense. The smell reminded him that, despite his appearance, he hadn't had a wash since he'd had sex six hours before. Time for a shower; time to wash off the smell of the girl from the lodge and the smell of his own emissions.

He walked into the private bathroom, stripped and ran the shower. Even in this inner sanctum the walls carried the agency's campaigns: toilet paper, deodorizer, perfume, tampons, shower-gel. Although he had owned SB&H for five years, Siemens would struggle to name all its accounts. He just made the odd decision, some of them very odd indeed.

As he stepped under the scalding shower, he mused on the possibility that he might have ordered the death of two law-enforcement officers in order to cover up a vicious murder.

Try and sell that to the great unwashed American public, he thought, winking at a girl happily showering in a picture on the wall.

4

The unmarked McDonnel Douglas 500 dropped Stanley Fulbright at the same spot it had unloaded Kent Hollis six hours before. He walked away in a whirlwind of dust that got into his eyes, ears and mouth. It did nothing to lift his mood.

The pilot had pointed in the direction of Riva – he hadn't spoken for the entire two and half hours' flight from Fort Worth – then set about refuelling the chopper from a tank installed on the back seat, as Stanley followed the narrow dirt track which twisted up and over the hilly terrain.

Soon the chopper was hidden from sight, and Stanley was effectively lost. Not a nature boy by any measure, he found it easy to imagine taking a wrong trail in this dust and walking fifty miles before hitting another town, but he knew he wouldn't last that long anyway, because he was dressed in a suit and tie and he didn't even have a hat.

Five minutes, however, brought him to a metalled road, and ten minutes later he caught sight of Riva. Satisfied he was on course, he stopped for a moment to dust himself down. Bad enough to turn up without an official vehicle, but to turn up looking like he'd *walked* into town – well, it wouldn't help his cause.

He pulled out his authorization and scanned it. *Eminent Domain* it said at the top, followed by close-set legal jargon that filled three A4 pages with, at the end in red ink, *that* signature. Stanley was tempted to rub it to see if it smudged, but decided that government agents do not smudge the President's signature. He folded up the warrant, slipped it into its protective clear wallet and set off again.

Although the man who had sent him, Baxter, had said it was because of reduced manpower, Stanley wondered why he, a clerk with no field experience, had been charged with rescuing, from the custody of a sheriff, a *murderer*? And why he wasn't to ask questions of the man and was to ignore the inevitable outrage from the sheriff, his warrant providing all the authorization he needed.

He reached the town outskirts, if that weathered ragtag of buildings could be deemed outskirts when he could already see the far end of the main street. God knows how towns like this survived. There couldn't be any farming or industry within half a day's drive, yet this little town clung onto its existence like a thirsty man by a waterhole. It looked like the town had upped and died a long time since, but no one had remembered to inform its inhabitants.

Two police vehicles were parked outside the sheriff's office – a Dodge patrol car and a Jeep – which meant at least one deputy inside, and that could be a complication. He glanced at himself in the black-painted window that fronted the building. Did he look official enough?

Well, he was wearing a dark blue suit and tie in the desert, and he had no hat. Did that count, or did he just look stupid? He puffed out his chest – of which there wasn't a lot as, though tall, he had never had the build to match – and he grasped the handle of the door and walked in, suddenly aware that he had no idea what he was going to say.

The front office was hot and empty, an air-conditioner mockingly silent in the corner. Already he could feel sweat trickling down his cheek. For a government man, and this hick sheriff's superior, he didn't feel authoritative.

He checked his watch. 5:18 p.m. He had been told to get Hollis to the chopper by 6.00 p.m. He doubted he'd manage that, but he'd do his best. That was all you ever could do. (As his last foster father had told him many times: *if you don't do your best, don't bother doing.*)

'Hello,' he shouted. 'Anyone here?'

A young man about his own age appeared, sweat triangling on the front of his grey uniform shirt. 'Yeah?'

Stanley offered him his hand. 'Stanley Fulbright. Office of Central Intelligence. I'm here to pick up a prisoner.'

'We's only got the one – and he ain't going nowhere.'

'Mr Hollis?'

'That's the asshole. Now I don't care who you are or where you're from, but this guy killed a woman not six hours ago, and we're aiming to see he stands trial and fries.'

Stanley read his badge. '*Deputy* Penny, is the sheriff in?'

'He may be, but I don't see that it's no concern of yours. Now just take your suit and your—'

'I must insist on speaking to Sheriff Rawley.'

The deputy walked over to him and stared him in the face. He smelled of onions. 'The sheriff is busy. Take a hike.'

Stanley wasn't sure what to do.

'Sheriff Rawley, could you come here, please?' he shouted.

The deputy gave Stanley a shove that made him step back, but just as he was going to try again the sheriff entered.

'Hey Penny, hold that thought. Now.'

Penny lifted his hands and stepped back, grinning.

Stanley moved past him, aware he was flushed.

'Sheriff Rawley, your deputy has not exactly been—'

'He's here for that guy,' said Penny. 'To take him away.'

The sheriff, fat and red and tired-looking, seemed surprised. 'I don't think that'll be so Mr . . .?'

'Fulbright. Stanley Fulbright.' He showed his OCI identification to the sheriff, who seemed to recognize it.

'And what exactly is it you want, Mr Fulbright?'

Stanley nodded at Deputy Penny. 'Privacy for one.'

The sheriff nodded. 'Penny, go check out Six Mile Point.'

'What?' he said.

'I said go out to Six Mile Point and check for tipping. Stake it out for a couple of hours. Twilight's when—'

'You gotta be joking, sheriff.'

Sheriff Rawley caught Stanley's cye and realized he was being made to look weak.

'Get in your car, Penny, and don't come back till I radio.'

Penny cursed, grabbed a hat from a rack and stormed out, slamming the door hard enough to cause dust to rise.

'That's what nepotism gets you,' said the sheriff, shaking his head. 'Sister's boy.'

'Look, Sheriff, before we get into your family tree is there anyone else here?'

'I don't like your attitude, son.'

'Hey, I'm not your son, and you should be concerned about *your* attitude. I saw how you reacted when you saw the ID. You know I have authority here, so answer the question.'

Stanley could scarcely believe he'd just been so abrupt. Seems power does corrupt. But, then again, maybe it was just the heat and being made to look a fool by Elmer Fudd Jr.

'Radio's usually operated by Mabel. I let her go; she knew the deceased. One deputy off sick, other an hour in-country checking a rustling. So it's just me and Hollis.'

'And it'll just be you when he's released to my custody.'

'No,' Rawley said. 'I don't give a fuck what your badge says, who your boss is or whether the sun shines outta your shiny white butt. He killed a woman we all knew and respected in this town, and he's gonna be tried for it on my charges.'

'No, he's not. You're going to release him now.'

The sheriff exploded. 'Look, boy, you come in here in your cheap suit and city sweat . . . I got the state boys coming in, forensics from Lubbock.'

'They're not coming.' Stanley pulled out the wallet and slapped it in the sheriff's hand. The ultimate subpoena.

'Eminent Domain, Sheriff. All your calls were intercepted as soon as Mr Hollis went missing. All the authorities you have contacted have co-operated with OCI a hundred per cent. No state detectives, no forensics, no nothing, Just you, me and him – and me and him are leaving. Now.'

The sheriff was plainly appalled, and maybe a little bit frightened. He stared at the document.

'Eminent Domain? That's the government buying up land.'

'It was. It's more now. Read it. Check the signature. Ring the numbers. Do what the hell you want, but those papers give me the right to do anything *I* want! Now, are you going to co-operate or do *I* ring the numbers?'

It wasn't the heat, Stanley suddenly realized. It was the feeling of absolute right. Eminent Domain made him right and the sheriff wrong, regardless of who actually *was* in the right. It wasn't a good feeling, but it sure would be helping him get out of this tick of a town and back to Fort Worth.

Rawley was lost. He tried to speak but gave up. A welter of

emotions flickered across his ruddy wet face. Anger, fear, regret, puzzlement, hate, frustration and then, oddly, resolve.

'No,' he said, handing back the wallet. 'You can see him, but he ain't leaving.'

'Big mistake, Sheriff.'

'Not as big as the one he committed killing Ida.'

He led Stanley through the back.

There was a narrow corridor and two airless cells to one side. Only the furthest one was occupied.

'You claim he's yours, so you'll be safe in with him.'

The sheriff pulled his gun, a ludicrously big .44 Magnum with a ten-inch barrel, unlocked the door, and stood aside so Stanley could enter the cell.

Having made such a big show of his authority, Stanley couldn't really refuse the offer, despite a nagging suspicion that the sheriff might just lock him in with the killer.

Hollis sat up. He hurt all over and his chest was still tight from where the Taser had hit him. It was clear that, somewhere between the diner and the jail cell, someone had kicked the crap out of him.

The stranger in the sweat-stained suit nodded at him from the corridor as the sheriff opened the door.

'Mr Hollis, how are you? Stanley Fulbright, OCI.'

'As good as, considering. OCI? 'Bout time. You explained to this asshole what—?'

'This "asshole" ain't had nothing explained, ass-*wipe*,' said the sheriff, stepping behind the stranger, ''cepting this boy here flashing high-level ID and demanding your release, which is about as likely as me releasing a hold on my pecker when I'm on the job.'

'I'd hold that thought, Sheriff,' said Stanley.

This remark was as much for Hollis's benefit as the sheriff's, and it pleased Hollis. The man had a sense of humour.

Stanley was disconcerted by the amount of blood on Hollis's shirt but it wasn't unexpected. He didn't look like a killer, but to his knowledge he'd never met one before. He held out his hand and Hollis shook it limply and patted the bunk next to him. Stanley edged into the cell, but chose to stand against the wall under the small window.

'Got any beer? Coffee?' said Hollis.

'No. Got a good woman dead though – and you did it.'

'I did it all right, Sheriff. It's just there's fuck all you can do about it. Isn't that right, Agent . . .?'

'Fulbright. Stanley Fulbright. Yes, I'm afraid Mr Hollis is correct. This is strictly an OCI matter now; we have total jurisdiction. You are obliged to turn him over to us.'

'*Obliged*? I'd be obliged if you can explain to me why the government is interested in people who butcher waitresses!'

'We have our . . . that's *our* business,' said Fulbright, not wishing to betray his own ignorance. He was just a courier. Rule One at OCI, drilled into everyone from Day One: '*You don't need the reason, just the order.*' Stanley always obeyed the rules; he had made a point of it all his life.

'My papers authorize me to take Mr Hollis away from Riva, and for you to forget this ever happened.'

'*Forget*? Just like that? My Ida . . . Ida dead, and you . . . Where the hell do you think you are, boy?'

'I'm in Riva, Texas, which, if I'm not mistaken, is still a part of the United States.'

The sheriff was genuinely perplexed. He sat down on a wooden chair in the corridor outside the cell and kicked the metal door shut with his foot. It didn't lock but it put a barrier between him and the two freaks who'd just about fucked up the only good thing that had happened to him in the last three years. Since his Evelyn had died of cancer, in fact. He sat back against the wall and wiped the sweat from his bulbous face, the heat in the tiny cellblock stifling.

'He ain't going nowhere until I get me some answers,' the sheriff said after a long pause.

'Sorry, but you don't have to know a thing,' said Stanley.

'How do I know this is on the level?' said the sheriff, clearly upset. 'This could be some elaborate con. ID's only bits of paper. You could be his accomplice. You—'

'Grow up, Sheriff. How long ago did you call in the state troopers? Call any of the numbers on the paper; they'll all tell you the same thing.'

'Mainly,' interrupted Hollis, 'to keep your nose the fuck out of what don't concern you.'

'Hey, boy, I'm getting mighty tired of your attitude.'

'Attitude? You shitbrain! You're the one with the fucking attitude!'

'Er, that's enough, Mr Hollis.' Stanley was as flustered as the sheriff. He could see something unravelling that could never be rolled up neatly again. 'Sheriff, are we free to go?'

'This man, not six hours ago, nailed a woman to the floor, slit open her belly, shot her, gouged out her eyes and stabbed her in the head. God knows what else he would have done if I hadn't've gotten there. Now, if you've got the authority to haul this psycho away, I want to know why.'

'Sheriff, please, you don't—'

'No, no, Fulbright, let the man hear,' said Hollis with a smile. 'He wants to know. Let me tell him.'

'Mr Hollis, please—'

'If you've read my psych reports, Fulbright, you'll know "please" ain't in my dictionary. You ready, Sheriff?'

Psych reports? What were they?

'Go ahead, boy, and this better be good.'

'Oh it's good. And 'cause of your country ways I'll keep it simple. But first, you said this Ida woman was a friend. Just how good a friend?'

'None of your business, boy. Just get on with your story.'

'Good enough to be fucking her, despite her skinny tits?'

The sheriff let out an incoherent oath and pulled open the door. Stanley stepped forward to intercept him, but Hollis didn't even blink. He enjoyed goading people, was a master at it, and always knew just how they'd react.

'You little shit, you ain't getting out of that cell in one piece, so help me!'

'*So* ain't around right now. Just Fulbright,' said Hollis. 'And, appearances and weight to the contrary, he does outrank you. Now sit down and act like a peace officer.'

With some difficulty Stanley guided Rawley back to his seat in the corridor and placated him, he himself now being as angry at Hollis as the sheriff. Sweat was making his shirt stick to his back; heat or fear, he was just about swimming in his own perspiration. He leaned back against the open cell door like a referee trying to keep two contestants apart.

'Sheriff, please, we're all . . . we're both law officers here, let's try and keep emotion out of it. I understand you're upset . . . No, that's shit! I haven't a *clue* how you feel, but if you let us both go now, I'll—'

'I want the story. From *this*,' he said, pointing at Hollis, who still sat on the bed, leaning against the wall and staring at the sheriff, occasionally shifting to let his sweat chill his back.

'Sure,' said Hollis, a smile playing on his thin lips.

Stanley saw it and his stomach turned over. How the hell had he ever gotten into this mess?

'You've both got me down as Kent Hollis. Wrong. My real name's Kenneth Handry – "The Handyman" to some. Remember? Made the "most wanted" four years back?'

'"The Handyman"?' said the sheriff. 'That psycho killed all them women in the Southwest? Twenty or thirty of them?'

'Lots more than that, but then I got caught, tried, sentenced and executed. Except I didn't get executed.'

'But it was on the news, I remember,' said Stanley, his heart beginning to race. All wrong; this was all wrong.

'Faked. Instead the OCI made me a fully fledged Fed. Well, more than that, actually; I became a fucking star!'

'What is all this shit, Fulbright?'

Stanley didn't know, didn't *want* to know. 'That's enough, Hollis. Can we go now, Sheriff, before—'

'I think it's too late already,' said Hollis.

'Too late for what?' said the sheriff.

Hollis smirked at the increasingly frightened Stanley. 'These government guys offered me a job and all the money I need to take out whoever they tell me to.'

'What you saying?' said the sheriff, now so out of his depth he looked like a drowning man. Covered in sweat, gasping for breath, his piggy eyes squinted against the heat in a face as red as a weightlifter pushing his limit.

'What Mr Hollis is saying, you asshole,' said Stanley, angry at the sheriff for having put them both through this, 'is that he's a fucking sociopath. He doesn't give a shit about *anyone*. Us included.'

'Perceptive, Fulbright, real perceptive.'

The sheriff stood up. He was a sweat factory. 'I – I don't know what . . .'

'You let us go, that's what, Sheriff,' said Hollis. 'And do it now.'

'Sheriff, do as we ask, or it could . . .' said Stanley.

'It could what?' said the sheriff.

'It already is,' said Hollis leaping from the bed without any warning, dashing past Stanley into the corridor and grabbing the sheriff's gun. 'You should have listened to Fulbright. If you'd let us go everything would have been all right, but now you know too much. Can't have people running round knowing the government assassinates its own citizens.'

'Hollis! *Don't!*' shouted Stanley.

'*You* wanna do it?' said Hollis.

Stanley looked at his feet. Truth was he wasn't sure *he* would be getting out of the sheriff's office alive. It was clear Hollis could do what he liked, and what he liked was killing – and what kind of loss would Agent Fulbright be if Hollis took it into his head to vent his anger on him?

'Hey, I don't know what you have in mind . . .' The sheriff looked into Hollis's cold silver eyes, and saw his end.

Hollis shoved the gun into his expansive gut and cocked it. 'Want it quick or slow, Sheriff?'

'Hollis, please . . .'

'Shut the fuck up, Fulbright. You know I outrank *you*. Now, Sheriff, get in the cell!'

'Hollis, there's no need,' said Stanley. 'We can—'

'And you can walk out of that door, Not-Too-Bright, or stay in here with the sheriff. Now, what's it to be?'

Stanley had never been so scared in his life and had never seen a look of such utter depravity in an intelligent man's eyes before. It brought him out in goosebumps and made his bladder ache. He backed away, his body doing his thinking for him, and edged along the short corridor to the sheriff's office, tensing for the inevitable gunshot, though whether he expected to feel the bullet ripping through his own body he was too terrified to decide.

But no shot came. So why didn't he run back in there and shoot Hollis? Blow the maniac's brains out. He might not save the sheriff, but justice would be served. Yeah, and *then* what would happen? He would probably be executed for destroying government equipment! No, Stanley, for his sins, had only one choice: let Hollis do as he pleased and pray he didn't decide to get some more kicks by killing him as well.

He paced nervously around the perimeter of the hot empty office, waiting for the sound of the man's death, but there was nothing. Two minutes later, just as he was about to step back to the cells to see what had happened, Hollis walked out wiping his hands.

Stanley couldn't see any blood. 'Wh-what did you do?'

'Go see.'

Stanley didn't want to, but knew he had no say in the matter. He stepped through the door and spotted the sheriff lying on the bed in the cell. Taking a couple of steady paces towards him Stanley saw how he had died.

The last inch of the butt of his .44 Magnum was protruding from Sheriff Rawley's purple face. His hands were claws, his eyes wide enough to show white all round his pupils, the floor soiled with urine and excreta.

Hollis called from the office: 'Hey, Fulbright, why don't you pull the trigger, see where the bullet comes out.'

Stanley threw up.

Hollis laughed. 'Better call it in, kid – get the mess cleaned up. And not just yours. That deputy'll come back soon, and then look at the shit you'll be in. Besides, I want to get back to Clinger. Got an itch that's just gotta be scratched, if you know what I mean.'

For an insane second Stanley considered grabbing for the .44, but sense prevailed. Hollis might be mad but he wasn't stupid. And thank God: as he pulled off the pillow to cover his vomit, he found the gun's bullets. Sudden relief swept over him; what would have happened if he had stormed next door, shouting his hatred, only to click off empty chambers into Hollis's laughing face? It didn't bear thinking about.

No, Hollis might be insane, but he was probably brighter than Stanley and most of his superiors. That was usually the way with sociopaths. What was needed with Hollis wasn't a plan of attack but a plan of survival, and at the moment that didn't stretch further than prayer.

He slammed the cell door on the dead cop and walked out through the office into the street, where Hollis was already revving up the sheriff's Jeep.

'Next stop the chopper, right, Fulbright?'

'I have to call this in,' said Stanley, nodding at the sheriff's office.

'What do you want for dinner? I cook a mean steak.'

'You've got *your* job, Hollis, I've got mine. Enjoy the trip back to Clinger.'

Hollis leaned across the passenger seat and patted it. 'I said what do you want for dinner? You haven't seen where I live, have you? Do *your* duty on the chopper radio.'

'But—'

'Fulbright, no one says no to me.'

Not if they want to stay alive, thought Stanley. He climbed into the Jeep as it pulled away, dusting the street.

'Your first name's Stanley, isn't it?' said Hollis, for all the world as if they were two neighbours out for a Sunday drive. 'When I was a kid my momma bought me a little puppy. A Labrador. Black. I called him Stanley.'

'What happened to him?'

'Three guesses.'

5

The back lot of the Zebra Lounge was usually well lit by the security lights on the roof of the bar and by the streetlights on the expressway that hung above the place like the hand of God waiting to slap the den of iniquity into oblivion. Except tonight the expressway was closed for repair and its lights were off, and one of the security lights had been vandalized. This still wouldn't have been a problem for Cheryl Kenney – after all, she didn't exactly want to be in the spotlight when she fucked – but this store manager she'd met had suddenly found a couple of friends, and while she had nothing against pulling a train, she preferred it to be on her own terms with people she had chosen.

Okay, it was her own fault. She'd been in the mood for a quick ride with someone, anyone; someone who could take her over a car hood, give it to her hard and fast, with no commitment, no emotion, just two animals satisfying each other. As long as they wore a condom, she'd let them take her any way they wanted. That was half the fun. Knowing what you wanted and then seeing if it lived up to your fantasies. Like Christmas. When she was a girl, seeing all those wrapped-up presents, trying to guess the shape, the size, wondering if it was going to turn out the way she'd dreamed. Then the anticipation, the first sight of her parcels' contents – sometimes it was good news, but usually it was a disappointment: the economy size. Still, some times it came good, in a manner of speaking . . .

It wasn't the sex, she knew that now. It wasn't the orgasm – she always had better when she relived the event with her vibrator. No it was the risk. Not from AIDS – she wasn't that dumb, though she'd met some assholes who were willing to take that gamble for the thrill. No, it was the *wrongness* of it, the crudity. Two people humping hard in some dark corner like wild dogs rutting behind trash cans. It was always rough, rarely long or satisfying, but the experience was all stored up for later use. And when the guy had unloaded, that was it. He could compliment her or tell her how good he was or want to give her his telephone number, but she'd be smoothing down her skirt and walking away before he even had his zipper up. And tonight this computer store manager, Nathan Rorke – or Rorke the Ram, as he called himself – had been promising her a cock like a tyre iron if only she'd let him see her jugs.

Cheryl's breasts were her secret weapon: the kind of men she wanted didn't care about conversation or her mind; all they wanted was in her blouse, and what was there was plenty.

So she'd told Rorke the Ram she'd meet him out back at his pick-up in five minutes, promising him a ride he wouldn't forget. His eyes had nearly bugged out as far as his pants. So easy, so pathetic. He wasn't bad-looking, in a big way, but his come-on line had been to offer her a Power Macintosh on easy terms. What world did guys live in today?

She could tell the sort as soon as she walked in a bar: the look that lingered too long; the little smile that said 'we're made for each other'. Subtle ones sent a drink over, the rest sent themselves. Whichever, as her sole purpose was to get fucked, the charade of talk was soon dispensed with. The quickest she'd ever done it from walking through the door to parting her legs was eighteen minutes. The longest – well, the failures were too many to count; a lot of guys, when they had it offered straight out, either didn't believe it or couldn't take not being in charge. Not a few would assume it was a con: she was a hooker who'd hold a razor to their dick when they got outside, or there'd be a pimp with a gun. But those who took the bait got what they wanted and, most times, so did Cheryl.

So she had slipped into the Ladies on her way to the lot, and checking she had her protection, had adjusted her jeans, making sure her large red blouse covered everything it should. Her figure looked good and her tight blue jeans and white high heels made the most of her long legs. Her medium-length natural blonde hair was shaggy, and her eyes and mouth had undergone extensive work-outs with Revlon to appear at their best. She knew her overall look was cheap, but the men she was after didn't have much taste anyway.

As she walked to the red Ford pick-up she saw the guy stood waiting, dragging on a cigarette and rubbing his crotch. She looked back at the bar. It was a long way to run if something went down, and the music from the band was loud enough to mask the most heartfelt of screams. She glanced around. Maybe she had gone a bit too . . . She'd had four or five drinks, but she could hold her liquor. Or at least she thought she could: the fact she was out here proved she might need to watch her boozing if . . . *oh shit.*

Two other guys stepped out of the shadows on either side of Rorke. One tall and black, one short and white, both beefily built, working men, both with *that* look, visible even at twenty yards. One of them was holding what looked like a rag or a scarf. She could see it going in her mouth and then . . . well, it wouldn't be fun. She'd got herself raped before and hadn't enjoyed it, though she'd never reported it to the police. She knew it was her own fault; play with fire and eventually you'll get burnt, and there's nothing much hotter than a man's libido if you give him the nod. Switch him on and you'd better put out, or he'll put you out. She stopped walking.

'Hey, boys, I'm all for a party but—'

The black guy spoke. 'Shut up, bitch, and get over here.'

Cheryl didn't move. Once they were in striking distance she was lost; while there was space between them she had a chance. She could hear her heart thumping in her ears even above the thumping of the bar band.

Rorke opened his arms and threw her a counterfeit smile. 'Hey, babe, you got enough to go round. And I always share my good fortune with my friends.'

'Why? You need help to get it up?' She knew she shouldn't start with the insults, but she'd offered the guy a freebie!

Suddenly shortie darted out to her and, although she stepped back, he made a clean grab at her arm. She raised her fist to strike him and he brought his knee up into her stomach and knocked the wind out of her. Rorke then rushed over and grabbed her and they dragged her to the pick-up and threw her face down onto its wooden bed.

'Oh baby, oh baby,' said shortie behind her.

Pain rolled through her stomach, making her want to throw up, but she knew she had to keep her senses. The best she could hope for now was a gangbang, but the worst . . .

'Oh baby, oh baby,' chanted shortie.

'Come on,' said the black brute. 'Get her pants off. Let's get us some of that pussy.'

'Oh baby, oh baby,' said shortie as he clambered onto the pick-up and thrust his hands under her to get at her jeans.

Other hands then lifted her up by grabbing her voluminous blouse at either side, while someone else pulled her jeans down. Cool night air touched her bare legs.

'Oh baby, oh baby,' said the short man. He was beside her now, his trousers round his knees, his small erection pointing at her face. He grabbed her hair and lifted her head.

'You're gonna choke on this, then you're gonna *drown*!'

She spit at it and he slammed her head down once, twice.

'Turn the bitch over,' said Rorke. 'Let's see those titties she promised me.'

At last, she thought, *they're doing something right.*

They rolled her over and the black guy wrenched her jeans off her legs and threw them into the night, her black panties only just visible under her ballooning blouse. He unbuckled his own belt, his face set in a dangerous leer.

Rorke reached for her panties, his trousers already round his ankles, his penis semi-erect. His hands brushed the black material, as Cheryl put her own hand down them.

'*What the—*'

The bullet zinged past his ear close enough for him to feel its heat. He leapt back, caught his feet in his pants and tumbled into the black guy, who grabbed for the edge of the pick-up and, steadying himself, watched his companion crash out onto his back and try scuttling away, whimpering.

He looked back at the girl. She had sat up, the Smith & Wesson Special Airweight .38 she'd had stuffed down her panties now on clear view, its snub two-inch barrel swinging back from his crotch to the cock of the small man who was leaning back against the side of the pick-up burbling like she'd already shot him in the head.

'Five seconds, boys. Five seconds to get out of my world or I'll Bobbitt the lot of you.'

The tall black guy looked like he was going to discuss the situation so Cheryl fired the gun into the side of the pick-up, six inches from the dwindling bulge in his trousers. A splinter hit his hand and he got the message. Hoisting up his pants, he ran over Rorke and into the dark. Shortie in the pick-up rolled over the side, only to land flat on his face, squealing as gravel made contact with his penis. But it didn't stop him getting to his knees, dragging his pants up his thighs and setting off in the other direction.

Cheryl still had a painful stomach where she had been punched, and she wanted revenge. She crabbed to the end of the pick-up and let her shaking legs reach the ground. Then, standing upright, she pulled off her panties and tossed what was left of them at Rorke who was lying on his back, a cut dripping blood down his face, his penis hosing his belly with urine as he pleaded quietly for her not to shoot him.

'Souvenir,' she said.

She walked over to him and placed the barrel of the gun on his shrinking, dribbling cock and held it there for a full ten seconds until he stopped shrieking for mercy and fainted. Then, satisfied he wasn't faking, she slipped on her jeans and looked to see if anyone had come out in response to the shots, but no one appeared. Chances were they wouldn't even have heard shots let off *inside* the bar.

'All I wanted was a fuck,' she shouted into his face, as angry with herself as with him. 'You didn't even have to be *good*, you asshole! But you went and spoiled it.'

She fumbled in his pockets and found his wallet and a lighter. She opened the wallet, fanned out his cash and took ten for her panties and another fifteen for the drink tab he'd stiffed her with before coming out. Asshole.

She stood up. Clearly no one was coming, and the other two had long gone. She wouldn't be able to use the Zebra Lounge again, but it was a twenty-mile drive from Clinger, so that was no big loss.

She looked down at the pathetic bastard – Rorke the Ram? More like Rorke the Dork – and was tempted to kick him in the stomach, but then she thought of something better.

She pocketed all but one of his business cards, then took a pen out of his inside pocket and wrote on the last card I KNOW WHERE YOU WORK and slipped it into his top pocket. Then she picked up his lighter and set fire to his pubic hair.

She could hear his screams as she spun her Corvette onto the main drag. Well, they'd promised each other a hot time; at least she'd kept her side of the bargain.

Five miles on she had to slew the car to the shoulder and throw up. God, what had she been thinking? The same thing she thought every time: she liked the risk. Like her driving and her job, she needed all the excitement she could get – but, then again, you could also get too much of a good thing.

6

Stanley Fulbright had never been so scared in his life.

Not when one of his foster fathers used to beat him with his belt, the one with the eagle on the buckle. Not even the time he had been on a freeway outside Chicago and a sniper killed the guy in the Buick in front of him, and he and a dozen other motorists had been trapped for half an hour before a SWAT team took the bastard out. They had been heart-thumping, horrific moments: jagged marks in a relatively smooth life. They were moments which still woke him in the small hours, sweat dampening his bed, fear fudging his mind, but they were nothing compared to the terror he now felt sitting on one of the couches in Hollis's Winnebago.

They had driven to the helicopter waiting outside Riva, Hollis talking for all the world as if they were a couple of salesmen who'd just turned a good deal on water coolers. There they found the silent pilot ready for take-off, his extra fuel tank dumped in the dirt. During the flight back, Hollis had responded to Stanley's queries about their destination with a weird smile and a selection of disco songs: 'Disco Inferno', 'September', 'Backstabbers'.

Stanley's terror had been temporarily stayed when they had landed outside the Clinger Solardome. Until, that is, Hollis had guided him to an electric golf-cart and they had driven inside onto the field, past a couple of OCI agents in their bulletproof jackets emblazoned with the single word LAW. There they had pulled up outside a giant black Winnebago. *At least I'm among friends now*, Stanley had told himself waving at the nearest agent, but the man hadn't responded – and then Hollis had unlocked the door and ushered him in.

'Welcome to my home, be it ever so humble.'

It may have been a Winnebago, and Stanley may have been scared enough to have already pissed in his pants, but he couldn't help noticing the laser-disc player, the Dolby Pro-Logic surround sound speakers, the Bose hi-fi, the champagne and caviar on ice, and the expensive designer-label clothing lying about like so many old newspapers. Hollis lived like a king, even if his kingdom was mobile.

'Sit down, Fulbright,' he said, 'I'll cook us some dinner. Steak do you? Help yourself to caviar.'

Stanley could only nod, food the last thing on his mind.

He eyed the door, judging the distance. He was fit, he was wiry, he could probably outrun Hollis on the flat, but could he outrun a gun? And what about the OCI guys outside? Surely they would help him if they saw Hollis coming after him? But then again, Hollis got what Hollis wanted. Just look how they'd given him a football field.

Hollis popped his head around the fridge door, large raw steak in one hand, remote control in the other. He pressed a switch and there was an audible click from all the doors.

'Just in case you were thinking of leaving too early,' Hollis said, before diving back to look for the other steak.

Stanley kept quiet, unable to focus his attention on anything long enough for it to quieten the banshee screaming in his head. The only thing he perceived with any great clarity was that he was going to die. He could tell Hollis was unbalanced; he didn't need to have read any reports to see that. His casual manner, his sudden mood swings, the killings. Even his home seemed cast from his own thoughts: black, self-contained, abnormal.

Hollis slammed the fridge door shut, making Stanley jump, then slapped two enormous steaks on the kitchen counter and began to soften them up by pounding them with a tenderizer.

Stanley couldn't stop shaking, his hands fluttering as if he was wired into an electrical outlet. He was also afraid to open his mouth for fear of what might come out: either vomit or a hysterical plea for mercy. He watched the man pummel the meat and couldn't help thinking of his own flesh. His mind was fracturing, splinters of rational thought dancing amid the debris of wildest lurid fantasy.

Suddenly a song blared out. Disco music. 'Feel the Need in Me' by the Detroit Emeralds. The man had snapped a cassette into his Bose system and the Seventies were pumping out, the bass strong enough to vibrate the couch.

How many people had Hollis killed before he was caught? And how many since? Today alone it had been two, perhaps even three before dawn broke.

'Can I use the bathroom?' Stanley asked, his bladder full of fear.

'Sure. Just don't be smart, okay?'

Stanley nodded and headed towards the toilet.

'Leave the door open,' added Hollis, without looking up.

Stanley nodded, sliding the toilet door open, stepping in and taking a long pee.

Hollis finished tenderizing the meat. He liked his meat

rare so he would only flash-fry it. It never occurred to him to ask Stanley how he liked his.

As he got out the frying pan and poured oil into it, he glanced over at Fulbright, now returned. He was really scared. Hollis wondered what fear was. Even when he was due to be executed, fear hadn't been in his mind. The universe revolved around him, and so the thought of his nonexistence didn't worry him, particularly as everyone and everything else would be extinguished in that moment. He could imagine nothing, but *nothing* didn't hurt, so what was the worry? And as for fear, that was an emotion only others experienced, especially when they realized what he intended to do to them.

They sat at the table, two bloody steaks in front of them, a bowl of pepper salad in the middle, Buds on the side.

'Tell me your story, Stanley,' said Hollis as he nibbled on a chilli pepper.

'My story?' Stanley could hear his stomach grumbling.

'Yes,' said Hollis, slicing his steak into strips which he then proceeded to eat like bacon, dabbing the ends in a pile of English mustard, occasionally dipping into the salad for a piece of pepper. 'Your life? Where were you born?'

'San Francisco. Nineteen-sixty. September. My parents were killed in a car wreck when I was two, and after a spell with my mother's folks I was put in a home. They were too old—'

'Don't make excuses. They dumped you. Excess baggage.' He chomped noisily on a celery stick. 'Eat.'

'No. My grandmother—'

'Put you in a home when you were what? Three? Four?'

'Four.'

Hollis licked mustard from his knuckles. 'Then?'

'Foster homes. About one a year. Some good, some bad.'

'Tell me about the bad?'

'Beatings. Being picked on by the other kids.'

'Bad beatings?'

'Bad enough. For a kid. For a fostered kid.'

'Was it you or them?' said Hollis swigging on his beer.

Stanley didn't know the answer, and didn't offer one. Like any kid, he always assumed it was him. They didn't like him, he'd done something wrong, but he didn't know what. There were a lot of weird people out there, even those who profess to care for children. Just look at the creeps he had been collating these past months. How many times had the words Teacher, Nursery Help or even Child Psychologist turned up? He didn't tell Hollis, but by the age of twelve he had been in fourteen foster homes, only three of them happy, and even those sent him back within months.

Stanley decided to skip his childhood. What small comfort he had gained from engaging in conversation with Hollis – it was better than the alternative – only served to remind him of other fears, and he had enough of those.

'I left the home at sixteen for a job in Miami in a hotel. One of my better foster parents offered me a job with his brother-in-law. I took it; anything to get out into the world. I worked in his hotel for nine years, until I was deputy manager. It was long boring hours, badly paid, and I had to be polite all the time, but it was respectable work.'

'So you had a career. What stopped it?'

'A girl. I got her pregnant. I wanted her to have an abortion, she refused. I'd seen enough unwanted kids to know that this was just another, and I knew we weren't going to have any kind of life together. When she said she was keeping the baby, I left.'

'Abandoned your own kid. History repeats itself.'

'Something like that. I found out she lost it after I'd gone. Blamed me for the shock; but to be shocked by someone leaving, you've got to care – and she didn't care about me.

'I bummed around for years doing anything I could turn my hand to. Finally got arrested for vagrancy in Seattle, and did twenty-eight days. When I got out, this guy offered me a ride. I wasn't going anywhere so I thought, what the hell, maybe I could bum a meal out of him. He took me to an office, got me a burger, a change of clothes and offered me a chance at a real job. He made me take some tests, plus a long interview with a shrink. Then he made me an offer. Did I want to work for the government?'

'OCI?'

'Yes. He explained how city, county, state and federal authorities haven't the time or resources to cross-index information without there being a good reason. Interstate felonies where the felons are known are dealt with, but when it comes to small-scale crime, child abuse, abduction, sexual assault—'

'Save the job description. You're a fucking clerk, logging statistics so you can find out Mr Jones in Galveston used to be Mr Smith in Pontiac and he likes slipping it to boys. Well, whoopee, ain't we just solved a major crime wave.'

'It helps, not that you'd—'

'Hey, remember you're a guest here.'

'Some guest.'

Hollis leaned forward jabbing his beer bottle, his eyes

boring into Stanley. Curtis Mayfield was imploring them to 'Get on up'.

'Ever occur to you that for every Mr Smith and Mr Jones you put away, there's another hundred, another *thousand* ready to take his place? Ready to stir the shit with their dicks? You're fighting a losing battle, Fulbright.'

'One pervert put away is—'

Hollis laughed loudly, but it was the sound of a man who had learned to laugh through copying others, not because he had ever found anything amusing. 'What's perverted? In a world gone wacko, what's right and what's wrong?'

'I'm right and you're wrong,' said Stanley.

'Yeah, but who's going to get to tell anyone tomorrow?'

Stanley snapped. 'Look, why don't you just kill me now, so I don't have to listen to this bullshit!'

Hollis bared his teeth in imitation of a smile. 'You're looking at a car, a Cadillac. You think it's red, then twenty guys come along and swear it's green. What colour's the Caddy?'

'Red.'

'Because that's what you see, and you're always right? So *they're* all liars?'

'Yes.'

'You're colour-blind. Now what colour's the car?'

'This is stupid.'

'Is it?' Hollis dabbed his finger in juices and licked it. 'Just thinking you're right don't make it so. What makes it so is what *happens*. If every man fucked his own kid, wouldn't that make kid-fucking normal, and those that didn't weird? What's right is what the majority do. I just do what most men, the majority, wish they could do. Keep the bitches in their place with fear and pain. It's what men are, if only they'd own up to it. All I am is honest, Fulbright; I do what I want, not what I should. You see, they still burn heretics – just nowadays they do it with electricity.'

'You're not a heretic. You're a madman.'

'*I'm* the madman? *Me?* I was offered four hundred thousand dollars for the film rights to my story so the network can sell airtime on a Sunday night. Go figure. You're not one of the good guys, Fulbright. You're one of the losers.

'I had fucking *fan mail*, can you believe that? Women wanted to meet me, guys wanted me to be their buddy. A couple of kooks wanted to watch me doing it, one even wanted me to do her! Fucking weird, man. So you sit at your computer, Fulbright, and you round up the facts that help pull down some nobody because he likes sticking it to teenies, but don't fool yourself into thinking it means anything.'

All the while Hollis had been leaning closer and closer, until Stanley could smell his breath. Suddenly the man sat back, his bad smile back in place.

'They send you to that school?'

'What? Yes, Washington State. Middle of nowhere. Secret. About two hundred of us. We were there six months, but by the end only about eighty of us made it.'

'Did you notice anything odd about the other recruits?'

'No. Men, women, white, black, ages from twenty to forty.'

'Their backgrounds?'

'A lot had come from broken backgrounds. Agents I've met since then, too.'

'Doesn't that strike you as significant?' Hollis finished his last piece of steak and licked his lips.

Stanley thought about this. No. He had a pretty jaded view of the world; he believed everyone was a fuck-up, and those that weren't were either lying or were just plain lucky. Happiness was *not* the norm. It was as if misery was a disease that would inevitably infect everyone, spreading from person to person, home to home. Some people might have been immune, but he was damned if he had ever met them.

'No,' he said finally.

'They programmed you well.'

'What?'

'Nothing.' Hollis finished his Budweiser and snared Stanley's untouched bottle. 'How's the steak? You haven't eaten any.'

'Not hungry.'

'Why?'

Stanley was angry. Not only at his own terror and the man's intimidation but also because he had revealed so much of himself in so short a time to a complete stranger. He'd had relationships with women that had lasted for months where he hadn't said as much as he had in the past half hour.

'Why am I not hungry? Isn't that fucking obvious?'

'You're scared?'

'Yes.'

'And you should be.'

Hollis got up, taking both their plates and tutting at the waste, then returned with a tub of ice cream and two spoons. The Tramps were trying to 'Hold Back the Night'.

'Dig in.'

'I told you I wasn't hungry,' said Stanley staring at him.

Hollis matched his glare, then spoke without a flicker of expression:

'Woman once tried to stare me down. I had a spoon then. She stopped staring.' He picked up a big scoop of green pistachio ice cream to show how he had stopped her, then he slowly licked it.

An uneasy silence fell between them as Hollis ate his ice cream and Stanley swallowed back his bile.

The music slowed and became more soulful. The Pointer Sisters' 'Slow Hand', James and Bobby Purify's 'I'm Your Puppet' and The Delfonics' 'La La Means I Love You' all played through without interruption. And all the time Stanley was getting closer and closer to breaking point until . . .

Suddenly he snapped and tried to grab at Hollis, but the man dodged the blow as he if had been expecting it from the first moment they had set eyes on one another, and punched him in the gut in reply, then grabbed his jaw and slammed his head against the wall.

'You're beginning to annoy me, Fulbright. Here I wanted a pleasant conversation and all I get is abuse. I may prefer killing women, but they ain't all I do. Understand?'

He pulled out of his waistband a Smith & Wesson 67 .38, its long silver barrel glistening in the subdued light, and held it under Stanley's chin.

'You could die in five seconds, five minutes, five hours, depending on where I shoot you. But just think what you'll feel and what I'll get to see before you die.'

'Give you . . . a feeling . . . of power does it?'

Hollis considered this, looking into Stanley's eyes, then at the gun. He slowly raised his revolver until he was pointing it at Stanley's forehead. He dug it in painfully.

Stanley held his breath.

'Bang,' said Hollis.

Stanley let out a gasp, his whole body limp, his heart beating faster than he could have counted.

Hollis smiled an alien grimace, then slowly slid the gun barrel from side to side on Stanley's sweat.

'B-bastard,' Stanley managed, his bottom lip trembling.

Hollis's smile became broader and even more maniacal. 'You ain't seen nothing yet.'

He pulled the trigger.

Stanley screamed, a short howl of animal terror.

Then he realized the revolver had simply clicked instead of blowing his head off.

Hollis whispered. 'Your face . . . what a picture.'

Stanley couldn't speak, couldn't breathe.

Hollis flipped open the gun and debated whether to put bullets into it.

No, he decided, *not yet.* The time would come when he would have to do it, but it could wait because it would keep Siemens waiting. Fulbright could live a little longer.

Stanley voided his bladder again. If Hollis noticed, he gave no indication. He stabbed the barrel of the gun into the ice-cream tub and licked it clean.

It took Stanley a long while to recover. Never had he been so certain of death. He felt like one raw nerve – one touch would send him into orbit. Then he slowly realized that Hollis was talking.

'. . . good delaying procedure; your new defence team have to have time to get to know your case. But, finally, it was decided. They were *desperate* to execute me. I had no regrets about what I'd done—'

'What about the girls you kill? Don't you feel anything?'

'Everybody dies some time. Cancer, AIDS, car wrecks, war, flood, tornado, fire . . . What's one or two girls being in the wrong place at the right time? Now, can I continue?'

Despite his predicament, Stanley couldn't avoid getting angry with the man. And the disco music was obscenely at odds with his situation. Currently Odyssey's 'Native New Yorker' was mixing into the Hues Corporation's 'Rock the Boat'.

'I was found guilty and no end of appeals could help me, not when they saw the video.'

'Oh God, I remember that now . . .'

'Stupid. Got caught on a security video, killing a girl. Smashed the camera when I realized, but by then the tape had done its work. I might as well have done the girl right there in front of the jury.' He sat back shaking his head.

He had been sloppy, but the girl's hair had been just so perfect and when she'd tilted her head *that way* while she sold Passion to some old broad what could he do? That was why, when she quit work, he'd cornered her in the parking basement and run his knife down between her breasts, slicing through the material of her pink uniform like it was a second skin, and then he had got her on her back and quickly found out what she looked like naked. And once his knife had let him see her true colours – her reds, her pinks, her browns – he had decided to save her the trouble of praising the majesty of his desire by slicing her throat and liberating her essence . . . And then he had seen the security camera pointing straight at him. He was arrested within ten minutes as he hailed a cab, the girl's blood still sticky on his hands.

'But you were . . .'

'What?' Someone was speaking.

'You were executed.' It was Fulbright.

Hollis came back to the present, aware of an ache in his groin. Sweet memories . . .

'Yes. Lethal injection. I didn't know what they were going to do. Went through the rituals, all that crap . . .'

Stanley could see Hollis was lost in thought again, but instead of dreamy pleasure his face showed a fearful introspection. Clearly he was remembering the moment when he had been killed in front of witnesses in the name of justice.

'You didn't know?' said Stanley, relishing the man's discomfort; knowing there had been a time when Hollis had believed he was going to die as surely as had his victims.

'No. They'd fixed the doctors who certify death in the chamber. Instead of poison they gave me a drug to shallow my respiration and reduce my heartbeat. To anyone stood nearby I was a gonner, except to the doctors they'd bought off.

'They wheeled me to the infirmary, the certificate was signed, I was dead. Hours later they revived me, substituted some poor schmuck's corpse for mine and smuggled me to a secret address where they showed me the needle with the real stuff. Said if I didn't cooperate they'd inject me and no one would be the wiser, but do as they ask and I'd live. Well obviously I said yes, and they made their proposition: keep on killing, but *they* choose the victims. Sold me some bullshit about taking down people unofficially. Couldn't be done by the police or the FBI, but they had been sanctioned "at the highest level". Eminent Domain, right? Said this shouldn't worry me because I'd been doing American girls for years. I laughed; they didn't. They said if I agreed they'd give me anything I wanted, but in return I had to kill when they said. I was a gun and when they pulled the trigger I wasn't going to jam, was I? No, sirree, I says, just let me at 'em.

'Well the first one they gave me was a guy lived out in Raleigh. They showed me his home, told me when he'd be in, and how he had to be dead before I left the house. Turned out it was one of the doctors who'd certified me dead!'

'Didn't that strike you as odd, them killing their own people?' said Stanley. He himself had been working for these people.

'No.' Hollis was genuinely puzzled by this.

Stanley almost laughed. The expression on the man's face: he couldn't see what was wrong with killing people who were supposed to be on your own side.

'I used knives,' Hollis continued, his mind again fixed on rewind. 'Four of them. Cut him up *real* good. I spent a good twenty minutes cutting him before he died. By that time he was in – what? – nine different parts? No, the tongue was last, so that would make ten. That I put by the phone. Little humour. Then I got out of the house, met the car, and they drove me away to an empty motel.

'Once the murder had been confirmed and the local police revealed what I had done, even they looked at me with respect – and when the local police concluded it was some psycho satanists they were ecstatic! They even gave me a hooker, told me I could do what I wanted. I did.'

'What if she'd recognized you?'

'Wake up, Fulbright. Who was she going to tell? St Peter?'

Stanley's heart leapt. 'So . . . so how many have you . . .?'

'Terminated?'

'I was going to say butchered. I presume you don't just shoot them? That woman in Riva . . .'

'Shoot them? And miss all the fun? It's sixty-eight now. Sixty-nine if you include that sheriff. Seventy with you.'

Stanley began to shake again.

Hollis laughed. It was so easy. He had nothing against Fulbright, no real reason to kill him, but he would do it. No loose ends, Siemens always said.

He took another shug of beer. Alcohol sometimes helped him to be creative, and he had decided Agent Fulbright should have something special. Something really *inventive*.

He reached inside his pocket and pulled out a pair of handcuffs and dangled them in front of Stanley's ashen face.

Stanley shook his head. 'You don't need those.'

'No, but you do. People tend to turn uncooperative when you start slicing them. So give me your hand. *Now*.'

7

Cheryl Kenney didn't like her breasts. They were fine caged in a bikini or Wonderbra, but unleashed they headed south faster than a retired New York tailor. Yes, they made many a slobbering male's eyeballs pop upon being revealed (though, by that stage of the game, aesthetics were never high on her admirers' list of priorities). Unfortunately now, standing in her bedroom with bright morning sun highlighting her frame in the mirror, she was disappointed.

Okay, if you're nearing forty and you've had some kids, tits take a turn for the toes, but she was twenty-six, fit, childless and still in the market for Mr Right. She began to check the rest of her body but decided she was depressed enough. Cellulite and lines came with age but, while lines were up front and honest, cellulite was sneaky stuff, turning up just where a girl wouldn't see it – but others plainly could. She knew her sunbathing days were numbered.

She slipped on her bra and picked through the panties on the floor until she found a pair that looked clean, then clambered into her light-blue jeans and her yellow blouse – the sweat stains didn't show so much – and walked from the stifling atmosphere of her boxy bedroom into the greasy confines of her equally small kitchen. There she pulled out a carton of Florida orange-juice from the fridge, found a glass that wasn't cracked or covered in greasy fingermarks – she really would have to lay off the Colonel's chicken at least for a couple of days – and poured herself a full measure. She considered dropping in a couple of Alka Seltzers, but decided the noise would be too great. Instead she took a swig and bathed in the coolness that wafted over her from the still open fridge door. Her air-conditioner was on the fritz, and finances dictated a straight choice between getting that fixed or a new muffler on her Corvette. Her car won every time.

It was only after the second gulp that she remembered she had spiked the carton the night before with vodka to save time mixing it. She checked the clock over the stove: 6:48 a.m. She'd only had three hours' sleep, which didn't really count, so either this was a very late drink or a *far* too early drink. A too late drink. If she admitted to herself that it was actually the first of the day she'd have to acknowledge that she did have a problem. So, a late late nightcap it was.

She took two more swigs, belched, and put the carton back into its cold lonely home, with only a jar of peaches in Kirsch and two cans of Coors for company. She then grabbed her brown leather jacket off the back of the chair, checked the windows – Mikey, her cat, had a habit of sneaking in when she wasn't around – then it was out into the morning sun. She decided it was still early enough not to worry about those carcinogenic rays, so she took the hood off her white '86 Corvette and climbed in.

She gunned the engine, only remembering, as she let the tyres bite into the tarmac with their customary squeal of delight, that she would be disturbing the neighbours. But by then the car had a life of its own and she went with it, spinning right onto Echard and down to the junction with Maidstone, where she turned left and let the Chevy have its head. It was a good twenty minutes to the airfield – a bad forty-five in the rush hour – and she needed waking up.

She switched on the radio to her favourite station and let the heavy metal throb through the speakers. Soon she had forgotten about her figure and was remembering instead the disaster of the night before.

She couldn't believe that Rorke creep, after being handed a hot piece of ass on a plate, wanting to share it with his Neanderthal friends. If it had just been *him* in the parking lot, he wouldn't even have found out she was armed. Stupid prick. (Carrying the piece down the front of her jeans had proved a useful precaution before – a guy gets too fresh with his hands and comes across a gun, he's apt to think twice before coming on strong again.) She laughed as she remembered Rorke's screams when he woke up to find his balls burning, but it was small compensation for wasting a good pair of panties and near enough blowing her box off shooting at him the way she had. She picked up one of his business cards from the ashtray. He was manager of a computer store. HASKINS HARD BARGAINS & SOFT DEALS. Maybe she'd give him a ring, scare him a little . . .

The radio brought her back to the present. Whitesnake were blasting out a demand for her to 'Slide It In', and she would have been only too willing to oblige Mr Coverdale, droopy tits and all. Oblige his whole goddamned band, come to that! Now *there* was a thought.

Seventeen hot minutes later brought her to a sliding halt at the gate of Daniels Air Park – a record if she wasn't mistaken. Lucky the Highway Patrol hadn't been out. She smiled at the geek in his too-big blue uniform on the gate as he waved her through, reading his mind as he stared at her cleavage.

Dream on, dweeb. Dream on. She drove along the dusty perimeter road to the second of the three hangars on the right of the field, and parked the Corvette outside.

Inside it was cool, like a giant cavern, but she knew as the sun rose, so would the temperature and the poor guys inside would be sweating like crazy. Most of them worked wearing only shorts, and there were times when the smell of aviation oil, sweat and all that naked burnished flesh, some of it extremely cute, almost made it worth the hanging around waiting for a call. But today she wanted work. Standby pay was shit-all; she needed the mileage. Billy the head mechanic was already in – his wife had died a while back and he had little reason for going home – and he was tinkering with something on a bench. He threw her a hello which she returned two-fold, then walked into the office.

The room was a mess, and so disorganized it was probably FAA illegal. She parked herself on the desk next to Mulligan, her fat boss, and stared over his shoulder at the manifest.

'So what is it today?' she asked, taking a drag from the cigarette he had left in his stolen Miller ashtray. It made her cough. (She'd long quit smoking, but knew it annoyed Mulligan if he saw her doing it.)

True to form, he snatched the cigarette out of her hand like a disgusted father then sucked on it as if trying to inhale the remaining inch. He half succeeded, then stubbed it out, his ruddy face even redder.

'Bad for you, Cheryl,' he gasped. 'Give it up.'

She tapped his balding head. It was damp. 'Of course it is, Mulligan. Name one thing that's good that ain't bad.'

'Sunday gospel meetings.'

'Depends on the singing.'

She peered at the scrawl that passed for information on the clipboard in front of him.

'Take him where? San Antonio?'

'You wish. No – the Solardome.'

'*Our* Solardome? But it's all locked up.'

'He wants dropping inside on the field. The roof'll be open.'

'That's a help.'

'You pick him up at the airport, deliver, wait, take him where he wants to go. Billy's got number two all fuelled up. It's been valeted too, so watch the candy wrappers. The man's private flight gets in at 7:45. He doesn't like to be kept waiting. And he doesn't like to talk, so button it.'

'What, no politics?'

Before he could slap her rump she hopped back and grabbed a paper cup and poured herself a coffee. It smelled fresh enough not to be yesterday's brew warmed over – one of Mulligan's little economies – so she braved a sip. She pulled a face. He'd economized on the brand again, but it was bearable; she was dehydrated so anything wet would do. She needed a Tylanol as well, but knew better than to let Mulligan see that she had yet another headache. (She'd only remembered just in time to chew some Wrigley's Spearmint in the car to mask the alcohol on her breath.)

She checked her watch: 7:18. Time to go. She dropped the cup into the wastebasket – Mulligan tutting at her blatant profligacy – and headed for the door.

'How about combing your hair?' said Mulligan. 'Make-up wouldn't hurt either.'

'Hey, you want glamour, *you* supply the cosmetics.'

Mulligan shook his head, his red jowls wobbling. He was

an okay guy – if she chose to forget how he came to own the business – but he was fighting a losing battle. They were down to three charter choppers now, and one of those wasn't fit for a trade-in. However, Cheryl made a point of sliding a comb through her hair, trying not to wince as it caught on tangles. She supposed she liked Mulligan, despite their history, and liked her job, but they didn't make up for that big hole in her life. Trouble was, she didn't know what the hell the hole was!

She blew Mulligan a kiss which, as always, he caught and stuffed in his top drawer, then she walked out to the yellow Bell 206 Jet Ranger with MULLIGANAIR stencilled in green on the door, parked alongside the hangar.

She climbed in, slammed the door and shrugged off her jacket. She'd been in a hurry the evening before, and had parked the chopper exactly in the right place to catch the sun – consequently it was like an oven. She slid open her window and began her start-up procedure. Just as she was about to fire up the engine, Mulligan came waddling out of the hangar, waving a manifest at her. Shit. Where was her head these days?

She made sure the engine had started before Mulligan reached her, so that she didn't have to listen to his abuse. Then she opened her door and snatched the clipboard, pointing at the whirling rotors above. Dropping the clipboard on the passenger seat, she noticed a yellow Post-it note and its message, PLEASE BE POLITE, as she began to accelerate rotation. Wasn't she always polite? Suddenly she jerked open the door and hawked a greeny near Mulligan's retreating feet, pleased he didn't see her unladylike behaviour – but when you've gotta spit, you gotta spit.

Slamming her door, she eased forward the collective pitch lever and throttle in her right hand so the chopper would rise, letting it hover noisily ten feet above the ground as she assessed her feel for the controls, then she called the tower for clearance.

Clearance granted, she played the tail rotor pedals to swing the Jet Ranger through ninety degrees to point it towards the open field, then, increasing engine power and pushing gently on the cyclic pitch column in her left hand, she was rewarded by a surge of power that had the helicopter zooming across the airfield, its nose down, but her spirits only slightly raised.

She might fly helicopters – which were a sight more sexy than fixed-wing aircraft – but she was no more than a glorified cabdriver. Christ, even her Jet Ranger was painted yellow like a checker cab!

8

Stanley was shaken awake in the dark. Christ, how had he fallen asleep? He looked at the laser-disc player, its clock showing 6:23. It was the only light visible in the darkness of the Winnebago. Suddenly a shadow loomed over him, obscuring the clock. It smelled of alcohol, its breathing heavy. He sensed it move to his right and settle.

Stanley was sitting on the couch with his back to the wall, his legs stretched in front of him, his left arm handcuffed to a lamp above him and long since numb. Hollis was seated beside him on his right on the floor, his back also to the wall, his head on a level with Stanley's waist. They were sitting like two old friends sharing a bottle and remembering old times, except Hollis didn't share his drink and Stanley didn't want to hear any more stories.

'You never knew your momma did you, Fulbright?'

'No.' Terrified as he was – he fully expected to be shot or stabbed – Stanley knew he had to stay calm.

'I knew my momma, Fulbright. Right up to the moment she died, when I was twenty-two. Right up to that last gasp and that last wide-eyed look. Her pupils slowly opened up as she died, like light didn't matter no more. Funny that. When people die you close the shades, but their own shades open.'

Stanley heard the sloosh of liquid as the man swigged from a bottle. He wished to God he could see, but he might as well have been blindfolded.

'I knew momma every day of my life,' said Hollis. 'From the day I was born she was there, loving like no momma ever loved her son. She was strict but she was fair.'

Another swig. The man was beginning to slur his words which meant he was half way to being full-out drunk – and that Stanley did not want to see. He couldn't decide whether this gave him an edge or had simply shortened his period of grace. He decided to egg the man on in his ramblings.

'You loved her?'

The stink of alcohol blew in his face. *How close was he?* ''Course I loved my momma! Doesn't everyone? Well, 'cept you 'cos you never knew your momma.'

'How did your momma die?' asked Stanley and knew immediately he had made a mistake. He wished to God he could remember more of Hollis's exploits prior to his execution.

'She died of love. *My* love.'

Now Stanley remembered. Hollis had murdered his mother. Tortured her to death. It had taken *days*. He felt the urge to vomit again but he knew his stomach was empty.

Hollis started to whine. It was a weird sick sound, and in the dark doubly frightening. As he keened he began to call for his momma, like a little boy after a nightmare, afraid to lower the sheets and go to her room. Except Hollis was the nightmare and there was no mother and Stanley knew that being privy to such a display was his death warrant. *Try and steer the conversation away from his mother, you fool.*

'What about your father?'

Another swig and, judging by the loud splashback when he lowered it, the bottle was well towards being empty.

'Dead. Plane crash. He was a deputy sheriff. Hitched a ride

taking a suspect to Lincoln. Plane hit a storm. Took them a week to find the wreckage. I was six. That left just momma and me.'

Another swig, and a belch. Smelled like bourbon. Stanley had seen a bottle of Jack Daniels somewhere. Why couldn't it be bloody beer? He had to keep the man talking. He closed his eyes tight, then opened them again. No difference. *Jesus . . .*

Okay, Stanley, think it through. Work out your position: where things are. This is his home. He knows his way around in the dark but he's also canned, so that could make us even.

An image flashed into his mind of two blind swordsmen lashing out at each other, desperate for their blades to find flesh, but hearing only the whistling of steel and the stumbling of misguided feet, until one was impaled or sliced by the other's weapon. He felt a wet tap on his cheek; Hollis was nudging him with the bottle, its suddenness like walking into a cobweb in the dark. He shuddered.

'Momma did everything for me, every day. Dressed me, washed me, fed me, taught me. Punished me if I was bad. And I *was* bad. Used to wet the bed all the time. Used to make me go to sleep with a rubber band wrapped round my little pecker. "Plug up that leaky tap", she said. Hurt sometimes when it woke me up. I'd lie there waiting for her to let me use the bathroom. I didn't dare take it off. Did that one time – sewed up my foreskin, threatened to make it permanent.'

'She *what*?'

'Sewed it up. With cotton. Learned my lesson that night. But it was all because she loved me, wanted me to grow up right. Taught me everything she knew. How to use a knife and fork, how to read and do math, how to keep my room tidy, the proper way to bury animals. Told me all a boy needs to know. Taught me hard but she taught me well. 'Course I was clumsy, made lots of mistakes and she had to punish me, but she *always* said it was because she loved me, and I knew the hurting was good. Even when she let me sleep with her, the lessons didn't let up. Or the pain. Soon got to enjoy that part, once I'd turned ten – the things she did. Never let me touch her, said it was dirty for a boy to poke his momma, but she said I needed regular cleaning; needed to have the demons in me released into the world so they didn't fester. Needed them demons releasing every morning and every night and, if they didn't want to come out, momma had her ways. She had her ropes and her pulleys and her plug. Knew how to keep a boy interested. And I loved her. The best momma a boy ever had, all that pain and love, couldn't be bettered.'

'Did . . . did you go to school?'

Hollis sounded positively wistful. 'No need. We lived out aways and momma taught me. I passed all the tests the local schoolboard set and, as momma only had to make sure I was educated, they let me stay at home. Never left the house. No need, momma said. I didn't believe her, so every so often I would sneak out and when she caught me, whooh boy . . .'

As his mind wandered off down some byway of hell, Stanley tried to remember any details of Hollis's trial. He murdered women in their twenties and early thirties. Never raped them, but semen stains were always present at the scene; part of the forensic evidence that trapped him. Early thirties?

'How old was your momma when you . . . when your daddy died?'

'How old? When daddy died? Why nineteen, of course.'

Nineteen? And he had been six? That meant she gave birth to him at thirteen, and was thirty-five when he killed her.

Hollis sat up and grabbed Stanley's face and squeezed his cheeks painfully. 'My momma was the best momma that ever lived! She *loved* me. She was just. Right. I loved my momma. I deserved everything I got. From the first day I spilled my demons and she knew I had to be cleansed, from that day on she worked to clean me, to rid me of the badness. And it worked. Came a time only momma could get them demons riled and spitting. Came a time only my thinking of momma could scare them enough to spit.'

There was a final swig, a burp, and the sound of an empty bottle rolling across carpet until it hit something solid.

'Need me a bottle,' said Hollis, getting to his feet.

Stanley squinted in the dark but only heard the man crashing towards the bar. Tugging as hard as he could at the handcuffs, he realized they weren't going to be pulled apart and whatever they were attached to was equally obstinate.

There was a bleeping. A phone. Somewhere near Hollis. He swore and fumbled the receiver from its cradle.

'What?' he barked. 'No! No, not . . . When I'm . . . Don't push it, remember who . . . Fuck you, man!'

The phone slammed down and Hollis mumbled incoherently as he stumbled towards the refrigerator.

Stanley heaved himself as far forward as he could to see, but the blackness was so all-pervading that, if it wasn't for the faint glimmer of the clock, he could have been led to believe that the ghost of Hollis's momma had stitched up his eyelids while he slept.

He heard a bottle being cracked open, then he saw a thin

white strip of light, and silhouetted fingers snagged around the neck of a bottle as Hollis's hand reached into the fridge. The door closed, but as the pencil line of light shrank and disappeared it reflected off something in the man's other hand. Something metallic and sharp.

A knife. Oh God.

Stanley found himself shrinking back along the couch and curling into a ball, his knees drawn up to his chest, free hand wrapped round his shins. This was it – the end. Stabbed to death in the dark by a drunken maniac in a closed building full of OCI agents, not one of whom apparently was going to raise a finger even if he screamed himself hoarse.

Hollis was speaking, his words slurring into one another.

'Orders. Fuck orders. Yessir, nossir . . . I do what I do 'cos I wannado it, not 'cos some fuck inna suit tells me!'

He sat down heavily on the end of the couch, oblivious to the fact that Stanley had only just moved his legs out of the way.

'You,' he said in a rough whisper. 'You gotta go. Orders.'

'Who . . . whose orders?'

'The big man. Mr Siemens. Ol' baby-juice hisself.'

'Siemens?' Stanley didn't know what to think; things just kept getting worse. 'Siemens has *ordered* you to kill me?'

'Orders is orders.'

Hollis fell silent. He wasn't bothered about the killing – Stanley could tell that – but that he had been ordered to do it, and it was then that Stanley knew he only had seconds to act. He slowly edged his left leg down the slab cushion of the couch until he felt resistance. *Hollis's thigh. Don't press too hard; you know where he is now. Assume he isn't sitting upright, but slightly slumped: that's how he tends to sit, isn't it?*

Listen to him: his breathing, his drinking. Get his attention, for God's sake. Talk to him.

'Hollis, what will you do when they want rid of you?'

'Take as many of them as I can.'

'But what . . .?' He'd got a fix on where the voice was coming from, but it was muffled. Was he holding up a glass? *Damn this darkness.* 'What if they just strafe this RV?'

There was a long pause. Invisible ice chinked in front of a hidden face. There was a snigger. What was he thinking?

'You couldn't do—'

'What's going on?' said Hollis, cold and calm.

'What?'

The voice turned towards him. Oh God, he was *facing* him. Stanley was convinced Hollis had night vision, that his eyes had yellowed and his pupils were constricted to vertical slits and he was staring at him, seeing the sweat running down his temple. Hollis's other senses would be heightened as well, the alcohol irrelevant. He'd be able to smell the piss in Stanley's trousers, hear the racing of his heart and know his plan, because in the dark the madman knew all and was simply waiting for the right moment to deal with him.

'Why the talk, Fulbright? What's the game?'

Stanley held his breath. There was a buzz from the fridge, but otherwise the world had died and all that was left were two voices, one hunting the other like disembodied spirits. The awful silence continued, Stanley willed himself to make out the man's shape, but saw only coloured sparkles and flecks he knew were in his optical nerve and not in the Winnebago. The dark had become a cocoon – or a shroud – that was wrapping him tighter until he would be ready to burst like rotted fruit at the first touch from Hollis's knife.

Then he heard the sound of ice sliding in a glass, as ominous as the cracking on an ice-bound river at the dead of the night – and then, worse, Hollis's voice, quiet and knowing:

'You can start breathing again, Fulbright.'

God, he can hear me holding my breath.

'You're going be a long time not breathing.'

As Stanley began to tremble, he heard the chink of ice again, closer to the voice, the last syllable muffled. Then a swallow. He was drinking from the glass. *Now.*

Stanley brought his right foot up and across to his left as hard as he could and felt something solid dig into the front of his ankle but it gave immediately and there was a sharp gasp and then breaking glass and he felt an arm flap past his face and thump into the dividing wall behind the couch. He pulled his foot back and kicked twice more, each time making contact with the man's face – then he heard a thump and felt the couch rise, as Hollis's weight left it.

There was an agonizing pause as he waited for the man to leap on him in fury, slashing and carving his way up his body to his eyes, but nothing happened.

Stanley swung himself off the couch, but couldn't find the floor. Hollis was lying alongside the couch. Stanley felt down, touched the man's chest, found wetness – the spilled drink – and carried on up until he touched a jaw – rough, needing a shave – and on up to a mouth, open, and he heard the heavy breathing, a rasping. He felt the cheek. Wet. Warm. He felt up along Hollis's nose. It felt hot and unnatural. Broken? Then the eyes. Closed. The man was out. But for how long? And what would he do once roused, with Stanley still tethered to the couch? Suddenly Stanley realized what he had done.

Key! There must be a key to the cuffs!

He felt down, remembering the man was wearing just a shirt with one top pocket. And jeans – four pockets there.

There was nothing in the top pocket.

He ran his hands down to Hollis's waist, found an empty hand. The knife. Where was that? At least he would have a weapon if Hollis woke up. *Woke up?* Fuck that, stab the bastard. Right in the heart. End any chance of him rousing. He was going to do you, Stanley – so do him first. He touched the man's arm, still unable to see anything, but found Hollis's other hand empty as well. A cursory fumble on the carpeting revealed only broken glass and an ice-cube. Shit.

Back to the jeans' pockets. Stanley sat up, placed both feet under the other man's back and slowly lifted, leaning down as best he could to feel in his back pockets. Unfortunately, they too were empty, but he did find something else: a small pistol, tucked in Hollis's back, underneath his belt. Even if he had wrestled the knife from him, Hollis would have pulled the gun and blown him away, no doubt laughing as he did so. Stanley pulled it out.

It was small, snub-nosed. He cocked it and aimed it in the dark at the man's face. It would be so easy – and so right – to blow the cocksucker away. Self-defence. But, thinking it through, he envisioned himself sitting in the blackness next to a corpse, his situation untenable. No, never mind getting Hollis; all he wanted was to be out of the RV. At best now, he could hold the man hostage . . . Would that be possible? Bargain for his release?

He couldn't help laughing – and the sound hung in the air like a sneering stranger in the dark ridiculing him. Then it came to him: *shoot the handcuffs!*

Stanley couldn't believe he could have been so stupid. If he could lose the handcuffs, he could make a run for it. It was a slim chance, but what other option did he have?

He edged up against the Winnebago's outer wall and pulled the stiff shade aside and looked out onto the field. To his surprise the place was relatively light and seemed deserted. Siemens must have had the other agents moved away, so they didn't hear or see anything untoward. All he had to do was get to the spectator seats without being seen. *Yeah, that's all . . .*

Stanley wanted to debate his actions but he heard Hollis groan and knew it was the cuffs or the man, and either way he would be alerting those outside.

He sat as far away from his hand as he could, pulling the cuff taut and, praying that his aim was true in the dark, he pushed the barrel of the gun against the short steel linkage, felt it give, then – holding his hand upwards, and turning his face to look downwards – he fired.

His hand came free instantly but the flare from the gunshot revealed in its single nightmare strobe flash the face of Hollis looking up, his eyes open, the lower half of his face covered in blood as if he had just torn the throat out of some animal. But it was those eyes that Stanley carried with him as the darkness returned. Hollis had been staring straight up at him, hatred like a living thing hunkered and waiting in the blacker black of his wide pupils. In the darkness the man hissed – an inhuman venting of hatred and evil promise. Stanley felt as if he was trapped in a deep cave with an inhuman creature who existed solely to burrow its way through his flesh and tear at his heart. He crawled along the couch towards the kitchen area in the darkness, sheer terror fuelling his actions, but as he stepped off a hand grabbed his trouser leg, nails digging in.

Stanley thrashed out with his other leg and his hands, but his left arm was numbed from being held up for so long, and was useless. He batted at the man's spider-like grip with the revolver, but it would not release, so he fired the gun down onto the floor where he had seen Hollis's face.

Another flash, another thunderous roar, a mouth open in a snarl, eyes promising a retribution unimaginable to sane men.

The hand on his leg suddenly jerked away, knocking the gun out of his hand, as blackness crashed back into the room. Stanley didn't wait to see if it was the death throes of the man. Instead he hurled himself into the main gangway and crawled on his belly for several feet, then staggered up and charged for the central side door, fumbled for the door handle, then pulled it down.

And he was out into the light, falling face first onto the turf, its smell a beautiful clean normal thing after the sweat and dead meat and alcohol stink he had been confined with for the last few hours. He stood up and tried to get his bearings. He had been in pitch darkness for hours and his eyes were finding it hard to focus. He needed to reach the cover of the seating because he had no way of knowing where anyone would come from, or how soon they would appear.

It was twenty yards to the nearest sideline and he covered it faster than any wide receiver had done since the Solardome had been home to the Clinger Coyotes.

He heard a shout a long way off but he ignored it and he crossed the line, hit the bleachers and took a flying leap onto the third row of seats, landing full-length on his right side. Despite the pain, he forced himself to roll out of sight underneath the seats.

Peering over the top of the seats, he saw a ring of men forming around the Winnebago, some staring at the van while others, ominously, were scanning the 'Dome, but none, as yet, were looking his way. It was only a matter of time before someone entered the RV and found out whether Hollis was dead or not, and then all hell would break loose. He had to find a way out – and find it fast.

9 Siemens walked the short distance from his parked Lear Jet to the chartered helicopter at Clinger Airport. It was going to be another scorching day, and he got to see daylight so rarely even these five minutes were welcome.

He had made it company policy to use small-time air charter or car-hire companies. The criteria for their selection would have raised eyebrows in certain quarters, were they known, not least among board members of SB&H who were paying for today's trip.

In most cases the charter companies were run by people who had something to hide, and could be leaned on to ensure discretion. Others were in such tenuous financial circumstances they were willing to do anything with no questions asked – or records kept. It also cut down on overheads, a constant source of worry to Siemens as he tried to juggle his legitimate enterprises and his other work. So far he had succeeded, but it was always a battle, particularly as even secret work has to be paid for.

There were those who thought this added to the risk of exposure, but Siemens saw it as the expeditious use of resources: the more people owing you favours, the more chances you had of garnering the kind of loyalty that money can't buy. Take the charter company who owned the yellow Jet Ranger he was heading for now: Mulliganair.

It was operated by ex-Vietnam vet Frank Mulligan who

had been cashiered for black-marketeering in '72 and who had since managed to cover his tracks pretty well, until Siemens found him. His outfit was run on the very edge of FAA regulations and would probably be shut down if it was looked at closely but, in return for no-questions-asked ferrying work at low rates, Siemens kept the FAA off Mulligan's back. Subsequent OCI investigations had shown it wasn't only Mulligan who was contravening the rules; one of his pilots shouldn't have been flying either.

Siemens reached the Jet Ranger, its rotorblades turning slowly, suddenly regretting his short excursion in the sun – he was still wearing his blue Gaultier duster coat. With a curt nod at the female pilot, he climbed in and settled in a rear passenger seat.

Cheryl wondered why the man hadn't sat up front, then saw him open a briefcase and decided he wanted to do some work. Fine by her. Her headache would give her enough problems just concentrating on flying – never mind talking as well. She climbed in, slammed her door, belted up, contacted Clinger International tower for clearance, then throttled up and took off.

Siemens scanned the report that was scrolling up on the laptop computer in front of him, and his anger grew. The fiasco at Riva had gotten out of all proportion, their agent actually allowing Hollis to kill the town's sheriff! Baxter had some explaining to do.

He erased the report – standard procedure – and slammed the lid, pondering what to do next, tapping his jaw with his balled fist. Containment of the incident had continued after Hollis and his 'rescuer' had left, but the situation had demanded drastic action. There were at least five witnesses who had seen Hollis, and others who had seen this Fulbright moron. Siemens had debated alternatives; he didn't care about the people involved, it was purely the practicality of the exercise, as cover-ups have a habit of becoming bigger nuisances than the original problem – just ask Nixon. The fuck-up in Riva had become a boil that needed pricking; the question was how big a knife to use in lancing it?

He looked out of the window onto the hot city below. It looked like a hundred other cities he had seen from the air. So many people doing so many different things for so little purpose. At the end of it all, every single one of them would die. What difference if a few died sooner rather than later? And who was there to care, when they lived out in the middle of nowhere? Ants, they were all ants. This colony might be a thousand times larger than the speck that was Riva, but two million, two thousand or just two inhabitants – what were numbers? What counted was the agency's work; if ever ends justified means, it was OCI's true purpose.

He had made his decision eight hours before and was sure it had been the right one. All he had to do now was dispose of Fulbright and placate Hollis. For at the end of the day, whatever happened, Hollis was what mattered. Without him OCI and Siemens were a gun capable only of firing blanks; but with Hollis and his loving they were a weapon that had true potency and true worth.

He locked his briefcase and settled back and closed his eyes. He rarely slept – such a waste of time. Naps were all he needed and, if the unsteadiness of their take-off was anything to go by, the settling of the chopper as it landed in the Solardome would rouse him.

They were flying east and the cockpit was hot, and Cheryl

was glad she had removed her flying jacket. It was against company policy not to be uniformed when carrying passengers, but she really couldn't give a shit. The guy was hardly likely to get up and walk out was he?

She yawned. Last night's 'excitement', her lack of sleep and the vodka were playing havoc with her biorhythms. In fact she couldn't remember the last time she'd worked a straight eight-hour day and had a good six hours' sleep. What she needed was a vacation: a couple of weeks in Hawaii or a cruise. Laze in the rays, check out the talent; two weeks of bed and booze. The risks she had taken last night proved just how desperate she was for the former.

Christ, she could be lying in a hospital bed now, nursing God-knows-what injuries. Or worse, she could be lying in a morgue. Still, she couldn't help smiling. If those boys hadn't come on so rough she'd probably have let them do her anyway. Sometimes she wished she didn't like her sex hard and heavy; there were times she wished she could see the appeal of good wine, a log fire and slow lazy lovemaking with a good-looking guy who whispered her name and told her he loved her and cried when he came. But then she would remember that she didn't love anyone, and that what she wanted was to be *fucked*. Big as she was she liked to be used, although even she knew her size meant she always retained that element of control.

Take the time she'd kicked the crap out of that guy who started using a candlestick on her. Or that creep, the airline pilot, who'd tied her over a coffee table, then spent a couple of hours jerking off on her back. As soon as he had untied her *without having laid a finger on her*, she'd punched him out. But, for all the disappointments, there were some moments she always came back to in her fantasies.

The busboy in Denver, the monster truck mechanic, the two dentists, that time after the Prom . . . Now *that* was one time she would give anything to relive.

She spotted the Clinger Solardome glinting on the horizon by the interstate, and it broke her reverie. She shouted the appearance of their destination but got no response. A quick glance over her shoulder told her the man hadn't donned his earphones and he seemed to be asleep.

From watching him approach the chopper, she had estimated him to be six-two or six-three, and very well built. He was good-looking too. His clothes spoke money, his manner said authority, his eyes forbade conversation. He was a man used to getting his own way. She braved a second look. Yes, if he wanted to have his way with her, she wouldn't say no.

Listen to yourself, she thought. *I'm hot – and it isn't just the sun!* She worried at times that she was too obsessed with sex; it was in her thoughts all day, whatever she was doing. She wondered if she was a nymphomaniac and, while the idea always made her laugh, there were times when she would take a closer look at herself.

If she went more than a few days without sex she would become real antsy and unpleasant to be around, and masturbation just made things worse. If only she could relieve the pressure that way, things would have been fine but, no matter how good it was, when it was over it just made her yearn for the real thing. A while back she'd shared an apartment with another girl, and once or twice they'd made out with each other, but neither of them were really dykes and it ended up just plain embarrassing. No, she was straight; it was just her approach that was a bit crooked.

She circled the Solardome, checking there was adequate clearance and that the field below was empty, then she slowly descended through the roof into the huge arena.

She could see uniformed men dotted around the perimeter of the field, wearing dark blue jackets with LAW on the back. There was also a large black Winnebago parked towards one end of the field. A man was guiding her down, waving his arms, and she decided to trust his judgement.

She managed a gentle landing, but even before she had secured the helicopter, the rear passenger door was open and the man had stepped down onto the field and was walking quickly over to a shorter man in a grey suit who was limping slightly as he made his way to meet him.

'Thanks for the ride,' she said sarcastically, taking off her headphones and wiping the sweat out of her ears.

Checking her watch, she filled in the manifest. Eleven minutes' flying time. Maybe she should have taken a roundabout route but, then again, her instructions were to wait.

She turned on the radio. The Red Hot Chili Peppers were demanding she 'Give It Away'.

For you boys, she thought, *any time, any time, any time.*

10

Stanley knew it would be pointless to try and run from the Solardome. It would be surrounded by OCI agents, each with orders to shoot him on sight. And, as the place was stranded in a ring of empty parking lots, he would be an open target.

He hurried down an exit to the main concourse that ran round the underside of the upper tiers of seating. Just getting across the concourse would be impossible as he would be visible for seventy-five yards in each direction, its sheer width negating any cover the curve might have offered. He reached the end of the passage and skidded to a halt and leaned against the wall. He braved a look into the concourse – and immediately whipped his head back.

There were six men, all dressed in blue LAW over-jackets. There would have to be similar numbers positioned all over the 'Dome. He edged up to the corner again and keened an ear, hoping to hear their conversation. Instead he heard someone running towards him, boots echoing loudly.

He turned and ran back down the exit, dashing through the first door he could find. Marked PRIVATE, it led him into a thin, curving corridor that approached a group of doors out of sight of the door he had entered by. He tried the first one.

Marked 11A, it was a storeroom. Paints, a lining cart, brushes, brooms. He considered grabbing something for use as a weapon, but heard the door at the top of the corridor opening. He didn't want to be trapped in a glorified broom closet, armed with a brush. He slid out and edged along the wall to the next door, aware of the entrance to the corridor closing. No turning back now.

As he reached for the handle of 11B, the door to 11A snapped shut with a bang like a rifleshot. The oncoming footsteps stilled. He held his breath. There was a long pause, then he heard a small metallic click and a scraping noise. Someone cocking an automatic pistol. They'd be able to spray the corridor by keeping their finger on the trigger – and there was no way they could miss him with the fifteen shots their OCI-issue Beretta 9mm automatics held.

Stanley couldn't risk crossing to the alternative doors on the other side of the corridor, or the one at the end, so it had to be 11B, assuming of course, that it was even unlocked.

He pushed the handle down and felt the door give. It *was* unlocked, but he didn't move. Instead he tried to hear his pursuer, but all was silence. He couldn't see anything either: just the bare cement floor, beige brick walls and neon tubes marching the length of the ceiling. But then he saw a shadow move on the far wall: the man was nearly in sight. Another couple of seconds . . .

Stanley stepped into 11B, shut the door and leaned against it. He'd thought 11B couldn't be worse than the closet that was 11A, but it was. It was a shower room.

Two rows of benches, separated by a head-high wire frame with hooks for clothing, led to a communal shower area with three showerheads. On his right were a dozen metal lockers, on his left two toilet stalls, both with modesty panels instead of full-length doors and – other than a dirty towel hanging from a hook near the showers that must have been used to mop the floors – it was bereft of anything portable. It also offered no viable hiding place.

Stanley started to shake. At least in 11A he would have had weapons to hand, but here . . . all he could hope was that the guy would slip on some soap and bang his head! He leaned against the door, fighting to keep from being sick. Another thirty seconds and he could be dead. He had to do something. How about surrendering? No. Siemens was going to have him killed, come what may. He had to fight; there was no alternative.

He moved to the lockers and tried each of the stubby metal handles, but they refused to open. He looked back at the door. There was a sound out in the corridor. A careful, slow sound, and then a gentle creak. The door to 11A. It would take the man ten seconds to realize it was empty. Stanley considered hiding in one of the stalls but, even if he squatted up on the toilet seat, all the guy had to do was push open the door and unload his clip into him. Then all the others would have to do was cart his body away and mop up the blood – on a floor designed for easy cleaning. The irony was not lost on him, despite his terror. Then he heard the adjoining door slam open, the man bustle in, the clatter of a bucket and a muted oath. *Think, Stanley, think!*

Two minutes later the door to 11B slowly opened and the black muzzle of a gun poked its way through the three-inch gap between it and the doorframe. Then the door was flung open with a crash, and a man in black jeans, black boots, black shirt and a dark blue jacket with the word LAW in foot-high yellow letters front and back burst in, his pistol sweeping the room at chest height, eager to sight a target.

The room was empty except for a man having a shower so, training his gun on the naked man still standing with his back to him, he quickly checked the rest of the area. Lockers on the right, toilets on the left, both gates open, a guy in the shower, steam rising, clothes on a hook at the end of the benches, the guy singing tunelessly and soaping his body.

Relaxing slightly, the man with the gun walked the length of the room until he had reached the clothes hanging on the last hook. As he was about to check them out, the man turned round and began soaping his penis and balls right there in front of him. The man with the gun froze. Who was this guy? Why was he showering now? This was a groundstaff restroom, but there shouldn't be any groundstaff around, not since OCI had commandeered the place.

Just then the guy started to stroke his penis. He was talking to it too; calling it his 'big big pal'. Oh, Jesus. The man with the gun didn't know what to do. He had his gun trained on a man who looked about to jack off! So he coughed, then spoke.

'Hey you, fella, what you doing?'

The man in the shower froze and slowly looked up, his hair plastered down by the water, most of his body covered in soap. He let go of his penis and slowly held up his hands.

'Hey, don't shoot. I didn't know you were there. I wasn't coming on to you or anything. I'm not even like that. I—'

'Shut up. Who are you? What you doing here?'

The guy looked down at his penis and offered a weak smile as if to say it was pretty obvious.

'Name?' barked the agent.

'Ch-Chandler. B-Bill Chandler. There's no need for . . .'

'ID?'

The man shook his head. 'Look, pass me the towel. I'll sort it all out. I know I'm not supposed to be here . . .'

The other man hesitated, then, shifting the gun into his left hand, reached for the towel hanging on the last hook, his eyes never leaving those of the man in the shower.

He gripped the dark blue towel, lifted it off the hook and held it out to the man. It felt heavy. Wet. The man in the shower was rubbing his eyes. The man with the gun took one second to look at the towel. It was filthy. What was—?

The naked man grabbed the towel and, before he could loose his grip, the other man was pulled into the shower and head-butted.

Dazed, the OCI man tried to swing the gun up to shoot, but Stanley grabbed him by his collar and ran him back on to the metal frame dividing the two benches. There was a resounding twang as the back of his head made contact with the metal pole, and the whole frame vibrated with the impact. The man went down, his legs splayed out in front of him, the gun clattering across the floor to rest in a pool of water.

Stanley stood over him, water dripping off his body, unable to believe his luck – or that his plan had come together. *The element of surprise, Stanley, is all.*

However, he wasn't sure what to do next, so he squatted down and checked the OCI man's pulse. Slow and steady – good, he hadn't killed him. *Sorry guy, but it was you or me.*

He stood up and realized he needed to go to the bathroom. A long night of terror with Hollis and the tension of the last half hour were proving too much for his constitution. He debated whether he could afford the time but the growling in his bowels told him no contest, and he only reached the nearest stall in time before his insides emptied themselves.

His enforced evacuation gave him a moment to think through his next action, and by the time he had flushed the toilet he knew what he was going to do.

The OCI man was about his size, so Stanley stripped him to his underwear then tied him to the frame with his belt and gagged him with the towel. He donned the man's jeans, shirt, LAW jacket and his cap, put on his own shoes, pocketed the Beretta, and made his way into the corridor.

He tried the other three doors but found only a ladies' shower-room, and two more closets, so he had no alternative but to make his way back up to the exit.

He did have the advantage of looking like any one of a hundred other OCI guys in the 'Dome; but he also had the disadvantage of not knowing what his plan of action should be. Add to that the fact that he would be gunned down the second he was spotted, and Hollis's offer of the previous night to end it quickly took on a whole new appeal.

Some minutes later, as he crouched behind a parapet overlooking a second-tier entrance on the west side of the Solardome, he saw, to his dismay, twenty or so men on the field, with a cordon around the Winnebago and three men standing guard by a yellow Bell Jet Ranger helicopter parked in the centre. Looking around he could also see a search pattern had been instigated, and each row was being systematically checked. Eventually they would cover every row, so lying underneath the seating would prove futile. But what else could he do?

Bluff his way out? Offer waves and grunts to other LAW men as he proceeded to the outside of the building? Yes, he could do that, but to actually get out of the building would require him to give the password of the day – and that he didn't know. So what else was there?

He looked up at the 'Dome roof. It was half open, allowing clear blue sky and sunlight to pour through. So near yet . . . He lowered his gaze to the field. *The helicopter.* He might not be able to bluff his way out of the building but he might just bluff his way on to the field and into that chopper, and then . . . and then he'd need a pilot.

He squinted across at the Jet Ranger, too yellow on the too green grass. He saw a woman step out of the helicopter and trot over to someone he assumed to be Siemens, who was standing with Baxter – the man who had ordered him to Riva – about ten yards from the rear of the Winnebago. There was a heated exchange, but the Solardome swallowed the words before they could reach him. Baxter went inside the Winnebago, and the woman spoke to Siemens, then walked back to the chopper. *She* was his ticket out of here.

He edged along the parapet but, realizing that if he acted suspiciously he would be caught, he took a deep breath and began walking down the long stairway to the bottom tier of seats, pausing every so often to look along the rows and praying the chopper wasn't about to take off, because if it did and he wasn't in it, he was doomed.

As he began to walk onto the field he realized how vast a building it was. It was the outdoors inside, and he felt as exposed walking diagonally from the west ten-yard line to the centre of the field as a duck in the sights of a hunter – except that there were forty hunters here and he didn't have the luxury of flight. Yet.

He reached the twenty-yard line, now within the ring of

OCI men, in the heart of the beast so to speak. No turning back. Another ten yards . . . The woman had been fixing the door of the helicopter but had finished and was climbing back in. Never mind that; concentrate on getting there. Keep your mind clear, head up, don't look guilty. Look like you *belong*.

He passed an agent who nodded at him. He nodded back. Look like you're going somewhere; it's no different from walking a city street at night: got to look like you know where you're going, and not like you're a stranger. Blend in.

Another man, another nod.

Forty-yard line. Almost there. The chopper was starting up, its engine turning the rotors faster and faster.

Another man, holding up his hand. He had a radio. He wanted him to stop, to speak. Stanley didn't falter. Instead he pointed at Siemens and raised his eyebrows. The man followed his finger, nodded him through.

Close. Real close.

He was three-quarters of the way to the chopper, with Siemens directly in front of him, but he couldn't risk changing course for the helicopter if the agent he had just passed was still watching him. It would be so much easier to throw his hands up in the air, scream 'Don't shoot!' and surrender. Surely Siemens couldn't execute an unarmed man in front of thirty witnesses, even if they worked for him? But commonsense stood its ground and Stanley continued to walk.

The chopper's rotor was getting wound up, ready to take off. He walked past Siemens, who was looking away from him. Stanley pulled his cap down and turned ninety degrees. There was no going back now.

As he reached the front of the Jet Ranger he waved at the pilot and pointed at the passenger door, then walked round and opened it. He detected movement behind him. He glanced at the glass canopy, saw a distorted image of several LAW men walking towards him and Siemens waving his arms. Stanley pulled himself up into the passenger seat and slammed the door.

'Take off!' he shouted above the roar of the engine.

The pilot looked at him, unable to hear in her headphones, then looked at the men running towards the chopper. She looked back at Stanley and shook her head, relaxing her grip on the controls and letting the engine slow.

The men were nearer, all shouting, most drawing weapons. Stanley drew his own. He pointed it at her.

'Get us out of here! Now!'

She shook her head again. 'Shoot me and you don't go anywhere!'

He pulled the gun to the left and fired once, a neat hole and spiderweb appearing in the window in her door.

'If I shoot you you're fucking dead. Now fly!'

She took a moment then decided to comply, pushing the control forward, and Stanley felt the Jet Ranger lift off.

Immediately shots rang out and two holes appeared in his door and another high up on the windshield.

'Crazy bastards!' she shouted.

Stanley hadn't expected them to try and shoot them out of the sky. Suddenly the helicopter started to rotate.

'What's wrong?' he shouted.

Cheryl was too busy fighting the chopper to speak but, as it turned in a circle thirty feet above the field, the machine caught up with its own trail of smoke and the severity of the problem became clear: they were on fire and out of control.

There were more shots, then Stanley caught a glimpse of Siemens waving frantically at everyone to stop. He must have realized the stupidity of downing a helicopter on top of himself.

'Get it up, get it up!' screamed Stanley redundantly as the helicopter continued to spin.

'Tail rotor's gone!' shouted Cheryl, pressing the pedals futilely. 'Can't keep us straight! Might hit the roof edge!'

He pointed down at the field fifty feet beneath them and made a cutting motion with his hand across his throat, then pointed at the two of them. She caught his meaning as the field below disappeared in a haze of smoke, the blue jackets and the green grass rendered dark and distant.

The smoke made it impossible for Stanley to judge how high they were, and the rotation made it impossible to get his bearings. It was like being trapped in a howling whirlwind. All he could do was put his trust in this woman's abilities.

Occasionally the downdraught from the rotors parted the curtain of smoke and he saw men below scattering. His heart was racing and all he could think about was that the engine would suddenly stutter and they would plummet like a stone on to the field and do Siemens's job for him. He realized he was screaming when the woman yelled at him to stop.

'You got us into this! Just shut up while I get us out!'

He nodded dumbly, and rested the gun in his lap. Looking to the side he saw girders and steelwork so close he could have reached out and touched them.

Cheryl was fighting a losing battle. It wasn't just the tail rotor; the engine was beginning to cut out, and the vibration in the controls could mean a swashplate was loose. Suddenly the Jet Ranger burst into daylight, blue filling the horizon. They were out. Stanley let out a little whoop of triumph but he saw the girl shaking her head.

'Brace yourself, we're coming down!'

Before he could react the helicopter lurched backwards, pressing them both against their seats.

'Shit!' screamed the girl. 'Tail's hit something!'

She leaned on both pitch levers, desperate to get the helicopter up and away from the hole in the roof, but now it had a mind and momentum of its own.

The engine faltered, there was a clattering noise above them and then the roof of the cockpit was ripped off, showering them with glass. Stanley saw one rotor cartwheel away, followed by a terrible banging to his right. There was another desperate grinding noise, then the helicopter turned sideways, throwing the woman onto him and, as he realized she no longer had any control over the craft, he was peppered with hot liquid. His seat was ripped from its mountings and, shielding his face, he was catapulted through the now upside-down windshield into black smoke and pain.

Cheryl felt the machine fall over sideways, heard the rotors pound into the roof like hammers onto sheet metal, saw machinery and glass disintegrate about her, then felt a tremendous blow in her back and heat on her face. The next thing there was blue everywhere, and hot air blowing hard.

She quickly orientated herself and sat up. She was on the plastic canopy of the Solardome roof, twenty feet from the slumped body of the helicopter. One broken rotor pointed straight up, the other three were gone; the rear was burning, smudging the blue sky with black. The man who'd been with her was lying further down the slope, still strapped into his seat. He was looking at her with an expression of utter amazement: he too couldn't believe they had survived. After she'd checked herself for breaks and burns, and found only a cut on her left wrist, her next concern was whether the Jet Ranger would explode, so she walked over to the man and helped him unbuckle as far as her shaking hands would allow.

'You owe me a chopper,' Cheryl said as they limped unsteadily across the gentle curve of the 'Dome to the walkway that ran round its rim two hundred feet above the parking lot.

Stanley tried to think of something to say, but he was still coming to terms with his actually surviving a helicopter crash.

They were halfway between the burning chopper and the roof edge when there was a shout and, looking right, they saw a LAW agent standing on the walkway, pointing a gun at them.

'Stop right there, you mothers!'

'We need help here,' shouted Cheryl.

'Don't,' said Stanley. 'He'll kill us both.'

'I don't know who you are,' Cheryl said to Stanley. 'But the word LAW makes me think he may be police.'

'And maybe not. They've just shot your chopper down! You think they're going to compensate you?'

Cheryl couldn't understand what was going on. Worse, her legs were growing weak and she wanted to vomit, but the guy made sense.

The LAW man clambered over the low fence onto the roof.

'If you've got a gun,' he shouted, 'throw it down. Now!'

Cheryl looked at Stanley. Somehow he had kept hold of his Beretta, his clenched knuckles showing white through the smoke smears.

'Better do what he says,' she said.

Stanley looked at the gun, then at the man, then raised his free hand and let the gun fall. It clattered loudly onto the roof beside them.

'There,' shouted Cheryl. 'It's down! We surrender!'

The man laughed. 'Sorry, lady. Orders is orders.'

He raised the gun and aimed.

Stanley turned and stood in front of her as the gun roared, jerking with the impact of each bullet, then he fell against her and they both collapsed onto the roof.

She thrashed about under him, finally rolling him over to her right, where he lay cruciform beside her, staring up at the sky. She heard the LAW man running over the roof towards her. He was coming out of the sun, so she couldn't see him. She scrabbled backwards, her hands burning on the hot surface.

'Please,' she begged; this situation was a hundred times worse than the night before. Then she'd had an edge; here she was just a piece of meat waiting to be skewered on a hotplate.

'Please don't kill me, *please*!'

The man reached her and she saw his cold eyes. Even if he wasn't going to enjoy killing her, he'd feel no guilt about it.

'Don't kill me. I won't tell!' She knew it was pathetic, but she had nothing else to offer.

'Bye-bye, sweetcakes,' he said, pointing his pistol at her head. 'Pity but—'

He didn't finish his sentence. There were four rapid bangs to her right and the man's head disappeared in a frenzy of flesh and blood. His arm fell to his side, the gun dropped to the floor, and his knees gave way as if the joints had been removed. He fell forward, his face mashing into the roof between Cheryl's legs, gore splattering her.

Shaking and teetering on the knife-edge of an out-of-control screaming fit, Cheryl turned to see Stanley sitting upright, the automatic held in front him still smoking, his arms beginning to shake. He let out a big whoosh of breath, then gulped in more air, his face twisted in pain.

'But . . . but you were shot,' she finally managed.

Stanley lowered the gun and threw up onto the roof. He'd just killed a man. Blown his fucking face off. Another human being. *A man just doing his job.*

'He shot you,' was all Cheryl could say. 'In the back.'

'What? What?' said Stanley, aware someone was speaking.

She shook him. He jumped at her touch, hysteria close.

'He shot you.'

'Kevlar.'

'What?' she said, the tears finally starting.

'These jackets are made with Kevlar. Bulletproof. I felt the fucking things but they didn't penetrate.' He nodded at the man's gun, another Beretta 92F. 'Automatic weapon. Low stopping power. Still felt like being hit by a hammer.'

Before either of them could think of anything else to say, there was a dull *whummp* and the helicopter rolled over and disappeared into the 'Dome. There was a pause, during which they could hear shouts, then a large explosion, and soon fresh black smoke swirled up out of the open roof and fanned out across them like accusing fingers.

'We've got to get out of here,' said Stanley rising to his feet, his back in agony.

Cheryl joined him. She could see downtown Clinger to the south and a couple of blue flashing lights.

'Someone must have called this in. We wouldn't.'

'We?'

'I'm with them. Except now they want to lose my services.'

'Why?'

'I wish I knew and I hate to tell you this, but they won't want you around either.'

'But all I did was fly some guy in here.'

'Wrong guy.' He picked up the other agent's gun and handed it to her, then forced himself to check the body, finding a Colt .38 which he pocketed. Now, if the bastard had used *that* . . . Finally, he slipped the man's LAW jacket off and made Cheryl put it on. The blood didn't show.

'Every guy in a LAW jacket will shoot us on sight. Now, you can stay here and let them do it easy, or you can come with me and make it harder.'

She looked down at the dead man, his head a black wig on a bowl of scarlet Jell-O.

'What if I just plug you here, do them a favour?'

Stanley shook his head, ignoring the gun pointing at him. 'You saw what they did? That asshole shot me in the back and he was going to *execute* you. You heard him: *orders*. Now, do you want me to paint a target on your forehead with your lipstick, or do you want to find out *why* we're so unwelcome?'

He set off for the gangway.

Cheryl, with no viable alternatives, quickly followed.

They found a narrow ladder down from the roof to an

inner gangway that ran around the inside. Crouching low, they sprinted along the walkway, eyes constantly scanning the 'Dome for anyone looking towards them.

Luckily the crashed helicopter had thrown everyone into disarray. Its burning wreckage had forced them to move the Winnebago, and it was now driving across the field towards the north exit. Stanley saw there the possibility of escape.

The lack of firefighting equipment inside the 'Dome meant that the helicopter wreck was burning fiercely, pluming scuddies of thick pungent smoke around the field. Agents were running from the stands with fire extinguishers, but they might as well have had buckets of water for all the good it would do. Stanley guessed correctly that the chopper must have been carrying a full load of fuel. Keeping the smoke between them and the frantic agents below, running around like angry ants, they found a ladder that led down to a wired-off cement passageway behind the seating. The only problem was that they would be in plain view for the minute it would take them to clamber down.

Hunched down at the top, Stanley pointed out the risk, but Cheryl shook her head. Chasing after the man she had realized that, even though he had put her in jeopardy, he was also the only person in the place who wanted to keep her alive, and he had already saved her life twice. Besides, he seemed to have at least some idea of what was going on.

'Let's just get out of here any way we can,' she said.

'I'll go first,' he said. 'If they get me, you try some other way.'

She looked down at the spiralling black smoke and the burning junk that had been her livelihood. 'I think it's beyond repair.'

He grabbed her forearm and squeezed. 'I'm sorry but—'

'Later. *If* there's a later . . .'

She could see the fear in the man's eyes. Good. She never trusted macho bastards who claimed to thrive on danger. The only person who could deal with danger coolly was a head case. No one welcomes the chance of dying, no matter how much they enjoy the adrenalin rush of fear. She liked danger, but only when she was in control. A car, a helicopter, freefalling, the assholes she picked up. Ultimately she was always in charge: it was *she* who floored the pedal, twisted the throttle, packed the 'chute, made the pick-up. If her judgement was out, tough. But here she was just prey. Even the weight of the gun in her hand was no comfort; she could use it – and would – but they were outnumbered and playing on the home team's turf. Literally.

Luck was still a companion and they descended the ladder without being detected, and found their way down on to the main concourse via a flight of stairs. Fired by fear and their two recent triumphs, they proceeded boldly as if on some mission past several other agents.

They then found another set of stairs – wide and meant for the public – that ran down the outside of the building and opened out on to the huge empty parking lot. At the bottom there were a further three agents, one with a radio.

Stanley went on the offensive. He was sure no one knew what he looked like. He wasn't supposed to have got out of the Winnebago, so his picture wouldn't have been circulated.

'Hey, Siemens wants more men by the south entrance,' he said to the OCI men. 'Fire trucks coming. Wants them kept out.'

The three men looked at Cheryl. *Oh God.*

'Do it!' Stanley barked, waving them away.

The three nodded and ran off across the parking lot.

'Right. Back onto the field,' he said.

'*What?*' She swung him round and banged him against the wall. She was strong, and as tall as him.

She jerked a thumb over her shoulder. 'Out there's where we want to be. All we gotta do is walk out of here.'

'To get out you need to know the password,' he said, patting his jacket down. 'In the past people have impersonated OCI agents so, each day there's a password for the day. Every guy out there has orders to shoot anyone who doesn't know the word.'

'So how?'

'We drive.'

Before she could ask any more questions, he was off down the ramp towards the field.

At the bottom was parked the black Winnebago. A couple of agents stood at its rear but otherwise everyone else was on the main field or inside the building. Dressed as they were, no one would stop them getting into the vehicle.

Settling himself in the driver's seat, Stanley was glad to see the keys were still in the ignition.

Cheryl sat beside him. 'But what about the password?'

He switched the engine on and gunned it. '*That's* our password. Just be prepared to duck if they start shooting.'

He handed her his pistol and the .38, and she added them to the Beretta already on her lap.

'Quite a regular little arsenal,' he said.

'Oh, you ain't seen nothing,' she said, looking at her lap.

Too busy to ask what she meant, Stanley set off, wheeling round and heading up the gentle cement slope to the exit. As the RV crested the rise, an agent ran alongside shouting. Stanley ignored him and, shifting gear again, floored the accelerator and threw the Winnebago to the right, heading for the parking lot. The Winnebago was a bitch to handle, more like a truck than a motor-home, and the double wheels at the back gave it a grip when he didn't want it. Then a shot rang out.

'Hold on!' he shouted.

Pressing on the accelerator at the split second he felt the Winnebago straighten up, he headed for two agents now pulling their guns, who leaped aside before they could fire. Then the Winnebago was out into the open and crashing down a low, wide flight of stairs into the parking area. It grounded twice, sparks flying, metal screeching, then hit the roadway and bounced level. Stanley slammed on the brakes to regain a semblance of control, then drove on across the parking lot. There were cars dotted about, most anonymous agency vehicles, but he was able to weave a path without any collisions.

There were no more shots, which surprised him, but then he noticed the fire-trucks on his left, firemen arguing with OCI men. Siemens wouldn't want to attract attention outside in the real world with a shoot-out. Instead he would have the RV followed. That could be the edge they needed.

The entrance gates were slowly rolling together but the Winnebago would not be denied. Stanley slid through the gap, catching only one gate with the tail of the RV and jolting it out of its track. It ground to a halt and jammed, leaving a gap barely five feet wide, too narrow for a car to follow. He turned right, just missing a cab and a haulage truck then, on the straight again, began speeding up as he headed downtown. His heart was pounding and his chest and his back ached; he felt sick with terror. He glanced across at his companion, expecting to see an equally frightened woman clinging to her seat for dear life.

Instead he saw an eager face leaning forward, her eyes wide with delight, a big grin creasing her features, the occasional *whoop* escaping her lips like she was riding Space Mountain. The crazy bitch was *enjoying* it!

Siemens's anger was so apparent even those hardened to his rages were wary. He shouted commands into a radio, ordering the gate closed, and for all and everyone to shoot at the Winnebago on sight unless it got onto the street.

As he gave the burning wreckage a wide berth, the smoke choking in its intensity – the chopper had spilled its full fuel load over most of the right half of the field and the flames had reached the first half-dozen rows of seating – and then heard the fire sirens from outside, his rage increased geometrically. He screamed into the radio that '*No one, repeat no one!*' was to shoot at the Winnebago, his voice loud enough to demand little need for a transmitter.

Satisfied his message had been received, Siemens threw the radio onto the ground, grabbed a gun from one of the men standing behind him, and shot it to pieces, then he tossed the gun back at the astounded agent. His rage dissipated, he turned and smiled at his worried coterie.

'Been one of those days,' he said simply, then pushed his way through them and headed for the north exit.

As he cleared the smoke, he sniffed at the cuff of his Gaultier duster. Damn! Ruined. He ripped it off and threw it to the ground, undoing the buttons of his red Hermès jacket.

'Baxter!' he shouted, his anger returning.

Stanley slid from lane to lane, making progress as fast as he could without causing an accident. Luckily they weren't spotted by any Clinger PD cars and, checking his mirror, he couldn't see any vehicles in pursuit. Obviously it was only a matter of time before they were spotted – a speeding black Winnebago wasn't exactly inconspicuous – so he asked Cheryl to keep her eye out for accessible underground parking.

A minute or so later she spotted one on the other side of the street. *Kiley's Parking, 1200 spaces. Weekly Rates.*

Slamming on the brakes, Stanley threw the RV across the opposite two lanes, managing to miss the cars coming the other way, and he brought the Winnebago to a sliding halt by the pay-booth. The vacant-faced youngster on duty, wearing a Beavis and Butthead T-shirt, handed him his ticket without a word and Stanley drove off down the ramp, the RV's roof missing the garage ceiling by inches.

He drove the full length of the first level until, at the very end and before he would have to negotiate a tight spiral turn, he found four empty spaces and slid to a screeching halt, the back end threatening to whip around and clip a couple of parked cars, but stopping just in time.

Switching off, he sat back and wiped sweat from his face.

Cheryl shook her head. *What a trip!* 'Some driving, man! Couldn't have done better myself.'

Stanley didn't appreciate her praise. He had been

operating on pure survival instinct. They had come through because of luck, not any innate NASCAR driving ability on his part. He tried to steady himself, but he was *wired.* He gripped his thighs, his fingers digging in painfully. He felt as if he was going to explode. Even his teeth were chattering.

'Oh God, I think I'm going to be sick,' he gasped.

Cheryl, so hyped up she was almost orgasmic, didn't know what else to do so she patted him on the back. 'Hey, come on. You did good. We're safe for now. Take it easy.'

He swallowed bile, then threw his head back. He had to concentrate, get calm, think straight. Whatever the girl thought, they weren't safe; that much was crystal clear. And the truth was, unfortunately, that they were unlikely to be safe this side of the grave.

'Got to move,' he said. 'Got to get out of town.'

'Got to shut up, asshole.'

It was a voice from behind. A man's voice.

Cheryl spun around to see a blond man pointing a gun at her. He had a calm face but it was his eyes that drew her attention. Even as she noticed the red nose and bruised sockets and cheek, it was their silvery glint that made her catch her breath. They were robot eyes: purposeful and uncaring.

'Lady was right,' said Hollis. 'Good driving, Fulbright. Got a bit shook up back there but, hell, we're here now.'

Stanley looked into the mirror. He could see the man's bloodied face and his gun as he held open the curtain dividing the RV. He had never considered that Hollis might still be inside the Winnebago when they stole it.

He slowly turned to look up at him. The man's face was

flushed, his nose darkened, probably broken. It offered Stanley no satisfaction to know he had hurt him.

'I owe you, Fulbright. The nose, the humiliation, stealing my home. Long list of grievances. *Long* list.'

'Who are you?' said Cheryl.

'Introduce us, Fulbright. You know how I like the ladies.'

'Introduce yourself,' said Stanley, his mind a jumble of images, all of them terrible.

Hollis cuffed him across the head with the butt of his pistol. 'I'm Kent Hollis. And you are?'

'Fuck yourself.'

Hollis raised his eyebrows, then hit her too with the gun. 'I said, what was your name, girl?'

Blood trickled down Cheryl's cheek. Her head buzzed. 'Cheryl. Cheryl Kenney.'

'You flew the chopper in, right?'

She nodded.

'What do you want, Hollis?' said Stanley clutching a ragged cut on his right temple.

'Fun,' was his simple answer.

Stanley screwed up his eyes in pain. Got to keep alert. He forced his eyes open. Hollis's gun was still pointing at his face as he spoke to Cheryl.

'Looks like you've got a fine body there, Cheryl. After all this excitement I reckon you need to cool off.'

Stanley made to rise but Hollis hit him again, harder.

Stanley slumped forward, suddenly desperately weak. 'Leave her alone, Hollis. She's got nothing to do with . . .'

Hollis leaned down to Stanley's ear, as his gun rubbed along the curve of Cheryl's breast.

'One more word out of you and I won't let you watch.' He

stood upright again. 'Now, girl, get your clothes off. We've got some time before they track this heap down, and I'm in need of some entertainment.'

Cheryl shook her head, toying with the guns on her lap.

Hollis smirked. 'You really are loaded, aren't you girl! Now drop those on the floor and get your ass back here.'

Cheryl shook her head. No way was she going back there.

The man thrust the gun into her right cheek, hard enough for her to cut the inside of her mouth on her teeth.

'Drop the fucking guns on the fucking floor, then get your fucking ass back here!'

'Hollis, please,' said Stanley, unable to remain silent when he saw blood trickling from Cheryl's mouth.

Hollis pointed the pistol at Stanley's forehead.

'That's Mr Hollis to you,' he said.

And he fired.

Stanley felt heat and a sudden rushing emptiness and then everything went black.

Cheryl stared in horror as Stanley's blood splashed across the inside of the now crazed windshield, then she began to scream hysterically, her whole world suddenly an insane slaughterhouse polluted by madmen.

As Stanley slumped forward, Hollis was philosophical. 'I *told* you to shut up, jerk. Now, Cheryl, your clothes – off.'

The shock of Stanley's shooting caused Cheryl to drop her guns into the footwell, which was fortunate because at that moment she could have grabbed one of them and tried to shoot Hollis, although he already had his gun pointing at her head. Even so, her hands ferreted on her lap, like a blind child looking for its comforter.

'I'll count to five, Cheryl. *One . . .*'

Cheryl was hyperventilating, unable to comprehend.

'*Two . . .*'

She didn't know where to put her hands. The Winnebago's dashboard was streaked with Stanley's blood, her lap and seat splashed with blood . . . *She had nowhere to put her damn hands.*

'*Three . . .*'

She felt cold steel behind her ear. She instinctively jerked forward, but as she did she panicked.

'Don't shoot, don't shoot! I'm getting up, I'm—'

'*Four . . .*'

She stood up, trying not to fall forwards, then she slowly turned. 'I'm coming. I'm coming!'

'Not yet,' smiled Hollis. 'But you will be . . .'

Cheryl looked at him. He had the face of an evil child just before it sets fire to a kitten. Then she noticed a movement in the curtain behind him.

Hollis saw the flicker in her eyes, began to turn.

The portable TV caught him on the side of the head, the screen peppering his face with a hundred minuscule glass darts. He fell with the TV, banging the other side of his head on the back of Stanley's seat, before falling into the side of the RV. The television landed at the feet of a man with a face that had been beaten bloody and whose little fingers were missing from both of his bloody upraised hands.

Cheryl couldn't help it. She began to laugh.

And, even as she knew she had stepped into the darker side of her mind, she rejoiced in it. So much had happened so quickly; so much violence and horror. Then, as she stared at the stranger staring at her, she grabbed at Hollis's .38 and knelt over him and rammed the barrel into his mouth.

'*You bastard!*' she screamed. '*You're fucking dead!*'

But the man touched her on the shoulder.

'No,' he said, coughing up red spit. 'Not yet, not here. We need him. Please. If he's still alive, don't kill him.'

She looked up at his face. He looked like a businessman, his grey suit creased and streaked with blood, blue tie still tight to his collar. She didn't recognize the face, but she remembered a man like him arguing with Siemens just after they landed. He had been sent into the Winnebago. No wonder he had been arguing, if this was the result.

'You sure?' she said, her hand shaking.

He nodded, nursing his hands under his armpits, his voice cracked but calm. 'He'll make a fine hostage. Guaranteed.'

'Hostage?' was all Cheryl could say before her vision clouded and she felt herself tipping over into darkness.

11

The fire chief was not convinced by their story but when Siemens threatened him with Eminent Domain, and the Clinger PD captain explained just what that meant, the man stormed off in a huff.

'What really happened here?' asked the captain as they walked away from the smouldering remains of the helicopter.

They passed the two fire units Siemens had allowed into the Solardome to extinguish the fire, smoke lying in the air like mist, tainting their breath.

'A chopper bringing one of my agents hit the roof. We can handle it.'

The cop nodded at the retreating figure in the gold helmet. 'Didn't keep *him* out though, did you?'

Siemens pulled up short beside a fire truck and, grabbing the captain by his suit lapels, slammed him up against the truck's grille.

'I don't know why you're talking to me like this, Captain Schroeder. We got you out of that jam with that hooker, and you weren't required to do anything. But now, when I ask you to do one simple thing, all I get is snide remarks. None of my staff would *dream* of talking to me like that. A year last March you sold yourself to one of my agents, and now you're mine and you do what you're told. Understand?'

The captain stared back at him, his tough stance already looking brittle.

'Understand, *Detective*?' emphasized Siemens.

The man finally offered a quiet 'yes', aware of the implied threat in Siemens addressing him by a lower rank.

Siemens smiled. 'Good. Now just go do your job and keep that fire chief quiet.'

Captain Schroeder stared at him, his face red with anger, but they both knew it was the impotent foot-stamping of a punished boy, and he finally walked away.

If there was one thing Siemens couldn't stand, it was people questioning his orders, especially cheap little whores like Schroeder. He needed time to think, and there was still work to attend to in Seattle. He retraced his steps past the helicopter wreckage and across the field, heading for the control room, thinking over all the details.

Someone had found a dead agent on the roof, and Siemens had ordered the body to be thrown down into the chopper fire. He had then called the Fire Department himself, just to avoid suspicion – having found out they were already on their way – and had ensured that OCI's local contacts in Clinger PD were involved to help smooth things over. He had also prepared a cover story about a simple accident caused by pilot error.

That he didn't have the pilot was a problem, but he knew the helicopter owner could be persuaded to back his story – why else would Siemens be using a two-bit outfit in the first place? – and if necessary he would even be able to produce a pilot who would claim to have survived the crash. All he needed now was to tidy up the loose ends and eliminate the real pilot. And to do that he would need to locate the RV – and also kill his own two men.

Fulbright he didn't care about – he was just a jumped-up

clerk after all – but Baxter was another matter. Siemens had never felt anything for the man personally, despite what Baxter assumed they meant to each other, but Baxter had been entrusted with almost all of OCI's secrets and were he ever to broadcast what he knew, there would be serious trouble. Siemens also suspected that the man might have found something even more damaging in File Seventy-Seven. He had been told to leave it alone but had gone back into it, even after the kid had died. Baxter simply couldn't be trusted any more; he needed to be erased, regardless of collateral damage, even if that included Hollis. After all, if Seventy-Seven got out, Hollis would be redundant anyway. He needed to know where the Winnebago was and that's where Schroeder came into it – or went out of it, permanently. It might be petty but right now Siemens was willing to surrender himself to any emotion that got the job done. There was too much at stake for there to be any more slip-ups.

In fact, everything was at stake. If only the stupid bastards he surrounded himself with could be trusted with his knowledge, then the work might get done quicker. But, then again, how many ordinary people could handle such knowledge? He wondered sometimes if his insight was a gift or a curse. Whichever, it was a burden he was glad to bear because, ultimately, he knew the rewards would be so inestimably high it was worth every risk, every dollar . . . and every life.

12

The man nudged Cheryl conscious.

'Come on, girl. No time for idling. Work to do. Come on.'

Cheryl came round to find herself staring into the pulped face of the man who had been about to rape and kill her. She forced herself up and looked at the dead Stanley.

Who was sitting up looking at her! His eyes were glazed, but they were definitely alive, even though blood sheened his face like a paint spill.

'*You're alive! He's alive!*'

Stanley managed to nod. He could see the girl speaking, but his head was buzzing like a swarm of bees had entered the bullet wound on his forehead. He tried to speak but his mouth was dry, his jaw muscles uncooperative. He tried to reason out what had happened. Hollis had shot him at point-blank range; his head should be somewhere outside on the parking lot, but while the windshield had gone his head had not.

A strange man in a grey suit bent towards him, and Stanley realized that his own vision was fish-eyed. Weird. He'd seen this effect in movies enough times when they wanted to show what it was like to be drugged – and the effect was accurate!

'Fulbright? Fulbright?' said the man in the grey, blood-spattered suit. 'Look at me, man. You have a bad wound on your scalp. Hollis was sloppy, lucky for you, but we can't wait here. Once Siemens locates us, we're his.'

'Em . . . Em . . .' Stanley tried to speak.

The man touched his shoulder, wincing as he did so. 'Yes, Eminent Domain. Right now we're the only friends we've got, and we need to move. Can you stand up?'

Stanley pushed down with his hand on the arm of his seat, and was surprised to find that he could stand. Blood coursed into his eyes and he had to rub it away – and that was when he realized how bloody he was.

'Don't panic,' said the man as Stanley began to jitter. 'Scalp wounds always bleed badly. Much worse than it looks. The bullet creased your forehead. Another half inch . . .'

Stanley heard him. Good, at least one ear was working.

Cheryl helped him up, her face a curious mixture of terror and relief, and the three of them stepped over Hollis, blood dripping onto the man from two of them. All could see that, despite the mess that was his face, Hollis was still breathing.

'We need the first-aid kit and a car,' urged the grey-suited man.

Stanley still had trouble concentrating, so it was left to Cheryl to hunt through the Winnebago's closets until she found a small green briefcase with a white cross on it.

'Grab some towels as well,' added the man.

She did and rejoined them by the side door.

The man winced and held his hands free of his body. The top joint of both little fingers had been severed.

'Can you hotwire a car, Fulbright?' he asked.

Stanley shook his head, and more blood seeped into his eyes.

'I can,' said Cheryl.

'Okay. Find one with a trunk. We need to stash Hollis.'

'He's coming with us?' Stanley managed.

'He's all we've got. He means more to Siemens than just about any man alive.'

Cheryl didn't waste time asking questions. She walked back to a closet, removed a wire coathanger and wrenched it out of shape as she stepped outside. Despite their hurried entrance and the subsequent shot, there were no sounds of running feet or sirens in the long, cool vault.

She scanned the assembled cars, looking like victims waiting to be mugged. Regal, Voyage, Plymouth, Saab, Toyota, Geo . . . then she saw it: a beige Chevrolet Cavalier, old and battered enough not to be alarmed.

She trotted over to the car, her footsteps echoing like a noisy shadow, and gave it the once-over. Slipping the wire down between the window and the doorframe, she hooked the lock arm and pulled, the internal door lock popping up.

Checking no one had appeared, she pulled open the door, slid in, kicked off the steering-wheel cover then, snatching out the ignition wires, she got them sparking and the engine turning over. She tooted the horn.

The man leaned out of the Winnebago. 'Pop the trunk!' he said.

Trunk opened, she helped them carry the limp Hollis down to the car. There the three of them unceremoniously dumped him into the trunk, grabbed the guns from the Winnebago, and climbed into the front, the grey-suited man wedged in the middle.

With Cheryl driving, they reversed out of the parking space, then set off up the ramp to the exit.

'Anyone got change?' she asked as they reached the booth.

She was suddenly worried. Both Stanley and the other man were covered in blood and would arouse the interest of even the most spaced-out grunger.

A wincing Baxter slipped her fifty dollars. 'Smallest I've got.'

They reached the barrier, the sunlit street ahead of them looking like another world. The kid in the booth was on the telephone and waved at them to wait. Cheryl parped the horn. He waved at them to wait again. It was Stanley's turn to slap the horn.

The kid came out muttering. 'I'm talking to the police.'

'Wanna talk to a paramedic, kid? Open it,' she said, handing him the fifty bucks and nodding at the barrier.

'Anything less?'

'Just do it.'

The kid smiled and pressed the button.

At street level, Cheryl turned right.

The man at her elbow suggested she drive easy and obey all traffic laws.

'Hey, I always do,' she said.

'Miss Kenney, you have had eighteen moving and twenty-three parking violations to your credit over the last four years. And those were just the times you were caught.'

'What? Who the fuck are you? And who's he?' she said nodding at Stanley, who was holding a black handtowel to his still bleeding head.

'All in good time. First priority is to get out of town.'

Cheryl looked at her two bloodied companions. 'First priority is a hospital for you two.'

The man pulled out his gun and held it clumsily, the pain from his mutilated finger apparent.

'Out of town is in *all* our interests.'

Cheryl nodded – she'd had enough of guns to last her a lifetime – and moving into the outside lane began looking for the first turn to the Interstate.

Stanley lowered the towel from his head. It was soaked. Christ, he was bleeding to death! He knew the man was right about getting away from Clinger as fast as possible, but what was the point if he ran out of blood on the way?

'I don't think . . . I don't think I'll make it . . .'

The man looked at his head. 'The bullet grazed you for about four inches. There's a long cut just above the hairline, but it didn't reach your skull. You'll be scarred but a fringe will hide it. Just keep the towel against it.'

Reassured, Stanley pressed the towel back to his forehead.

Cheryl changed lanes again, drawing a blast of horn, then slewed the car into a side street she knew would lead to a ramp onto the Interstate.

'You guys, do you know each other?'

Baxter spoke, his voice high. 'I ordered Fulbright to meet Mr Hollis.'

'Fucker,' said Stanley. 'You sent me out to meet that sociopath knowing he would—'

'I didn't want to. Siemens ordered me to send someone into Riva who was . . . expendable.'

'What?' said Stanley.

'Expendable,' he said quietly, then added: 'Like Riva.'

'Where the hell's Riva?' said Cheryl.

'Hollis is a very dangerous but very vital part of OCI's operations. Siemens would do anything to protect him,' said Baxter.

'Who's Siemens? What's OCI?' said Cheryl, swerving round a slow truck.

'Siemens is our boss. *The* boss,' said Baxter. 'And OCI? Well, call them super police.'

'Super police? Like the secret service? FBI?'

'More powerful than either. Less well known.'

Stanley was puzzled. 'You said Riva was expendable.'

'Did I?'

'Yes,' said Cheryl. 'You know you did.'

'There was an accident last night, after you and Hollis left. Getting caught was bad enough, but killing the sheriff was too much to cover up, especially with other potential witnesses. So OCI arranged an . . . accident.'

'What kind of accident?' said Stanley.

'It wasn't my idea. It came straight from—'

'*What?*' Stanley grabbed the man by the collar.

'A gas tanker!' Baxter blurted out, his face creased with pain. 'At the gas station. Blew up. Took out half the town.'

'*What?*' said Cheryl.

'Killed eleven people, injured another dozen.'

'Including everyone who saw us?' said Stanley.

'Yes. Drastic but necessary. Anyone we missed – well who cares about a couple of strangers in town? Both the sheriff and his deputy are dead and burned up. No one else knows. Sometime someone will remember the woman Hollis murdered, but no one'll care and the state troopers won't find anything.'

'Jesus.'

Cheryl couldn't understand any of this. All she'd done was ferry some guy to the Solardome. Now she was on the run with secret policemen and there were dead bodies everywhere. She slammed on the brakes, the car sliding to a screeching halt, cars behind braking and blaring their horns.

There was a thump in the trunk as Hollis obeyed the laws of motion.

'So who's the guy in the trunk?' she said.

'Please, Miss Kenney, continue to drive. We haven't—'

'We have. Now you explain.'

A car drew alongside, the driver swearing. Cheryl wound down her window and let rip with a string of obscenities that stopped the redneck in mid-sentence. He drove on.

Baxter patted her arm. 'Please. When we're somewhere safe, I'll explain everything. It's gone far enough, but not here.' He nodded at the drivers giving them the finger.

Cheryl stared at him, then looked at Stanley. The poor man was exhausted, his face and upper body sheathed in blood, but through his pain Stanley nodded for her to drive on.

She slipped the car into gear. 'Where should we head?'

'East. Avoid rush hour,' said Baxter.

Stanley leaned back. His head hurt, his mind was buzzing and a tide of guilt was about to engulf him. On the roof of the Solardome, a time that seemed to have been months before but couldn't have been more than an hour, he had vaporized the head of another OCI agent. Shot the man's face off. A fellow agent. That the man may actually have been in on the conspiracy did nothing to negate his guilt. He felt wetness round his eyes and couldn't tell whether it was tears or blood; whichever, both were inadequate recompense.

Cheryl found the freeway and roared up the ramp and across two lanes, until they were lost in eastbound traffic three lanes wide. They were headed out of town and traffic was relatively light compared to the opposite carriageway, where all four lanes were reduced to a crawl. As the Cavalier settled at a steady forty-five, she realized she owed her life to the two wrecks sitting with her; Fulbright had shot that guy on the roof, and Baxter had creamed the psycho in the trunk with the TV. So, for now, she would go along with them. Besides, what choice did she have?

For his part Stanley felt cold. Loss of blood? No, shock, he told himself. He was so damned tired, too. But he needed to stay awake. Talk. Keep your mind working.

'Baxter?' he said. 'Hollis did that to you? Why?'

'Because you had escaped and he wanted revenge.'

'And Siemens let him?'

'Yes. Hollis is everything to him. And Siemens used to be everything to me . . .' He fell silent as Stanley studied him.

He was in his late fifties, five-eight, not slim but not gone to fat. He looked like an accountant. His hair was thin and receding but dyed black. His flesh was untanned, like he worked indoors, but the torture he had recently been through could well have made him pale. His suit was expensive and well cut, but now just so much soiled cloth. His tie was silk – dark blue with a crisscross white motif, the knot perfect – and his collar still done up. For some reason the incongruity of it reminded Stanley of crossing the hands on a corpse.

They had travelled five miles, and all three were beginning to relax. The only police cars they had seen had been going the other way, no doubt in response to the smudge on the horizon where smoke from Cheryl's chopper escaped the Solardome. Baxter had found somewhere to rest his hands that didn't make them feel as if white-hot rivets were being hammered under his little fingernails – not that those fingernails would be a problem again. Only he had a real grasp of what they were up against, but he didn't dare tell the other two of his fears. Why let them know that they were only delaying the inevitable?

Cheryl's mind was on where they could go. She could see the Apple Grove Windfarm way out on the right, forty giant triple-bladed white windmills turning lazy circles in the breeze, and there was the flare from the refinery that blazed twenty-four hours a day (she often used it as her first marker for the city when coming in at night). At the precise moment she made out the fading word STAROIL on the giant flarestack, hell broke loose in the back of the car.

Two kicks and the backseat gave and Hollis was squirming his way up through the gap, and before anyone could react his hands were clawed around Baxter's face, his fingers in his mouth, and he was pulling himself out of the trunk and onto the folded rear seat. And he was screaming; screaming high and loud as the car began to swerve from side to side. He kept his grip on Baxter's face, even as Stanley and Cheryl batted at his hands and Baxter tried to bite down. But Hollis's bloodlust would not be denied: he was going to snap the faggot's head off his shoulders, and then watch the blood spurt like cancerous semen. He tugged even harder and Baxter began to choke.

Stanley had guessed what had happened even as he turned to see the bloodied nightmare of Hollis's face a foot from his own, the manic eyes wide and so bloodshot there were no whites showing. The killer's face was ripped in a hundred places, glass still embedded in the cuts, which had run and turned most of his face as red as his eyes – but it was the eyes Stanley would never forget.

The man himself had disappeared and something else was

in there, something that had one purpose only: to kill them all regardless of the cost, even Hollis's own life if the car crashed.

Stanley tried to prise the clutching hands from Baxter, but they might as well have been welded in place. Cheryl also tried hitting him away but she had to keep hold of the wheel or they would crash. They were in the middle lane, doing fifty, traffic on all sides. A Greyhound bus on her right, a rust-coloured Chevy pick-up on the other side and a Mack truck behind her hauling milk together formed an alley of metal with only the road ahead offering any kind of escape.

Stanley then punched at Hollis's screaming face, but his fist skidded off and he hit Cheryl instead.

The car immediately swerved into the pick-up on its left, then careened back and side-swiped the bus, both the drivers reacting by stamping on their brakes and causing vehicles behind them to follow suit. Cheryl let Fulbright deal with the madman; she had her hands full with the car.

Then Baxter slapped into her and she was banged against the window, the car careering to the right and sliding the length of the slowing Greyhound bus, its terrified passengers staring down at her. The impact spun the wheel in her hands, and her attempt to hold it almost broke her wrists as the wheel snapped full-circle. The car was beginning to slide. She realized the only chance to correct it was to steer into the car now on her left: a Cadillac. The chauffeur tried to ease away from her but he didn't have a chance, and with a thump the nose of their Cavalier dug into the Caddy's right front wing and tore it off, the metal whirling away over their heads and slamming into the windshield of the Mack behind them. Its driver, blinded by his crazed windshield, immediately lost control, his vehicle sliding sideways until it began to roll.

Cheryl caught sight of the truck rolling behind them, as big as a building being demolished, the huge trailer swinging round like a giant bat intent on slamdunking them off the freeway. She felt the car bounce away from the Cadillac, its rear gouging a line into the limousine's offside doors, before she again slammed into the side of the bus. Then, in a cloud of smoke, she found the bus slipping away, the rolling milk-tanker behind slamming into its rear and forcing it half off the freeway and onto the verge. The tanker stayed on its side, veered back across the freeway and batted a Ford tractor unit which mounted the central barrier, narrowly missed a couple of cars in the outside lane, shaved a Mustang in the middle lane which spun as if it was on ice, then ploughed head-on into a Peterbilt hauling wrecked cars, which began spilling its load like vomit over vehicles unable to avoid the rain of metal.

Cheryl had little time to take in the horror around her – there was horror enough in the car. She felt a hand on her face, Hollis's, and found her head wrenched to the right so that she was looking into his face, her hands still grasping feebly at the steering-wheel. His teeth were bared; he was going to bite her face. His breath stank of stale blood, his eyes were black crystals in red orbs; he wasn't human.

She screamed, pulled forward, then back, loosening his grip, but her attention had been taken from the freeway, and by the time she saw what was ahead she had no choices left.

Another bus was blocking the central lane, traffic ahead slowing to less than twenty. She glanced at the speedo. *Fifty*. There was a gap between the decelerating bus, which had steered back onto the inside lane, and a florist's van in front of it. If she could make it through, they'd at least make the verge. She stabbed at the accelerator and felt the car accept her instructions and surge through the gap. Relief that they had made it turned to horror as she saw there was no verge; they were passing an exit down-ramp and all that was left was a drop to the ramp twenty feet below.

She tried to steer back out of trouble but Hollis grabbed at her breast and dug his fingers in hard enough to make her yelp. He was screeching now like an animal high on the scent of prey, all considerations lost in the need to inflict death and taste blood. As horns, explosions, screams, rending metal and hissing air brakes filled the world outside, Cheryl knew she couldn't react in time.

The car left the freeway, mounted the shallow kerbing and took off over the grassed embankment to the off-ramp, and three seconds of flight were followed by a bone-crunching impact that had all four of them leaving their seats and hitting the car roof, Hollis coming off worst as he banged his face on the dashboard before falling onto the rear seats.

Cheryl stamped on the brake in an attempt to ease its speed, but there was no reaction. The speedometer was stuck at thirty, but she reckoned they were going faster – and the ramp had a sharp curve at the bottom that swung back under the freeway. They weren't going to make it.

She pulled on the wheel, hoping to broadside the restraining wall, but nothing happened. She pulled on the handbrake and although there was burning rubber and protests from the rear tyres, it was too little too late. Bracing herself, she shouted a warning, and then the car hit the wall.

The initial impact threw everyone forward, but the three

in the front were lucky. Cheryl slammed into the wheel and Stanley into the dashboard, and Baxter into him, but Hollis was launched through the windshield onto the car hood and then he was gone from sight, only splashes of blood – dark brown on the light brown hood – evidence that he had been in the Cavalier.

As steam wraithed up from underneath the car and drifted into the passenger compartment, its hot metallic stink stinging freshly torn skin, Cheryl was the first to come around. She sat back, her breathing painful. The top frame had buckled upwards and the door needed encouragement to open creakily. She then checked her companions. Stanley was awake but coughing, Baxter still.

She stepped out and fell to her knees, but forced herself to keep going, aware the vehicle might explode or Hollis might suddenly appear at the front of the car. This last notion made her reach back inside and grab a gun from the footwell, then walk past the crumpled hood to check.

The front wheels of the Cavalier hung limp in space over a forty-foot drop onto wasteland, and at the bottom lay the body of Hollis, broken bushes showing his route downwards.

She spat at him but her bloody phlegm only reached the car hood and was quickly lost amid the bloody trails the madman had left as his skin was sliced by the windshield.

She turned and stepped back to the Cavalier, aware that other vehicles were stopping, people staring, some getting out to help. She leaned into the car and grabbed Stanley's free hand.

'Out! Out now! We gotta move. Now!'

Stanley had also seen the crash coming and, free of Hollis's interference, had made a split-second decision that the footwell was safer than the windshield. He had been proven right, his saving of Baxter being coincidental. He dragged himself across the front seat and fell headfirst out of the door, every bone in his body feeling as if it had been stomped on by a crowd. Then he saw the onlookers, the two lanes of their cars beginning to back up the ramp. He grabbed Cheryl by the shoulder and pulled himself upright.

'Get him out,' he said.

Together they reached in and pulled Baxter out, his moans acknowledgement of his survival, if not his comfort.

As Baxter slumped to the ground, Stanley reached back onto the seat and picked up another gun. Then, turning, he hefted Baxter up and the two of them dragged him into the middle of the road.

'Car,' said Cheryl. 'Need a car!'

Cheryl pointed her pistol at a young woman leaning out of a Toyota Carina.

'This one,' she said, spitting blood onto the floor. 'Get out, lady. Now!'

One or two people made to move forward, but then thought better of it. The trio looked like armed fugitives, bank robbers maybe. The two lanes of vehicles had now backed up on to the freeway, and above them, out of sight, could be heard shouting and horns.

The woman edged her way out of the car as if her backside was zippered to it. Cheryl ran up to her, letting Baxter fall to his knees. She grabbed the woman's arm and hurled her aside. A burly guy in jeans and dirty T-shirt stepped forward, but Cheryl fired the .38 into the air.

'*Anyone moves, they don't move again!*'

She got into the car and, keeping the door open and

training the gun on the fat man, she slipped the Toyota into drive and let it roll towards Baxter and Stanley.

Stanley hauled the man over his shoulder and stumbled across to the car, pulled open the back door and threw him in, then shut the door and slipped into the passenger seat.

Cheryl slammed her own door, gunned the engine and floored the pedal, smearing the tarmac with rubber and powering the car down the hill, past the steaming wreckage of their Cavalier and on into the city.

Stanley leaned back and stared at the gun in his hand. The world had gone mad. There was a stirring from behind. He looked back over the seat and saw Baxter looking up at him, blinking blood out of his left eye.

'Dump this car,' the man said weakly.

'What?' shouted Cheryl over her shoulder as she overtook a cab on the inside, wheel-hubs screaking along the kerb.

'Too many witnesses. Police will have the description in five minutes. APB. Dump the car. Go to ground.'

'Go to ground?' said Stanley, his neck paining him from craning around. 'Where?'

'Park somewhere quiet, find a hotel. Need a rest – time to think.' The man scrunched up his face in pain.

Cheryl nodded. Despite the panic, she was thinking clearer now than she had in weeks. It was like the whole world had suddenly come into focus: colours were sharper, sounds more distinct, her body in tune with its surroundings. She felt . . . *alive.* What the man said made sense.

She checked her mirrors and, without signalling, turned sharp left and down a side road, then flicked the car into a back alley. It was a dead end, but that didn't matter. She skidded to a halt just feet from the stained brick wall at the end, then reversed up until she banged into the back of a yellow garbage dumpster. Straightening the Carina, she stepped out and checked her handiwork; from the side street the car was hidden by the dumpster.

Cheryl beckoned Stanley to get out, then helped the grimacing Baxter clamber out. He was unsteady on his feet but at least he could walk unaided, and together the three exited the alley and limped their way back to the main street. She was a native of Clinger but she only had the vaguest idea where they were. Somewhere on the east side, possibly Detravo. Wherever, it was a rundown area, not somewhere to hang out at night, even by Cheryl's low standards. She checked her companions.

They looked just like they'd survived a car wreck (or a shoot-out, she corrected herself, seeing as she and Stanley were still wearing their stolen LAW jackets). A better area, and someone might have offered to call the paramedics.

Baxter pulled out a wallet. 'Here. That should get us into a hotel.' He coughed weakly.

She opened the leather wallet. It was full of cash: fifties and hundreds – two grand's worth, probably more. Who *was* this guy?

She spotted a hotel one block down – the Rosemont – and they headed for it, their bloodied appearance and pained movements drawing stares but no reactions. This was part of town where everyone minded their own business – unless they had business to do.

Entering the Rosemont – an ugly five-storey red brick affair occupying a block of its own – they found a large foyer full of derelicts and winos sitting sprawled in chairs, watching TV and their lives dribble by. They proceeded past a row of broken candy machines to the desk, where a balding middle-aged Mexican sat in an undershirt and pants reading *Hustler*, some of whose pages were creased over. A connoisseur obviously. His undershirt and thick moustache were flecked with the remains of food; he looked like he'd suffered a nosebleed.

Cheryl banged the bell on the desk to catch his attention. He was about to get annoyed, then he saw her, and her two companions, and he was sufficiently puzzled not to formulate an insult. He had never seen LAW jackets before.

'Wha'?' he said, his accent a thick chicano drawl.

'Room. Now. For all of us.'

'Party time, eh?'

'Does it look like it?' said Stanley.

'Takes all sorts, man. Wha' this "LAW" shit anyways?' he said, pointing at Stanley's and Cheryl's logos.

'Room, shithead,' said Cheryl.

'Hey, lady, I don't think—'

Cheryl pulled out two hundred-dollar bills and waved them under the man's moustache. 'You gotta room or you got a rich relative keeps you in such luxury?'

The man snatched the money and slipped it down the crotch of his pants, in one practised movement. Then he turned and grabbed a key off a hook on the board behind him.

'Four-one-five. Facing back.'

Cheryl took the key. 'Anyone asks, you've never seen us.'

'Depen's, lady.' His eyes glittered greedily.

Stanley – tired to the point of pain – pulled out his automatic and pointed it at the man's belly. 'You never seen us, and if anyone finds us I'll find you. Okay?'

The guy looked at the gun, then at Cheryl. She pulled open her jacket and showed the butt of her .38.

The man nodded. 'Never saw you.'

They walked to the waiting elevator, ignored by everyone. As they stepped in, Cheryl saw the desk clerk sit down and resume his reading. What kind of life could that man lead if he could casually accept a bribe from a trio such as they?

The elevator was old and slow and matched their bodies perfectly, and they had barely made it to their room before both Cheryl and Baxter threw up in the bathroom, she in the toilet, he in the washbasin. Stanley tried to hold out, but he was soon vomiting into the shower stall.

Twenty minutes later Cheryl rang down to the desk and, after heated negotiation, the clerk agreed to supply antiseptic, plasters and bandages in return for another hundred.

Cheryl sat down on the end of the bed and eased her LAW jacket off. Her left shoulder ached and her breast was sore where Hollis had grabbed her in the car.

'Shock,' she said. 'Best to just lay low and let it pass. I'll slip the guy another hundred. That should keep him quiet. And then you can tell me what the fuck is going on.'

Stanley nodded, even though he was as lost as she was. This time yesterday he had been a clerk, checking crime figures for a tri-state area in the Mid-West. Now he was on the run, he'd killed a man, and been involved in both a car crash and a helicopter crash. He only needed a train wreck and he'd have the set.

He started laughing apropos nothing, and knew he was going into shock, as predicted. So he went with it, his laughter hollow, but soon he was in the bathroom again, retching his stomach empty, tears streaming through the dried blood on his face and dripping pink into the toilet bowl.

Baxter was propped up on the bed, his head slumped on his shoulder, asleep.

And Cheryl was weeping by the window, her head on the cold radiator, her body racked with sobs, her view a dirty, garbage-strewn alley that looked as bad as she felt. Whatever she had fallen into, it looked like they might be hiding away in the Rosemont for quite a while.

13

Cheryl helped Baxter to remove his blood-stained jacket, shirt and undershirt, each providing fresh agony as they slipped over his mutilated hands but he relaxed a little once naked to the waist and propped up on the bed. As he spoke, she dabbed his cuts with iodine and tried her best to staunch the weeping from his little fingers.

'The Office of Central Intelligence was founded in the early Eighties to help smaller police departments, state police forces and certain under-funded investigations by the FBI, Treasury Department, DEA, ATF, and even the Secret Service, to co-ordinate information that might lead to convictions.

'Under normal circumstances, the crimes we investigate don't warrant the expenditure required to do the legwork. For example, Fulbright here was co-ordinating data in the tri-state area of Utah, Wyoming and Idaho to see if there were any unsolved offence upswings when known sex offenders resettled. So far he had identified four men whom the FBI are investigating over alleged child abductions. The local FBI offices did not have the manpower or budget to do this research themselves, but OCI does.

'Another example— *Oh God! . . .*'

'Sorry,' said Cheryl. She had brushed against his right hand, and the result was now etched on his pale face. 'You really need a doctor to see to these.'

'I know, but right now, we've only got you, so . . .'

Cheryl nodded, took a deep breath, and began to dab at the small scratches on the back of his hand and wrist.

'There was a rumour of a child slave-labour ring using illegal immigrants operating along the west coast in packing plants and textile companies. Local police and immigration had enough trouble catching adults, so OCI were called in by the state police in California and New Mexico. By co-ordinating the efforts of twenty detectives spread across eight separate forces, we helped close down seven factories using children as young as nine. Good, useful work.'

Stanley and Cheryl both agreed.

'OCI is funded in part by a direct grant from the government. About one hundred and fifty million dollars annually. In addition we are allocated funds from the various law-enforcement agencies who use our services regularly – it's equivalent to about one quarter of 1 per cent of their annual budgets. In addition – and this is where Siemens comes in – OCI enjoys private funding.'

'Private funding?' called Stanley from the bathroom, as he downed two glasses of water.

'Wealthy businessmen who approve of OCI's aims either donate directly or provide money through channels. There are also tax breaks involved, so their help may not be entirely altruistic. Nonetheless, they add several million dollars a year to the agency's budget.'

'The money's traceable? OCI is accountable?' said Cheryl.

Baxter shook his head. 'You know those Russian dolls? Open one up and there's another inside, and then another and another? Siemens has organized OCI like that. The big doll is Fulbright's work. Statistical analysis. But inside that there is the second doll: the men you saw in the Solardome. They do the fieldwork, and most of it is legitimate: helping out other agencies, gathering information, tracking down fugitives. Then inside that doll is the work that requires the private funding – not that all donators know about it, but, well, some must do. And then, at the heart, there is the final doll – Hollis. Why he is used I don't know; why his victims are targeted, again I don't know. But I do know his funding comes direct from Siemens.'

'Siemens is rich?'

'Yes. He invested OCI money in an advertising agency in Seattle, called it his cover, but it's simply a source of money.'

'Where in Seattle?' said Stanley.

'Fothergill Building.'

'Know it. Big black building. Had a girlfriend worked for an insurance company there.'

'Yes, you lived in Seattle. He cooks the books, funnelling money from certain accounts to pay for his own "interests" – interests they know nothing about – but it's not for personal gain. Oh, he lives well, stays in the best hotels, he has his penthouse, the ski lodge, travels first-class, limos . . . but we're talking *millions*, and all of it spent funding Hollis's activities. Even the IRS can't touch it.'

'The IRS?' said Stanley, impressed.

'Eminent Domain can keep even them at bay. Speaking of which, I gave you an Eminent Domain when you went to Riva.'

Stanley was suddenly embarrassed. 'I know. Hollis, um, ripped it up. In the chopper coming back.'

'What is Eminent Domain?' asked Cheryl.

'Hand me my jacket,' said Baxter looking at his bandaged hand. 'The inside left pocket, if you'd be so kind.'

Stanley found a plastic wallet identical to the one he'd carried in Riva and handed it to Baxter, who gave it to Cheryl.

'Examine that carefully, my dear. There are only eight . . . now *seven* such documents in existence. Each is signed by the incoming President after his inauguration. His security advisors always assure him of its value.'

Cheryl had heard the terminology before. 'Isn't Eminent Domain the right of the government to buy up land for its own use? They used it for the railways and oil exploration, and to build defence bases and airfields.'

'True, but this Eminent Domain is far more powerful. It gives Siemens or his designated agents like Fulbright here – anyone with that paper – the right to fuck over anyone and anything they like, pardon my language. It gives OCI the right to overrule any investigation. Technically it's like having the President standing beside you giving the orders. Siemens will undoubtedly be using Eminent Domain to run the show here in Clinger – which is why we're in such danger.'

Cheryl finished wrapping his other damaged hand and he thanked her, carefully laying them in his lap as she set to on dealing with the bruising and scratches on his face.

'The men wearing the LAW jackets are the elite: the ones who do the dirty work, the surveillance, the take-downs – and that would now include us. They keep out of the public eye, they're salaried through dummy accounts, they buy their own vehicles, they even have to source their own guns.'

'What if people see those? They're not exactly anonymous.' Cheryl nodded at the jackets on the bed.

'They quickly forget them. People assume it's the police. You've probably seen them on news report but they didn't make any impression. Only senior police officers know of OCI and the effect of Eminent Domain and, to be honest, it's usually only ever used to cover the agency's back – as in Riva. It can cover everything, including the media, but it would have to be relayed from the highest level for a reporter to obey it, so it's rarely used outside of law-enforcement agencies.'

'What about the armed forces?' said Stanley, amazed at the power he had been wielding.

'Yes. OCI will receive cooperation, but will not be in charge. Again, orders will be relayed.'

'God,' said Cheryl. 'That's some piece of paper. What about the fire services, paramedics, coastguards, the FAA?'

'Eminent Domain, shown to the right level of person, will have the same effect. It actually serves OCI to have its demands directed through the chain of command; that way we're not seen. We could use that phone right now and surrender to the most honest policeman in Clinger PD, but I guarantee that within hours we would be dead.'

'But why?'

'I don't know. I was as ignorant of OCI's darker side as Fulbright until about two and half years ago, when Siemens took me into his confidence after his assistant was killed. They were in the middle of an operation, and he wanted me to help him sort it out.

'At the time we . . . we were lovers, and he based a lot of his trust in me on my love for him, and he knew I would do anything for him. He didn't tell me everything at first but eventually I came to grasp the depths to which OCI will descend.'

'Depths?' said Stanley, swabbing at his forehead with the iodine and trying hard not to yell out in pain.

'The elimination of enemies of the state. Normally we accumulate evidence against an individual and pass it on to the relevant authorities, and let them pursue the criminal through the courts. However, for Siemens and his field agents, that same information could lead to assassination.'

'Oh, come on,' laughed Cheryl. 'Assassination – give me a break. Shit like that you get in the movies, but—'

Baxter shook his head, 'Oh, my dear, don't be so naïve. Look around. *Anything* is possible in this madhouse.' He seemed genuinely exasperated at her ignorance.

'White cops beat Rodney King half to death on video and get acquitted? Evangelists are caught with hookers and are plied with cash by their poverty-stricken followers? The Mayor of Washington is caught using crack and gets re-elected? People line up for their fifteen minutes on air to tell how they're sorry for sleeping with their mothers . . .? For God's sake girl, a quarter of the nation still believe Elvis Presley is alive! So when I say that, to my knowledge, Siemens has ordered the murders of three hundred and eight individuals, you'd better wipe that smirk off your face and listen up.'

Cheryl wanted to come back at him, but was too surprised by his vehemence to think of an answer. Instead she let the madman carry on. But, then again, some guys *had* tried killing her – one of them wearing one of those LAW jackets. Was it possible Baxter wasn't two cans short of a six-pack?

'Most of them were clean kills,' Baxter said. 'A gun, a bomb, an "accident". I also have little doubt that the death of my predecessor was anything but an accident. As proven by Siemens sending me in to face Hollis. Siemens knew what he would do to me, but knew I had no alternative.'

'Who *is* Hollis?' asked Cheryl, screwing the cap onto the iodine bottle, then remembering her own cuts needed tending.

'A sociopath,' said Stanley. 'A convicted serial killer who was supposedly executed four years ago, but has been working for Siemens, carrying out murders to order.'

'How could you put up with this?' she said to Baxter.

'What choice did I have? I . . . loved Siemens. He slept with me, used me. It was . . . And what could I do? Who would I tell? One wrong move and I would be added to the list.'

'But murder? In the name of the law?'

'Hollis was due to be murdered in the name of the law.'

'But that's an execution – after a trial, appeals . . .'

'So OCI cuts out the red tape!' said Baxter. 'I felt the way you do, at first, but a lot of OCI's victims *deserve* to die. And don't give me that liberal bullshit: there are people walking the streets who openly flout the law – look at the Mafia, racketeers, street gangs, Hell's Angels – yet the law requires the burden of proof to be on the prosecution. The defence doesn't even have to establish innocence! OCI solve the problem, usually when there is foreknowledge of something major about to happen involving known criminals. We've taken out child molesters who would eventually kill; hold-up artists with itchy triggers; rapists set on increasing violence; drug pushers; Mafia, Tong, yardie and terrorist group members. We've eliminated wife murderers, professional hitmen . . .'

'Hitmen?' said Cheryl. 'That makes you as bad as them!'

'Listen, girl! There are five billion people on this planet, half of them starving and half of the rest dying sooner than they should – victims of war, disease, crime. In the big picture a couple of hundred people dying is nothing.'

'This is—'

Stanley could see that Baxter was angry, though whether it was from conviction or the need to convince *himself* of the right of his master's actions, he wasn't sure. Stanley was going to need some convincing himself if he was ever to accept that he had been working for a bunch of murderers.

Baxter leaned forward, his bandaged head stabbing at Cheryl, who had now stripped down to her bra and panties, a not unattractive sight despite the blood and bruises.

'Let's say you two get married. You have a child. At five that child is abducted, raped and murdered by a group of perverts who are known to have been involved in paedophilia for twenty years. What if I then told you that we could have "removed" the man who stole your child and that he could have been "disappeared". Now, would you protest their rights? Picket City Hall? Go on *Oprah* and scream they were as much victims as was your child? No, you wouldn't. You'd just feel let down by the system, but at least your child would be safe, and those bastards would have got what they deserved.

'Now, carry that further to the people who might lure your child into prostitution, turn him on to hard drugs, shoot him during a mugging, drag him into some sick cult, blow him up with a terrorist bomb . . . Now things start to look different, don't they? And that's exactly what Siemens did to me; he convinced me that what he was doing was right, but because it was illegal he'd had to set up an elaborate framework to mask his activities. If I didn't like it, I was free to leave but – and he made this *abundantly* clear – were I ever to go on record about what I knew, he would have to protect the interests of OCI, whatever the cost. And I believed him.'

'So why the change of heart?'

'File Seventy-Seven.'

'What's that?'

Baxter relaxed a little, testing his neck. Stanley, meanwhile, was stripping down to his own underwear, careful as he peeled his trousers over the cut on his right shin.

'I was supervising a programme to discover flaws in our computer security. We'd been hacked into and, although no damage had been done, we had tracked one of the hackers down.'

'What happened to him?' asked Stanley, fearing the worst.

'We gave him a job! He was a damn good operator and, like a lot of hackers, he was a loner: those are the very people best suited to working for OCI. Like you, Fulbright.'

'Hollis mentioned the kind of people OCI recruits.'

'Hollis is astute. Very mad, but very astute. Loyalty comes from love or need. My loyalty to Siemens was based on love. Like a housewife who refuses to admit her husband is a brute, I forgave every new horror I discovered, partly because Siemens is so plausible, and partly because well, let's just say pillow talk. The other kind of loyalty is based on need: the need for a family, to belong – the gang mentality. Most of our office people like you come from broken homes, bad backgrounds, orphanages. They're people who *just* missed out on life's opportunities, failed to make the grade in a police department, were too short or too fat, didn't have quite the right SATs. We take them, train them up, pay them well, give them responsible work and inculcate in them a loyalty McDonald's would kill for. And all we ask in return is for them to shut up about what they do. We pay well, with good health and dental care, the works.'

'He's right,' said Fulbright. 'I've lost a lot with this. I was happy with my work – *and* I believed in it.'

The scale of destruction of his life's fabric was suddenly apparent to Stanley. He eased himself onto a chair by the table next to the bathroom door. Even if they survived this storm, the aftermath was bleak: no career, no pension, health care or references. He looked around the room.

Fading paintwork, peeling wallpaper, ages-old furniture, the view of an alley, the sounds of other failures echoing down the corridors. This was his future now, back to where he was before he was recruited, but this time it would be infinitely worse: he had seen what he *could* be, and that would be denied him. In one fell swoop Baxter and Siemens had contrived to destroy his whole existence. Had he felt stronger, he might have taken his outrage out on the man facing him, but for now he'd let him talk; let him explain why honest people work for murderers, and why good, decent people like Cheryl and himself were on the run, and under sentence of death.

Baxter continued to talk, staring up at the ceiling, his arms limp by his side, the painkillers Cheryl had given him having some effect – though he secretly doubted that any over-the-counter drug could kill the pain of amputation.

'This young hacker I employed found File Seventy-Seven. I'd given him the most obvious job for his talents: finding flaws in our system. His job was to try and break into all our most classified data. Kid was a damn genius. Each time he found a way in, I'd get him to devise a lock so no one else could do it. The one problem, of course, was he could devise back doors for himself. I warned him against doing it, but then he discovered File Seventy-Seven.

'He called me up, really excited. It was encrypted and needed decoding, but it was huge – as big as any of our other filebanks. I knew nothing about it, and I was stupid enough to ask Siemens what it was. He was surprised we had found it but said it was simply a political file, giving details of past political affiliations of prominent figures. It had been "borrowed", he said, from the FBI – a euphemism I took for stealing. Seemed fair enough; a valuable tool in fact. He asked me to get the kid to close it and leave it alone. No problem, I said. But the kid, arrogant little fool, wouldn't.

'Couple of days later he fell down an escalator in a mall and broke his neck – died instantly. At the time I thought it was an awful accident, but when I went to clear his desk I found it had already been emptied. All that was left was personal stuff like his Walkman – kid worked with heavy metal blasting through his skull fifteen hours a day – but all printed documentation had been removed. I took the Walkman and the half-dozen tapes to give to his mother. On the way home I was stuck in traffic and I flipped through the cassettes. They were just tapes, no boxes. One I noticed was Black Sabbath, but it had sticky tape over the tab. Pre-recorded cassettes lose the tab so they can't be recorded on, but he had recorded over *this* tape. For some reason I slipped it into my cassette player and found the voice of the kid reciting a sequence of words. Fourteen of them.'

'Passwords?' said Stanley. He was trying not to stare at Cheryl's deep cleavage, her breasts being constricted by her arms as she bent down to fix a split toenail.

'Exactly. He'd kept a record of all the levels he needed to get through to access File Seventy-Seven.'

'So you wrote them down,' said Cheryl to her feet.

'Precisely. By now I was paranoid about what we were really up to. I worked late a couple of nights after that and got into File Seventy-Seven but I was scared of being caught so I downloaded the first batch of documents onto a CD-ROM. *This* CD-ROM.'

From his jacket lining he carefully extracted a compact disc.

'Information stored optically and read by laser. Virtually indestructible. No trouble with magnetic fields or ageing.'

'So what's on it?' said Stanley, purposely turning away so that he could no longer see Cheryl's breasts, but then suddenly aware that a confessed homosexual would be looking at him in his Y-fronts. Not that he had anything against homosexuals but . . . well, he felt uncomfortable, not least because, to his surprise and embarrassment, Cheryl's near nudity was causing the first stirrings of an erection.

Stanley's dilemma was not missed by Cheryl, who herself was surreptitiously taking in his own body. It came as no surprise to *her*, however, that she should be thinking of sex so soon after a disaster and while still in the middle of a crisis. Tension did that to her. One time in high school her fear of exams became so acute she spent the entire morning masturbating herself into unconsciousness (that she had then failed was probably as much due to exhaustion as ignorance).

'I don't know what's on it,' said Baxter, aware of how stupid he was going to sound. 'I panicked and shut down after a few minutes. That was . . . five days ago.'

'And you think Siemens knows you've read it?'

'I'm sure he knows someone accessed the file; whether he knows it was copied, I can't say. But the fact that he fed me to Hollis suggests he doesn't trust me. Besides, that kid gets killed a couple of days after I tell Siemens he'd broken into his most secret files – what do you think?'

'So we need to read that?' said Cheryl.

'Need? I don't know. It may well be exactly what Siemens says it is, and the kid may have died by accident, and I have betrayed his trust. A lover scorned and all that . . .'

Cheryl stood up, rotating one shoulder and then the other, making her breasts jiggle excessively in the process.

'Look, I don't want to be personal, but you keep going on about how you love the guy,' she said. 'Surely you—?'

'Four years ago, Siemens and I were in Las Vegas. Routine business. We were drinking in a motel. He switched on a cable show. It was gay porn. I watched him watching it and made some unsubtle comment, and before I knew it he was kissing me. Now, I'd seen him with women and assumed he was straight, but I wasn't going to complain if he wanted to come my side of the tracks. He is extremely good-looking.'

'That I'll give you,' said Cheryl.

Stanley stared at her, then looked away.

'We ended up in bed, I doing everything he asked. And that night became a regular occurrence. We didn't live together, but two or three times a week . . . I gave, he took, he said all the right things, and I fell in love. Hopelessly in love, for the first time in my life, like a schoolboy with a teacher. I would have done anything for him. For a year or more it was all I could have dreamed of, he confiding in me, telling me all of OCI's secrets and I accepting them on trust because, well, when you're letting someone fuck you, trust is part of the package. But then, three times a week became once in a while, became now and then, became . . . and like any lovestruck fool I made his excuses for him: pressure of work, OCI came first, all that crap. Until I confronted him, and he rejected me out of hand. Said it had been good but it was over; I'd misread the signals, let my heart rule my head – all the usual clichés when someone wants to end an affair. He wasn't nasty: just get back to work and pretend it never happened.

'I took it like any jilted lover would. Tried begging, pleading, but it didn't make any difference, so I lost myself in my work, hoping he would reward me in some way for my dedication, but nothing changed. He'd read me well, knew I believed in OCI and that I wouldn't betray his trust, knowing how much good OCI did. And, like a fool, I bought it: if I couldn't have him, at least I could do his work, dirty though it was.'

'*That's* damned naïve,' said Cheryl, sitting on the edge of the table, only a couple of feet away from Stanley. She enjoyed making men uncomfortable.

'Have you ever been in love, Miss Kenney?'

'No,' she said honestly.

'And you?' he asked Stanley.

'Yes. A long time back.'

Both Stanley and Cheryl eyed each other.

'And?' prompted Baxter.

Stanley remembered Gail. How, after she had dumped him, he had hung around outside her home for three days hoping to catch a glimpse of her, to explain how much he needed her. Until the police dragged him off, in fact. And then, even after a beating at the back of K-Mart from a couple of her father's friends, he wasn't deterred. Only Gail spitting in his face the next time he saw her persuaded him he was onto a loser. Since then he had been careful to shield himself from his emotions. Naturally his girlfriends complained that he was cold. He knew he wasn't, he was just being careful but none of them appreciated his sense of self-preservation. So yes, he had been in love; and yes, he understood how Baxter must have felt – and, for the first time since he had met him, he felt sorry for the bastard.

He offered the man a nod, and Baxter accepted it.

'But now you've changed your mind?' said Stanley.

'Changed my mind? No. Woken up, maybe. The killings I could stomach; they were acceptable in the scheme of things.'

'In the scheme of things . . .' said Cheryl with a sigh.

Baxter was incensed. 'Oh, grow up, Miss Kenney! I checked on you – routine when booking freelance services. We know all about you and your father's accident, and the way Mulligan operates his helicopter hire business. The only reason you've still got your pilot's licence is because your father lied before an FAA investigation after that man was killed.'

Cheryl was dumbstruck. How could he know that? She remembered the day: it came back often enough in her nightmares.

Her father had been a lifer in the Marine Corps, and had been honourably discharged after twenty-five years. She had worshipped him, especially after her mother had died when she was eleven. He had lived and breathed choppers and had passed on that love to Cheryl. They went flying every chance they could, her father eventually setting up an air-ferry service with an ex-army buddy, Mulligan. It was a March afternoon, light poor, weather worse, and she had persuaded her father to let her take up one of the helicopters, saying she needed bad-weather experience if she was ever going to be able to cope with it. She was fifteen.

Everything went fine until a gust of wind blew them into some trees. She clipped a tall pine and the chopper rotated to the ground, crashing into a farmhouse, killing an old man, breaking her arm and crippling her father. The whole thing was an accident, could have happened to anyone, but on a day when they were supposed to be grounded, and she hadn't got a licence, it meant the ruin of her father.

From his hospital bed he had made her say he had been flying, that he'd blacked out and it was his error that had caused the crash. She had wept for days, knowing what it meant to him, but he had explained that, with his back shot, he wasn't going to be flying again anyway, and why should the company go down and she get into trouble for something that wasn't her fault? So the investigation was held, he was found liable, his personal insurance paid up for the old man, and the company and Cheryl were saved.

Two months later he died of an overdose in a VA hospital, a copy of one of his old flying logs on his chest, a single sentence scrawled across its base: SORRY CHERYL, GOT TO FLY.

Since then the only thing Cheryl had ever respected or cared about was her flying. She still blamed herself for her father's death, and that of the old man. Deep down she knew it wasn't so, just one of those unlucky things, but like Baxter she could ignore the truth for the sake of love.

'I'm sorry,' said Baxter, seeing how distraught he had made her. 'We do deep research on anyone we use. Your boss told us the full story in return for contract work.'

'Cheap bastard.'

'Not that cheap, but loyal. Anyway, where were we . . . ? I had joined the team, learned OCI's secrets, and had come round to Siemens's way of thinking. But File Seventy-Seven . . .'

'What?' said Stanley.

'The day before he died the hacker came to me with a print-out. It was a name and a background. Man in Grand Rapids. Hollis had killed him four months previously. I made a note of the details, shredded the print-out, and ordered the boy not to print anything more. I then did my own work-up.'

'And?'

'And he was completely innocent. No criminal record, no involvement with known felons; he wasn't suspected of wife-beating, adultery, child abuse or dishonesty. He was a teacher, married for eight years with twin daughters aged four. His wife worked in a florist; he had no debts other than his mortgage and his Mastercard. He was a churchgoer, a Lion, an all-round decent, upstanding American citizen. There was no logical reason why he should die. So I checked with the local police about his death. He had been stabbed twenty times, case unsolved.'

'So why did he die?' said Stanley.

'I don't know! Using that password I accessed other files at random. Again none of the details were relevant, other than – over a period of three years – these seven people had been murdered by Hollis. I made a list of their names but, because I had no intention of announcing that I had suspicions, I let it drop. I still have that list.'

He pulled out his wallet and extracted a small piece of folded paper. Wincing with the effort, he opened it out, and showed them the seven names and seven cities written on it.

'Any more detail, I could talk to the local police. Pull Eminent Domain on them if needs be, but I don't see why.'

'But you suspect . . .'

'I don't know what I suspect.' Baxter was weary; tired of talking, of reasoning. 'File Seventy-Seven might tell us. That Siemens gave me to Hollis today, and the mess we made up at Riva, both lead me to think Seventy-Seven holds some secret even worse than legitimate assassinations.'

'Innocent people?'

Baxter shrugged. 'Every one was an ideal citizen. None particularly rich, not all married, one gay, but all law-abiding citizens. Unusually law-abiding in fact: not a parking ticket or missed book club payment among them.'

'And no links?'

'Nothing. Different incomes, sexes, educations, jobs . . . No common denominators other than they were all in perfect health – the autopsy reports were included – and of course they all died brutally, the women in particular seeming to have been subjected to incredible violence. But that's it.'

Stanley took the list and scanned it. He might as well have been looking at a page from a telephone book.

Michael Warriner,	Tuscaloosa, AL
Catherine Ginever,	Glasgow, KY
Anne Holbro,	Queens, NY City
Brim Le Seur,	Fort Pierce, FL
Foster Selvadurai,	Fresno, CA
Josephone D'Mello,	Tacoma, WI
Haroldine Trelivin,	Salem, OR

'If I had my computer I might be able to run a program to isolate common traits,' offered Stanley fruitlessly.

'But there *is* a common trait,' said Cheryl, reading the list and handing it back to Baxter.

'What?' said Baxter.

'They were all murdered by Hollis.'

She grabbed the CD-ROM. 'And Siemens ordered him to do it, and this might tell us why. And if we know why, we might . . .'

'. . . have some ammunition against Siemens,' said Stanley.

They looked at the CD-ROM.

'We've got to get into that,' said Stanley.

'But first we've got to get out of here,' said Stanley.

Unfortunately both courses of action seemed about as likely as getting the compact disc to work by spinning it on a finger and running a pin over its grooves.

14

After they had tended as best they could to their wounds, Stanley took a shower while Cheryl and Baxter got dressed.

Examining his body limb by limb, Stanley found that he was bruised but nothing was broken and none of the cuts were serious. Even his head wound didn't seem so bad since it had stopped weeping. He leaned against the shower wall and let the hot water dash over him, idly probing the plughole to see what was backing up the water. He was standing in three inches already and it was in danger of overflowing onto the floor. Although the LAW jacket had stopped the bullets, he felt as if he had been given a good kicking. He rubbed his back, wincing as his fingers prodded the eggshaped bruises. He was *more* than lucky to be alive.

Stanley switched off the shower, narrowly avoiding causing the grey water to overlap the stall, and stood dripping, a tired battered man lost in a world of violence and pain. He wondered what their next course of action should be. Baxter had been damning about their chances, but surely to get on TV with a reporter would be safe enough. Name names, point fingers – then, if anything did happen, the culprits would be known. Some comfort; how many victims rest easy in their graves because their killers have been caught? Besides, it all depended on what Baxter had downloaded onto his disc. For all they knew it could be the OCI payroll!

Face it, Stanley, we're all screwed. He didn't even feel sorry for the girl, if he was honest; he was frightened enough for himself, and as innocent as she was. Baxter, on the other hand, seemed to know more than he was telling, or suspected something beyond Siemens's megalomania. At least Hollis, his number-one killing machine, was dead.

It was as he at last stepped out of the shower stall and reached for the remaining handtowel that there came a knock at the door. The guy on the desk had been bribed not to let anyone up, and he wasn't due to deliver anything. Besides, their phone was working and he didn't look like the kind to make unnecessary trips upstairs. He peered through the steam into the main room and saw Cheryl walk to the door and listen intently.

Who is it? he mouthed silently.

She shrugged her shoulders.

Baxter got off the bed and picked up one of the guns.

Stanley's stomach turned over but he knew there was no alternative. He stepped out of the bathroom and over to the table and picked up the other gun. He was naked but right then he didn't care.

The knock came again, firmer this time.

All three looked at each other, Stanley and Baxter both drawing a bead on the door.

'Who is it?' said Cheryl in a surprisingly calm voice.

'Jesus – from the desk.'

'What do you want?'

'Gotta little somet'ing for you.'

'Like what?'

'Like food. Said I'd try and get you a little somet'ing. Got tacos, corn dogs, burgers, the works.' There was a pause. 'Only cost you another hundred.'

Cheryl smiled. The creep had them over a barrel and knew it. This time she'd let it go, but the man needed a lesson. She looked at Stanley, unable to avoid dropping her eyes to his crotch – *hmmm* – then gestured for them to relax.

She opened the door, ready to pull the creep into the room and scare him, but it was she who was suddenly frightened. The Chicano was there all right, but so was a Clinger police officer, gun drawn and pointing straight at her face.

'Don't move!' he said. 'Anyone else in the room, drop your guns so I can hear them hit the floor.'

Stanley was shielded from sight by the half-open door and he edged back against the wall to give himself better cover. But just as he was about to edge forward, Baxter on his left stepped into plain sight of the door.

Cheryl saw the policeman's eyes catch a movement behind her and his gun panned away from her. The instant it was off her face, there was a loud report behind her and the cop's shoulder exploded blood across the wall behind him. He was forced backwards by the impact and, hitting his head on the wall, slowly slid to the floor, a smear of blood staining the grey surface behind him. The creep receptionist instantly fell to his knees and started praying to a God he probably only mentioned when orgasming, obviously fully expecting to be shot too.

'Jesus,' gasped Cheryl, 'you still want another hundred?'

Baxter stepped to the doorway and dared a look down the corridor. He then poked his gun into the Mexican's ear.

'Disappear,' he said.

The man crawled away on his hands and knees, praising God and Baxter in equal proportions.

'Is he dead?' asked Stanley.

Baxter shook his head. 'Not if they get to him soon, which they're bound to with the noise we've made.'

Just then there was a shout from behind them. As one, they spun around to see another cop on the fire escape, pointing a gun at them through the open window.

'You, shortie, drop the gun! *Now!* You without the clothes, drop yours too. Do it!'

They had no choice. Baxter let his .38 drop onto the floor, Stanley placed his on the table beside him. With Cheryl between the two men, they were sitting ducks.

'Kick it over here,' said the cop, nodding at Baxter. The light was behind him so his features were indistinguishable, but his voice betrayed no fear.

'You, get that gun off the fucking table.'

Stanley pushed the Beretta onto the floor.

'Kick it, fuckhead!'

Stanley kicked it, stubbing his toe, but making no noise.

It was over. Their weapons were nearer the cop than themselves and he would be able to plug all three if they made any move.

'Right, not one of you fuckers move an inch, or I'll shoot you where you stand. I'm coming in and then we wait.'

Baxter and Cheryl were standing three feet from the door, a second from possible escape but neither of them dared to move. Stanley was midway between them and the window, the table on his left, the bed on his right as he faced the window. Never had he felt more naked.

The cop put his left leg through the window and steadied himself. The only sound was the beating of their hearts in their ears, and the metallic clatter of the fire escape as the cop dragged his right foot across its latticed platform. But as he lifted his right leg there was a noise from the shower: the water finally emptying itself down the blocked plughole.

The cop stopped suddenly but found himself unbalanced, his coolness evaporated. 'What was that? Someone else?'

Stanley took his chance without thinking. He stepped over to the bed and grabbed the two LAW jackets that lay across the end. He scooped them up and held them in front of him as a shield, and ran to the window.

'No!' screamed Cheryl seeing Stanley's bare back and buttocks rippling as he darted towards the cop.

'Run!' Stanley shouted.

Cheryl hesitated but Baxter grabbed her arm and pulled her into the corridor, where they stepped over the slumped cop and ran on down the hall towards the stairs, Baxter limping and gritting his teeth against the pain.

The wobbling cop raised his gun, pointed it at the charging Stanley and fired.

The jackets were wrenched from Stanley's grasp and slammed into his face and chest, as if by a hurricane wind. He was blinded but he didn't stop.

There was another shot and one of the jackets flew past his head and then he made contact with the policeman.

The jolting impact knocked the breath out of him, and he yelped in pain as the policeman shouted his own shock, and then the two of them were tumbling through the window and slamming against the unyielding, rickety frame of the aged fire escape, three floors up.

The second jacket fell away and floated down into the garbage-strewn alley below, landing on the hood of the patrol car parked underneath. Suddenly Stanley's world turned upside-down, and searing pain ripped through his arms and pulled at his shoulders as he found himself hanging over the railing, the metal of the platform digging into his already tender abdomen, his hands chaffing on the rusted railing and his legs kicking into warm air. Looking to his right, he found the cop was also hanging onto the rail, but with only his right hand, his other arm and legs jerking furiously as they tried to find a hold.

'*Jesus, Jesus!*' he screamed. '*Help me, help me!*'

Before Stanley could do anything, the rail snapped, the cop lost his tenuous grip and grabbed at Stanley's ankle, the additional weight instantly pulling both his hands free, and amid a rain of rust both men plummeted in a tangled and screaming bundle the thirty feet into the alley below.

Baxter and Cheryl reached the third floor just as they heard the sirens and shouting from the lobby two levels down. Baxter instinctively turned around to run up towards the roof, but Cheryl grabbed him.

'There's nowhere to run,' she hissed. 'Have to bluff it.'

Baxter did a double-take. Their wounds were dressed but their clothes were still bloody.

'You can't have a shoot-out without guns,' she said. 'And you can't run when all there is is a dead end.'

She grabbed his forearm and headed down the long, dimly lit corridor. She knew she was being logical – keeping cool was a requisite part of her job – but in a flying emergency she would have her hands on the controls, and her past experience as reference; here she was little more than a pinball being bumped around a table, only luck providing a good score – and it seemed luck was running low.

They heard running somewhere below them, barked orders, and doors being kicked open. Shit. They were going to do the entire building. Head down, she charged on.

Suddenly she ploughed into a startled middle-aged man in a brown suit with an oversize briefcase. She skirted him and ran on, and they were halfway down the corridor, with shouting coming from the stairwells at both ends, when she stopped, a breathless Baxter bumping into her.

'He was a bit too well dressed for this dump,' she said.

'Fashion tips? Just what we need right now . . .'

'He's up to something. And at this time?' She looked at her watch, 1:54 p.m.

'So what?' said Baxter, his voice rising.

Cheryl forced herself to be calm. Surprise, that's what they needed. Surprise was the only advantage they had left.

'Come with me.'

Too rattled to argue, Baxter followed her to the room the businessman had entered, his leg giving him yet more pain. Cheryl proceeded to rap on the door.

'What are you doing?' hissed Baxter.

The door opened a crack and an eye surveyed them. Cheryl pushed and the door swung open, the man behind it staggering back – he hadn't had time to fix the chain – and she pulled Baxter into the room and slammed the door.

The man was in his early fifties, well-dressed, his hair too abundant to be entirely his own, his face nicely tanned. His hands were the real giveaway however, the fingernails long and beautifully manicured. He was about to protest but Cheryl put a finger to her lips.

'Give me the briefcase.'

'No!'

'Give me the briefcase or I'll give you some of this.' She held up Baxter's right hand so the man could see the fresh dismemberment of his finger. He turned white and sat on the bed, his worst nightmares suddenly a reality.

As Cheryl unclipped the fat briefcase she explained. 'Well-dressed guy coming here this time of day can only have one thing on his mind. Am I right? And such a big case, it's not going to have a packed lunch, is it? Aha!'

She emptied the case onto the startled man's lap. Women's clothing: red high-heel shoes, a red miniskirt, black fishnet stockings, black underwear and a long red wig.

'What's her name?'

'Cathy.'

'And yours?'

'El-Eloise.'

Baxter leaned against the door.

'TVs, Baxter. You should know the type.' She had never understood some men's fetish with dressing up as women, especially if they then want sex with a woman anyway. Still, who was she to question weird sexual peccadilloes . . .

'Right, the both of you strip.'

'What?' the two frightened men said in unison.

'Any minute now some goons are gonna come slamming in here, looking to shoot two of us. We've got to convince them we ain't who they're looking for. Now strip!'

Even as she spoke, she began to take off her clothes.

'Hey, Eloise, you into CP? S and M?' she said, pulling off her jacket and blouse.

'N-no,' he said, unclipping his tie.

'Well, you are now. How about AC/DC?'

The man was most affronted. 'No, I am not.'

She looked at Baxter. 'Well you are now.'

She unclipped her bra and stuffed it, and her blouse and jacket, under the mattress.

'Come on, come on,' she urged as the businessman stared dumbfounded at her full swinging breasts.

He began undressing. He didn't know what was going on but there was a naked woman involved – and he was all for that.

It was the chant that woke Stanley up.

'My leg, my leg, oh my leg. My leg, my leg, oh my leg . . .'

He opened his eyes and saw dirty water, an empty Cheetoh's pack, a milk carton, a used condom. He was lying on his front on top of something. He turned his head to the right. A face, creased in pain, white with shock. The cop.

Stanley rolled off and sat up, his buttocks in soggy paper and plastic. The cop was lying on his back, staring up at the sky, his face a picture of torture. Stanley ran his eyes down the man's body and saw the cause of the repetitive chant.

The man's left leg was twisted completely around the wrong way. God knows where it was broken – his hip, his knee – but wherever, it must hurt like a sonofabitch and if the guy wanted to chant he wasn't about to stop him.

Stanley stood up, his own knee feeling as if a nail had been driven into its side and was being waggled by some sadist. He leaned on the hood of the car, aware of the large dent and the spidered windshield, both of which must have been caused by their fall, and bent down to the guy, hoping he hadn't broken his neck, but if the poor bastard could feel his leg, he was probably okay. He looked him in the eye and, even though he received no response, he apologized.

'I'm real sorry for this. Hope it ain't too bad. Sorry.'

It was pathetically inadequate – a leg injury like that could cripple the man for life – but what else could he do? He sure as hell wasn't waiting around to give first-aid.

He spotted the cop's .38 and, picking it up, was debating whether to try and steal the man's pants, when he heard a siren and, whipping round, saw a squadcar flash past the end of the alley, followed by a squealing of tyres. Damn!

He limped off, aware he was naked except for a gun, which meant one less hand to cover his embarrassment.

The sight that confronted Officer Jimmy Ellis when he kicked in the door to Room 317 was pretty goddamn amazing – and he had seen some pretty goddamn amazing things in his time with Clinger PD. He might be in pursuit of armed felons, but this was something he needed to commit to memory.

There were two naked middle-aged men lying face-down on the bed, both with their hands tied behind their backs and gags in their mouths. Standing the other side of the bed, facing him, was a red-haired woman in high heels, fishnet stockings and black suspenders, and nothing else. She had tits to die for and a lightly downed pussy with a crease you could park a BMX in. In her hand was a leather belt and she was laying into the two guys like there was no tomorrow. There were angry red welts striping both men's buttocks, and he could see the guy nearest to him was weeping.

She stopped in mid-lash and stared at him, eyes blazing, her breasts lightly banging together with each heavy exhale. Her areolae were large and dusky, and looked like two big eyes trying to stop going cross-eyed.

'Seen enough? This ain't illegal; no money's involved. I do it because I like it.' She raised the belt and leathered the men's backsides. Both let out whimpers. 'And *they* do it because they've been naughty boys – haven't you?'

She raised the belt again and the two men nodded frantically. She stared at the cop, making sure he could see everything she had to offer, glistening with a sweat she had worked up surprisingly fast, though probably more through fear than exertion, but it did the trick. If his eyes had bugged out any more, they would have rolled down his face.

'Well?' she repeated.

'I—' Jimmy Ellis was speechless.

She peered at his badge. 'Officer Ellis. Maybe you'd like to shut the door and join in?'

The two men nodded their heads, but she stilled them with another thwack. She was enjoying this; maybe she had missed her vocation. Ellis was tempted, she could see, but commonsense ruled – especially when his sergeant appeared.

'Seen enough, Ellis, or do you want me to jack you off?'

'Yes, sarge. No, sarge. I mean—'

'Move it, Ellis!'

Ellis backed out of the room to be replaced by the big sergeant, sweat staining the underarms of his beige uniform shirt, his bald red pate gleaming, a grey moustache like a limp raccoon on his lip. Despite being indoors, he still wore mirrored shades. He shook his head in disgust at the two men.

'What a fucking waste. All that tit, all that pussy, and you just want your tushes smacked. What a world. Sorry for interrupting, ma'am. Go right ahead. Damn wimps deserve it.'

Cheryl was amazed, but hid it and nodded a thanks, rewarding the cop's generosity by leathering the two men again.

The sergeant was about to leave the room, when he paused. He looked even sweatier than when he had walked in, and Cheryl surmised that it was more than the pressure of work.

'You haven't got a card, have you?' he said in a low voice.

'Sorry. It's all on recommendation, and all like this.'

She slapped the crying men yet again.

'Shame, shame,' he said, scratching his crotch. He gave her breasts one last lingering look, then left the room and closed the door.

Cheryl dropped the belt and felt her whole body go limp. Not only had it been close, but she also knew such a potentially serious situation was more than likely to end up in her repertoire of masturbatory fantasies.

She gave the cops five minutes, herself sitting on the end of the bed, the men remaining bound and gagged. She examined the red marks on their white cheeks. In an odd way she had enjoyed hurting Baxter. Serve him right for playing his part in getting her in this fix. As for the other guy, well, maybe it would make him think twice about cheating on his wife. (She'd seen a picture in the briefcase of him and a couple of kids and a friendly looking, plump woman.) Then, when she judged it safe, she finished dressing in Eloise's clothes, and let the men go.

They, of course, were both outraged, insisting she needn't have gone so far or been so vicious, but when she pointed out the two fresh stains on the bedding, they both hushed up. It seemed all three of them got a kick out of danger in the sex department. *What a fucked-up world we live in*, she thought.

She instructed Baxter to dress in the businessman's suit, and for the businessman to stay behind in the room. He nodded his vigorous agreement, particularly when she promised more of the same on his balls if he didn't do as ordered.

Checking the coast was clear, Cheryl and Baxter walked down the corridor to the window at the end, and clambered down the fire-escape. But as the reached the bottom, a hand clasped Baxter on the shoulder and spun him round. It was the sweating sergeant.

'Got you,' he said.

Wary that the policeman might recover from his shock sufficiently to direct others after him – and needful of getting as far away from the hotel as possible – Stanley had little choice but to run down the alley to the street.

He came to a halt and peered round the corner of an empty store. The street wasn't very busy, with only a handful of pedestrians, but it was definitely a bad area, and he could see only one white face – and he was lying on his back on a bench.

Stanley, completely naked, had no option. He scanned the far side of the street and spotted a secondhand clothing store a hundred yards to the right and, thankfully, away from the hotel. Waiting until there was a gap in the traffic, he set off, almost immediately having to slow as he spotted broken glass on the sidewalk. There was no way he could risk running; he would have to judge every step.

The first to spot him were a pair of black hookers who seemed to have won joint first prize in an eating contest.

Stanley could do little but smile at them and cover his crotch with his pistol.

'Hey, honey, don't hide it! You got it, show it!'

Most other occasions Stanley would have been pleased to draw a compliment on his penis, but right now he would have been grateful if it could have just crawled up inside his body like his balls already had.

An old Korean couple stared at him from their grocery-store doorway, the woman tutting, the man smiling. Stanley suspected his behaviour confirmed a certain racial stereotyping on their part, but he didn't feel it incumbent on himself to explain his unusual circumstances.

He crossed the road, his progress applauded by a group of black teenagers playing craps in a doorway.

'Hey mister, you forgotten something?'

'Go for that tan, man!'

'I seen bigger clits than that!'

More than once he was tempted to reply, but decided he was lucky they found the situation funny. Right now he was a fucked-up white dude, but what if they chose to see instead a sex-crazed rapist fleeing the scene of one of his attacks. After all, he was naked and armed!

He let a cab pass then had to suffer the ignominy of a rusted Cadillac stopping to let him walk to the other side of the road. He didn't know what to cover, his balls or his ass; what he didn't do was wave his thanks.

A wino slumped in a doorway grinned toothlessly at him. 'Hat.'

'What?'

'Need a hat in this weather.'

'Sure.'

'You got a helmet. Need a hat.'

As Stanley was trying to decide if the man was raving mad or knew a good pun when he saw it, a heavy-set black kid on a Cannondale mountain bike slewed to a halt in front of him, pushed his shoulders back and stared him in the face.

Stanley tried to walk round him but the boy rolled the bike into his path.

'What is it?' Stanley said, hands on hips, uncaring any longer of what people saw. The kid was getting him steamed.

'What's the story?' said the kid with a sneer. He was dressed in so many branded items – Kangol cap, Russell Athletic T-shirt, Levi baggy jeans, Dreadly jacket, Cat boots – he could have been sponsored.

Stanley heard the kids across the street cheering. He looked past the boy and saw the safe harbour of the clothes shop just ten seconds away. So near and yet . . . He scanned the street in both directions. Traffic was slowing to look at him but none of the vehicles was, as yet, a police car.

'The story?' said Stanley, glancing at the .38 in his hand. Anger was giving him a bravado his exposure had until then denied him. 'The story is you're standing in front of your homeys talking to a naked white guy who's pointing his dick at you and who might just have the hots for your black ass.'

It was an insanely stupid thing to say but Stanley hadn't the time for politeness and, besides, he had the gun.

The boy stared at him, absorbing this information.

Stanley saw the name on the boy's chain. 'You go for white, Dwight? Or do you like to jack black?'

Dwight looked into Stanley's face and saw desperation. He didn't know the cause but he could see its outcome if he wasn't careful. He looked at Stanley's gun, then looked at his friends and saw humiliation – and decided to cut his losses.

He walked his bike into the road, trying to maintain his cool. 'Cross me again, freak, and you gonna pay.'

Stanley decided to leave it at that, and the kid pedalled away. He let out a long breath and realized his legs were shaking. He needed cover, in more ways than one.

He walked on to Honest Bob's Clothing Mart and, just as he stepped through the doorway, he turned and waved. It was a gesture that was appreciated and gained him several cheers. As idiotic as it seemed, despite being totally naked at midday in a neighbourhood he would normally have nightmares about venturing into, he was more in control than he had been since he'd walked into Riva the day before.

Inside Honest Bob's it was dark and cool and, quite logically, it smelled of old clothes. Racks of pants and jackets and shirts ran parallel with the street to a small window on the right, with shoes of all colours, styles and sizes lined up along all four walls. There was only one other person in the store: a bearded black guy tall enough to be a basketball pro standing in front of the cash desk, dressed entirely in black.

'Need some clothes,' said Stanley by way of introduction.

The guy raised an eyebrow. 'You don't say.'

'Quick.'

'Looks like it.'

'Now.'

'Quickest there is.'

'So?'

'So what?'

'Well I don't have any money.'

'Everythin' here looks to have price tag.'

'Obviously, but as you can see I haven't any money.'

'I see what you got man and, to tell the truth, I ain't impressed.'

'But can you help?'

'If'n I was to walk into a Jaguar dealer and say I hadn't got any money, do you think they'd give me an XJ6?'

'No.'

'Get the picture.'

Stanley was trembling with frustration, but the guy continued to lean against the counter, his expression unchanged.

'But I can't go out there like this.'

'You came in like that.'

Stanley toyed with the gun. He wanted to shoot him.

'Tell you what,' said the man. 'You can either hold me up or trade.'

'What?'

'The .38. Either point it at me and say, "Gimme some clothes m'fucker," or swap it.'

Stanley was so exasperated he simply handed the man the gun and waited for instructions.

'Nice piece,' he said. 'And I mean the gun.'

'That's a relief.'

'So?'

'So what?'

'So you gonna get dressed or are you really a pervert?'

'Oh. Right.'

Five minutes of hunting found him a pair of patched black 501s, a white T-shirt, a grey striped shirt, a grey hooded jogging top, a Coyotes baseball cap and a hideous pair of brown leather shoes that were the only pair in the shop that were an immediately comfortable fit.

He walked back to the black man who hadn't budged an inch from his lazy stance in front of the cash register.

'Well?' said Stanley.

'Shame about the shoes.'

'Yeah. Right, I'll get along.'

'Fine.'

At the door Stanley stopped. The guy's lack of reaction was irritating. He was acting as if armed naked men dropped in on the hour. Mind you, in this neighbourhood . . .

'How come you call yourself Honest Bob when I've given you a three hundred and fifty dollar gun for – what? – fifty dollars' worth of clothes.'

'Good point, man, but who said *I* was Honest Bob?'

'What?'

'He's in the john. Bad buritto. Can't get his ass off the can long enough to wipe it.'

'But you'll give him the gun?'

'No.'

'So I've stolen these clothes and you've stolen my gun.'

'Seems that way.'

'Well, the least you could do then is give me the gun back and let me square it with Bob.'

The man pointed the .38 at Stanley. 'I think not. Now, you got what you came in for. Be grateful you're leaving.'

Stanley dithered, then shrugged and walked out.

'Have a nice day,' shouted the man.

'Yeah,' muttered Stanley. 'Missing you already.'

He walked up the street, an eye on the teenagers in the doorway, keeping his hands in his pockets so they wouldn't see that he was no longer armed.

Sirens could be heard in two directions. Shit. Back in the real world. For a moment there in the shop, he had been in another dimension, without time or logic, but now he was back on the run and needing to find the girl and Baxter.

The problem was that, in order to discover their fate, he would have to travel back into the war zone and, clothed or unclothed, armed or unarmed, he would still be naked.

'What would you do?' said Baxter, explaining why he and Cheryl were running from the hotel. 'I've got a wife and two kids and a cat. If they found out about this, I'd be ruined.'

'Even the cat?'

'What?'

The sergeant's gaze bored into Baxter's bruised face.

'And me,' said Cheryl, ensuring the cop could see her cleavage. 'I've got a business to run. Schedules to keep.'

'You said you weren't doing it for money.'

'A little white lie. The other guy was paying. George here was on a freebie.'

As soon as she said it, she knew she was getting into deep water. Her lie would soon become a story that at some point was bound to fall apart.

'Him? Why?' The word 'freebie' had obviously sparked the sergeant's interest. Cheryl decided to fan the flames.

'He helped me out of a jam. We got stopped on Second.

George told the officer I was his niece. Gave me a lift home. We got to talking and I figured I owed him a favour.'

The cop shook his head. 'Beautiful broad like her and all you wants is your ass whipping.'

She ran her fingers over his nameplate. 'So what would *you* do with me, Sergeant Renfrew?'

'Run your tits into the station house and book you.'

Bang went Plan A.

'Why?'

'Because I don't like whores.'

'That's a bit strong,' said Baxter.

'Shut up, George. You I still ain't sure about, but this little lady is going for a ride.'

'On what?' said Cheryl, finding herself turned on.

A big guy who obviously would not have read Dr Ruth was threatening to take her somewhere and fuck her. Another time she would have been really pleased to be come on to this way, but now was not the time. She tried another tack.

'What was all the shooting?'

The cop tore his gaze from her breasts and frowned. 'You see anything?'

They both shook their heads.

'Fuck it. Get out of my sight.'

Cheryl nodded gratefully. The cop turned away, but, just as they were about to head up the alley, he turned back and reached over to Cheryl's head and snatched the red wig off to reveal her wet, plastered-down blonde hair.

She could see the policeman running over in his mind the descriptions from the APB: *Tall, blonde Caucasian female, twenty-five, hundred and forty pounds, plus two guys, one of whom would be a five-eight, fifty-year-old Caucasian, last seen in a suit, white shirt and tie. May be bloodstained . . .*

The cop ripped open Baxter's shirt and found a bloody undershirt underneath and immediately stepped back and reached for the revolver in his waist holster but, before his fingers made contact with the butt, a large piece of wood smashed across the back of his head, knocking him cold.

Stanley dropped the wood beside the stilled policeman. 'I'm getting too used to violence I think.'

'Thank God for that,' said Baxter, reaching down and extracting the cop's .38.

'Where've you been, and where did you get those clothes?' said Cheryl.

'I could ask the same of you,' said Stanley. She looked real sexy, in an extremely cheap sort of way. All tight and red with shapely stockinged legs that seemed to reach all the way up to her shoulders.

He explained what had happened to him and how he was walking back when he had spotted Baxter and what looked like a hooker talking to a cop at the side of the Rosemont. Thanks to cover provided by the blocked-off base of the fire-escape, he had edged his way along the alley without anyone seeing him. The rest had been straightforward and brutal.

'Enough talk,' said Baxter, in charge again, as Cheryl was about to explain their appearance. 'We've got to get away.'

'Most of the cops seem to be around the back.'

'Right, lead the way,' said Cheryl, bending to pick up her wig, and adjusting it as best she could.

'Nice legs,' said Stanley, her short skirt showing all.

'I charge very reasonable rates too,' she said as they jogged towards the street. 'Just ask Baxter.'

'Pity I've got no cash.'

'Baxter has.'

'A threesome? Not my scene.'

'It is for Baxter.'

'Don't remind me,' he said. Then turning to Stanley he added, rubbing his backside, 'And you – don't ask.'

They reached the street. There were two police cars parked half on the sidewalk at the front of the hotel.

'How are we going to play this?' Stanley asked Baxter.

'I have no idea,' said Baxter.

'Might be quicker just to give up,' said Cheryl. 'They're Clinger PD not OCI.'

'No!' said Baxter vehemently. 'Doesn't matter who you surrender to. Eminent Domain gives Siemens the right to lift us from any cell. We'd be dead in hours.'

Just then a cop exited the front of the Rosemont and walked over to one of the police Plymouths.

'Better get moving,' said Baxter.

They set off in the opposite direction, hugging the shop fronts, Baxter, with his sore hip, struggling to keep up.

Cheryl suddenly stopped. 'A bus!'

It was true. A Clinger TA bus was pulling into the kerb fifty yards ahead of them, people dismounting.

Without another word, they broke into a canter and waved the bus down just as it was setting off. Stanley was the first up the steps, stopping as the driver demanded the fare.

The driver was fat and harassed and would be expert at dealing with recalcitrant passengers.

Stanley patted his empty pockets, then turned to Cheryl on the step below him. She turned and looked to Baxter, still standing nervously on the sidewalk, who fished out his wallet and passed up a hundred-dollar bill.

Stanley offered it to the driver, who gave him a practised look of contempt. 'I can't change that.'

'No need,' said Cheryl. 'Just take us as far as you're going and keep the change.'

'No route costs that, even for three.'

'Does it matter?' said Stanley, eyeing the cop standing by his car, talking into the radio.

The driver considered the bill and smiled. 'A hundred dollars to go as far as this route goes?'

'*Yes*,' said Cheryl.

'It's *your* money.'

Stanley led the way to the back of the bus.

There were only four passengers, two old black women, a black teenage girl, and a drunk. They had all observed their boarding, and were staring.

'Lottery,' said Cheryl.

The bus set off just as Cheryl sat down near the back, with Baxter gingerly parking his bad leg next to her. Stanley chose the centre back row, facing down the bus aisle.

Each found they were sweating profusely and, as they wiped their faces, they hunkered down as the bus cruised past the front of the Rosemont. At last something was going right.

Then the bus slowed to a halt with a hiss of air-brakes.

'End of line!' announced the bus driver.

What?

Stanley looked through the grimy back window. They had stopped a block from the Rosemont, still in sight of the cop standing by his car, who had now been joined by two other officers, both carrying pump-action shotguns.

The other passengers got up and walked down to the front and stepped off the bus – including the drunk, determined to find the nearest lottery-ticket vendor.

The driver looked up into his mirror as he pocketed the hundred-dollar bill. 'End of line. Everyone off!'

'I don't fucking believe this!' said Stanley, charging down the aisle and thrusting his face into the driver's.

'We gave you a hundred fucking dollars, and you drive a hundred fucking yards!'

'If you want to pay me a dollar a yard, that's your problem. We had a deal. I stay here twenty minutes, then drive back out to Fair Canyon. You're welcome to wait.'

Stanley was apoplectic.

An unmarked police car screamed past, its red flasher clinging precariously to the roof over the driver's side.

Cheryl joined him, Baxter remaining in his place, slapping his forehead on the back of the seat in front of him.

'You thieving scumbag!' she started.

'Hey, lady, I did you a deal in plain English. Cash for as far as I was going and this—'

The barrel of Cheryl's revolver stopped his talk.

'You have three seconds to get this heap moving or you're going to be able to see out the back of this bus without the aid of a mirror. Understand?'

He answered by turning on the ignition. 'Wh-where?'

'Ahead'll do fine,' said Stanley, once again impressed by Cheryl's forthright thinking.

He sat on the seat on the other side of the aisle, then leaned towards her. 'Where *are* we going?'

She shrugged. 'How far does a hundred bucks go nowadays?'

15

The window blinds were drawn, the room in half-light, the TV on but the sound turned down. *Ricki Lake* re-run. The man in the bed was naked and propped up on a shelf of pillows, tubes running into his arm, wires plastered to his chest, a monitor by his bed bleeping a low but insistent, steady sixty beats per minute. Hospital sounds and hospital smells circulated the room, unable to escape the double glazing.

The man's face looked like a freshly ploughed field, his white skin scored by angry stripes, some stitched, some open. There was a dressing on his right temple and a bandage encircled his hair-line. One arm was bandaged, the other raw, several layers of skin scraped off. His bare chest bore more fresh bruising that crescented his heart.

His visitor stood by the window in a burgundy suit that seemed to mock the patient's ripped flesh. He was staring out through a gap in the blinds towards the car park. He felt the electronic instrument in his pocket, still unsure. Siemens prided himself on his decisiveness, but even his cool confidence had taken a battering over the last day or so. He turned back to the man in the bed and smiled.

'Not what I would call a hundred per cent success.'

Hollis tried a smile but his face hurt. 'Fuck you.'

'On the contrary,' said Siemens, crossing to the bed and settling on its edge. 'You're the one who got fucked. First by Fulbright, then Baxter, then by the girl. Sloppy?'

Hollis made to punch him, but Siemens grabbed his fist and held it. 'Keeping you under wraps is costing me money, favours and an unacceptable level of risk. I've given you a lot of breaks over the years, Hollis, but I'm about out of them now. You have only one last chance to redeem yourself.'

'So where are they?'

'I can get you to them,' Siemens said cautiously.

He had taken a call from Captain Schroeder and knew where they had gone after the freeway smash. The question was: did he have the nerve to use Hollis?

'It's up to you what you do to them,' he continued. 'I've little doubt you'll be inventive, even in your present condition. But it mustn't get back to me or to OCI. If you fuck up, you run. If you're caught . . . well, don't get caught.'

Hollis nodded. He hated the prick but knew he was talking sense, and he also appreciated the fact that he himself was still alive. Despite the battering he had taken from Baxter, and going through the windshield and that fucking drop, he was still in one piece, even if his epidermis wasn't. And now Siemens was giving him a chance not only to clear the account but also, more importantly, to exact revenge. If he offed those three, then he would still be a lover – and still be alive.

Siemens let go of his hand and stared up at the TV. Some fat bitch complaining about date rape – as if. He picked up the remote and flicked channels, finally settling on a local news show. Shots of a freeway smash-up and ambulances and eye-witnesses anxious for their moment before the cameras.

'Eliminate the problem, Hollis. Take a vacation. And when you're fully recuperated, you're back in. Screw up and—'

'Just get me some clothes. And get me some aftershave.'

'What?' said Siemens.

The other man wouldn't be shaving for weeks – unless he wanted tissue dotting his face like confetti at a wet wedding.

'You heard,' said Hollis, ripping out the intravenous needles and pulling the heart monitor off his chest. The bleep became a flat tone, but he hit the OFF button and silenced it. He never had liked being hooked up to electricity; not since his childhood.

Siemens went to the door, opened it a crack and spoke to the uniformed OCI agent on duty outside, as Hollis pushed back the bedcovers and rotated his legs until they touched cold floor. The contrast with his hot face made him sigh.

'How'd you pull that? OCI outside. What about Clinger PD?'

Siemens shut the door. 'We have our contacts. The paramedics brought you to this dump before we could get to you, otherwise you'd be in a private sanatorium. There are police in the lobby but their commanding officer understands Eminent Domain as well as the dollar sign, and so isn't going to cause trouble – despite that freeway crash. No one died, but ten people were injured and fifteen vehicles were wrecked. Hard to hide that kind of thing, even for OCI. Officials we can coerce or corrupt; TV news is entertainment and questions get asked that usually need an answer.'

'*Your* problem. If you hadn't let Fulbright and the bitch hijack my Winnebago, none of this would have happened.'

'And if you'd taken out Fulbright and Baxter clean and quick instead of toying with them, you wouldn't be here!'

There was a knock on the door. Siemens answered it and came back with clothes and a bottle of Brut Aquatonic.

'They'll fit. Don't know if it's your brand. Doesn't matter really; looks like you won't be shaving for a while.'

'On the contrary,' said a naked Hollis as he stood up.

He took the Aquatonic, unscrewed the cap and dashed a generous measure into his palm. Then, dropping the bottle, he walked over to the oval mirror over the washbasin.

He saw his face for the first time. There were at least fifty vertical cuts, varying in length from a quarter of an inch to three inches, as well as severe abrasions on both cheeks, jaw and forehead. Obviously his face had made contact with the ground. He didn't know what Baxter had hit him with, but the right side of his face was peppered with lots of little cuts, skin flaps hanging like a hundred miniature open doors. It looked like someone had sandpapered his cheek. And his eyes – he looked like a fucking vampire.

His left eye was totally bloodshot, no white at all, and his right eye, the lid puffed up, was mostly red too. Dark glasses would be essential. He had stitches everywhere, mostly in twos or threes, but there was also a ten-stitch scar on his head in the middle of a shaved circle. He looked freaky and it made him angry. Were they ever going to pay . . .

He poured the aftershave into his other hand, dabbed his palms together, then, watching his face in the mirror, slapped it all over his cheeks and chin and forehead.

The pain took his breath away and he staggered back, his face feeling as if acid had been sprayed onto it. Every cut was on fire, the red heat carving its way through his skin to his tissue and on into muscles. The red of blood became the red of agony and, resist as he might, he had to scream.

He turned and grabbed Siemens by the shoulders and thrust his own face at him and shrieked, his eyes like scarlet marbles, teeth bared, spit flying.

After five seconds he quieted and, pushing the man away, staggered to the window, gasping for breath, his hands shaking, his body trembling. His face was untouchable: he might as well have poured boiling oil over it.

The door burst open and two armed OCI men came in, but Siemens waved them out and closed the door.

Hollis was insane. Maybe he was wrong to trust him with taking out the three. Perhaps he should cut his losses and rid himself of all liabilities. Baxter, Fulbright and the Kenney girl would be found in time and, whatever course of action they had planned, he was certain damage could be minimized, particularly if Hollis himself was dead – and right now the man would probably be better off that way. Siemens patted the silenced Sig Sauer .38 in his shoulder holster.

Hollis snatched at the blinds and hurled them aside, and looked out into the afternoon sun. A bright, dusty world stared back at him from the other side of the fire that was consuming his face. But it was working, it was *working*. He spun round and leaned back against the crumpled plastic louvres, their crackling matching the bones in his clenching and unclenching hands. Hollis was remembering.

'Momma used to say you could beat pain with anger,' he said breathlessly. 'Didn't need pills – just anger. Get angry with your pain, then take it out on something. Or someone.'

He remembered the times his momma had hurt him real bad, and he had done as she had told him and turned his pain to anger and spent his rage on an animal – the cats he'd burned and dismembered – and all because momma had hurt him. And then, another trick, he recalled a worse pain, when his momma had pricked him with her sewing needles.

She'd strung five of them together in a line and tied him down, like she always did, to the kitchen table, naked, his legs strapped open. Then she had set to, stabbing him with the needles, each time going in a little bit further. She'd kept it up for ten minutes, each stab accompanied by an admonishment for some transgression he had committed, followed by her insistence that she still loved him and that it hurt her as much as it hurt him, but bad boys must be punished even if their mothers love them. Eventually she had stopped, and all the little pricks of blood had run together and his lower stomach, inner thighs and genitals had been sheened in red. As she studied her handiwork she occasionally added a prick here or a stab there, paying particular attention to his scrotum – his Sack of Satan as she had called it – and then, when she was satisfied, she had promised to let him up, but only after she'd washed him clean. Hollis remembered being surprised that she had relented so soon.

And then she had produced the bottle of rubbing alcohol.

The first time she had done it, he had been eight. He had screamed himself hoarse and couldn't speak for days. It was a torture that was to be repeated several times each year. She had finally stopped it in his fifteenth year, when he had ejaculated as she poured the spirit onto his balls, and he hadn't screamed. But he could still remember that first time. The mind-scarring unbelievability of the pain and how deep it had cored into his being. And, remembering that now, he realized that the pain of aftershave on his face was nothing, but it had served to raise his anger and focus his mind.

He stepped away from the window, stalked over to the bed and snatched up the clothes and proceeded to get dressed.

Lee jeans, a white cotton shirt, black Harley-Davidson bomber jacket, Converse sneakers and Cons baseball cap made him look human again – at least from the neck down. He grabbed the Ray-Bans from the still startled Siemens's top pocket and carefully slipped them on.

He checked himself in the mirror again, and smiled. His face was livid red; he looked like the Red Skull, Captain America's sworn enemy. He was not unflattered by the comparison; after all, he had been at war with America for as long as he could remember.

'How do I find them?' he said.

Siemens sat on the bed, still undecided. He had a hundred men he could trust to find the three escapees, so why put it in the hands of a madman? *Because he trusted Hollis more.*

He was an animal but, like any animal, train it up, keep it fed and comfortable, and it'll do as you want. OCI men, on the other hand, fell into two distinct categories: the dedicated backroomers, like Baxter and Fulbright, who thought they were doing something right and proper in a world strapped for cash and hidebound by bureaucracy; and then there were his *active* field agents.

Most of them were rejects from other agencies or the armed forces, and most of them enjoyed the money or the power; few were dedicated to any cause other than their own self-interest. They needed watching but they got the job done, yet Hollis was something special. *Unique.* He had his own very special kind of greed, and that served Siemens's ultimate purpose even better. And if no one else knew what that ultimate purpose was – not even Hollis or Baxter – then it didn't matter. As long as the job got done.

So he would send Hollis to eliminate the three fugitives, then whisk him away and allow him time to recover. Hollis wasn't recognizable as his original self: his fingerprints had been etched away with acid, his facial structure altered. If he was to turn up dead, questions might be asked precisely because his identity had been erased, but they would still find no answers. Siemens's other agents, however, were all ultimately traceable – and the killing of three people would attract attention no matter on whom he laid Eminent Domain. Better a lone madman than armed units: hadn't anyone learned anything from the Kennedy assassinations?

He fished out a small black box from his pocket, about the size of a Sony Watchman, and handed it to Hollis.

'There's a bug. When you're within three miles, you can trace it using this directional finder.'

The screen showed a compass with eight points in green.

'Now, they're obviously more than three miles away. The closer you get, the nearer to the centre the light gets, and the faster it flashes. When you get a constant light in the centre, you're within a hundred yards of the transmitter. After that it's up to you. If and when you get them, find a clean phone and call the number. I'll have you picked up inside the hour. Look for the usual licence plate.'

Hollis pocketed the gadget.

'They were last seen in a hotel on Garrison: the Rosemont. After they dumped you they hijacked a car and holed up. Desk clerk gave them away when Vice tried to bust him for pimping under-age girls. Descriptions match. They left on foot. Clinger PD have lost them for now. They're hurting.

The cops have roadblocks, and they're covering the airport and railway station. Make sure you eliminate any IDs they might have, just in case they're found before we get there.'

'Oh, I'll eliminate their IDs.' Hollis picked up the aftershave. 'And this'll make sure I'm in the right mood to do it.'

'What's the trick with that? Do you really need it?'

Hollis turned and grabbed the hanging saline drip and before Siemens could stop him he punched the needle into the flesh between Siemens's left thumb and forefinger. Then, holding the man's hand steady with one hand, Hollis flicked the drip-rate regulator to full and ran his pinched fingers down the length of the tube, forcing the clear saline into Siemens's hand, where the flesh swelled visibly, the liquid unable to find an exit.

'Pain's all in the mind, Siemens, and you can control it.'

Siemens was beginning to grit his teeth, his hand trying to pull free, but finding Hollis's grip too tight.

'What you do is take that pain and focus it into rage. Forge the pain into hate. Focus it. Imagine worse pain, and inflicting it *on me.* Imagine doing this to my balls. Picture it; think it. Want it so bad the pain doesn't matter.'

Siemens clenched his hand, but it made the pain worse – yet it also made his anger grow as he thought of how he could hurt Hollis. All he would have to do was pull out his .38, stuff it in the man's grinning wound of a mouth and blow the fucker's brains out. Or Siemens could order him eviscerated, electrocuted, burnt alive, razored . . . And, sure enough, as hate overwhelmed him, and Siemens's mind filled with images of a writhing Hollis, the pain lessened. The man had been right; pain could be used to catapult emotions into action.

Hollis read the man's eyes, felt the hand relax, and knew he had made his point. Pulling the needle out he squeezed the swelling between his fingers, so saline, mingled with traces of blood, spurted over his hand in a thin fountain.

'Simple conversion. Take pain and direct it.' Hollis walked to the door. 'I presume it's okay to leave?'

Siemens blinked back tears. 'They won't stop you. Turn left and use the stairs. There are cops at the elevators. There's a black Olds outside. A Cutlass.'

He tossed him the keys.

'There's a weapon in the trunk, cash in the glove box. The tank's full. It looks normal but the engine'll give you one-thirty flat out. And don't fuck up.'

Hollis prodded the scar on his forehead, pulling back his finger and looking at the fresh blood on it. 'You thought of bad things to do to me because of what I did, didn't you?'

Siemens nodded.

Hollis tugged one of the stitches out of his cheek. 'Just think what I'm dreaming up for those three.'

He flicked his bloody stitch at Siemens and left the room.

As the door slowly closed, Siemens sat back on the bed, nursing his hand, and shivered violently. He cared little for others, but even he could summon up sympathy for Fulbright, Baxter and Kenney, knowing what he had set loose on them.

16

Hollis parked his Cutlass and picked up the bug tracer from the passenger seat. Still nothing. He had cruised past the hotel Siemens had told him about and, although the place looked like a cop convention, there wasn't a blip on the screen. Tossing it back onto the seat, he leaned back against his head restraint and closed his eyes.

He had to be logical about this, even if anger was eating at his gut like an ulcer. Hollis forced himself to concentrate. Once he found them, he would loose his rage, confident that Siemens would be there to pick up the pieces. And if the cocksucker crossed him, well, he'd go to ground. He'd been on the run before – no big deal.

He opened the door and breathed in fresh exhaust fumes from the van idling in front of his car. It was a hot day and his face was itching like hell. He stepped onto the kerb and walked over to a payphone and dialled up Siemens's secure number. After Hollis had been routed twice through bogus switchboards, Siemens answered.

'Anything?'

'Gone,' said Hollis, still amazed at the condition of his face as it reflected back at him in the booth's glass door. 'If your tracer's working, they're out of range.'

'Well, I can't help you. I've heard nothing from the PD. They shot one cop, clocked two others. The girl's dressed in red, looks like a hooker. Baxter's in brown. Other than that, nothing . . . hang on. Call on another line.'

Hollis nearly threw the receiver down but controlled himself. To be kept waiting by that—

'North on Egmont. Witness saw them take a bus twenty minutes ago; laid a hundred bucks on the driver. My PD man can't keep it quiet for long.'

Hollis didn't waste time replying. He slammed the phone down hard enough to chip the receiver, and walked back to the car and edged it out into traffic.

He drove at a steady forty, the bug tracer on the dash in front of him. It took eleven minutes for the first signal to appear. And six minutes later he had narrowed the signal down to a computer store: HASKINS HARD BARGAINS AND SOFT SAVINGS.

He drove along its front, unable to see anything beyond the products stacked in the windows and the multitude of offers. He hung a left onto Fifty-eighth Street, then another, and cruised the rear parking lot, the Cutlass's throaty engine growling like a prowling beast. Then he drove around to the front again. The green light remained constant in the exact centre of its compass points. *Got you, fuckers.*

He eased the car to halt, pocketed the tracer, then walked back to the trunk and popped it open.

Inside he found a black attaché case. Unlatching its twin catches, he raised the lid and couldn't help smiling. Much as he wanted the trio to suffer, he also wanted them dead, the sooner the better, and with this baby he'd have some fun, do the job, *and* give Siemens the headache he deserved.

He lifted out the Ingram M10 with its Sionics Suppressor and nine spare clips, slapped one home, and put the others into his jacket pockets. *Nice weapon.* With thirty rounds of

9mm ammo per clip firing off in less than three seconds, nothing – and nobody – would be getting in his way.

He dropped the lid on the trunk and, concealing the weapon under his jacket, walked the short distance to the store entrance and slipped inside. There he turned and slid home the bolts, top and bottom, of the double doors, effectively locking everyone inside the building and, to keep everyone else out, flipping the Apple Mac sign to CLOSED.

Walking through waist-high swinging metal gates, he found himself standing at the corner of two aisles, a row of work-stations stretching to the back of the store in front of him, with half a dozen people operating keyboards. To his left, eight-feet-high shelving stacked with stationery and plastic containers running parallel with the fifty-feet-wide store-front window display, two students checking prices.

Hollis doffed his baseball cap, unscrewed the Brut, and upended it over his head and let the flaming liquid dribble over his torn scalp and into his sliced face, its sting razoring its way into every nick and cut, as his world became as red as his bloodshot eyes and weeping wounds. A scream welled within him as pain-drenched images of his mother and the joyful cruelties and ecstatic miseries of her love pricked the bubble of his humanity and he surrendered to the blackness that always lay waiting inside his skull.

He announced his presence to the world with a long piercing shriek, then levelled his Ingram's and squeezed the trigger as lovingly as if it were his mother's teat.

The students were cut in half and, before what remained of their bodies hit the ground, Hollis turned his many bullets and terrible wrath on the other customers.

17

They needed to access Baxter's disc. So, when Cheryl saw the computer store, she'd made the driver stop, threatening serious retribution if he revealed where they had got off. That the store was HASKINS made her quest even easier.

It was a big store, all on one level apart from a large office in the centre that sat above head height atop a storeroom. With its long, angled black windows, it looked down on all sides of the store like an Amtrak signal-box. Before Stanley or Baxter could question her further, Cheryl, aware there were video cameras operating, and that speed was of the essence, led the way towards a young man with long hair, rimless glasses and bad acne.

'Hi, Kyle,' she read his badge. 'Looking for Mr Rorke.'

The boy pointed up at the office. 'He's up there.'

Cheryl led the way across the store to the stairs leading up to the office. Its base was painted black, and covered in large hand-painted logos. At the door she paused.

'Keep that ID handy, Baxter. It may work yet.'

She ignored the KNOCK AND WAIT sign and walked in, closing the door when she saw why they should have knocked. Mr Rorke was getting a blow-job.

Rorke saw them and shoved the girl kneeling behind his desk away, as if he hadn't noticed her sucking on the end of his penis until that moment. He was about to launch into a tirade of abuse when he saw Cheryl removing her red wig.

'We meet again, Nathan,' she announced, tossing the wig onto his exposed member and recently scorched pubic area.

Whatever had happened the last time these two had met, Stanley was glad he hadn't been there. The man just stared, eyes wide, his hands fluttering on top of his desk, mouth as wide open as his fly.

The girl tried to say something but Cheryl gave her a smile. She felt sorry for her. 'Don't you worry. We'll make sure Mr Rorke gets finished off. Won't we, Nathan?'

Rorke looked like he was going to burst into tears.

Cheryl scanned the room. It was an office furnished in light oak, blinded windows on all four walls that, if open, would afford uninterrupted views of the entire premises, the angle obscuring any view back up into the room itself. In one corner stood a bank of video monitors offering a continually changing selection of panning shots of the inside of the store. Rorke's absurdly large desk occupied almost half of one wall, with a couple of red leather chairs and a coffee table in front, stocked with various computer magazines. A coffee machine gave the room a lived-in smell. But it was the remainder of the room that held their interest: a varied selection of screens, drives, keyboards, modems, printers and other computer accessories sat gleaming under the neon.

Cheryl spoke to Baxter. 'Well?'

Following her nod at the computers, he realized what she was asking, and he walked over to the machinery, nodding.

'Yes, yes. Fine. Perfect,' he said patting an IBM screen.

Rorke found his tongue.

'Take it, take it. It's yours. I'm sorry. Real sorry.'

Stanley looked at the creep. *What was going on?*

'Hey, we don't just want your gear,' said Cheryl. 'We want your co-operation. Put your pecker away and come out and meet these agents.'

Stanley waved the badge on cue.

Rorke clutched his chest. 'Hey, there's no need for—'

'Get out here!' Cheryl shouted, pulling her gun out.

Rorke fainted.

'I think you pushed him too far,' said Baxter, already trying to extract the CD-ROM from his pocket. He gave up and beckoned Stanley to fish for it once again.

Cheryl tutted in annoyance and crossed to the desk and began slapping Rorke awake. As he mumbled his re-emergence into consciousness, Cheryl caught sight of the girl still standing by the door.

She was attractive in a bimbo sort of way, and Cheryl doubted she had the brains to plug in a word processor, let alone operate one, but for all that she looked scared, her bottom lip trembling, her hands trying to hike down her short black skirt. She wasn't some tough hooker – just a kid making do with what she had. Cheryl felt sorry for her.

'What's your name?'

'Anne-Marie,' the girl said, her eyes rimmed with tears.

'Well, Anne-Marie, don't you worry. Mr Rorke's been a little lax with his parking tickets and we're here to make sure he pays up. So don't worry none, okay? You just go off and do . . . whatever you do, and we'll be out soon.'

'Mr Rorke will be all right?'

She sucks his cock and calls him Mr Rorke? 'Do you care?'

She frowned, her opinion apparently rarely sought. 'No.'

'Well, there you are.'

'Okay,' said the girl, and left.

'What if she calls the police?' asked Stanley.

'Three digits? Don't think she can remember that far.' She looked at Baxter. 'Is that thing what we need?'

'Better than that. It's got a 4000 with rip.'

'Does it do fondue too?' she said.

'It means we can print out whatever we need, fast.'

'Sorry,' she said. 'Come on, Nathan, time to repent.'

'What did he do to you?' whispered Stanley.

'It was what he was *going* to do that counts. Nathan likes to share his women, don't you?'

Stanley had been knocked about a lot that day, but even his befuddled thought processes could work out that Cheryl must have been planning to have sex with this guy.

'You and him?' he said, genuinely amazed.

'So?' she said, kicking Rorke as he edged across the room.

Okay, thought Stanley, looking the guy over. He wasn't so much fat as big, but he was obviously a sleazeball . . .

'Hey, don't fret. It's not like you and me are engaged or anything,' Cheryl said, interested that he had an opinion.

They both stared at each other, unable to read the other's thoughts, until Baxter interrupted them.

'More pressing matters here,' he said.

'Right,' said Cheryl to Rorke. 'Can you operate it?'

'Yes.'

'Well, you might just live through this.'

The man was terrified.

Cheryl smiled. 'Now you know how I felt last night.'

He stared at her, sweat coursing down his face.

'You're given it on a plate and . . .' She became aware that Stanley was looking at her, and was suddenly all business.

'Right, Nathan, we've got us a CD-ROM and we want to

read it, and then print out any relevant pages. Can you do that?'

'Y-yeah, sure. No problem. Anything.'

'Then load the thing and get it up on screen.'

Rorke did as he was asked, anxious not to anger the mad bitch any further.

Cheryl sat back on his desk and let them get on with it. Eyeing her ludicrously short hemline, she realized she looked every inch a working girl. Then she caught sight of her face in a mirror. She looked wrecked, her hair shabby, her face with no make-up. She leaned over the desk and spotted the girl's handbag. Inside she found a bundle of cosmetics, and while the boys played with their toys she made up her face, grateful the girl had a complexion bad enough to need foundation and powder, which helped cover Cheryl's bruises.

As she finished, and was checking to see if she had missed anything, there was a cry of despair from Stanley.

'That's it? *That's it?* That's what we've got!'

'It's coded. We need the passwords.'

'You had the pass—'

'They've been changed! Probably as I was downloading.'

'What's up?' said Cheryl.

'We can only read three pages.'

'Hey, pardon me if I'm wrong here,' said Cheryl, her heart racing, lipstick clattering to the floor. 'But those CDs can hold hundreds of pages of info, can't they?'

'Thousands,' said Rorke, eager to be seen on her side.

'And this is supposed to be a master file, just bursting with incriminating goodies?'

'Yes, but—' started Baxter.

'But nothing! *Three fucking pages?* Can't you get anything else out of it, Rorke?'

The man turned and backed away as if about to be shot. 'Hey, I only drive the things. I ain't no mechanic.'

'What about one of your geeks outside?'

Baxter interrupted. 'No good. It's encrypted. Unless we've got the right words, phrases, letters, we'd be here forever, and I can virtually guarantee it's got a permanent lock.'

'A what?'

Rorke was eager to help. 'Give it the wrong password too often and it freezes you out.'

Baxter: 'Use the wrong key too often, the lock *disappears*.'

Cheryl stalked over to the three of them, each cowering back. In her high heels she was actually the tallest.

'You and me and him are up against all the shit OCI can call down on us, and all we have to appease their asses is three fucking pages?'

'*Yes!*' all three said.

'But that's like . . . like wearing a bulletproof *button*!'

They all nodded vigorously.

Suddenly she pulled out the .38 she had been carrying in her waistband under her blouse, and pointed it at them.

'Hey!' shouted Stanley. 'We're in this together!'

'I'm not!' said Rorke.

'Don't shoot the messenger!' said Baxter.

Cheryl was outraged. To have come this far and to be let down so hard. The CD had held talisman-like qualities and she'd banked on it to provide a map out of the chaos they were living through. But now *three lousy pages* . . . Her shoulders slumped and her gun arm fell limp by her side. She wanted to cry but she'd long since lost the knack.

Stanley patted her on the shoulder. She didn't object.

'So what are these three pages?' she mumbled.

'We don't know.'

Cheryl shrugged Stanley away. 'Show me.'

Rorke punched keys and a page formed on the screen.

File Seventy-Seven AO/12123-WW-ABB-4
A Eyes only A Eyes Only
Report intrusions.

'*It's a title page!*' she yelled.

Rorke instantly stabbed a key and a second page appeared.

Standard Format G2.
6.26.77
45 01 15   124 10 11
Ref NH: Gudgen
Ref W: Boscome, E
    Paalborg, J
    Paalborg, A
    Contreras, L
Contact Success: 1, 2, 3, 4
Containment: AAA

'Great,' said Cheryl. 'Now stun me with number three.'

The third page formatted itself and she groaned and laid her head on her hands.

The screen showed a line, running from the bottom left-hand corner to slightly below the top right corner. From it diverged four lines of almost equal length, two on each side, with lots of figures, some in brackets.

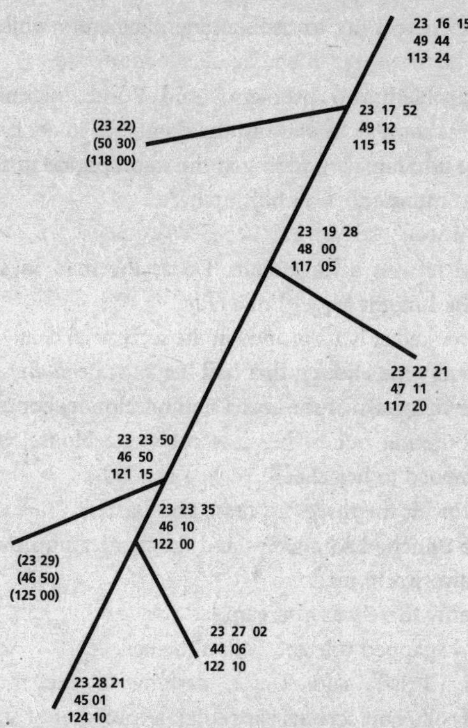

She waved the .38 in the air. 'Shoot me now! End it all!'

Baxter was eager to placate her. 'We may still be able to read the CD. We just need to work on the encryption.'

'And who can do that?'

'Kyle Tanner,' offered Rorke, even more eager to please the madwoman with the gun. 'He could do it. Smart kid.'

'We'd need a set-up like this, and some time,' said Baxter.

'How much time?' said Stanley.

'Best ask Kyle, but we'd be talking hours. At least.'

'What do you say to us camping out here a while?' said Cheryl.

'No problem, no problem,' said Rorke, planning on running as soon as he was out the door. 'I'll go get him.'

'No,' said Stanley, nodding at the microphone in front of the video monitors. 'Call him up here.'

'He's not—'

Cheryl let out a huge sigh. 'Do as the man says, okay. Otherwise I might forget I'm a lady.'

They looked at her slumped in the secretarial chair, fishnet legs spread wide enough that had her skirt been any shorter they'd have known if she was a natural blonde, her cleavage all but bursting out of her low-cut white blouse, the gun barrel pressed to her cheek. Yeah, a real lady.

'We'll print the three out first,' said Baxter.

Rorke punched some keys and the printer hummed into life. 'Got to warm up.'

Suddenly there was a scream.

Cheryl snapped upright. 'What the hell—?'

'Jesus Christ!' said Rorke, dashing to the monitors. Suddenly all eight screens zapped up a mid-shot of someone dressed in black firing a machine-gun, and the sound of crashing glass and shattering plastic reached their ears, as did other screams, but no gunfire.

'Who?' hissed Stanley.

'*Your* lot,' said Cheryl.

Baxter shook his head. 'No. Over the top.'

'A robbery, then?'

But then they saw people starting to fall, blood spurting from bodies and faces.

Cheryl flipped open her revolver. Three bullets.

Rorke punched some more buttons. Images flashed up of cartwheeling customers, bloody corpses, electrical equipment exploding, sparks and papers flying.

'*Oh God, no . . .*'

They saw the blonde girl take a hit in the back and catapult over a desk, her naked bottom exposed for a second before three more bullets ripped into her buttocks and propelled her head-over-heels onto the floor, out of sight.

'*Jesus!*' screamed Cheryl. 'You got any guns up here?'

The man continued to punch buttons, hoping to find a screen without murder on it.

'*Guns!*' shouted Stanley. '*You got a gun?*'

'Desk! Yes! Gun!'

Stanley ran to the desk and pulled open the drawers until the bottom one revealed another .38. He checked it: loaded.

'This all?'

A face exploded but the man's body kept standing upright for too long, as if he didn't realize he was dead.

Stanley ran over to Rorke and pushed him out of the way, desperate to get a view of the whole store, but already two monitors offered only snow.

'They'll get up here soon enough. We need to be ready. Rorke, get me a shot of the store,' said Stanley, grabbing the trembling man by the collar. 'Show me where they are.'

'Yeah, yeah,' said Rorke, happy to be told what to do. He selected a camera that gave a view from outside the door. A man was walking the length of the store, shooting everyone.

'Call the police!' said Stanley.

'You got a silent alarm?' said Baxter.

Rorke nodded.

'Hit it! It's quicker than the phone.'

Rorke reached under the console and pressed a button.

'Why's there no firing?' said Cheryl, watching in horror as a man's hand disintegrated as he held it up.

'Silencer,' said Baxter. 'It won't last but it works.'

Cheryl ran round the room, looking through the windows. The only door in or out was the one they'd come through. Shit. Step out and they were dead. They'd have to wait for whoever was out there to come up, and then they would have to defend themselves as best they could with two .38s.

'Baxter, what's the best way to wait for him?'

'You're asking me? How—?'

'Pretend you were second in command of an organization that kills people, huh?'

'We need cover, so either side of the door, behind the desk, or in back of the computers, but any shot you take has to hit the mark first time. Miss and he'll cut you in half.'

'So we won't need our other nine bullets, then,' she said shaking her head in disbelief.

'Great odds,' said Stanley weighing the .38. Mandatory training in self-defence had made him familiar with guns, but he didn't like them. It was like an alien artefact, and he felt as competent to use it as he had the first time he had driven a car with a stick shift after a lifetime of driving pick-ups: he knew the principle but . . .

Suddenly it fell quiet except for distant whimpering. The screens revealed something like a scene from an old Western, the high-resolution monochrome images showing a black-clad invader, his finger tight to the trigger of his weapon, surveying the carnage.

Stanley pressed ZOOM, wondering aloud how many more OCI people were there.

'This is too heavy for OCI,' repeated Baxter.

'Yeah? Well, it ain't a Domino's delivery!' said Cheryl.

'There are people *dead* down there!' said Baxter.

'Tell that to Riva,' said Stanley.

'If that alarm's ringing outside, we've only got to wait until the cops arrive,' said Rorke, his words almost a prayer.

'Shouldn't we warn them?' said Cheryl. 'About all this?'

'Yes,' said Stanley, aware that the cavalry could be wiped out before it reached the beleaguered pioneers.

He grabbed the phone and punched for a line. It was dead.

'They cut the wires.'

'No, they shot the junction,' said Rorke, pointing at one screen where sparks cascaded from a large grey box.

'Hey, there's something not right here,' said Stanley.

'You've noticed?' said Cheryl.

'No, look. It's just one guy. There's no one else.'

They scanned the monitors showing six different areas of the store. They showed corpses, wreckage, terrified cowering survivors . . . and the lone figure in black.

Cheryl stared at a back shot of the man with the gun. 'Turn around, you fucker. Turn around.'

As if on command he slowly spun on the ball of his foot.

'*It's Hollis!*' Cheryl gasped.

His face was a bloody dripping mess, his eyes pinpricks, but it was the madman all right.

'He survived that crash?' said Stanley.

They watched in horror as he stared straight into the camera, then looked up to his right, at the office. He then looked back at the camera, smiled, and walked out of vision.

'Oh Christ!' said Stanley. He ran to the desk, trying to push it towards the door, but it was too heavy.

'Help me, help me,' he hissed at Rorke, aware for the first time of the uncanny silence in the store. All they could hear were Hollis's footsteps crunching on glass.

Rorke shook his head and instead crawled into a corner and hid his head in his hands.

'Big man,' said Cheryl, spitting at him. 'Baxter, you any use with a gun?'

He looked at his bandaged hands. 'No, sorry.'

'Okay. Stanley, you take mine, give me the full .38.'

Stanley didn't argue: when there's a tidal wave coming who cares who has the biggest hat. He caught the revolver, rolled out the cylinder. Great. Three bullets. He slapped it back, spinning the chamber as he did so.

'Either side of the door,' Cheryl hissed. 'Try a cross—'

The windows suddenly imploded, showering all three of them with glass, the blinds unravelling and fluttering across the room like the wings of a giant crippled bird and, as the last piece of glass tinkled, and they could hear muted screams from customers to their rear, Hollis shouted:

'Can't think of anything clever to say, you fucks! I'll see if I can come up with anything before I get to you!'

He fired another burst, the ceiling panels shredding and falling like snow, the sound of destruction at odds with the muted purring of his gun.

Stanley crawled over to the right of the door, while Cheryl edged herself to the other side. But Baxter, on his knees in the middle of the room, waved his hands at her.

'No! The walls are too thin. He can shoot *through* them.'

Cheryl and Stanley looked at each other and as one dived into the middle of the office, just as Hollis opened fire again and thirty holes punched their way through the door and the walls where they had been standing.

Baxter was breathless. 'Soon as he's on a level with the floor he'll cut us off at the knees. And if you shoot back you'll just give him somewhere to aim.'

'So what are we going to do?' said Stanley, suddenly aware he had dropped his gun by the door.

'You two are the fucking pros!' hissed Cheryl.

Baxter and Stanley looked at each other, ducking as another burst of gunfire ripped through the walls, but this time a good foot lower. He was coming up the stairs.

Hollis gasped as his hand brushed the silencer. Shit, it was *hot*. He wrapped his hand in his T-shirt tail and unscrewed it. Thing would be blown by now, and what was a bit of noise? Couple of minutes he'd be out of here.

He tossed it away, slipped in a new clip and knelt down, examining the shredded door. Enough of it had been hit to make it almost invisible. Good move – shred the fucker, get it *open*. He wondered if there might be another exit but decided he didn't have time to find out. Besides, whoever was up there hadn't left yet. He paused for a moment.

In the eerie silence that pervaded the store, he thought he could hear a dozen rapid heartbeats, the gurgling of bowels, the welling of sweat, the sudden religious thoughts of atheists . . . Yes, he could, he could! *The place was his.*

He stood up and loosed the entire round into the wood, the door exploding off its frame into the room, smoke and dust everywhere, the air rent by the gun's deafening roar.

He coughed, but smiled as the debris drifted down and he

saw the roof inside the office. Whatever weapons they might have, he'd be seeing them before they saw him clear enough to fire, and then he'd cut them in fucking half.

God, but this felt so *good*. He'd wanted their deaths to be slow and juicy, full of pleas and whimpering, but a good old-fashioned knee-trembler can be just as satisfying if you're in the mood – and right then he was in the mood.

He dropped the clip and packed another in. He had three left. More than enough. He took another step, lifted the gun above his head and, holding it on its side, let rip a burst, the recoil strong enough to blur his aim, and he saw bullets thudding into the mangled ceiling and, a moment later, water beginning to fall. He'd hit the sprinkler.

He turned and checked the aisles. Someone was crawling away on their belly, but the wide bloody trail on the grey floor said they weren't going far. A woman nearby was sitting upright, her wide uncomprehending eyes fixed on the bloody stump she held on her lap that was pumping her life away. *Nice tits*, he thought.

'Okay, people! Get ready! Payback's coming!'

'Fuck you, Hollis!' shouted a male voice.

At last, proof *they* were there. It had been Fulbright.

'Sorry, no requests,' he said.

Oh God, he was going to mess them up but good. Stick his gun up the girl's wet cunt, see the bullets come out the top of her head. Fire up the fag's ass, give him a reaming his fisting faggot friends couldn't begin to dream of. *Yeah!*

He dashed up three steps firing a continuous stream at the open doorway, everything above waist height inside exploding into shards or flames; furniture, walls, computer screens, everything succumbing to his deadly hail. He paused, fired another burst until the gun silenced again, flicked out a clip, stuffed in another, took two more steps, fired again.

The back wall caught fire – he must have hit wiring – and it lit up a dark area at its base, and he saw someone.

Yeeeesss!

He aimed at the figure and fired half the clip into it. His victim didn't have a chance, but the jittering and the blood sprays were fun – like shooting a sackful of kittens.

Hollis stopped and only just remembered to duck down, hardly able to stop laughing. Christ was he ever having a good time here!

'One down, two to go!' he taunted.

Two shots rang out in reply but thudded into the ceiling near the entrance. Blind, they were firing blind.

'Either of you fucks left got tits?'

He took careful aim at the wall beside the door on the right and sliced it in two, then did the same with the wall on the left. The noise was incredible but he didn't notice it. All he understood was fire and pain and blood and death and his own sweet satisfaction.

Smoke started filling the room, despite the sprinklers' rain. It would soon be difficult to see. *Finish it, Kent!*

He edged up until he was only two steps from the top. He thought he heard a siren in the distance, but the fizzing sparks and cascading water masked the outside world. With a howl of triumph he leapt into the room and sprayed left to right then stopped. There was no one there.

Just a lot of wrecked equipment and some guy. Might be Fulbright, too big to be Baxter, but in his heart he knew it was neither. He looked up and rain fell on him. He was pleased the cold water dashing on his face was stinging him but then, screaming in frustration, he fired off another squeeze, peppering the now blank video screens, causing them to explode one after the other.

Be logical. There's no other door out of here. So they could be behind those computers on your left, cowering like the little insects they are, just waiting to die.

Good. He didn't like to disappoint people.

He turned to face the computers and printers on his left, dropped the spent clip and reached for another, but as he was slotting it home, a screaming blur flew at him out of a grey cabinet at waist height.

Cheryl hit Hollis square in the midriff and the man crumpled, slamming back against Rorke's desk, its shattered edge ramming into his kidneys. Pain stormed through him and he fell over her shoulder and landed with a splash on his face, his senses jumbled.

Cheryl rolled free and while still crouching kicked him in the head once, twice, then standing tall, kicked him in the ribs a couple more times.

'*You fucker, you fucker!*' she screamed.

She looked around for her gun. Shit! *Where was it?*

Then she remembered dropping it after she'd fired her two futile rounds as she scrabbled to the cabinet. She could see it sitting now by the wrecked laser printer, its handle turned temptingly towards her. But as she ran to get it Hollis, who was lying on his own gun, grabbed at her ankle and she fell headlong inside the printer's cupboard, banging her temple on its metal rear wall and dazing herself.

Then, as Hollis rolled back and forth on his back like a drunken tortoise, trying to regain his balance, Stanley rushed round from behind the shattered printer, revolver in hand.

Skidding to a halt at the man's shoulders, he fixed his aim on his sneering, bloodied face. For a second he was stunned by how much it had been ravaged – but only for a second.

'*Die*,' he commanded, and pulled the trigger.

Both men locked eyes as the revolver's cylinder slowly rotated until it was lined up with the descending hammer and impact was made with the chamber's contents.

And it clicked.

Hollis could see there were only three bullets left in the gun and they were two chambers away. He lifted his Ingrams up and pointed it at Stanley's face.

'Your gun's not empty, Fulbright, but it sure ain't full. And you don't know how many rounds *I've* got left. Might be one, might be thirty, but one's enough to send your pea brain into orbit. Now, you so much as twitch that trigger finger, or any of you other fucks makes a move, Fulbright won't have to worry about hair loss no more.'

Stanley stared down at the man's upside-down eyes, but even at such an odd angle he could tell he spoke the truth. A madman's eyes always do, the one thing they never learn to disguise; look long enough into them and you can see hell or your own death – and right then Stanley could see both.

'Now get rid of the gun,' said Hollis.

'Don't,' hissed Baxter from behind the computers. 'I've got him covered.'

Stanley knew it was a lie – the man couldn't cover a bed with his hands, the way they'd been left by Hollis – and he wasn't going to try and bluff Hollis.

'Got to,' Stanley said. 'No choice.'

'That's right, fuck,' said Hollis.

He slowly pointed his revolver to the side.

'Toss it,' growled Hollis.

Stanley lobbed it towards the flaring video screens.

'Good boy,' said Hollis. 'Now step back to the bitch.'

Stanley looked behind him to see where he could stand. Cheryl was kneeling directly behind him, holding her head. In the distance the siren became clearer, moments away.

'And you, faggot, come out here where I can see you.'

As Stanley stepped back in the rain splashing on the soggy carpet, Baxter came into sight, his hands empty. Stanley edged towards Cheryl and leaned down to help her.

'Leave the bitch. You, faggot, over here.'

Still on his back, Hollis kicked himself around until he could get to his knees without taking his M10 off them.

'You're going to die first, Baxter. I'm only sorry it's going to be quick, but then how fast is gut shot?'

Baxter came into view on Stanley's right, his trousers stained by urine.

'Golden showers, eh, Baxter?' laughed Hollis.

Baxter stopped and looked towards the shattered doorway.

'Go on, go for it,' offered Hollis. He shook wet hair out of his face. The sprinklers were still going full pelt.

Baxter looked at the gun, then at Hollis. He surprised himself by actually calculating if Stanley could jump the man while he himself was being shot at the door.

'No,' said Baxter. 'Just do it now.'

'Your wish is—' He didn't finish his sentence, even if his gun did fire.

Cheryl had grabbed a live cable from one of the printer terminals. Yanking it free of its pin plug and diving at Hollis, she jabbed it at his exposed and wet right leg.

The shock caused him to spasm, and as he did he fired, the bullets slicing an arc from the floor to the ceiling between Stanley and Baxter as he fell juddering onto his back.

As the firing stopped, the clip spent, Stanley ripped out another wire and thrust it into the man's left ear.

The man's hand shot open, dropping the gun, his back arched, his face muscles rippling as if in a wind tunnel, his eyes wide and teeth chattering hard enough to crack their enamel. Within seconds there was the smell of burning flesh and smoke frizzed about his hair.

But as they watched the man reap the fate he had eluded at the hands of the state four years before, there was a cry from behind and, turning, they saw Baxter leaning against the metal frame of the wall, his left leg straight, his hand clamped to his thigh, blood spurting between his fingers.

'Hit,' he gasped.

'You're a master of the obvious,' said Stanley, peeling off his jacket, rolling it up, and holding it to the wound.

'Hold that tight!' he said to Cheryl.

There was a siren outside.

'There'll be ambulances,' said Cheryl.

'And OCI,' gasped Baxter. 'All this will be down to us.'

He looked over at Hollis, who had stopped jittering and was staring at them, his eyes wide open, unseeing, his lips curled back in an animal-like snarl that said more about the man's mind than any psychological evaluation.

'Siemens . . . will do anything to . . . hide him. Got to go.'

'A hospital, then,' said Stanley.

'No,' insisted Baxter. 'Leave me. I'll use a gun.'

'Fuck that,' said Cheryl. 'You got us into this; you're going to get us out.'

Stanley looked around at the wrecked equipment and furniture. 'This stuff's too big to get through that door. There must be another way . . . the roof!'

He looked up. Daylight.

'There must be a trapdoor,' said Cheryl. 'They crane the stuff in through the roof!'

He walked to the far corner of the room, climbed on top of a metal desk and saw for the first time the base of a wide ladder disguised by panelling in the ceiling. He grabbed the bottom rung and pulled it. It glided down and hit the floor with a splash.

There was no need for words and Cheryl put her shoulder under Baxter's arm and helped carry him to the ladder.

'The CD,' he gasped.

Stanley went to the computer, but it had been destroyed, the CD lost somewhere inside the shattered drive slot.

'Oh shit,' he said.

'Did it print out?' said Cheryl.

It had. He grabbed the three wet laser proofs, folded them and put them into his pants pocket. Then, getting underneath Baxter's other shoulder, he helped carry the man up the steps to the roof.

In hot delicious daylight, they breathed in warm air, imbibing with relish the smells of the city. There were more sirens now but they were some distance off.

'How do we get out of here?' said Stanley.

Cheryl pointed at a fire escape at the building's rear and they hobbled across, Baxter groaning with every step. At the bottom Cheryl leaned Baxter against Stanley while she hot-wired an Audi 80, then, skidding to a halt in front of them, she waited until Stanley had bundled Baxter into the back and climbed in after him, before she floored the accelerator and roared out of the lot.

'Where are we going?' said Stanley pressing his hand as hard as he could against the hot hole in Baxter's thigh.

'Not a hospital . . . Siemens . . . find us,' groaned Baxter.

'Well, where?' shouted Stanley in exasperation, as his lap turned red with the man's blood.

'Let me think,' shouted Cheryl as she zoomed across an intersection, uncaring of the red light. 'You don't get seen to soon, you're gonna croak,' she said.

'Thanks for breaking it . . . gently,' said Baxter, scrunching his face up as pain crashed over him in wave after wave.

'He might have hit an artery here,' said Stanley, his hands gloved in blood.

'Shut the fuck up!' said Cheryl, barely missing a semi hauling a bulldozer. She thought she had an idea.

It was crazy but it was all they had and, besides, Clyde owed her a big favour. Only problem was he was ten minutes away. Did Baxter have that much blood in him?

She floored the pedal and zipped past a cab hogging the outer lane. She'd try and make it in five.

18

Their destination turned out to be a large ranch-style house in a street of similar expensive housing.

The Audi lurched up the short steep drive and slewed to a halt inches from the rear of a large white BMW.

They carried Baxter round the side of the triple garage, following the signs for SURGERY ENTRANCE until they came to a large red door with CLYDE HETHERINGTON, VETERINARY SURGEON on a brass plate.

'A vet?' said Stanley. 'A vet?'

'Doctors have to report gunshot wounds. Vets don't.'

Cheryl buzzed the intercom and a man answered. 'Sorry, surgery's not until five.'

'It's Cheryl Kenney, Clyde. Better let us in.'

'Us?'

'Yeah, me and the Veterinary Ethics Committee.'

'Jesus, what—?'

Ethics Committee? mouthed Stanley. Cheryl shook her head. The door buzzed open and they entered.

It was a waiting room, modern black plastic seating and old magazines, posters of pets happier than any animal who had ever waited in there, and an odd meld of tobacco and ether.

Another red door at the end of the room opened, and a dark-haired, handsome man in his thirties with a moustache and green cardigan came in, pipe clutched in his hand as if it could be useful as a weapon. He looked like he might well be able to handle himself but his eyes betrayed fear.

'Cheryl, I don't know what kind of joke this—'

'No time for explanations,' said Cheryl. 'Man's been shot in the leg; need you to fix it.'

'I'm a vet. He needs a doctor.'

'He needs fixing and you're going to fix him. *Now!*'

'Let me call the para—'

'Fine, you call them. I'll call Renee.'

'No!' The man looked as if *he* had been shot. 'Okay, okay. Get him into the surgery.'

He pointed to a door on their right and Cheryl opened it and together she and Stanley carried the almost unconscious Baxter into the next room.

Apart from the small size of the operating table, it could have been a doctor's surgery: the lights, the equipment, the smells. Hetherington came in after them and flipped on the lights, making them squint.

'What happened?'

'You don't want to know,' said Stanley. 'Check his leg.'

'And you?' he said to Cheryl, looking at her sodden hooker's clothing. 'Are you okay? You look messed up.'

'I'll live. Him – he needs the help.'

'Okay, get his pants off,' he said, handing them a large pair of scissors.

He went to a sink, washed and dried his hands, then put on disposable gloves. Looking down at his clothes, he let out a sigh of resignation and returned to the table.

Meanwhile, Cheryl had cut the seam of Baxter's pants' leg and laid bare his thigh. It was bloody, and looked bad.

Hetherington grabbed a roll of tissue and mopped around the wound, then, using a bottle of saline, squirted away at the bullet hole, Baxter's hands digging into the table-sides, his teeth gritted against the pain. Hetherington then got them to roll Baxter over so he could check for an exit wound.

'Straight through. Should heal but I'll take an X-ray; bullet fragment might still be lodged somewhere, or the bone might have been fractured. Luckily it missed the artery, otherwise you wouldn't have gotten him here. He could still do with blood . . . I'll give him something to knock him out.'

'No!' said Baxter. 'Need to stay alert. Painkillers okay, but nothing that sends me under.'

'Okay, but whatever I give you, you'll probably feel something. There's some work needed here. And after, you're not going anywhere. You'll need complete rest.'

He placed two pressure pads, one in front and one to the rear of the leg, and taped them on.

'That's not a problem, is it?' said Cheryl.

'Renee's off with the kids for three days to Disneyworld so, no, it isn't. Luckily. Right, X-ray first, before I start digging, then you tell me what's going on.'

Cheryl grabbed the vet's elbow. 'You patch him up, we lie low, we leave – and the debt's cancelled, okay? And this never happened. Believe me, you don't want to get involved.'

Hetherington studied her. Such a pretty face, all fessed up, but it was her eyes that hurt the most to see: they looked on a world away from the cosy wife-and-two-kids world he inhabited, where his biggest fear was his daughter's crooked teeth – and that Cheryl didn't come around while his wife was in. So he nodded and ushered them out while he fixed up the portable X-ray camera over Baxter's leg.

'You'll find some coffee in the kitchen.'

They left Baxter, and Cheryl led Stanley straight to the kitchen where she immediately found cups and poured them coffee from a percolator.

'What is it with you and this Clyde anyway? Guys you introduce us to seem to shit their pants when you turn up.'

Both of them were still shaking after what had happened, and were keen for the distraction conversation would offer.

'If you must know, my cat Mikey got hit by a car last year, busted his leg. I brought him to Clyde but I couldn't afford the six hundred dollars, so we made a deal.'

'Which was?'

'I think you can guess. You've had enough trouble dragging your eyes away from my cleavage.'

Stanley's red face gave him away. 'You slept with him.'

'Why not? Hundred dollars a time off the bill. He's a good-looking guy.'

'But that makes you . . .'

'A girl who cares for her cat more than her decency.'

'Makes your cat a pimp though.'

They both laughed. She had a nice laugh; pity he hadn't been able to hear it more often.

'So why the panic when you turned up?' he said.

'He's married. I "worked" off my debt in motel rooms until Mikey got better. Then the stupid cat got sick again. Eyes running with what looked like blood. Clyde told me it was a rare cat virus which needed expensive drugs . . . four hundred and fifty dollars. I should have guessed.

'After I'd paid off that little bill and everything seemed okay, Mikey got ill again. Same problem. Clyde was away so I took him to another vet, and gave her this story about a rare disease. She just laughed, said white cats are prone to conjunctivitis and this dribbling, which looks bloody but it isn't. Forty-four dollars please.'

'Oops. So when Clyde the Cad came back, you . . . ?'

'Threatened to tell his wife, hit him where it hurts.'

'In the divorce courts.'

'Exactly. He went to pieces, offered me money.'

'Which you took?'

'No. *That* would have made me a whore.'

'I don't see . . .'

'While I'll admit Clyde was a good lay, I only did what I did for Mikey. But the second time round, the rat *lied* his way into my pants; he played dirty.'

'So what did you do?

'Got free veterinary care for Mikey for all time!'

'Now *that* sounds like a good deal.'

'Would have been, 'cept Mikey hasn't so much as coughed up a hairball since! Apart from his goddamn booster, Clyde's not paid a cent. Damn cat. Sometimes wonder if he and Clyde came to some secret agreement.'

Stanley sipped his coffee. He still didn't know what to make of Cheryl. Either she was a slut, or a girl making the best use of what God had given her. But then there was Rorke, the poor bastard, who had obviously been slime in a suit.

'Don't fret it, Stanley,' Cheryl said, draining her cup and reading his thoughts. '*You* live alone, your best friend is a Labrador called Rex. He breaks a leg, you go to this nice lady vet and she says she can fix him for six hundred dollars, but you haven't got a bean. You explain your problem and this nice lady vet – good tits, great legs – she says, "No problem,

Stan. You're a hunk, how's about hitting the sack." Now, are you going to let your Rex suffer, or are you going to ball the lady vet?'

'Put it that way . . .'

'Put it that way, you'll probably break the dog's other leg! There's no problem, Stanley, long as people are honest with each other. Which is where Clyde fucked up.'

Stanley finished his coffee and was rinsing the cup in the sink when Hetherington came in, looking uncomfortable.

'Well, I've stopped the bleeding and taken the X-ray to check for fractures. No bone damage. Here's the X-ray.'

He held the plate up for them to see against the kitchen's neon ceiling light.

'Now the guy's got an artificial hip, which is why it shows up so well, but what I can't fathom is this here.'

There was a small black shape about half an inch under the surface of the skin halfway down the thigh.

'Looks like a bullet.'

'It's not. Wrong shape. Look closer. I may be losing it, but it looks like it's got wiring.'

Another minute of staring and Stanley suddenly grabbed the X-ray and rushed back into the surgery.

Baxter appeared to be sleeping.

'You've doped him up?'

'No,' said Hetherington. 'He's just wrecked.'

'He's not the only one,' muttered Stanley.

He grabbed Baxter by the shoulders and shook him, shouting at him to wake up.

'Baxter, come on, not yet. We need you. Baxter, Baxter!'

The man's eyes opened and his eyeballs swivelled around like a doll's. 'What? What?'

Stanley held up the X-ray. 'That's your leg.'

'I'm not stupid . . .' he yawned.

'Stay awake, goddammit!' said Cheryl. 'What is *that*?'

Baxter squinted his eyes to try and focus, then snatched the X-ray and looked at it closely.

'Jesus Christ . . .'

'What?' said Cheryl.

'It's a transmitter.'

'A what?' said Stanley.

'I had my hip fixed a couple of years ago. Had trouble with arthritis. OCI paid. While they did it, Siemens must have had that implanted.'

'So what does it do?' said Cheryl.

'It's a bug!'

'What? Like a tracking device?'

'Yes. *Exactly* like a tracking device.'

'Which means OCI can trace you? Find out where you are?' Cheryl was astounded.

Stanley kicked the table. '*That's* how Hollis found us at the computer store; he must have been able to track us. Didn't even need to follow that bus. Jesus, that means—'

'OCI could track us here too!' said Cheryl.

'What are we going to do?' said Stanley.

'Get it out,' said Baxter.

'*Get it out?* How?' said Cheryl.

'With a knife!' said Baxter. 'Come on doc, dig it out.'

Hetherington backed away. 'I don't think . . . It'll take time to prep, I don't have the right anaesthetic—'

'Forget anaesthetic!' said Baxter. 'You've got to do it now! Hollis may be dead but OCI could be outside. Get the damn thing out *now*! My leg's still numb from the shot you gave me.'

'What do we do when we get it out. Smash it?' said Cheryl.

'No,' said Stanley. 'Stop it transmitting and they'll know we've found it.'

'And they'll still have this location,' added Baxter.

'He's right,' said Hetherington, his face ugly with worry. 'You need to take it away – lose it somewhere.'

'But what about you?' Cheryl said to Baxter. 'You won't be able to move.'

Hetherington took a deep breath. 'He'll have to stay here; leave him with me.'

Everyone reluctantly agreed, although who regretted it the most would have been hard to tell.

'Get your gear,' said Baxter. 'The sooner it's out of me and this house, the safer we'll all be.'

'I'll need some help,' said Hetherington as he dropped metal instruments into a small sterilizing autoclave.

'You did the OCI first-aid course,' Baxter said to Stanley.

'That's a recommendation?'

'You passed?'

'Yes, but—'

'But nothing. You'll assist.' He turned to Cheryl. 'Nothing personal, my dear.'

'Hey, the less blood I see the better. Stanley, give me the print-outs from the store.'

Stanley carefully pulled them out. 'They're wet.'

'I'll dry them on a radiator. I think I've got us a way out of Clinger.' And with that little bombshell, she left them to their gruesome work.

Hetherington removed the dressing, tutting as he saw the wound still weeping, then, calculating where the transmitter had been placed, he sliced into the leg with a scalpel.

'Need you to keep washing away the blood, otherwise I'm fishing in the dark,' he said to Stanley.

Stanley did as he was asked, despite his rising bile, and squirted saline solution from the straw in the top of a plastic bottle. Blood ran down the man's thigh and collected in a growing pool on the flat surface of the operating table. Baxter was conscious, but as soon as he caught sight of his flesh being cut open he fainted. Stanley could only sympathize.

Hetherington used a metal clamp to hold open both sides of the three-inch cut and slowly cranked them open, cutting through sinew deeper and deeper into the leg until something glinted amid the blood and saline.

Another minute and he was able to pull out the object with a pair of long tweezers and drop it into a kidney dish.

'Incredible,' was all Hetherington could say.

'Incredible,' was all Stanley could say as he stared into the deep wound.

'Okay, I need to do some stitching, but it won't be enough. He'll need all of this looking at by a real doctor soon, just to be on the safe side, otherwise he'll scar up badly or there might be permanent muscle damage.'

'Whatever you say,' said Stanley, anxious to leave.

As the vet threaded a needle and began closing the wound, Stanley washed down the transmitter.

It was clear acrylic, lozenge-shaped, a third of an inch deep by an inch long, with four watch batteries, one pair on top of the other, taking up one half, the other containing a microchip and a series of thin gold wires.

'Those batteries?'

'Yes,' said Stanley, 'for distance or long service.'

'Some employers.'

'You're telling *me*?'

Stanley took the transmitter into the kitchen to show it to Cheryl, but he found her on the phone and immediately his heart leapt: was she making a deal? Turning them in?

'Right,' she was saying, 'give us twenty minutes. and remember, log it as if you were going to make a flight. I owe you for this, Brian. What? Well, we'll see.'

'What? Who?'

She hung the receiver back on the wall. 'We've got to get out of Clinger; I got us an escape route. Is that it?' She took it from his hand. 'And this is telling them—'

'That we're here? Yes.'

'Better move.'

She picked up the three A4 sheets, now warm and crisply rumpled, and they walked back to the surgery, where Hetherington was sewing up Baxter's leg.

'Very neat, Clyde. Very neat,' she said. 'Look, we've got to go get this thing away. Baxter, will you be okay?'

The man had come round. His voice was slurred, his eyes fixed on some faraway point, but he could hear them.

'Yes. Clyde's going to let me camp out here for two days, then he'll drive me to a motel out of state and I'll call a doc in and recuperate there. Don't know if we'll be able to get in touch again.'

'Best not,' said Cheryl. 'OCI seem capable of anything.'

'Where are you going? On second thoughts, don't tell me.'

'Out of state,' said Cheryl. 'I've been looking at those print-outs. I think I know where they're talking about.'

'Good. Just be careful,' said Baxter, wincing with the pain.

She leaned down and kissed him on the cheek. 'Look after yourself. And I'd change your healthcare if I were you. Maybe go on Pet Plan.'

'He couldn't afford the payments,' said Hetherington.

'I know,' said Cheryl cuttingly.

Stanley took Baxter's hand. 'I don't hold it against you that you dropped me in all this by sending me to Riva.'

'Riva?' said Hetherington, tugging up another stitch. 'Wasn't that on the news? An explosion?'

All three looked at him.

'Never heard of it,' Hetherington said, raising an eyebrow as he tied a final knot, the wound continuing to weep.

'If you could help me get him into the lounge . . . There's a sofa there. I've got my regular surgery to deal with.'

Very carefully the three of them carried Baxter into the lounge, where Hetherington arranged pillows under his leg and began to dress the new wound.

'Go,' said Baxter simply. '*Now*. And take these.'

He fished inside the pocket of his jacket – which Cheryl realized he was still wearing even though he had been operated on twice – and pulled out his wallet with his ID, six hundred dollars in cash and his Eminent Domain warrant.

As Stanley took them Baxter grabbed his hand.

'I'm sorry for getting you into all this,' he said. 'Truly. Siemens wanted a "rip up", and you were top of the list. It was just bad luck. I didn't even know you.'

'Rip up?'

Baxter took a deep breath. 'Expendable. No wife, no kids, no parents . . . no one to miss you if you . . . your past life's been ripped up and thrown away. Like mine.'

Stanley clasped his hand all the harder. He believed him, and that made Baxter as big a sap as him.

'I don't think either of us is expendable,' he said, then left the room with Cheryl.

As they reached the back door through the waiting-room, Hetherington caught hold of Cheryl's arm. 'Need anything?'

She shook her head. 'You've done enough.'

'Clothes,' said Stanley. 'She could do with clothes.'

Both men surveyed her. Torn fishnet stockings, a skirt short enough to prove she was wearing stockings, and a ragged white blouse designed to reveal what it concealed.

'Preferably something that covers up everything.'

Cheryl gave Stanley a look, but he grabbed her bare arm. It was scratched and dirty.

'No time to change,' she said.

Hetherington held up his hand. 'Get in the car.'

A minute later he was leaning in through the driver's door and handing Stanley a bundle of clothes.

'Some for both of you. I don't know what's going on and I don't want to know, but this is our debt cancelled.'

Cheryl pecked him on the cheek. 'Truth is, Clyde, if we get out of this, *I* owe *you*.'

The man's face brightened.

'But don't hold me to it.'

He stepped back as the car reversed down the steep incline. He waved them away and turned back into the house.

'Think he'll call the cops?'

Cheryl thought for a long moment. 'No.'

'Too scared of OCI?'

'No. He'd have to explain to his wife why I came here in the first place.'

She selected first and they drove off.

'Women,' said Stanley, sorting through the clothes.

'Men,' said Cheryl.

19

He found the street very easily, the grid layout leading him in almost a straight line to his quarry.

Eskdale Road was a rich neighbourhood, with large houses, wide sidewalks, lots of trees and lots of quiet. The kind of street where they rang Armed Response if they saw a coloured kid.

Hollis didn't know what car the fuckers were in and the four vehicles in sight were no guide, so he cruised the length of the street to check if the tracking light moved.

His head was still fuzzy, his hearing shot. He remembered the bitch zapping him and the world becoming just so much fucking pain and then there was a blackness he just *dived* into and then it all went quiet. *Real* quiet. And he'd have been happy to stay there except there was a light which just wouldn't go away and so, finally, he'd reached for it, but as he'd come back into the real world he'd found out it was just some fuck with a torch and he'd been *so* pissed off he'd lashed out and punched the fuck's nose right into his brain!

After that, despite being disorientated and hurting like a mother, he'd realized he'd killed a motorcycle cop and that where there was a motorcycle cop there's usually a hog. So he'd pulled off the guy's helmet and jacket and stumbled up the ladder to the roof and then down to the Harley in the parking lot, just as the troops arrived.

He'd ridden round for God knows how long, a bug tracer stuck on the gas tank, trying to pick up a signal until, finally, praise the fucking Lord, he'd found it, over on the west side. Then it hadn't taken long – despite the buzzing in his head and the stink of burnt hair and whatever the fuck that gunk was leaking out of his ear – to narrow it down to Eskdale fucking Road.

He rode the two hundred yards the street extended without a turn-off, counting more than forty homes, the bigger and more expensive two-storey numbers congregating at the top end of the long curving road. He found the signal had moved south, which meant he had already passed the house where they were hiding out. He wheeled the bike round in the street, accepting a wave from a middle-aged woman washing a Cadillac – didn't they have help for that? – and slowly cruised back in a rumbling second gear. But then the signal began moving away from him again.

He looked up from his miniature TV screen. He just caught sight of a blue car hanging a left and disappearing onto the street that crossed at the bottom. He slowed to a halt.

The blinking light began to move to the left on his monitor. That was it all right. Shit, it would have been easier if they'd been indoors, but at least he hadn't had the problem of identifying the right house.

He looked at the nearest house on his right. Belonged to a vet. The one next to it looked the same, but no sign. On the other side of the road two more houses, the same design but painted slightly different shades of cream, both driveways empty. Could have been in any one of them, or one further down. Fuck it, just follow them.

He gunned the engine, checked the tracer was still firmly stuck to his petrol tank, and roared off after his quarry. This time there would be no mistakes, guaran-fucking-teed.

20

'I must have been stupid not to notice,' said Cheryl.

She was driving across town, avoiding the main routes for fear of encountering police cars. Chances were they were driving a car belonging to someone who had been killed at the computer store, which would make them prime suspects – and prime targets.

She told Stanley to get out the pages they'd printed off the CD. 'Right, ignore the first one, but the second one, those figures . . .'

'Six, twenty-six, seventy-seven?'

'It's a date. The twenty-sixth of June, 1997. File Seventy-Seven okay? Now the other figures?'

'Forty-five, zero-one and fifteen; one hundred and twenty-four, ten, eleven.'

'Map references, longitude and latitude. If I remember right, that'll put it somewhere in the northwest. Northern California, Oregon maybe.'

'And "Gudgen"?'

'Could be a person, or a town.'

'Never heard of it. What about the drawing?'

'A map.' She leaned over and stabbed at the third sheet. 'Those figures also look like references. If we got a map we might be able to plot it.'

'Plot what?'

'No idea, but it near enough got Baxter killed, and God knows how many others – to say nothing of us.'

'So what are we doing?'

She had to stop at a light. 'Shit!'

'What?'

'Check your mirror. There's a cop on a motorbike.'

They had stopped at a light with Hollis about five cars behind. He debated whether to drive up to them and pop them through the window. He had the cop's Magnum; one bullet would probably take out the two in the front, but he'd give them all six to be sure – and all any witnesses would see was a cop!

He sniggered, a high-pitched exhalation he hadn't heard from himself in a long while. Not since momma used to make him laugh over what she did to the rabbits before they ate them. Just imagine the looks on their stupid faces when Fulbright and Baxter saw him. And that bitch. He'd shoot her tits off first, let her see all that flesh exploding on her lap, her nipples hanging off, and then . . . He was getting hard at the thought.

The lights changed. So, should he or shouldn't he?

'He's staying with us,' said Cheryl, eyeing the cop in the rearview mirror. 'Get your gun out.'

'It's only got three bullets in.'

'He won't know that. Just in case we have a stand-off.'

She drove carefully, within the speed limit, obeying all the traffic laws, determined to give the cop no reason for stopping them, unless he'd checked the licence plate . . .

They came to another intersection. Traffic was heavy, the light against them.

Both stared at the cop in their respective mirrors.

'So where are we going?'

'Daniels Airfield, where my company works out of.'

'I think OCI will have that covered.'

She shook her head at his patronizing tone. 'They have. I rang the office and a voice I didn't recognize answered, said my boss had stepped out and could I leave a message. One: Mulligan never steps out, not while any of us are up in the air. Two: he always uses an answering machine; that way he gets the message straight not secondhand. Then I rang a friend who runs a Cessna charter service on the same field. He said our hangar door was shut. We never shut that door – never. Saves on air-conditioning keeping it open.'

'Which means OCI are in there.' Stanley realized what he was saying and tried to think of something encouraging to add but knew it was pointless.

Cheryl was silent for a while. Finally: 'I liked Mulligan, the fat bastard.'

'He'll be all right.' *Lame, Stanley, lame.*

'No, he won't. The others maybe, but you heard Baxter: he sold out me and dad for cash. Too big a liability . . .'

The lights changed.

She checked the cop again.

'If he follows us, we're in trouble. Just to check, I'll take a left, then two rights, get us back on Fourmile.'

*

Hollis guessed, as soon as they turned left, that they'd seen him so, patting his tracker, he continued down Fourmile, confident he would be able to pick them up in a couple of minutes. He'd hang back, see where they went.

'He's gone,' said Stanley.

'Hope so. My friend's gonna have a Cessna cranked up and ready to fly and packed with charts, but we've got to make it look like we stole it.'

'What?'

'Brian's a good guy. I don't want him to get landed in all this shit. We'll have to punch him out. Chances are there'll be OCI men about watching.'

'All the more reason—'

'Hey, Stanley, we get airborne, no way they're gonna track us. I'll keep low, circle the city three or four times, you drop that bug, then we fly northwest under the radar. Tankful of gas should get us most of the way there.'

'Most?' said Stanley, the word hanging in the air like a hammer ready to fall.

'Hey, don't worry. I'm a professional.'

'Professional what? What kind of guy lets you punch him out for a favour?'

'You'd be amazed what some guys'll do to get hold of this bod.'

'You'd be surprised what some of us wouldn't do.'

'Well, you've got no worries on that score, Fulbright.'

'Thank God for that.'

They drove on in silence.

'Still no cop,' Stanley finally announced.

'I'd noticed. Now, we're only a couple of minutes from the airfield. The creep on the gate will recognize me, so there's no point in bluffing. We'll just drive straight through. The Cessna will be on the far left of the field, right by the runway. It'll be all black.'

'Apt,' he nodded vaguely. For some reason her plan didn't fill him with confidence.

Hollis was cruising parallel to his prey about two blocks behind. He couldn't figure out where they were going.

The fastest way out of town was just about any route but the one they'd taken – and no one's cool enough to try and shake off a tail by driving through enemy country. By now Siemens would have an APB out on the three of them and any vehicle they were in. Given the shit he could pull, first time they stopped for gas it'd be like the St Valentine's Day massacre – and there was every possibility he'd be next to go.

He didn't blame the man for it; he'd have done the same after what had gone down in the computer store. Hollis smiled; just how would the prick cover that up? But that didn't excuse his vindictiveness. No, if Hollis got to these three first, then he'd go looking for Siemens.

Cheryl pulled the car over to the verge in a cloud of dust.

'That's the airfield. Gate's about two hundred yards on the left. Now, you're sure about what we're going to do?'

Stanley disliked being treated like a little kid. 'Yes, I'm sure what we're going to do.'

He smiled, even though his heart was racing. He was looking forward to decking one of her boyfriends.

'And don't forget the clothes,' she added.

Stanley *had* forgotten about them, and leaned across to the back seat to get them. Bitch.

They'd stopped. Hollis pulled in behind a Mack tractor and peered round its bulk. Where the hell were they? He looked through the chainlink fence on his right. An airfield.

An airfield. If they got airborne he was fucked. He'd have to do it now.

He eased the bike along the inside of the tractor, then, bumping over the roadside, steered back onto the road just as the Audi set off, its wheels spinning, a cloud of dirt dusting the hot afternoon asphalt. Damn!

Cheryl zipped through the gears, knowing the entrance to the airfield was at an angle and that to enter she wouldn't have to reduce speed and, as luck would have it, the gate was up.

She roared through, the creep in the box leaping out when they were already well onto the airfield and slewing a long lazy left across the parched grass towards the end hangar.

The man belatedly dropped the barrier, just in time to force Hollis to slam on his brakes and skid, his face heading straight for the wooden bar.

He threw the bike onto its side and just managed to slide underneath, his trousers ripped by the road.

The guard ran out towards him.

'Hey, buddy, I'm sorry. I—'

Hollis sat up, unclipped his holster, drew out his gun and shot the man in the mouth.

'Not sorry enough, asshole.'

He got to his feet as the man stumbled back into his hut, his hands clasping at the air in front of him for support before landing in his own brains.

Hollis jumped astride the Harley, flipped on the lights and siren and, after skidding in a smoking circle, regained control and roared off in pursuit of the car.

Cheryl brought the car to a sideways sliding halt at the rear of the plane and leapt out, leaving the motor running.

Stanley joined her and together they ran up to a man standing by the plane, clipboard in hand.

'Hi, Cher—' he managed before Stanley punched him on the jaw and he fell, pole-axed, his clipboard flying.

'Jesus,' said Cheryl. 'You got something against my friends?'

Yes I have, actually, thought Stanley. Brian was a tall, balding Italian with the look of a boxer gone to seed. What did she see in these guys?

She climbed into the cockpit, Stanley running round and getting in the other side.

The plane was prepped and ready, the engine turning over. She flipped some switches, grabbed the control column and set the plane speeding out towards the runway.

'That cop's back!' shouted Stanley above the engine roar.

'Too late!'

'Not if he's got a gun.'

He looked back through his still-open door. The man had his lights on; he was standing, his arm extended over the bike's oval windshield.

'He *has* got a gun!' warned Stanley, but his shout was lost on the wind that whirled past the door beside him.

Then he saw the flash, but didn't hear the shot – the engine was too loud.

Cheryl swung the plane to the left, then back round to the right. She could see the cop to her left and, to avoid being shot, she swung the plane back towards the left again, causing the cop to swerve out of sight.

'Need to shoot him!' she yelled.

Stanley nodded, though he had no intention of shooting a cop. He pushed open his door and, despite the buffeting from the propeller's backdraft and the sight of the ground sliding past at sixty miles per hour, he took careful aim at the Harley-Davidson's tyres.

The first shot went God knows where, but the second took out a chunk of the bike's windshield, and the cop slowed out of range. But then Stanley slipped, and in righting himself dropped the gun, which bounced on the taxiway behind him.

Hollis saw his clumsiness and immediately accelerated.

'He's not stopping!' shouted Stanley.

Cheryl swung onto the runway, gunned the engine, watching as the cop started to come alongside, gun pointed at the cockpit. As he got within fifty feet, she opened the throttle and let the plane begin its take-off run.

The backwash from the propeller caused the bike to wobble and the rider swung in behind them, letting off a shot as he did so. Stanley's still open door took a hit, as did the wing above his head.

'Throw something out!' shouted Cheryl, her eyes fixed on the gauges, judging the best point to lift off.

Stanley grabbed the bundle of clothes and one by one

tossed them out on the off-chance that some item might hit the cop in the face and blind him.

At first Hollis tried to dodge them, but when he realized it was only clothing he kept on coming in a straight line.

'No good!' shouted Stanley. 'That's the last of it!'

He threw out a pair of shoes and, with it, the transmitter he had hidden in the toe.

'Shit, there goes the bug!'

'Doesn't matter now, does it!'

Then she let out a whoop of triumph as the plane began to lift and the ground slowly receded – and, with it, the cop.

Hollis fired one more shot after them, but it was futile. The bastards had made it.

In the distance Stanley could see a police car charging after them as well, its lights flashing, but, as Cheryl had said, it was too late now.

Stanley gingerly reached out for the door handle and slammed it shut, grateful just to be inside the plane, regardless of his having no idea of their destination.

Hollis knew he'd missed them and he brought the Harley to a slow stop. *Fuck*, *fuck*, *fuck*.

He stared up after the plane, and watched as it circled to the south, gradually disappearing in the afternoon haze. A police car was now within earshot and he cursed his continuing bad luck.

He wheeled the bike round and it was then he noticed his bug scanner. It showed a flashing light within a hundred yards, and not off the screen as should have been expected.

He rode on until he was directly over the signal. The clothes. It must be in the clothes they threw out!

The police car screeched to a halt twenty feet in front of him, and the lone driver jumped out, gun in hand, and ran over to him.

'Missed them, eh?' he said excitedly.

Hollis looked up at him. Young, keen, hyped up. Stupid.

'Tough luck, buddy,' the cop offered.

'Yeah,' said Hollis, shooting him in the balls. 'For you.'

Then, because he was so angry at losing the three in the plane, he drove the Harley over the squealing cop's legs, then stopped to consider the next move.

He looked at the police car. *Aha!*

He got off the bike, dropping its full weight onto the patrolman's head, then climbed into the cop's car and headed off across the field at speed, aiming to crash through the perimeter fence.

He needed a new strategy.

21

It was a quiet sound: a sound that Baxter instinctively knew was wrong, even though he was on a strange couch in a strange house. And he was right.

The torch flicked on in the pitch darkness, blinding him.

'Hello, David. You've been in the wars.'

He recognized Siemens's voice.

'I am privileged: your coming here in person.'

'Truth to tell, David, it should have been Hollis, but he seems to have got himself lost somewhere.'

'How did you find me? We removed the transmitter.' The light from the torch was rendering his world a mixture of flashing colours and white light that hurt his eyes and made him feel nauseous. He shielded his face with his hand.

The voice moved to his right. 'Lucky you found it when you did, otherwise Hollis would have been here sooner. And with you three together, and the veterinarian . . . very messy. He had a tracer. You must have got it out of the neighbourhood just in time, and he followed it to an airfield.'

'They got away?'

'That would be telling.'

'But if he followed them—'

'His tracer was also bugged. I'm not about to let Hollis off the leash entirely. I had his movements tracked from when he left the hospital to the computer store to here, and then to the airfield. When I found out you weren't with them, I guessed what had happened. Guy they decked said a young man and a woman. Didn't take long to re-trace Hollis's route. Your idea remember: programming a computer to keep a log of all bug movements in case we picked up someone who dumped evidence en route. Only way that bug was coming out was on the end of a scalpel, and the only scalpel in a four-block area belongs to the late Dr Hetherington upstairs.'

'You killed him?'

'A drug-crazed burglar broke in, slashed his throat. Shocking. I may even supply the OD'd junkie tomorrow – I haven't decided yet. You know how I like to be creative.'

'And me?'

'You're going to tell me what you know.'

The torch panned down to Baxter's exposed leg and illuminated his heavily bandaged thigh and the two bloody stains that showed his wounds. The pain had forced Baxter to drop his blanket onto the floor. Siemens reached out and stroked the leg, Baxter clenching his fists in anticipation.

'Not yet, David. I'll save that for if you're stubborn.'

Baxter dropped his hands by his side, his right arm trailing on the floor. New sweat dampened his brow, and his heart began to race. He hadn't seen a weapon in Siemens's free hand, but knew he hadn't any chance of jumping the man.

'So, where have they gone?' said Siemens.

'So they *did* get away.'

'Very good, David. I always underestimated you.'

'Yes, you did.'

Baxter brought up the revolver Hetherington had given him and pointed it at Siemens's face.

The man smiled.

'Get the torch off my face and onto yours,' said Baxter.

'As you wish.'

Siemens seemed mildly irritated by this turn of events, as if Baxter was offering him the wrong wine at a dinner party rather than threatening to shoot him.

'A lot of people have died because of you,' said Baxter.

'Oh, don't moralize, David. You were happy enough to go along with our work. You actually relished it. Remember that time we got that killer in Ohio? You actually danced in my office when he burned to death in his car. *Danced*. Right after your hip operation. So don't start with the—'

'What went wrong?'

'I presume we're being personal here – with the tears.'

Baxter was indeed crying.

'Nothing went wrong,' continued Siemens. 'Mind if I sit down? Been a long day.'

Without waiting for an answer he parked himself on the arm of the couch, Baxter training the gun on his smiling face. In a theatrical gesture, Siemens pointed the torch directly into his own face and opened his eyes wide in mock terror.

'Everything is going according to plan, David. *My* plan, that is. Oh, you've caused a little hiccough, but this will all soon be cleared up and forgotten.'

'And File Seventy-Seven?'

The smile faded; Siemens's eyes took on a quizzical cast. 'What is this obsession with that damn file? Is that why you were at the computer store? Trying to access it? Well, you could have saved yourself the trouble: it's locked up tight.'

Baxter didn't answer.

'Or was it something . . . you had a *disc*, didn't you? Again I underestimated you. Foolish of me. So what now?'

Siemens stared down at his jacket cuff and played with a stray thread.

'I kill you.'

Siemens shook his head. 'I don't think so, David. Not *you.* You love me, remember. However bad a boy I may be, you'll always love your daddy, won't you?'

Baxter gripped the gun harder, his hand beginning to tremble.

Siemens looked directly at him, the torch beam reddening his pupils satanically. 'You see? You couldn't kill me any more than a wife could kill the husband she loved. Or a son the father he adored.'

'True, you bastard, but I can shoot someone I *hate.*'

'Oh, and who might that be?'

'Me.'

Baxter turned the gun to his face and fired into his right eye, blasting the back of his skull across the television sitting behind him, his head whipping back onto his pillows, his hand and gun falling onto his crotch.

Siemens sat very still for several seconds, his gaze fixed on the rills of blood that were patterning the TV screen, then he patted the hand that still clasped the gun.

'I really *did* underestimate you, David.'

He switched off the torch, crossed the room and left the house via the front door, making sure it locked behind him.

No lights had come on in the other houses in the street, and he took advantage of the anonymity the night afforded him to quickly walk the block to his car. As he drove away, he phoned a very specialized cleaning company.

COLD

A man may build himself a throne of bayonets,
but he cannot sit on it.

DEAN INGE

22

Stanley was in a light plane and it weighed heavy on his mind. Airliners were okay – they were like buses with wings but with plusher seats, in-flight movies and reassuring TV commercials – but in the cramped cockpit of the Cessna 152, with its deafening drone, unpredictable motions, worn seats and battered instruments, it felt as if they were in a VW Beetle with a kite tacked onto the roof.

It wasn't just that propellers were something from another century or that the goddamn wings kept moving; it was also the fact that it was dark, the weather was doing its best to batter its way in, his pilot was a hyped-up adrenalin junkie, and he had no idea where they were. He also needed to go to the bathroom and the noisy night mocked him, peeing on the windows.

'You okay?' asked Cheryl.

She had been studying him out of the corner of her eye. Flying the plane wasn't as easy as she remembered – she hadn't flown a plane in four years – but, knowing Stanley was a nervous flyer, she hadn't given any hint that she was unhappy with the plane's sluggish response.

'Me? Fine. Couldn't be better. What's that smell?'

There was a gasoline odour which he hadn't had the nerve to ask about. Cheryl cocked a thumb over her shoulder.

'Spare fuel tanks. Brian likes to fly down to Mexico and land in places where they don't have refuelling facilities.'

Stanley looked back. The whole rear of the cockpit was filled with welded-together oildrums. *Jesus!*

'What does he fly to Mexico for?'

'I never ask but I doubt it's the cuisine. All that back there gives us an extra three hundred miles. Range of about nine hundred miles at a steady one-forty – or so he claims.'

Claims? 'Is it safe?' Stanley said, sniffing the air.

'Yes, as long as you get some fresh air.' With which she opened her window, and sucked in icy, wet wind.

Stanley followed suit and nearly had his eyeballs blasted into the back of his skull. He didn't speak for another half hour for fear of what other gems Cheryl might spring on him.

It was a moonless night and the rainclouds effectively obscured any starlight there might have been. The altimeter showed they had risen to five thousand feet, but as he couldn't see the ground he didn't know if they were a mile up or about to land. It was frightening, like being in a blackout. There were moments when, as the plane was buffeted by a strong crosswind, he was tempted to open his door and hurl himself into the night. That way lay certain death but, as the chances were they were never going to outrun OCI, a short fall from the skies would solve all this torment once and for all. Eventually, however, Cheryl made an announcement.

'We've got about another hour or so's flying and then, by my calculations,' she handed Stanley a chart, 'we'll be able to land somewhere.'

She flipped on a small light attached to the dashboard and he edged the chart into its welcome beam.

'Don't see any airports.'

'You know OCI will be waiting for every airport within range to report our landing; so we'd be arrested before we got off the field. No, we'll have to land somewhere else.'

Somewhere else?

'A road probably. A field. Though, without daylight . . .' She let it trail off as if this was a minor inconvenience.

Stanley stared at the map. They were *nowhere*: he didn't recognize any names. Moab? Bonanza? Apparently it was Utah.

'How will you find anywhere to land in this?' he said, indicating the night.

'We'll manage.'

'Manage? *Manage?*'

'Yes. Trust me. If you hadn't hijacked my chopper I'd be in some bar now having a good time.'

'Don't you mean out the back of some bar?'

She shook her head. 'I'm here saving your life and you've the nerve to criticize my sex life.'

'Hey, you want to screw assholes, that's your choice.'

She dipped the plane and Stanley panicked.

'So they're assholes,' she said, smiling at his fear. 'Doesn't give you the right—'

'You mad bitch! What's your problem? Ever since I've met you, you've got into all this like it's a wet dream! This isn't a game. We're going to die. DIE!'

Cheryl controlled her temper. 'I'll get us down and we'll make it to Gudgen and we'll find the answer.'

'Just wish I knew what the damn question was. We're going to get killed, and not even know why.' He remembered Hollis saying something similar and it made him shiver. 'And what do we do with it anyway? Who do we go to?'

'FBI? TV?'

'You heard Baxter. Eminent Domain can get Siemens anywhere.'

'Well, what about the Federal Witness Programme?'

Stanley didn't answer and Cheryl looked at him. 'Is that possible?'

'Not with what we know.' He thought it through. 'Siemens could cover it up easily. To get on the Programme you have to have solid evidence that'll get a conviction. Being in danger isn't enough, otherwise half the urban population would be on it.'

'But if we had the evidence?'

If – and it was a very big if – they had enough evidence, they might be able to rescind Eminent Domain and so escape Siemens's wrath, but it would all depend on their finding more information, and then finding someone to trust but – Catch 22 – Eminent Domain meant they couldn't trust *anyone*.

'It's worth thinking about,' he said finally. 'Besides, if we do get out of this we'll need something. Everything I've got is gone. My job, apartment, car, healthcare . . . even my vacations have gone. Company man, you see, like Baxter. My bank account'll be frozen: no cash, no credit cards. All I've got is what I'm wearing – and even that's not my own! Christ, I don't even have any ID.' He was *fucked*.

'Oh, stop complaining. *I've* lost everything too.'

'Like what?' he said angrily, as the full import of his situation began to sink in.

Cheryl thought about her own losses. A new flying job was easily found, and without a rat like Mulligan as boss she'd probably be better off; her house was a mess and cost more to maintain than some places rent for; her cat was never home; she had no steady boyfriends – no friends of any kind come to that: she'd never been much able to stomach the company of women. It was okay when they were talking about men or flying, but when it came to clothes and TV she couldn't care less. She'd rather sit on her own with a Coors and her Walkman blasting out Aerosmith than listen to silly bitches whining on about tampons versus pads. Bank account? She lived from week to week, had never had more than a couple of hundred dollars on deposit in her life. She didn't even own a share of the chopper business – Mulligan had screwed her out of that when she had still been getting over her father's death. About all she would be leaving behind was her 'Vette – and OCI would have that by now, the bastards. She actually had very little to lose but, instead of admitting this aloud, she jerked the control column and pretended to cope with a mini-crisis. She just hoped Gudgen held something that could help them both, otherwise . . .

As for Stanley, he looked at his door handle again. It would be so simple, just a quick twist, then to jump and kiss the cold, dark rain before the earth kissed him.

'Right. Start looking.'

'For what?' said Stanley, pulling his eyes away from the windshield. He had been staring mesmerized at the streaks of rain for God knows how long.

'Headlights.'

'We're *that* low?'

'No, you dipshit. We're running low—'

The engine faltered, then picked up.

'—on fuel. We've got ten minutes yet. Don't panic.'

Stanley had long ago learned that whenever someone told you not to panic they invariably knew something you didn't and that there was *every* reason to be worried.

He looked out of his steamed-up windows, frantically rubbing at the condensation. He had been dreading this for over four hours and, as the engine sputtered again, he still hadn't spotted anything.

'We're going to crash, aren't we?'

Cheryl had had enough. 'Yes, we are.'

Stanley laughed. She was joking? Suddenly he saw a flash, small and distant and probably in his imagination, but he pointed at it through the windshield anyway.

'There. Was that . . .?'

It flashed again, then became constant. Headlights, moving in a straight line. Cheryl kept her eyes on them, slowly easing the plane down. The rain had stopped but it was still dark, and the headlights were the only illumination. She knew that landing in a field was suicide, but a straight highway would serve. All they needed was to be sure it was long enough.

She concentrated on the light, annoyed that it kept disappearing then reappearing, but at least it continued in a direct line. It might be a hilly road but it seemed like it didn't have any curves. Her only problem now was that they had overflown it and she had to bank through three hundred and sixty degrees to see if she could find it again.

Unfortunately the lights had now gone, and the world below was once more a black blanket. She checked the compass and flew a north-northwest heading. The engine coughed again and she tapped the gauge, but of course that did no good.

They were at six thousand feet, so she had room to play with and, if needs be, she could feather the engine, but she would have to have sight of her landing strip.

She banked around a second time – better to go with what she knew was there than try and hunt out another road – and the engine coughed another threat.

Lights. Excellent.

She pushed the Cessna's nose down, praying there was no high terrain between them and the lights she judged to be about a mile and a half away.

Stanley gripped both sides of his seat and clenched his teeth, his breathing fast. *They weren't going to make it.*

Cheryl played the controls, keeping the plane square on to the lights, compensating for the westerly wind, and keeping the nose down enough to see but not enough to dive. The engine whined again. She tested the throttle but there was no response.

'Gas is going,' she announced.

Damn! The lights had gone again . . . no, there they were. That road must have a *lot* of dips. She prayed they would land in a dipping section; land on a rise and they might plough straight into the tarmac and find themselves smeared all over Idaho.

She dropped the plane again, the engine choking, and then came the sound Stanley had been dreading. Silence. Apart, that is, from the rush of the wind and the propeller continuing to revolve, like the wheezing of a terminally ill patient.

In seconds they were almost level with the headlights, and a head-on collision seemed inevitable – and with a combined speed of maybe two hundred miles per hour no one was going to survive – but at the last second Cheryl pulled back her control wheel, screaming her demands to the plane.

'Lift, you bitch! Lift!'

Stanley actually heard the car's brakes screeching as its driver spied the giant black bat, then it was gone and the Cessna was descending again, Cheryl begging the plane to respond, its propeller stilled, as if awaiting the outcome.

There was nothing ahead, just more black and the sound of wind, and then a bump. And another, heavy enough to jerk Stanley against his seatbelt. Then the plane was on the ground, its wheels zinging on highway, Cheryl whooping for joy, but as the aircraft crested a rise it took off then crashed down, jostling the two of them and giving Cheryl a fight to keep it straight, and then they were barrelling down an incline, the small lights from the plane revealing a two-lane blacktop.

They began to rise again and Stanley braced himself for another lurch into the air but Cheryl slapped his thigh.

'Nearly done, kiddo,' she said.

They slowly coasted to a stop, and then began to roll back, but Cheryl turned the wheel and they swung to an unsteady halt, nudging the roadside.

They both sat for a moment, their hearts stilled in gratitude, and then the party began, with shouting and cheering and hugging and holding. They were *alive*.

'Right, let's find us a car,' said Cheryl.

'Easier said than done, but after—'

A light flashed across the horizon then dipped down.

'Oh shit,' said Cheryl.

The light appeared again then blinked out.

'What?'

'Black plane, black night, and that's a truck. He'll be doing sixty. You know how long it takes for one of those babies to stop? And we're on the other side of a rise.'

The light appeared again, brighter, like the eyes of a carnivorous beast.

They unbuckled, kicked open their doors, then dropped onto the wet road, both yelling in pain as shock thundered its way up through under-used ankles and calves. They then limped as fast as they could to the tail of the plane, desperate to get away from the thundering truck they could now hear charging towards them on the other side of the rise.

Then it was on them, its six headlamps blazing, the rows of orange and green decorative lights on its cab and trailer like the landing lights on a DC-9, spray from the wet road arcing behind it like jet plumes. Then the beams came down from the heavens and onto the road and spotlighted the plane blocking its path, and as the driver hit his brakes there was a horrible screeching and a timeless moment as Stanley and Cheryl hurled themselves into the darkness.

There was a terrible impact as the two machines mated, the Mack hitting the Cessna broadside, its wing just missing the driver's cab as the fuselage behind Stanley's seat took the full brunt of the collision. The Cessna was cleaved in two, the tail section whirling up into the night forty yards further down the highway, only to be run over by the truck as it slewed to a stop. The wings and cockpit and engine were hurled to the right, the trailing edge of a wing catching on a rock and cartwheeling the plane into the night, where it exploded with a dull *whuump*, sparks and flames shooting into the sky as it continued to roll towards a line of trees.

The truck finally halted, its smoking headlights blinded, its windscreen shattered, the driver swearing hysterically.

There was a long silence as Cheryl and Stanley kept their heads down in case of flying debris, and the truck idled, its air brakes hissing, the Cessna put-putting a series of minor explosions like dud fireworks, flames already dying on damp vegetation. Cheryl rolled over on her back.

'Trees,' she said.

'What?'

'There's trees. We could have clipped them.'

Stanley started to laugh. 'Now she tells me . . .'

Soon they were both laughing – and trying to stop at the same time.

The driver of the truck opened his door and looked about. He probably didn't know what he had hit.

'Better see if we can help,' said Stanley, aware his bladder control had let him down, but he was unconcerned: wet trousers were a small price to pay for survival.

He helped Cheryl to her feet and found she was shaking.

'You okay?'

'Stupid question. Yes. It's cold, or haven't you noticed?'

He thought she was trying to hide her fear, but then he realized it *was* cold. He pulled off his jacket and wrapped it around her. She was still dressed like a hooker and the damp would worm its way into her faster than a pimp with a habit to support.

They walked up to the driver who was standing in front of his rig, checking the damage. As they drew level with the cab they saw the shattered windshield and the steam rising from the crumpled hood. To wreck a Mack takes some doing, but their Cessna had done it. Cheryl slipped free of Stanley's arm and mounted the steps to the cab's open door.

The driver turned and saw Stanley. He was a big bearded bear of a man in blue denim, his face white and shiny.

'Jesus, man, what was that?'

Stanley held up his hands. 'Sorry. It was our plane. We had a forced landing.'

'You were in it?'

'No. We got out. I'm sorry . . .'

'How the fuck am I gonna claim this on the insurance? Hey, you said *we* . . .'

He advanced menacingly. He *was* big. He was also angry. Stanley stepped back.

'Yes, my . . . my girlfriend. She was—'

'Stop right there!' shouted Cheryl from the cab.

Stanley turned to see her leaning through the gap between the cab and the open door, pointing a shotgun at the driver.

'Sorry we messed up your rig, but we didn't have much choice on where we landed.'

'Just so's you're around to explain to the police.'

He couldn't help looking at Cheryl's long legs as she worked her way one-handed down the cab steps onto the road.

'Sorry,' she said, 'but we're not talking to the police.'

'So what you gonna do? Ain't no courtesy bus to get you to the terminal, and my rig's shot.' He patted its crumpled fender like an old friend.

'Wait till we get a ride,' said Stanley, walking back until he was standing beside Cheryl.

'You assholes, you wanted or what?'

'Could say that,' said Cheryl.

'Shee-it,' said the man. 'Mind if I smoke?'

He pulled a pack of Camels out of his top pocket and lit up, using a disposable lighter.

There was a dull crack to his left and he looked over at the burning wreckage. Not much more than a campfire now. Ten more minutes and it wouldn't be there.

'See what we can take,' she said, nodding at the cab.

'You're not gonna rob me as well?'

'Whatever we need. Sorry,' said Stanley.

The man stroked his truck while he smoked. 'Painted her myself you know. Took over a week. Sacrificed two Ohio runs to get it done.'

Cheryl said, 'You're insured.'

'Yeah, but your boyfriend dies, what money's gonna replace what you done together? Cash can't replace history,' he said, fondling his punctured front tyre.

Cheryl didn't know if he had a point or was just weird.

Stanley came back out with a map and an overnight bag. He dropped it to the ground, and by the light from the open door of the cab he unzipped it and found clothes, toiletries and porno mags. There was also a wallet.

'How much cash?' said Cheryl.

'Three hundred, three-forty.'

'Take two hundred.'

Stanley did as he was told, shrugging his shoulders at the trucker as if to say 'She's the boss.'

Lights suddenly pricked the horizon.

'Looks like our ride,' said Cheryl. 'Okay, you, get back up there, but give me the keys first, just to be sure.'

The trucker edged past them, his fear clear despite his size. He reached up into the cab, switched off the ignition and dropped the keys into Cheryl's outstretched hands. She tossed them away into the darkness.

'Right. Sit there and do nothing, and no one'll get hurt.'

The car's lights rose and fell with the road, until they slowed to a halt fifty yards ahead of them. Cheryl stood with the gun behind her back, Stanley in front waving his hands.

The car slowed to a halt and a man stepped out.

'You got trouble here?'

'Yeah,' shouted Stanley. 'We just hit something. Don't know what. You see anything?'

'Hot dog! I told you I saw a UFO,' the man said, diving back into the car and bringing it level with Stanley and Cheryl.

He was middle-aged, bald, dressed in a cheap suit, shirt and tie. His companion was a girl of about twenty, road-tired, her eyes smudges, her equally cheap clothes creased.

'We was driving a couple of miles down the road and this *thing* flew right over us. Candice was asleep, but I saw it. I saw it, by God, and I says to Candice that was a UFO, didn't I? And then you hit the damn thing! Where'd it go. You folks okay? This truck's a wreck. O god, I wish I had my cam—'

'What's your name?' interrupted Cheryl.

'Sydney. Sydney Iselbaum with an "s".'

'Well, Sydney Iselbaum with an "s", just shut the fuck up and get you and your daughter over here.'

Candice dragged her weary frame out of the car, as if this was a nightly occurrence. 'I ain't his daughter.'

'Shame,' said Cheryl. 'At least you'd have an excuse.'

Five minutes later they had stripped the couple down to their underwear and requisitioned their clothes, Stanley now wearing a blue striped shirt and a dark blue suit two sizes too large, with his own ugly brown shoes, Iselbaum's being too small.

For her part Cheryl was dressed in a medium-length blue

skirt, yellow blouse and red velvet jacket and shoes. She wasn't wearing any pantihose.

They then took Sydney's wallet and Candice's purse and their car, tossing out their suitcase. As Cheryl ripped out the truck's CB radio, she asked the driver where they were.

'Twenty miles west of Burley.'

Burley? 'That's a big help,' said Cheryl as she drove past the broken Mack in Iselbaum's new gold Saturn coupé.

Stanley checked the salesman's well-thumbed road atlas.

'Well, I reckon we've got six hundred plus miles to go. We'll take it in turns. Twelve hours should get us there.'

He then looked at the speedometer. They were nudging eighty.

'Okay. Eight hours.'

Cheryl switched on the radio just as there was a time-check. It was 10:30. She rolled through the stations until she found one playing an old Led Zeppelin track: 'Black Dog'.

'You like Led Zeppelin?' she said.

'Can't say I do.'

'So what kind of music do you like?'

Stanley thought for a while. 'Slow music.'

23

Hollis finished masturbating, his head full of bloodied breasts and stifled screams, and ejaculated into the tissue, grunting his relief.

Careful to have caught all his semen, he delicately folded the tissue and, wrapping sticky tape around it, slid it into an A4 envelope alongside a small plastic bag, a piece of Playdoh and a hand-written note. He then licked the gum on the envelope, sealed it and placed it on the bed beside him. Good. It was done. He sat back and wiped the sweat from his brow, sniffing the odour from his fingers as he did so.

His face stung and his head ached. He had been concentrating on his fantasies for a long time. Too long probably. He forced himself up off the bed and walked to the window, where he pulled aside the grimy shade.

Daylight stabbed at his eyes and he winced, dropping the shade and shutting out the parking lot of the Six Star Motel. He checked his watch. Shit, he *had* spent too long jerking off.

He walked into the bathroom and washed his hands and face and dabbed himself dry. His orgasm over, his skin was tender, and the cuts on his face and hands were suddenly a source of simple pain not enjoyment. Then he dressed in the clothes he had stolen from the man who had lived in this room and who was now face-down in the bath, his blood long since drained away from the single knife wound in his neck.

Hollis had driven from the airfield the evening before in the stolen police car, back into Clinger, abandoning the car on the southside and walking fifty blocks before he found this motel and the man parking up his Regal outside Room 22.

Using his police uniform, Hollis had engaged the man – Bill something, a cookware salesman – in a conversation about burglaries in the neighbourhood and had asked if he could check if his room had been disturbed. The rest was easy.

Assured of privacy and, equally important, time, he had then stripped off and lain on the dead man's bed and tried to think of a way out of his mess, but he knew he had gone too far in the store and Siemens was not going to help him this time. Or ever again, come to that. Unless . . .

He was surprised to find he didn't actually care, but then he'd always gone with the breeze, doing as he wanted when he wanted. Okay, it had been a whizz for a while there, with Siemens handing him it all on a plate and a lot more besides, but now it was gone he'd just have to find other ways to have fun. But first he had a score to settle. Correction: *three* scores.

He pulled on the man's shoes, pleased that his clothing was a good fit, then went back into the bathroom and did his best to cover his scarred face. It was a futile task.

Combing his hair forward did little to help, and dark glasses actually drew attention to the fact that he looked like a bowl of salsa. Best just to wear the guy's cap and make do. Anyone stared, he'd stare back – that usually worked.

He checked the room over, just to make sure he hadn't left anything, then locked it and walked out to the man's Buick. It started first time – not bad for an '82.

Hollis reversed across the lot, then drove out onto the main street and headed for the nearest post office.

Siemens swallowed the last of the lobster and wiped his chin. He offered a napkin to the man who was sitting up in the bed next to him, but the man refused. He'd only had a couple of mouthfuls and wasn't hungry. When he had gone up to Siemens's room he had suspected that it was for something more than official business, but nothing so brutal.

Siemens stroked the man's naked thigh and smiled at the snail-trail of dried semen, but his smiles had ceased to be valid currency once he had sodomized the man against his wishes. He stood up and surveyed himself in the tall mirror.

Still in good shape; he wondered why the boy hadn't been more aroused – it was obvious there was mutual attraction – but the young man hadn't even moved when he'd given it to him hard, just made that weird catching sound in his throat like he wanted to speak but didn't have the nerve. Maybe he wasn't as bi as he thought. Siemens would probably get him to jerk off for him before he threw him out: show him who was the boss. He was walking to the toilet when the telephone rang.

He picked it up, turning to admire again his flat stomach in the mirror.

'Yes?' he said.

'Hi. Recognize the voice?'

'Hollis. I wondered when you would—'

'Shut up Siemens, and listen. I'm standing outside a post office and I've just dropped a package in the mail. Inside the package there's a sample of my blood, a sample of my semen, and an impression of my teeth. Oh, and a note promising the package will be explained in a letter I'm holding in my other hand right now. This letter gets posted in four days, and it will tell whoever received the package that they should get DNA tests done on the blood and semen and check them against the DNA of the late Kenneth Handry – and then to contact you personally to explain how someone executed four years ago is still able to bleed and come. Now, I'm as keen as you to keep this quiet, but I'm even keener to stay alive, so this is the deal. You tell me where Baxter, Fulbright and the bitch are, I kill them, and we're quits – and the letter doesn't get sent.'

'Who are you sending it to?'

'As if I'd tell you that . . . It could be the FBI, state police, newspaper, TV, a politician, *Hard Copy*, *People*, Geraldo, Steven fucking Spielberg . . . could be any one of maybe ten thousand addresses. But when they realize what they've got they'll drop everything to find out the truth. Make O.J.'s trial look like *Night Court*. Now, have we got a deal, or do I just drop this envelope in the box right now?'

'I don't know where they are.'

'That I believe, Siemens, but you'll find out. You'll have people on the job everywhere. All you do is tell me where they are when you find them, and let me get to them without interference. Then, when I've done them, you try and get me.'

Siemens let the receiver rest on his chest. 'Get out, now,' he said over his shoulder.

'My clothes . . .' said the man.

'*Get out now!*'

He watched as the man grabbed a bundle of clothes and fumbled his way out of the hotel suite into the corridor.

'Why should I trust a fuck-up?' Siemens said to Hollis.

'Because you got no one else you can trust. Even your pal Baxter's had enough.'

'Baxter's not a problem.'

'And how do you figure that? I saw the three of them take off from that airfield.'

'You obviously need glasses. You saw Fulbright and the Kenney girl. Baxter I finished myself. Properly, like *you* were supposed to.'

Hollis was silent for a moment. Siemens could imagine the conflicting emotions: rage at being thwarted, yet pleasure that the man was dead.

'Give me those two, and this letter disappears.'

'Okay, okay.'

'Stay in that room – and don't get any ideas about rigging a relay. I'll know if you move out of the hotel, and then the deal's off, and then someone's got a scoop bigger than the time they find a woman Clinton *hasn't* felt up.'

The phone went dead.

Siemens hurled the receiver down. Wanting Hollis dead as much as he did, he couldn't help admiring the way the man thought. He and Hollis were more alike than either of them would care to admit.

He picked up the telephone and called control at the Solardome. First to see if there was any news on the Cessna the fugitives had escaped in; and second, to track down all samples of semen and blood belonging to the late Kenneth Handry currently held by the FBI and local police departments – and also the address of his dentist.

24

The drive to Gudgen was tiring if uneventful.

They had picked up US20 at Mountain Home and taken turns at the wheel, the driver having the choice of radio stations. Cheryl chose rock, Stanley the OFF switch. They stopped four times for food, drink and gas.

First at Nampa, where Cheryl swapped their plates for those of a Cougar from California; then Vale; then Burns where, to their horror, they caught an item on CNN in an all-night diner about a massacre in a computer store in Clinger: nine dead, eight injured and initial reports suggesting there were three gunmen, two men and a woman, who 'as of this hour' were yet to be apprehended. Careful after that to mind all speed limits, their final stop had been at a grocery store in Sisters where Cheryl disappeared into a restroom to emerge, half an hour later, a cropped brunette. It didn't suit her but it was an effective disguise. For his part, Stanley bought a cap and pulled it over his scar.

They made the Oregon coast about lunchtime and, turning north, travelled the last stretch of their journey on 101, passing through towns with names like Seal Rock and Otter Rock with, on their left, the sparkling vista of the Pacific Ocean and, to their right, rolling hills populated by spruce and larch and fir with the breathtaking backdrop of the Cascades rising up to kiss the near-empty blue sky. Either sight would have fooled the most desperate of people into thinking their troubles weren't quite as bad as they imagined, but together they made the hearts of Cheryl and Stanley ache at the injustices that had conspired to ruin their lives.

Finally reaching their destination mid-afternoon, they found Gudgen to be a minor coastal town boasting a small harbour protected by a low headland to the south and by a large bluff to the north on which sat an automated lighthouse. Highway 101 ran right along the harbour edge with only a boardwalk between it and a stone jetty. The harbour was dotted with dinghies and small boats plus the odd jetski and powerboat, the boardwalk offering a parade of semi-clothed vacationers of all ages.

The bluff at the northern end of the harbour was so steep that the coastal highway had to double back on itself and rise up through the town for half a mile before it was able to resume its run to Lincoln City. As a result Gudgen was built on a lazy Z, tri-sected by the highway with, on the ocean front, obvious tourist development in the shape of souvenir shops, arcades and a range of folk-art shops offering woodcraft, textiles and pottery, many with a Native American flavour.

Above the ocean boulevard there rose more general stores and housing and a parade of guesthouses and small hotels, all in keeping with the town's somewhat timeless appearance.

(It seemed clear the town council had issued ordnances prohibiting buildings rising higher than three storeys; in fact, nothing looked to have been built since the Sixties, wood and brick beating out glass and chrome at every view.)

And at the top were the grander houses, the social structure of the town clearly echoed in its vertical rise, and in these buildings' distance from the highway. Those nearer the highway tended toward the shabby and commercial, as if they had given up the fight to remain untainted, while those further back looked more genteel and dignified.

All in all it looked little different from any one of a dozen Oregon coastal towns they had passed through. However, first impressions can be misleading and both Cheryl and Stanley soon noticed that, on closer inspection, Gudgen showed subtle differences from those other resorts.

There were more esoteric items on offer – crystals, tarot and palm readings, New Age books, 3-D posters, oriental arts, even drug paraphernalia – all targeted at a younger audience, and an audience with money. The crowds that milled the length of the sidewalk supported this view. The majority were under thirty, some with kids some without, most dressed in T-shirts and jeans or shorts. Mingling with them was a smattering of older couples who, with expressions of mild disdain, tried too hard to ignore what offended them.

Stanley pulled across the highway and halted in a recently vacated parking bay on the ocean front – waiting restricted to half an hour. They stepped out of the car and stretched. It had turned into a nice afternoon tempered by a cool breeze and humidity that hinted at rain later.

They scanned the stores along the opposite side of the road: *Toomorrow*, *Medusa*, *Gem Heaven*, *FFRREEKKZZ*, *Capricorn*.

'Could do with a change of clothes. Maybe a suitcase, if we're going to stop somewhere,' said Stanley.

'Right. Here's the cash. Go get them.'

'While you . . .?'

'Call Clyde. See how Baxter's doing. Remember?'

Stanley hadn't thought about Baxter in a while, because he was too scared about his own circumstances, but he wasn't about to admit that to Cheryl. Instead, he dodged the light traffic and ran across the road and set off towards the U-turn at the north of the town.

On the outside of the bend, nestling beneath an imposing rocky outcrop, were the town's municipal buildings: the library, a blunt box with its porticoed entrance facing the street; a small sheriff's office with parking for three cars out front; and a meeting hall not much bigger than the sheriff's office, its noticeboard promising *Equus* from the Gudgen Players. Gudgen was not a large resort.

Stanley walked past Adobe Arts, Indian World and Made in Oregon, until curiosity got the better of him and he stepped inside one of the New Age shops.

Incense brought back memories of dull parties and failed liaisons, and he quickly stepped out. He had always wondered just how much Eastern junk people could stomach before they realized their homes looked like bad Indian restaurants.

But, mixed in amongst the exotic array of hippie shops were the more obvious stalwarts of Main Street USA – Eddie Bauer, Pizza Hut, J. C. Penny – and he finally found a Nordstrom store selling discounted clothing and walked in.

Meanwhile, Cheryl had found a telephone booth near the ramp leading down to the jetty, had dialled up the operator, and got the listing for Clyde Hetherington in Clinger.

Dialling direct, the phone was answered after five rings by an unfamiliar voice.

'Hello.'

'Could I speak to Mr Hetherington.'

'I'm afraid the vet isn't available. Could I take your name, please?'

Only Clyde and Baxter were supposed to be there. Cheryl looked at the receiver as if it were alive.

'Hello, caller. Hello? This is Detective Knox, Clinger PD. Can I have your name, please?'

Cheryl slammed the phone down and stepped back from the booth and ran back up to their car, looking for Stanley but he wasn't in sight. Damn.

Now, why would the police be answering Clyde's phone? She could guess at the answer, and it frightened her. It seemed that everywhere they went, people were dying just because they *talked* to them. What about Clyde's wife? When had he said she was coming back? His kids? And Baxter? What about him? Was he still alive? Had *he* talked?

She suddenly felt sick and leaned over a hood of the car to catch her breath. A middle-aged woman touched her arm and asked if she was all right. Cheryl snarled at her to fuck off, then dashed across the road and stood in front of *FFRREEKKZZ*, her eyes running over the bewildering array of painted Chinese massage balls, not taking in what she was seeing. Surely they couldn't have done anything to . . .

Suddenly she heard her name being called and, turning, saw Stanley coming towards her, a carrier bag in each hand, an Adidas tote-bag over his shoulder.

'Convincing enough?' he said.

'What?'

'The bag looks like we're on—'

'Police. Answered the phone,' she said.

'At the vet? Shit. Well, there could be a dozen reasons.'

'Don't patronize me.'

She stalked off, and he followed. But what could he say? If the police were there, something bad must have happened. He caught up with her as she fiddled with a gumball machine.

'Have you got a criminal record?' he asked.

'What?' she said, smacking the machine in irritation.

'Have you ever had your fingerprints taken?'

She kicked its stand. 'Have you?'

'I'm in OCI. Course I have.'

'Busted for grass when I was seventeen. Drunk driving when I was eighteen . . .' It suddenly dawned why he was asking.

She looked around at him, but all she could see was the Hetheringtons' home and the doors and chairs and kitchen surfaces and cups she had touched while they were there.

'Oh shit.'

'And the computer store,' he said, fear rising. 'Bound to pick up latents there. We're *wanted*. Not just by Siemens but by the cops. Can't shut them out of something you've seen all over CNN . . .'

His voice trailed off. How many times had he watched TV and seen mugshots on *Most Wanted*?

Instinctively he looked round at a newsstand near him, but it only carried the *Gudgen Oracle* and the *Portland Oregonian*, one majoring on new parking restrictions, the other on the President's threat to tax 'Ecologically Unsound Lumber'. But how long before their pictures were released? Christ, the store was a *massacre*; place him and Cheryl there and the media could make up any old shit, all of it sensationalist and guaranteed to get them shot on sight.

And suddenly the friendly faces about them housed a myriad disguises; smiles hid plans, laughter concealed threats, and beach bags and baggy clothes contained weapons.

He hustled her back to the car, convinced all traffic was about to stop as someone yelled 'Freeze!' and everyone else would drop to the floor and there they would be, surrounded by itchy-fingered local cops, desperate to make a name for themselves beyond their dull jurisdiction.

But they made it unmolested, and he got the key into the ignition and pulled out into the traffic and drove up round the bend until Cheryl persuaded him to loosen his grip on the wheel and get out of second gear and pull up.

'We need a drink,' she said. 'And I don't mean booze.'

She pointed at a space in front of an REI store and, once parked, she led the way to the café next-door.

Halliberry's had a certain faded splendour. A big one-room affair with a single high, wide window looking out over the houses and stores further down the hill and on to the ocean, it was on the second leg of the highway, packed in between less touristy shops – grocers, clothing stores, a bookshop, candy stores. It was emptying, the handwritten sign on the door reminding people 'WE STOP SERVING AT 5.30, SO YOU CAN STOP EATING BY 6'.

They found a booth near the back and settled in, trying to look inconspicuous. The whole place looked like a salesroom for a gingham manufacturer: red gingham tablecloths, blue gingham seating, even gingham-covered staff. It was only after their waitress – a large and pleasant middle-aged woman called Mabel – came over and asked what they wanted that they realized they looked like any other average couple out for the day, and they relaxed.

Mabel brought their coffee, and as they sipped it they discussed what they should do. By the time Mabel came with their omelettes, they were in agreement.

'Nice-looking omelette,' said Stanley by way of introducing himself to Mabel.

'Must be the eggs,' she said.

'What my husband means,' Cheryl began, then leaned forward and added conspiratorially, 'is he sells cars.'

Mabel nodded as if this did indeed explain everything.

Cheryl continued. 'We want to know more about Gudgen. We were passing through, but we might stay a couple of nights.'

'Yeah, Gudgen's nice. A few too many hippies, but they keep the place going. About all we got now, tourists. Fishing's dead; just got the views and the junk souvenirs. Couple of nights, you say?'

Mabel reached under her apron and drew out a card. It read: *Pacific View Guest House. Great Food. Good Rooms. Low Prices.* There was a hand-drawn map on the back.

'My sister-in-law's place. It ain't got a view but she's a mighty fine cook. Specially with omelettes.'

Stanley smiled weakly and continued to eat.

Mabel left them to finish their meal, then they paid, leaving Mabel a good tip and walked out into the sunshine.

Orientating themselves and their map, they got into the car and drove the half mile to the guesthouse, just off the third leg of the highway.

It was a big bland affair in light blue and cream, large bay windows on every floor, facing every direction *except* the ocean, which was blocked from sight by other, more salubrious guesthouses. However, the initial doubts were soon dispelled by the hearty greeting they received from Mabel's sister-in-law, Henrietta – she'd received a call that they might be coming – and her friendliness more than made up for the ramshackle appearance of the house.

She was another jolly middle-aged woman, and she showed them straight to their room. It was big and airy and smelled of roses, and the high bed and plump lacy pillows looked like a corner of heaven plonked down on earth.

Stanley paid for two nights in advance and, with a warning not to be late for supper at 6:30 sharp, Henrietta left them in their room. But they were asleep in minutes, and only the knocking on the door from Henrietta's husband woke them up.

There were eight other guests, and Stanley and Cheryl said little for fear of stumbling over each other's stories.

It was as they finished dessert – a blueberry pie with so much fruit it made the pastry redundant – that Cheryl asked Henrietta about the library.

'Oh, that closes Sunday and Monday I'm afraid. Is there anything I could lend you? We have a lot of books upstairs.'

'No, no, thanks. It was newspapers and magazines I was after. Wanted to see about property in the area.'

'Thinking of moving here?'

Stanley was puzzled, and Henrietta caught his look.

'Your husband doesn't seem . . .'

Cheryl stroked his forearm. 'My mother. She wants to retire to Florida, but that's too far. I was wondering about this coast, checking out the prices. Gudgen looks nice.'

'It is, 'cept during tourist season. Too many young folks about, with their hair and motorbikes and—'

'Dollars,' said Henrietta's husband. 'Only reason the town

keeps going is the summer and the kids with their cash. Never bite the hand that feeds you, I always say.'

Henrietta frowned at her husband, then turned back to Cheryl, her smile in place again as if by magic.

'Well, as I say, the library's closed. You could try the realtors. Don't think they open Sundays but—'

'What about a newspaper?'

'The *Oracle*? Sam's open most days. Since his Liz died, he don't seem to have much interest in going home. He publishes Wednesdays, so Sundays you might find him open unless he's out on a story. He writes most of the paper himself, has done for the last thirty-five . . . no, thirty-six years.'

Stanley finally saw the point of Cheryl's question.

'Where is the *Oracle*'s office?' he asked.

After supper, they went back to their room, anxious not to be drawn into any further conversation, and equally eager to avoid being seen in the town until absolutely necessary. They soon succumbed to tiredness again, and adjourned to bed early.

The night was warm, so Stanley slept on the floor, wrapped in the bedspread, while Cheryl covered herself in a couple of sheets and enjoyed the soft sinkiness of the kingsize bed.

Glimpses of Cheryl undressing had found Stanley regarding his companion with more than just an accomplice's eye. He had to admit she had an attractive body; it was just a pity about her personality: she was like a sleek Afghan hound, athletic and gracefully proportioned, but blessed with the personal charm of a rabid Dobermann. She was too hard, too unfeminine. He had nothing against assertive women; it was just that Cheryl was likely to assert *her* opinions with a boot in the groin. So, despite his erection, and his juvenile efforts to catch a glimpse of her breasts and buttocks as she undressed, he knew there was no danger of involvement. Not that he considered sex appropriate to their circumstances – and then he remembered their talk in the hotel when he had also got a hard-on, even though Baxter had been laying it out in plain English that they were doomed.

For her part, Cheryl too had sneaked the odd glance at Stanley as he stripped, but her interest was marred by the bruises on his body. The guy had taken some beating, and it was probably only their desperate plight that gave him the strength to carry on. She was battered herself, but not as badly. She caught sight of him furtively ogling her and did nothing to discourage him. It just meant he was normal, and she had to admit it gave her a cheap thrill. So she gave Stanley one last flash of her breasts as she tumbled onto the bed, bade him a tired goodnight and hoped he wasn't going to be so crass as to jerk off.

Returning Cheryl's goodnight, Stanley was grateful for another glimpse of her incredible cleavage, and hoped his erection would let him sleep.

At it was, they both fell asleep in minutes.

25

Hollis had stayed in the Six Stars Motel, cold water covering the weighted corpse in the bath to keep the smell down. He had been calling Siemens every couple of hours until he learned that Cheryl and Stanley had crashed their plane in Idaho and were heading for Gudgen, a town on the Oregon coast. Realizing it would be stupid for him to fly from Clinger for fear of being followed, he had driven up to Amarillo.

The flight for Portland left Amarillo Airport at 11:30 p.m. and he booked his ticket with All Western by telephone, using the Visa Card of the man he had killed, then waited until five minutes before the flight was due to be called before collecting his ticket. That way, he figured, if OCI had any ideas about tailing him, anyone who picked up a ticket after him would be a prime suspect.

And, lo and behold, as he hovered by a flight-insurance machine, he saw a furtive-looking man in his late twenties dart forward and pay for a ticket with cash. As the man turned with his boarding pass, his eyes caught Hollis's boring into him, and he looked quickly away. *Amateur.*

Hollis spotted a washroom and made a beeline for it, making sure he crossed the path of the same man, and caught his eye again.

He reached the Gents and strode in, pleased there was only one other occupant, an elderly man rinsing his hands. Hollis walked past him to the urinals and stood as if peeing, but didn't bother to unzip.

Sure enough, fifteen seconds later, as the old man finished drying his hands and exited, the guy who had bought the late ticket came in and gave the room a look over – then, spotting Hollis, feigned disinterest and walked over to the washbasins and fiddled with his hair.

Hollis shook his head in disgust. He had expected better of Siemens.

He pretended to shake off, then walked over to the basins and stood next to the man and ran the hot water. The man avoided his gaze in the mirror. He was late twenties, scruffy and thin. He'd pass as an undercover narc cop (his eyes were shifty enough).

The room was silent save for the gentle hubbub of people outside, and a jet whining away as it became airborne. Then Hollis heard his plane being called over the tannoy positioned above the mirrors.

The other man stopped combing his hair, and took his turn at the urinals. The instant his back was turned to him, Hollis grabbed the man by the elbows, jerked them backwards until they almost met and propelled him to the nearest stall, where he pushed him through the door until his knees cracked on the bowl and his face was smudged up against the white-tiled wall.

Hollis slammed the door behind him and slipped the bolt, then spun the man round, dragged his leather jacket down over his arms so the man couldn't use his hands, then grabbed his hair and pulled his head up.

The man's eyes were watering from the sudden pain.

Hollis peered into his face, his teeth bared. 'I expected more.'

'I'm not . . . I . . . ' The man seemed genuinely frightened – or was it just a good act? Didn't really matter now, did it?

'Save it,' said Hollis. 'You got a pen?'

'What?'

'A pen! A pen!'

'Pocket. Inside pocket.'

Hollis pulled open his jacket and found a blue Parker ballpoint. He clicked it out and, wiping his sleeve over the man's sweaty face, wrote the word FAIL in scrawling capital letters across his forehead.

'Siemens's standards have really slipped.'

The man looked at him, his eyes wide with terror, his nose running with blood and mucus. 'What? Who? I—'

'Deaf too. Must be too much wax.'

Hollis slid the pen tip into the man's left ear and jiggled it. 'Yeah, just as I thought. Too much wax.'

Suddenly he cupped the man's other ear with his left hand and, letting go the pen, slammed the man's head against the right wall of the cubicle, forcing the entire length of the pen into his head.

The man died instantly, his eyes continuing to stare in puzzlement at the man who had just murdered him.

'There,' said Hollis. 'That should have shifted it.'

He let the man slump onto the toilet, ignoring the smell from his voided bowels, and felt for his OCI identification.

Instead, however, he found himself pulling out three wallets, all belonging to different people. And, instead of them being the alternate IDs an agent might have carried, Hollis realized they were stolen.

The man wasn't OCI, just a thief, probably grabbing the

first flight available out of town, using someone else's money.

Hollis leaned back against the door. Shit. Much as he had enjoyed offing the guy, he could have done without the distraction. He heard the final call for his own flight, the announcer's voice sounding as if she was standing right outside the stall door. For a moment Hollis was startled, but then sense prevailed.

He took all the cash and credit cards and the driving licence of one Laurence Granville, who bore a passing resemblance to himself, then wiped his prints off the wallets and dropped them on the guy's lap.

He pulled open the door, checked the washroom was still empty, then walked out onto the concourse and headed for his boarding-gate.

He was the last to board the half-empty 737 and smiled at the double-take by the stewardess when she saw his scarred face.

'Never get drunk when you're lying under a sunlamp,' he said.

'Oh, heavens.'

'You should see the rest of me.'

She pulled a face.

'Only joking.'

She relaxed and he found his seat.

26

They found the murdered man in the washroom at Amarillo airport an hour after Hollis's flight had taken off. There was little doubt who was responsible, the method of murder being particularly bizarre. The agent following Hollis had boarded his plane without being spotted, but Siemens held out little hope of his keeping track of Hollis once they had touched down in Portland: the latest murder was proof that Hollis was alert to being tailed.

Once he knew Hollis was on his way, he had chartered a Lear jet to take him back to Seattle, his intention being to get to his office in the advertising agency and wipe everything on his private computer about File Seventy-Seven. He had already ordered the destruction of all relevant files at OCI's headquarters in Fort Worth, and was confident that this time his orders would be carried out without question. That just left the small matter of Fulbright, Kenney and Hollis.

A day had passed since they had crashed their plane – it had taken too damn long to trace the thing – and the pair would have reached Gudgen by now, with Hollis not far behind. So where could they get information from in Gudgen before Hollis got to them?

The sheriff? No, he had been bought. The local newspaper? They'd sewn that up too in '77. And all the people on the boat were taken care of. Plus the fact that Fulbright and

Kenney were in Gudgen proved they hadn't accessed much of the file. Good, it still looked containable.

He opened his laptop and punched up the first forty or so pages of the file, skip-reading as it scrolled up the screen. He couldn't see anything that led directly to the lodge, but what if they got there anyway, despite the security? Or if Hollis didn't keep his word? After all, he had never questioned why an organization like OCI should be using someone such as him. What if he became curious about that? Curious enough, maybe, even to let the two fugitives live until he could find out the truth?

Siemens slapped the computer lid shut, tossed it aside and called up the pilot on the intercom.

'Change of plan. Get me to Bend airport in Oregon.'

'Bend? It'll be closed, sir.'

'Well, get it open, or get me somewhere close, but do it!'

He snapped off the mike and sat back, rubbing his eyes. He'd go to the lodge, just in case, then secure the mountain and exterminate anything that came within a mile of the place. He had come so far with his work, he wasn't about to risk losing it now. He would let Hollis have his head, but the instant he failed to keep his side of the bargain, Hollis was out of the equation. Permanently.

27

They both woke up aching – Stanley from his bruises and lying on the floor, Cheryl from her bruises and sleeping without the benefit of firm springing – but both genuinely refreshed by their much needed sleep.

After a hearty breakfast and little conversation, they ventured out into the morning air and walked down the long winding main street to the newspaper offices at the end of the line of the shops leading down to the bend in the highway at the ocean's edge.

It was an overcast day, with rain threatening, but that didn't worry them. Their immediate concern was finding the *Oracle*'s office and talking to its owner and editor, Sam Dinkley.

There weren't many people about but, without fail, everyone they met offered a hello or a friendly nod. Stanley couldn't help comparing Gudgen with Riva, and the price *that* town had paid for Hollis's mistakes. What if Siemens decided to exact similar vengeance on this little town just because he found out they had been here? It wasn't just the cold morning air that made him shiver as they paused outside the offices of the *Gudgen Oracle*.

It was a one-storey building, not much more than a shop really. The window was covered in numbered photographs of local people and events, and handwritten notices about the local theatre group, kindergarten arrangements and a trip to Portland for the sales. Inside there was a small room with a high desk and, beyond that, an office, its door slightly ajar, a light on.

The notice on the door said CLOSED, but when Cheryl tried it, she found it swung open.

They went in, a bell tinkling gently above them.

'Come in, come in,' hailed a voice, male and hoarse.

They stepped through the bare room, its purpose now made clear by the rates for advertising on the wall behind the desk, and by the advertising forms and cheap ballpoint pens littering its counter. They found Sam Dinkley already in his office, even though it was only a little after 9:00 a.m.

He was in his sixties, tall, thin and white-haired, with a straggly beard that probably served to hide a weak chin. He was dressed in crisp blue jeans and a shirt so white and starched it looked like a method of torture. Halfmoon glasses dangled on string from his neck, and he wore a battered Beavers baseball cap.

The cramped and chaotic room was encircled by shelves jammed with books and old newspapers, with every available surface smothered in typed copy and photographs. It looked about as old as its occupier, apart from a small Apple Mac keyboard and laser printer at one end of the large battered desk in front of Dinkley, and a coffee machine on the ledge of the painted-out window behind his desk. The room didn't smell of coffee, however, but of sweet tobacco, a pipe-rack and smouldering briar on the desk where Dinkley sat providing testimony of the man's habits.

'Hi, folks.' He gave them a quick glance, decided they would make a suitable audience, and continued. 'D'you know when you're getting old? When you start writing about people you know in the *past* tense, and people you hated all your life suddenly have good points.'

'We—'

'Come in, come in.' He stood up and beckoned them to enter. 'I'm just writing an obit for someone I went to school with. Complete waste of space. He spent the last forty years looking at the insides of upturned beer bottles while his wife ran their shoe store. Now I've got to find something good to say about him. All I can think of in his favour is he hated basketball . . . ' He nodded at Stanley's Trailblazers' cap ' . . . present company excepted. And he always organized the Fourth of July fireworks, and that only because his brother could get them cheap and he could rook the council. Still, all in a day's work. Now, what can I do you for?'

'Well, we were passing through and we wanted to know a little bit more about Gudgen.'

Dinkley rolled two hardback chairs their way and they sat down, while he turned back to the coffee machine.

'Liar. Cream? Sugar?'

'Pardon? Cream, no sugar,' said Stanley.

'Black as it comes,' said Cheryl. 'What do you mean, liar?'

'Henrietta called, said you were looking for property for your momma?'

'Yes,' said Cheryl.

'Well, Mabel told Henrietta you were passing through.'

'Both,' said Stanley.

'Don't kid a kidder. Forty-one years I been reporting – thirty-six of them here on the *Oracle* – and not a day gone by without someone trying to put something over on me, whether it's on a story or advertising space. If you'd wanted property, you'd have said so to Mabel. But you didn't so you're not doing either.'

'Very astute,' said Stanley.

'Here's your coffee. It's crap by the way: I've had to economize. Not astute, son, just experience.'

'Okay, we'll give it to you straight,' said Cheryl.

'No you won't. Get caught in a lie, you'll invent another. Then another. So let's skip the next three explanations and get onto the real one.'

'You're wasted in this town,' said Stanley, warming to the man.

'Town's wasted on me, more like. Small places have as much right to the truth as big cities, just so happens people think what goes on in cities is more exciting, more important, but it ain't. Someone in Gudgen spends thirty years growing pumpkins, then one year they grow the biggest in town and they win the annual prize and they get their photo on the front page of the *Oracle* and everyone they know reads it and knows they achieved something. Damn sight more exciting then reading about some guy you didn't know being blown away on the subway, or some councilman being on the take. News isn't important, because you can't do anything about it. But when it happens to *you*, then *that's* fun. That's what people want: to read about themselves and people they know doing righteous and simple things. That's why the *Oracle* has the highest circulation per capita on the entire west coast.' He pointed at a framed certificate on the wall behind them. 'Ninety-six per cent of residents subscribe.'

'How many is that?' said Stanley, keen to encourage him.

'About nine thousand for the county, but the sales and the ads are enough to keep me in business.'

'So you would be the person to talk to about Gudgen.'

'Sure. What do you want?'

'We're in big trouble,' explained Stanley. 'Trouble you don't want to know about, believe me. The only chance we have of, well, surviving I suppose, may be here in Gudgen.'

'You the bad guys or the good guys?'

Cheryl said, 'If we said we were the good guys, would you believe us?'

'Yes.'

'Well, we are the good guys.'

The man laughed.

'It's the truth,' said Stanley.

'Oh, I believe you. It's just that if your salvation lies in Gudgen I think you'd better keep on running.'

'There's nothing . . .?'

'Gudgen's nowhere. A nothing town, one of a hundred along the coast. Nothing special. People live, people die, people visit. End of story. Oh, we get the occasional murder or rape – last killing in Gudgen was '85, I think, and that was a pair of tourists arguing.'

'You get a lot of tourists?'

'Yeah. Not the right ones mind. Lot of youngsters, New Agers – not as much cash as oldsters. Lot of the businesses fold after a couple of seasons. Just so much Indian and Alaskan folk art, cheap jewellery and astrology charts people want. They look nice, the shops smell nice too, but most people browse, especially the older visitors. Half the town's simply gawking at the other half. But everybody has to eat, so if you're thinking of investing, a diner might work. Mind you, two have closed down already this year, and rumour has it Burger King are looking to open up soon.'

'There do seem to be a lot of youngsters around,' said Cheryl. 'Must be the views.'

Dinkley laughed, a throaty rasp that Cheryl found rather sexy. She didn't have a thing about older men, but she didn't have anything against them either. Men were men, whatever their age.

'You can see the ocean. Big deal. We used to have eight fishing smacks, now there's two, and one of those is for seasick tourists to pretend they're up against the elements. Inland there's great scenery, but it don't belong to Gudgen.'

'So why so many young people?'

'You don't know, do you?'

'No, apparently.'

Stanley drained his coffee. It was foul; tasted as if it had been made with the ashes from the guy's pipe.

'One time, and one time only, something happened in this town made it famous for a minute, and it's stuck ever since. Whole tourist trade thrives on it. You've seen the shops, the stalls, all the crystals and tarot cards and runes and books. Lots of telescopes too. They're all here for one reason.'

'What?'

'The UFO.'

28

Hollis sang along with Edwin Starr's 'Contact', the door speakers pounding with the beat, then the song ended and he was alone with his thoughts again.

He had rented the Oldsmobile '88 at Portland airport, using his stolen ID and cash. Suspecting he might still be followed, he had driven at random for over an hour until he was sure he had lost any tail and then, stealing the licence plates from a Mustang, he had set off south.

City or small town, which was best to find victims in? Hollis debated this rather specialized quandary with himself as he continued driving down the coast towards Gudgen.

Obviously cities had the advantage of anonymity – people could be picked at random and their disappearance not queried for days. He could pounce any time, day or night, with almost total certainty that he wouldn't be noticed but, fun though it was, there was something unsatisfying about the ease of an urban kill. Slay a hooker on the Strip or a housewife out shopping in a mall in Inglewood, it would get twenty seconds on the news and only her immediate family or friends would worry. But in a small community the reverberations of his deeds were far more impactful.

In a small town, hundreds of people would be traumatized. Schoolchildren would be met faithfully at school gates, women would shop in convoys, police overtime costs would rocket. *Everyone* would suddenly become aware of just how fragile their existence was whenever clever men stalked women. True, there was more chance of eyewitnesses coming forward, but if he was careful . . . besides, of course, disposing of a body with country nearby was a lot easier than in a city: dumpsters and abandoned buildings were no substitutes for remote forest tracks and lonely highways.

Also, he'd noticed, quite a number of his city victims, despite their terror and agony, had an air of resignation; a belief brought about by years of urban paranoia that it was, after all, only a matter of time before it was their turn to be slaughtered, like they *expected* to die, because murder was part of the life cycle of cities: there's disease and old age and auto accidents – and murder. But in small towns and out-of-the-way places, it was a whole other ballgame, with murder an alien act that sat there on TV with *Seinfeld* and *Sixty Minutes*, as far away as any sitcom sofa or food riot in Somalia. And then *he* came into their lives with his knives and ropes and needs.

When all was said and done, it was the misery he enjoyed as he 'loved' them: showing them his power and his love and watching as they failed to conceive how such pain could signify loving attention. Momma would have appreciated his slicing and cutting; how the tears of gratitude would have flowed as she felt his devotion to her enjoyment . . .

His musing was interrupted by a large truck trumpeting a warning as he wandered across the yellow line. He whipped the Oldsmobile's wheel back and straightened his course.

Damn, he was tired, but he couldn't afford the time to pull off and rest. Not yet, not until *they* were dead.

29

They were in Gudgen Library. It turned out that Dinkley's late wife had been the librarian, and he still had a set of keys and full run of the place whenever he wanted. In return, the *Gudgen Oracle*'s archives, stored in the library, were readily available to the public.

The library had been built, despite its appearance, in the late Fifties, a gift from Gudgen's most famous son, Morris Applegate, inventor of the handleless doorlock. He had built the library, and donated his collection of books on the proviso that his collection always be 'front of shop'. The result of this was a gloomy, musty atmosphere that assailed the senses as soon as it was entered, since all the shelves were crammed with worthy but dull leatherbound volumes stretching back a century or so. The new books, the ones the townspeople actually borrowed, were towards the rear of the building, and in the single-storey extension behind the sheriff's office.

'Don't believe for one moment old Applegate even so much as opened one of these books,' Dinkley explained as he led the way to the central counter. 'He just wanted to impress people. Well, people are impressed all right. So impressed they just turn around and leave.'

'Any of them valuable?' asked Stanley.

The shelves rose eight feet high, and were full of dark green and dark blue and red and black books bound in cloth and leather, not a bright colour or picture in sight. It was like a writer's graveyard, the library a mausoleum, the books headstones stacked neatly one on another.

'Only because of their age. He bought them by the boxful just to fill up his library at home. My late wife was cataloguing them but she gave up; said it was a waste of time, like panning for gold in a monsoon.'

They reached the central desk and Dinkley leaned over and flipped some switches, and lights illuminated a corner of the library facing the ocean.

He led the way over to a large flat chest containing dozens of wide but shallow drawers, each dated with two or three years.

He reached down and tugged out one dated '77 and extracted a large broadsheet-size, red, leatherbound volume with the *Oracle* logo inscribed in gold on its front.

He dropped it on to the top of the table with a loud bang, and then stopped to recover his breath.

'Weighty words,' he joked and reached in his pocket for a handkerchief.

'You all right?' asked Cheryl.

'Forget I only got one lung sometimes.'

'And you smoke?' said Stanley before he could stop himself.

'Doc told you not to touch your dick again just in case it dropped off, would you go celibate?'

'Point taken,' said Stanley, reddening.

'Okay, so what is it you want to know?'

'What happened on 26 June 1977 in Gudgen?'

'You know the date but not the event. Odd.'

Dinkley hefted himself up onto the drawer chest and then,

like an uncle sharing a secret with his eager nephews, he told his story. Stanley and Cheryl both drew up red plastic shell chairs and sat down.

'It was late, eleven-fifteen. Gudgen was nothing then, and the place more or less dead. I was out with a couple of friends; been shooting a high-school reunion and we'd been drinking, not too much but enough that we couldn't rely on our word the next day. Anyways, we were walking down the front when Luther – he died in '87 – he stops and points up at the sky to the north, just east of the library.

'We all looked and sure enough there's this light: a streak like a meteorite, but it was green. At first I thought it was a firework, but it was moving, constant speed, and there was no way of telling how fast or how far up it was. This *green* streak . . . Well, I had my camera with me, but I only had three shots left and it was black-and-white film. Anyway I took all three. The first I missed because Luther nudged my arm; but the other two seemed fine – leastways till I developed them.

'Well, the light disappeared over the ocean and everything went back to normal. Except Luther. Never too bright, he went apeshit, and before we knew what had happened he'd called the police!

'Sheriff Tusa was in charge then and he just told us to go home – reckon he could smell the booze on us and thought it was a gag – but then state troopers came by about an hour later. Seems they'd had reports of a UFO from all across the North-West, but they had no point of impact. I told them it had gone out over the water; they didn't seem none too bothered.

'Later that night I developed the shots. The first was

useless, the second poor, the third missed; the thing had gone behind the library. But I knew I had something that might get beyond the front page of the *Oracle* – I still had ambition in them days – so, well, I cheated. I scratched the negative.

'There, I've said it. Always denied it all these years and me accidentally-on-purpose losing the negative didn't help none neither. I scratched it so it looked brighter, but I didn't make it any longer.

'The shot was analysed by NASA and a couple of university labs, as well as some guys from Kodak. They all said it was a fake: I'd scratched the negative. I called them liars and my friends backed me up. We got on TV in Portland, made thirty seconds on CBS, and that was it. I published the picture two days later on the front page of the *Oracle*, together with the statements of every person I could find who had seen it. Nineteen people all told, all seeing a green streak. Gudgen became famous for five minutes, people came at night to watch the skies, and I made something like seven thousand dollars selling that shot worldwide. And that would have been that but then that Spielberg movie came out – you know, *Close Encounters* – and, well, pow! The town went crazy, and anyone who could see a buck grabbed for it. And it stuck. You've seen the shops – all stems from that night in '77.'

He put his handkerchief away and resumed his story, his hands under his thighs, his legs swinging.

'Place has become a magnet for freaks and weirdos. They found what *might* be an ancient Indian burial site a couple of miles south, and there's a cave under the bluff got some markings on the wall at low tide that *might* be old too. All hazy shit but the word became that Gudgen was some kind of focus for weirdity.'

'Weirdity?' said Cheryl. 'Good word.'

'Like it? Not mine I'm afraid. It was the name of Luther's store. Lasted a season. Sorry asshole. Couldn't have sold water to a fish. Kind of guy, you'd give him a diamond and he'd drop it in a pile of broken glass . . .'

He hopped off the chest and pulled open the file drawer. 'Here's the newspaper.'

UFO OVER GUDGEN? ran the headline, followed by an extremely dull piece that would have kept people away from a free money handout. It was apparent Dinkley's remaining in Gudgen had more to it than a simple liking for small-town life; chances were he couldn't have found employment elsewhere even if he had wanted to.

'You did this pretty straight,' said Stanley politely.

'I'm a reporter: I say what I see.'

'Or what you fake,' said Cheryl.

'Didn't fake nothing. Just enhanced it a little. Everything's retouched these days.'

'And that's all that happened?'

Dinkley pulled up another shell chair and sat down, then leaned back, tilting it on its two back legs, the frame creaking, though from the look on his face it could just as easily have been his old bones.

'What's all this about?' he said finally.

'I told you,' said Stanley. 'You'd better not know.'

'I know, I know – and don't worry, I ain't after that one last story that'll see me settled in my grave with SCOOP DINKLEY on the headstone. Truth is, I ain't that interested in reporting.'

'Could have fooled me,' said Cheryl. 'Forty-what years?'

'Forty-one years, but here in Gudgen there ain't real news. I just tell people what they already know, firm up a little gossip, spread a little good news. I might as well be keeping the minutes of the community council. And you know what . . . ?' He let the chair slam back with a crack that echoed round the room. 'I'm proud of that. I don't believe I've wasted my talents; I don't think I've got that many. I ain't great shakes as a writer, ain't got a nose for news, I just do what I know best. So I ain't interested in your story so's I can see it in *People* magazine. I'm interested in it for myself; to know what I'm getting myself into.'

'You're not getting yourself into anything. And if ever anyone asks about us, tell the truth. Tell them *everything* we said and did. If you lie, they'll think you're trying to hide something and they'll *make* you talk.'

'Subpoena me? Now that would be something.'

'No, it wouldn't be legal. Believe me, what's going down is outside the law, even though the law is involved. "SMALL-TOWN EDITOR DIES IN CAR CRASH" is about as far as it would go. Please understand, the sooner we know all we can and we leave, the safer it is for *all* of us.'

'Okay,' he said. 'But it's not because I'm scared . . .'

'Of course not.'

'So long as that's clear.'

He didn't seem to have convinced himself, and Cheryl, feeling sorry for the old man, was tempted to leave straight away but knew they had nowhere else to go.

'What we've got,' said Stanley, pulling out the three laser pulls and unfolding them, 'is that date and four names: presumably people around here.'

'What names?'

'E. Boscome, J. Paalborg, A. Paalborg, L. Contreras.'

'Shit. Is this a game?'

'No game,' said Cheryl with a sigh. 'All we've got is a date in Gudgen, and these four names. We have no idea what it's about.'

Dinkley slowly nodded at Cheryl, after studying her for a while.

'Day after the UFO, all the cops and state people were down here, and some suits turned up. Washington they said. Had impressive badges – what was I to know? I told them everything. They had an Air Force guy with them too, now I remember. They chartered a boat. Old Josef Paalborg's boat, the *Carole*. He fished for crab and shrimp mainly. Barely paid his way, but it had been in the family. Ran the boat with his brother Axel and one other hand, Ernie Boscome. They went out the afternoon of the next day with two of the suits, the Air Force guy, and another man, younger. No more than a kid really. That'd be Contreras; remember it sounding Mexican. They had suitcases with them and radios. Said they'd be back the next morning.

'Well, next morning comes and no sign. I tried calling them on the radio but it was out. Talked to the suits who stayed behind and they said not to worry, they'd been in touch with them, they'd be back soon enough.

'Josef's wife came round about eight that evening, worried. Said she wanted the coastguard called out. Didn't trust them guys who'd chartered the boat. Just as I was about to call, *more* suits turned up. Told me to leave it, everything would be okay. Hey, I was gonna argue with my government?

'Next morning, about eleven, the boat comes back in. Half the town must have been waiting by the time it docked. Josef was dead, Axel badly injured, Ernie and the kid unconscious. The Feds rushed them off to the hospital and it was a couple of days before I was allowed to see any of them, and then only as a friend. There was going to be no story, and that was official.'

'What happened?'

'Two weeks later I wrote this,' said Dinkley, turning pages in the *Oracle* volume.

Stanley scanned the article: MYSTERY OF 'CAROLE' SOLVED.

'The story they fed me, and I believed, was that the boat had been almost overturned by a freak wave which had gotten into the engine and the cabin, knocking out the electrics and the radio. Axel had been swept overboard, his brother had tried to save him and had drowned in the process. Ernie and the kid had been hit by a boom.'

'What about the Feds: the guys in suits?'

'Those bastards were fine. They'd been in the cabin. Just the goddamn crew, the pros, *they* get hurt.'

'Didn't you suspect anything?'

Dinkley was angry, tears in his eyes. 'What the hell was I supposed to do? The police tell you something, you believe them.'

Neither said anything. Clearly a deep-seated nerve had been touched.

'Okay, I was a coward. They threatened me. Shutting the paper, screwing up my medical benefits – I'm a diabetic, my wife was developing arthritis . . . They could have railroaded me. I know I should have . . .'

'Hey, don't fret it, Sam,' said Cheryl, sorry the old man was upset. 'We know what they're like. Believe me, scaring you off is nothing. *Nothing.*'

'What happened to the survivors?' said Stanley.

'Ernie was killed in a car crash a week later.'

'*What?* And you didn't think that odd?'

'What's odd? People die. Life's a bumper sticker. My brother won the Silver Star in World War II, survived three years in the Far East, then he falls down the steps of the train bringing him home to Chicago, breaks his leg in four places, limped the rest of his life. He was a baseball player, great future as a pitcher, all wasted. No it didn't strike me as odd. Accidents happen. I hate candy and doughnuts, always have my coffee black, and at forty-five I turn diabetic. No, it wasn't odd, just tough.'

'So that was two of the four dead. What about the others?'

'Axel was as good as dead.'

'What do you mean?'

'He went insane. Whether it was shock or the amount of time he'd spent in the water I don't know, but once he left the hospital he had the mind of a child.'

'Once he left the hospital?' repeated Stanley.

'Yeah,' continued Dinkley, not catching the inference.

'Real slow, couldn't read or write – like a child. Might as well have had a lobotomy.'

'Yes . . .' said Cheryl. 'Where is he now?'

'He died. Three years back. Pneumonia. Lived with his mother out to Ridger. She didn't last much longer than him.'

'And you never got anything from him either?'

'Like what? The man's brain was mush. Never was none

too bright . . . sorry, that was uncalled for. I tell you, if I ever get Alzheimer's, I ain't gonna have it for long . . .'

'What about Contreras?'

'He upped and left a couple of days after he was admitted. Only had a concussion. Never knew where he went.'

Dinkley stood up and walked over to a stack of books where he rested his head against the shelves.

Stanley whispered to Cheryl as he watched the man. 'This is getting us nowhere. Unless there's more . . .'

'I might be a weepy old fart,' said Dinkley. 'But my hearing's fine. I'm sorry I can't help you but that's it.'

'No one pushed for an inquiry? To discover what happened?'

'Hey, when you got the FBI, state police, government people, the Air Force, the freaking coastguard, all telling you it was a tragic accident – and by the way there wasn't no UFO, just a meteorite – what you going to do? This is America, and we believe in our government, 'cause if you can't believe in that what the hell else is there? God sure as hell wasn't out there on that boat . . .'

'And you can't tell us any more?'

'No. All I've got is what's in the *Oracle*. I wrote everything I knew up, seeing as it was the biggest thing to happen in this town. I even wrote up the funeral. Only good to come of it was the UFO story sticking, despite their denials – or maybe *because* of their denials – and Gudgen's tourist boom starting, but that's it.'

Plainly annoyed, he pushed Stanley aside and turned the pages of the leatherbound volume until he reached an edition dated 24 July 1977 and there, on page two, were a series of shots of Josef Paalborg's funeral.

'Took a while to bury him,' said Stanley, noting the three-week delay.

'Yeah, they had his autopsy up to Salem.'

'You haven't got any medical examiners here?'

'The Feds said they wanted to be sure.'

'Ernie Boscome, the one who died in the car crash, they had him autopsied in Salem too?' said Cheryl.

Dinkley didn't answer Cheryl's question. It was another small detail he had succeeded in forgetting. He could see the wall he had built around his involvement in the accident being dismantled brick by brick – and it frightened him.

Long nights rationalizing past errors are wont to be rewarded if the nights are long enough and frequent enough, and he had buried 1977 several years back – not least because he could balance the mystery with the good it had brought to Gudgen – but was he a part of it or was he as much a victim in his own way as Josef and Axel Paalborg and Ernie Boscome?

They looked at the photographs of the funeral, Stanley trying to lighten the tone.

'Was the nightlife so bad round here then, you took shots of funerals?'

Dinkley was grateful for the man's kindness and sat down again. 'Round here a good funeral is a social occasion.'

The photographs showed limos, old but smart, lots of people in black. It appeared to be raining. Two coffins. A priest. The article contained tributes from friends, an address by Josef's father, one by the priest, and a complete list of those present. It was a long list.

'Whole town must have turned out.'

'Pretty much. Plus a few UFO nuts. Already they'd started coming.'

It was a sad page. Stanley closed it and apologized.

'No need,' said Dinkley.

Cheryl suddenly grabbed the volume and heaved it open again, then poked her finger at one of the photographs.

'Look!'

Stanley looked at the picture. It was poorly printed but the handsome face was clear enough. Younger true, but definitely the man.

'Who's that?' he asked Dinkley.

'There's a list. I do good lists. Main part of reporting in a small town, lists. Heaven help you if you . . . Yes, it's the young man from the boat. Contreras. Forgot he came back for the funeral. Shows respect.'

Cheryl and Stanley looked at each other. Although she had seen him more recently than Stanley, he remembered him from his own training at OCI's academy.

It was Siemens.

30

'Anything else?' asked Sam Dinkley as he put the bound newspapers back into their drawer.

Stanley answered him by producing their final print-out: the weird skeletal doodle Cheryl had decided was a map.

'Have you got an accurate map of this area?' she asked.

'Got all the maps you want,' said Dinkley peering at the sheet. 'Those longitudes and latitudes?'

'Reckon so,' said Cheryl, then she pointed at the bottom-most set of figures. 'This one's Gudgen.'

'Looks like you'll need an atlas for the rest. Hang on.'

Dinkley disappeared into another section of the library, his skinny frame soon lost amid the tall shelves.

'What do you make of all this?' said Stanley.

Cheryl shrugged. She didn't know; it had all got a lot weirder than they could have imagined – and looked like it was set to get crazier still.

Dinkley returned a couple of minutes later with two large atlases and several folding maps.

He slapped them down on the desk. 'Right, let's see where these take us.'

He opened a map of Oregon and its coast, and found that the longitude just encroached on its edge.

'Mile or so offshore. Must be where they thought the UFO

came down. Didn't see anything myself that night. You'd expect a big splash or an explosion, if it hit.'

'These other co-ordinates . . .?' said Cheryl.

Dinkley frowned, then opened an atlas. 'Smaller scale, but it'll give us a clue . . .'

Five minutes later they had plotted the trajectory of the UFO. Dinkley led them through it.

'It appeared here first at 49° 44′ North, 113° 24′ West at 23:16, which would put it near Fort Macleod, Alberta in Canada. And it hit the sea at 45° North, 124° 10′ West at 23:28. That makes . . . ' He pulled out a ruler and measured the atlas page. 'Six hundred and twenty-odd miles in . . . twelve minutes. How fast is that?'

Cheryl spoke up. 'Oh, only about three thousand miles an hour. Mach four.'

'No plane goes that fast, does it?' said Dinkley.

'None we've heard of, anyway,' said Cheryl.

'Three thousand miles an hour . . . shit,' offered Stanley. 'So what about these legs, the bits branching out?'

'I've been thinking about those,' said Cheryl. 'Some of the figures are in brackets – see, at the ends of the legs, the longitude, latitude and the times – but only these two here on the left side.'

Dinkley finished her thought. 'So the unbracketed figures are *definite* sightings or events, seen on the ground or on radar: the bracketed ones are what? Guesses? Estimates?'

'Projections,' said Stanley. 'If this end is where whatever it was came down at Gudgen, these could be places where they think others came down. It could have been breaking up, you know – an aircraft crashing, falling to bits.'

'Or a meteorite breaking up as it enters the atmosphere.'

'I may be no rocket scientist but even I know meteorites come in at a damn sight faster than three thousand miles an hour. Twenty thousand at least.'

Cheryl nodded. 'Whatever it was, it wasn't a meteorite. So what do we have?' She frowned at the map.

'If they were following it with radar they would lose it below a certain height, but they would assume a course, and they'd have a speed and rate of descent. That would give us all the end sites, including Gudgen.'

Together she and Dinkley went through the figures, leaving Stanley feeling like a spare part.

'This first one came down at 23:22 at Upper Arrow Lake in British Columbia,' said Cheryl. 'The second one also at 23:22 at . . . Moscow? Pullman? Didra? Somewhere round there on the border between Washington and Idaho.'

Dinkley took over. 'The third looks to have landed way out at sea, fifty miles at least off Portland at 23:29, the same time as this other one landed in the Cascades, nearest town probably . . . Ellert, here in Oregon. A minute later I sees it going over Gudgen, and a tourist industry is born.'

'And they never found anything?' said Stanley.

Dinkley sat back and shook his head. 'Not that I know of. They may have hired boats from other towns, called in Navy or coastguard, but I never saw anything. Didn't ask either.'

'Well, if they came to Gudgen, they'll probably have tried these other sites too.'

'Sure to have.'

'Looking for . . . ?'

There was a long pause, then Cheryl tried an explanation. 'Looking for an Unidentified Flying Object, which could be anything from a stealth bomber to a Russian spy plane – it was still the Cold War remember – to a satellite—'

'Ours or theirs.'

'Yes. Or something we don't know anything about.'

'It's the most obvious solution. Some secret NASA or Air Force project gone wrong. They need to get the flight recorder, cover their asses, or hide it from the Russians.'

'Yeah. Obvious.'

'And look where the southernmost bit landed,' said Stanley tapping the map. 'It's a restricted government area.'

'Could have been a plane,' said Dinkley.

'In *that* terrain?' said Cheryl.

'Could have been a VTOL, you know, like that jump jet Arnie used in *True Lies*.'

'Or a chopper,' offered Cheryl, knowing that it was lame when taken in conjunction with the speed the thing had come down.

Stanley continued to study the map and the lines drawn on it. He stared at the area shaded grey near the town of Ellert, emblazoned in red with GOVERNMENT RESTRICTED AREA.

'This map up to date?'

Dinkley checked the copyright. 'From '92. As up to date as it comes round here.'

'Would you have a map for '77?'

'This scale? Unlikely. I'll check, though.'

He walked back behind the shelves where they heard rummaging and cursing, and then he returned, rubbing his arm.

'Damn stiff drawers. Should be able to oil the bastards. No '77, but I got a '75. Will that do?'

Stanley nodded and took the proffered map.

'What are you getting at?' asked Cheryl as he unfolded it.

'Look there, where it came down, near Ellert.'

'What? There's nothing there.'

'Exactly. Nothing at all. It wasn't a restricted government area.'

Dinkley leaned over and agreed with Stanley. 'Meaning?'

'This thing, whatever it was,' explained Stanley, 'it comes down in the mountains, middle of nowhere, suddenly the government buys up the crash site, keeps people out. Sam, can you find out when the land was sold?'

'Maybe. Got my contacts, but on Sunday? I'll try.'

He walked off to a small office and sat down behind a desk and began telephoning.

'So what do you think?' asked Stanley.

'I don't know. I've got a bad feeling about this. If this is government shit, Siemens'll have more than his own say-so to pop us. We could just be about to step in the biggest pile of do-do there is. Secrets *stay* secret because no one spills the beans – or they're not *allowed* to spill them.'

'That's assuming this isn't just Siemens, but let's assume it is. File Seventy-Seven says all this shit with Hollis and the killings, and now us, started here in Gudgen and then moved on. We've got to follow the trail wherever it takes us because we haven't any other choice, bad vibes or not.'

'I know. I know . . .'

Dinkley returned, a smile on his face.

'Got a friend up to Salem. Works for the state land commission. He doesn't remember anything from '77, but he knows about the restricted area. The state kicked up a fuss when it was built in '81.'

'Built?'

'It's a ski lodge! Used by government people. It took the best view over the valley, then built down into the rock rather than on top of it. Looks like a bunker. Doesn't even have a window looking out onto the valley, apparently. Often crawling with security types.'

'Secret is as secret does,' muttered Cheryl.

'And it's used for skiing? By the government?'

'Once in a while. There's a cable car and a road, but they tend to use choppers. Locals complain about the noise – avalanche risk – but the town council won't do anything.'

'Can guess why.'

'Looks like we'll be going to Ellert,' sighed Cheryl.

'What about these other places,' said Stanley. 'Canada? Pullman?'

'We're after Siemens, not the UFO. We go where he goes, but even he couldn't fuck around in someone else's country. As for Pullman . . . would your friend know anything there?'

'Already asked,' said Dinkley, his grin even bigger. 'No government activity whatsoever, 'less you think closing down a cult a couple of years back is likely to be a part of this.'

'So, it looks like we *will* be going to Ellert,' said Stanley, his unenthusiasm obvious.

He forced himself to shuffle through the maps until he found the latest one showing the roads to Ellert, then folded it up and slipped it into his back pocket.

'Why do you want this Siemens guy so bad?' asked Dinkley.

'Can't tell you any more than we have,' said Stanley. 'It wouldn't be in your interest. Let's just say, if we don't find anything at this ski lodge, we'll be running for quite a while. Pity we're driving a stolen car.'

Dinkley fished in his pocket and pulled out a set of car keys and handed them over.

'It's a bit old, but it goes. A Chevy Blazer out back of the office. Do what you have to do. I may be no shakes as a newspaper man but I think I know people, and you two, well, I trust you.'

'You *do* know people,' said Cheryl, giving him a hug and a peck on the cheek.

'Hey, I'm real grateful too,' said Stanley. 'But you won't be getting a kiss from me.'

'That's a relief. Handshake'll have to do.'

They shook hands, and Stanley and Cheryl walked back through the library to the entrance.

'Don't waste any time, either,' Dinkley shouted after them. 'Just get in the Chevy and drive. Don't worry about anything you've left up to Henrietta's; I'll get that myself later, make your excuses for you.'

'If we get through this, Sam, we'll let you know,' said Stanley.

Cheryl added, 'And remember: anyone comes, tell them the truth. Promise?'

'I promise.'

'Including we stole your car, okay?' added Stanley.

'Right.'

They took one last look at the man as he began to put away his maps. They only hoped he wouldn't be found.

'We could take him with us . . .' offered Cheryl lamely, as she read Stanley's thoughts.

'I know what you're saying. No, he'll just have to take his chances.'

'But it's so unfair.'

'Tell me about it. Look, the sooner we find something on Siemens, the better for all of us. So let's get moving.'

The sign read: *Gudgen. Population 6,456. Elevation 25'*.

At last, thought Hollis, his face itching, his body cramped from the long drive.

He slowed his rental car down to twenty and idled along the highway edge, eyeing the town ahead. It was nothing special. He wondered why the two of them had come here of all places. They had a whole fucking continent to go hide in, but they made their way to this sorry excuse for a resort.

He pulled to a stop outside a general store and walked in, picking up a four-pack of Coke and a local tourist map, and dropping them on the counter. The store was old, small and empty, the tubby elderly woman behind the counter looking as if she'd served in it every day since it opened. She gave his face a long hard stare.

'Got some ointment for that face, young man?'

'This? No. Have you?'

'Burn, is it?'

'Sunlamp.'

'Got just the thing.'

'I'll take it.'

As the woman hunted for the ointment, she regaled him with a story about her getting a 'bitch of a burn' from an Elect Eisenhower barbecue. She even offered to show him the scar on her thigh, but he declined.

'Don't want to get too excited before I get to meet my girl. She might not live up to the standard set by you.'

'She in town?' the woman asked, bagging the carton of ointment and Cokes.

'Yeah, in a hotel, but I lost the address. Any way I can find out? People to ask?'

'There's a lot of guesthouses, bed and breakfasts, hotels even. Could ask the sheriff.'

As if. 'Where's he at?'

'Office on the bend, down on the front. Can't miss it.'

'Got "Sheriff" written on it?'

'You're smart.'

He pointed at his face. 'Not smart enough.'

'True. Turned down a chance to see my scar, too. You'll never know what you've missed.'

He picked up his change and the bag and walked to the door, stepping aside as a teenage boy came in.

'Neither will you, dear. Neither will you.'

He got back into the car, reversed into the road and carried on down into town. Obviously he wasn't about to knock on the sheriff's door and ask if he had seen two fugitives, but at least now he knew where to avoid.

It was muggy, mid-morning, and the town gave the impression of still being half asleep. That said, there were people about, most of them dressed in the bright colours and baggy shapes of tourists, with a smattering of tight tops. He saw several women he found very desirable and regretted for a moment that he had other work at hand.

But if he found the two he was looking for, and disposed of them, he'd have a whole country of tight tops to rip off, and tits to slash. Yes, things would be decidedly on the up once he had eliminated Fulbright and the bitch.

He spotted the ocean over the houses on his right, and

slowed as he reached the first U-turn on the highway. He spotted a café and decided he was hungry. He wheeled the Royale to a halt outside the Happy Plateful and entered, the smell of bacon persuading him that he did have time to eat.

He chose a table in the window that looked down the road to the bottom bend where, as promised, sat the sheriff's office, together with a couple of ugly civic buildings.

A cheery waitress – little more than a schoolgirl – asked him for his order and he ran his finger down the menu until he found the breakfast and asked for it with double bacon. A scene from *Five Easy Pieces* did not ensue: the service industries were learning. He also ordered orange juice and coffee.

He sat back and stretched. Yes, couple of hours, couple of days, whatever, soon he'd be a free man. Much as he'd liked being lord of the Solardome, he was after all just another civil servant. Okay, maybe a secret civil servant, but not much more than a glorified grunt when it came to it. Do this, do that. Fuck it.

His orange juice arrived and he drained it in one and ordered another, much to the girl's amusement. He went along with her giggles. It was a good day.

He watched the traffic slide by, most of it on foot, and most of that fat American or lank hippie. Weird mix, like they'd screwed up the dates for a Grateful Dead and a Wayne Newton concert: the people just didn't go together.

A couple of beach-blonde girls caught his eye and he followed them as they wiggled their dumb way down the hill like cellulite bombs waiting to explode as soon as they'd cured their acne. His mind began to wander back to Valley girls he'd put out of their ignorance, but then the waitress came back and placed the biggest breakfast he had ever seen on the table in front of him. He knew it would give him indigestion and he was tempted to stop before he started but, damn, the bacon looked so good – and the eggs over easy just as he'd asked.

He nodded his thanks and picked up his fork in time to see a deputy walking up the hill, his eyes plainly fixed on his Oldsmobile. Shit. If ever a situation needed heading off at the pass, this was it.

He slapped his napkin on the table, pointed at his car so the waitress would understand he wasn't running out, then he walked out to meet the man, taking his knife with him just in case. It wasn't sharp, but a strong enough punch to penetrate the skin, and it would slide on through a stomach or a liver as well as any shiv.

They found the Blazer where Dinkley had said it was. It was a bit the worse for wear, and the inside would probably have defeated the bravest of valets, what with its candy wrappers, old newspapers, crumpled Post-it notes, beer cans and assorted ash deposits, but it started first time, and the throaty growl of its engine promised a faithful response. Stanley started to drive, leaving Cheryl to navigate – she was more used to map reading – and he steered the four-by-four out of the small parking area behind the *Oracle* office and up onto the highway, where he turned left and headed up the hill.

*

'Problem, officer?' said Hollis, all smiles.

The deputy viewed him over his rimless glasses. He was young and fit – could mean hard work if it came to a fight – but his holster was still strapped, so they were even.

'Your car?'

'Yes. Taking a tour down the coast. Just dropped in for breakfast. It's going cold right now.' He nodded into the café. The deputy looked over his shoulder at the huge meal.

'You'll need to adjust your seat after you finish one of Frank's meals.'

Hollis laughed. It was surprisingly convincing.

'No Parking Zone,' explained the deputy, pointing up at a sign. 'In the a.m., parking's the other side. After noon it's this side. After 6 p.m. it's both sides. And don't ask me why: I'm new here myself.'

'Oh, sorry. Just saw the space, went for it. City living.'

'Well, you'll have to move it.'

'How big is the fine?' said Hollis eyeing his cooling breakfast.

The deputy smiled. 'Twenty-five dollars. Be cheaper to order up another breakfast when you've parked.'

'It would. Any suggestions?'

The deputy turned and pointed at a side street on the other side of the road. Hollis tensed, his anger coiling him to strike. It would be so simple – and so damn *satisfying* – to reach round and twist the man's neck and hear that odd little crack. Just to reach round and—

'Allen Street. You'll be parked up in no time.'

'Okay.'

Hollis got into the car. The deputy leaned down to the window and Hollis wound it down.

'Sunlamp?'

'Yeah. And a run with some smartass in a bar.'

'Who won?'

'He cheated.'

The deputy smiled and tapped on the roof.

Hollis dropped into first and set off, only to hear a blast of horn. He slammed on his brakes just in time to see a red Chevy Blazer miss his offside wing by inches. It slowed down enough for Hollis to make out the word ORACLE on its door before it sped past, the passenger leaning out of the window and shouting 'Asshole!' at him.

He calmed himself, then drove on up the side street and, finding a space, parked up and walked back to the highway, where the deputy stood with his arms crossed.

Just as he reached him Hollis stopped and looked up the street where the Blazer had disappeared from sight.

The passenger who had shouted at him. A girl. He'd heard that voice . . . *the bitch*! It was the bitch! But what was she doing in a pick-up with ORACLE on the door? He turned to run back to his car but the deputy caught his arm.

'Hey, not so fast. Now that was mighty careless.'

Hollis had two options: he could kill the deputy now and go after the Blazer, or he could avoid attracting attention, chill out, and ask some questions and pick up their trail later. The animal inside him was campaigning for the former, commonsense voting for the latter. The next five seconds would tell how close-run a contest it would be.

The route to the ski lodge was pretty direct. They would drive to Newport then take US20 to Albany, I5 to Eugene, and pick up 120 to Ellert. It would take four hours. What they would do when they got there, they didn't know, especially with all the security Dinkley's contact had mentioned, but if it took them one step nearer an answer, it was a step worth taking.

Hollis knocked on the library's glass door and waited.

The deputy had told him the Blazer was owned by one Sam Dinkley, editor of the town's newspaper. He had let Hollis off with a warning about his driving and pointed out the library as the place he had last noticed Sam. Hollis had thanked the policeman and gone back into the café but, as soon as the cop had gone, he had paid his check, run to his car and drove to the library.

Letting the cop go had been a wise move, but it had done little to quell the murderous desire that welled within him. Like a vampire in search of prey, Hollis needed the release only the dispatch of a victim could bring – and in the quiet confines of a library he might well have the ideal location. After, of course, he had found out where the bitch was headed in the newspaperman's Chevy.

He remembered a line from one of his favourite movies, *Manhunter*. Someone asks if they've ever seen blood in the moonlight and the guy answers no and he says it looks black. True, but Hollis knew something even better about blood. The smell . . .

He rapped on the glass again, and saw a figure moving in the semi-light inside the building.

The smell of fresh blood, that was something else. The hot

coppery tang of it, a scent that was almost electric, like that of new leather.

A man approached the glass door.

'Yes?' he said.

'Mr Dinkley? My name's Laurence Granville. Deputy Knox sent me. I was wondering if I could have a word?'

The man surveyed him.

Yes, the smell of fresh blood, thought Hollis. *And the smell of leather.* After all, leather was the hide of an animal that had once been full of blood. Gallons of it.

The man hesitated, then smiled and unlocked the door.

No, he thought, *nothing beats the smell of fresh blood on old leather.* Nothing.

The man pulled opened the door.

'Come in, Mr Granville. Always pleased to see new faces.'

Hollis matched his smile and walked into the library, the scent of a thousand leatherbound volumes wafting over him like the promise of an old lover's perfume.

31

Stanley and Cheryl decided to stop about ten miles from Ellert and have some food. Phil's Diner was a large wooden chalet affair that seemed transplanted wholesale from an Alpine ski resort, but for all its European styling its food was pure American – burnt beef and ice cream.

Parking at the side, they walked in to find the diner half full, most of the customers sitting at the tables that ranged in an L round the south and east sides of the diner. Here they were able to enjoy uninterrupted panoramic views of the surrounding woodland and across the highway through the dozen or so large windows. In contrast, the jumble of tables in the middle of the diner were empty. The pair chose a seat that faced onto the road, and ordered steaks.

Stanley nodded over at the cashdesk near the door heading to the kitchen at the rear, his foot involuntarily tapping along with a Country and Western song playing in the background. There was a rack of postcards, brochures and maps.

'Looks like they've got maps,' he said. 'Someone might know about the place. We'll check it out when we pay.'

'Fair enough, but if this lodge is government property, I can't see us exactly strolling in there, can you?'

Stanley avoided answering. He had Baxter's OCI identification and the Eminent Domain warrant in his pocket, but they would carry little weight with OCI people! So they would have to wing it, and the one thing he had always hated was doing things without planning ahead. Even a trip to the 7-Eleven had to be thought out, a list made, parking considered, the time of day studied. Late night was not a good move. He didn't live in a bad area of Fort Worth but it wasn't exactly swank city. With drive-bys, carjackings and robberies on the increase, and freeways log-jamming like they were in an inconvenience contest, it was a military operation just to get to and from work in one piece.

Their food arrived. It was big and bland but filling, and they tucked in hungrily, both surprised that they could stomach food with their nerves stretched to snapping point.

They were just finishing their meals when a black Pontiac Grand Am drew up right outside their window. Several cars had stopped off while they had been eating, but they had paid them no attention – just vacationers and truckers – but this was different.

The first thing Stanley noticed was the man who got out. He was tall and athletic and dressed casually in jeans and lumberjack shirt, not unlike Stanley himself. Very neatly pressed jeans and shirt, as if he wasn't used to wearing them – just like Stanley's ensemble.

Stanley pointed him out to Cheryl.

'Him? OCI?' she said. 'He doesn't look anything like a cop.'

'Exactly.'

'You're getting paranoid.'

'Well, you know the old saying: "Just because you're paranoid—" '

' "—doesn't mean they're not out to get you." '

'And let's not forget, my dear,' he said, turning so he couldn't be seen by the man, who was now looking up and down the front of the diner, 'that they *are* after us.'

'But he seems normal.'

'Too normal. He looks like he bought those clothes five minutes ago.'

'Maybe he did.'

'But why? You dress casual for the way it feels, not the way it looks. Look at us: we could have just walked out of a changing room. And so could he. Now *we've* got a reason. What's *his*? He looks like he'd be more at home in a suit – or a uniform.'

'So he's a stiff.' She dismissed his worry.

Stanley persisted. 'Washington State plates.'

She confirmed the fact, but so what? Within sight were another two Washington plates, a California and a Georgia.

'Siemens is only going to send in people he trusts, right?' he said. 'He's got something to hide which most of OCI don't know about. Even his Number Two, Baxter, doesn't know.'

'Or didn't know.'

'Yes . . . He's Seattle-based, not Fort Worth, so his aides are going to be Washington State platers.'

'And so are three million others! Half the people in here are probably from Washington,' she hissed. Didn't she have enough to worry about without him seeing bogeymen all over the place?

'But what if I'm right? Look at the guy. You stop for food, you park, you get out, you get in. He looks like a goddamn realtor the way he's measuring the place up.'

The man had taken off his sunglasses and had turned his back to them.

'What if he *is* OCI?' said Stanley. 'What kind of satisfaction am I going to get saying "I told you so" when they dump us down some gully for bear meat?'

'Well, let's just—'

She stared at the man. He had leaned into the car and pulled out a jacket, but then she saw him slip something from the glovebox into its pocket. It could have been a gun. It could just as easily have been a packet of cigarettes, or a lighter, but there was something furtive about the movement, and no one feels that guilty about smoking.

'Okay,' she said. 'Just to be on the safe side.'

Stanley was surprised by her change of heart but didn't waste any more time. They got up and went to the cashdesk. Stanley grabbed a map of Ellert while Cheryl paid their tab.

'Is there a back way out of here?' she asked the woman as she took her change and made a point of dropping a five into the tip glass.

'Only through the kitchen, but . . .'

Cheryl dropped another ten into the tip glass.

'Just don't tell Phil I let you through,' said the woman grabbing the bills.

Stanley and Cheryl walked through the kitchen, stepping aside as a girl carrying three orders of ribs came out, then let the door swing shut behind them.

The large balding cook dressed all in white saw them immediately and began to ask what they were doing.

Stanley went straight up to him and handed him a twenty-dollar bill. 'Health inspection. This look healthy to you?'

The cook took the twenty bucks but didn't move.

Stanley handed him another twenty and the man shrugged his shoulders and stood back.

'Health inspection complete,' said Stanley and ushered Cheryl to the back door.

They pushed open the door and walked into the sunlight, the smell of fresh garbage assaulting their nostrils.

'Okay,' said Stanley, leading the way along the rough-hewn wooden wall to the corner of the diner. 'I'll go first. If anything happens, you just get into the woods and wait.'

Cheryl handed him a steak knife.

'What's that for?' he said.

'Well, it isn't for your nails, is it?'

He was reluctant to take it but saw the sense, not that he would ever use it, but as a threat it might suffice.

'Okay, if I get to the car I'll drive it round here and pick you up. But if I shout, run.'

Cheryl nodded, pulling out another steak knife.

'Going for the set, were you?' he said.

She nudged him to move.

But as he stepped out into the parking lot, he felt a gun press behind his ear, and heard a quiet commanding voice: 'Mr Fulbright, I presume? Drop the knife. Get down on your knees. Don't speak.'

Cheryl saw the arm extending from around the corner and was about to rush and stab it when she heard a gun cock beside her own head, and another voice say: 'And you must be Miss Kenney. Let me introduce you to my friends here, Mr Smith and Mr Wesson.'

Cheryl dropped the knife. 'That's a Clint Eastwood line.'

'So sue me. Now move!'

32

Hollis drove flat-out all the way but, as the road climbed, the weather became worse and the temperature dropped and there were a couple of occasions when he nearly lost the Oldsmobile on the many bends. He had wasted too much time with the newspaper editor, which meant Fulbright had a good forty-five minutes on him. He knew they were heading for a town called Ellert and some ski lodge – he'd heard Siemens mention a lodge up in the Cascades before, so he assumed it was the same place. All the better if it was; he might get to meet Siemens sooner than he had expected.

He almost missed the Blazer, parked as it was on the far side of the diner. Only a fortuitous glance in his mirror revealed it to him. He slammed on the brakes, did a U-turn and parked up beside it. At last . . . those fucks were in the diner.

He considered what to do as he idly played with the release on the glovebox, then something caught his eye. Complimentary windshield wipes. He pulled out the pack, split it open and extracted a couple of tissues. They smelled of pine. Unfolding them, he pressed them to his face, letting the disinfectant soak into his cuts, then he vigorously wiped his cheeks and forehead and neck, feeling the pain and anger rise. Suddenly he heaved back against his headrest and punched the roof lining as a scream welled in him and then died as, his mind set, he kicked open the door, jumped out of the car and trotted around to the front of the diner. He counted thirteen other cars parked outside Phil's. Unlucky for some. He quietly entered the low building and surveyed the customers.

He reckoned the diner could hold upwards of a hundred people but was currently only a third full. Most seemed to be families with young children. A couple of honey-mooning couples – who else hold hands over burgers? – and several older couples, some scrawny, some fat. It looked homey. No bikers, no freaks, no niggers, and with gentle country music to aid the digestion. Glen Campbell if he wasn't mistaken.

He checked every table in one long sweeping glance, but failed to spot Fulbright or the girl. Damn. Maybe they were in the can.

He walked over to the cashdesk and smiled at the woman on duty. She reminded him of the skinny bitch he'd killed in Riva, but at least this one pretended to smile.

'Good afternoon, sir, and how can I help you?'

'The red Chevy Blazer outside. Have you seen the couple driving it?'

The woman looked over his shoulder and shook her head. 'I only see customers when they come in. Don't know what they're driving. Sorry.'

Hollis stared at her a long while. Was she telling the truth? Didn't matter much; he'd be finding out soon enough.

He pointed over her shoulder at a shelf of cigarette packs. 'Twenty Camels then,' he said.

As she turned he leaned over the chest-high counter and felt underneath it and found what he was looking for. Even up here in Nowheresville they had to be prepared.

He pulled out the baseball bat as the woman turned back to him.

'Lites or . . .?'

'Forget it,' he said. 'Trying to cut down.'

He turned to face the diners.

'Listen up, people!' he shouted.

Only a few looked at him.

He swung the bat round and slammed it into the cash register with a crash.

'I said listen up!'

The hubbub of conversation died and all that could be heard was Glen Campbell singing 'Galveston'.

'I'm looking for the driver of the red Chevy Blazer out there.'

Some people looked towards the car he was pointing the bat at, but most just stared at him dumbly.

He walked into the middle of the diner, the bat held out in front of him, its weight a satisfying reminder of his power.

'I do not like to repeat myself. The red Blazer. Whose is it?'

The silence was only disturbed by Glen Campbell and a child whimpering and a mother's shushing.

He shook his head and walked over to the window and tapped the glass impatiently.

'See it? Big red motor, four wheels? Comes out of Detroit. Here, just in case you *still* can't spot it.'

He swung the bat full force at the window and it shattered, spewing a blizzard of fragments out over the Blazer's hood.

Several women screamed.

As the tinkling settled, he knocked the remaining shards of glass out of the frame, then swung the bat until he was slapping his left palm with it, the threat clear.

'This red Blazer – whose is it?'

Cold air drifted in hesitantly, as if wary of the scenario the newly opened window had revealed; a baby cried out, its parents desperately trying to quiet it. One woman was becoming hysterical. He walked over to her – a fat, middle-aged, ugly – and let the bat drop onto her mound of pancakes, where he rolled it in the syrup, then lifted it up and held it to her quivering lips.

'Come on, porky, eat your lunch.'

The woman stared at him wide-eyed, unable to move.

'Lick it, bitch.'

She eased a tongue out like a nervous slug and after several attempts managed to touch the bat and quickly steal a dab of maple syrup before she threw up in her lap.

Hollis shook his head in disgust. 'Bulimia. Worked for Jane Fonda but obviously not for everyone.'

He walked on. The woman's even fatter husband bristled with bravado but a touch on his bulbous red nose with a sticky bat stilled his jittery hands and he deflated like a balloon, a loud fart venting the air.

Hollis did a slow circuit between the occupied window tables and the empty inner tables.

'Imagine you're back at school, people. It's SAT time – if any of you motherfuckers got that far – and what I want is an answer, and what you want is to give it to me because the consequences of failure are far far worse than your current miserable existences.'

Suddenly a tremulous voice behind him called out.

'Freeze!'

Hollis stopped and smiled, then turned.

A nervous young man in his early twenties sat pointing a

small revolver at him, his face running with sweat, his hands trembling. Hollis could see that the gun wasn't even cocked. Amateurs.

He walked back towards him until he was standing four feet away and staring into the boy's eyes.

'Don't show what you ain't going to use, boy. Ain't your girlfriend never told you that?'

'Put it down,' said the girl sitting across from him, tears running down her not unattractive face. 'I'm sorry, mister. He doesn't mean it.'

'Do as your girl says, boy, or things are going to get a whole lot worse.'

The boy's eyes whipped from the girl to Hollis and back again. He tried to speak but the effort was too much.

Hollis spoke instead. 'Judging by your haircut you're a military man. Army?'

The girl answered for him. 'National Guard. Illinois.'

Hollis feigned terror. 'Whoah, Illinois National Guard. Maybe I'd better put up my hands now and beg for mercy.'

The girl let out a nervous gasp of laughter.

'Or maybe you should act your age, boy, and go back to Illinois and get out your GI Joe and play with *his* gun.'

The boy finally relented and slowly laid the gun on the table, his girlfriend covering his hand and saying it was all right, it was going to be all right.

Hollis smiled. 'Very sensible, but didn't they tell you in the Guard never to relinquish your weapon?'

The boy offered an incoherent whisper.

'Can't hear you.'

'Yes.'

Glen Campbell announced he was a lineman for the

county. The baby had been persuaded to hush up, but a woman was quietly sobbing.

'You're pretty goddamn useless, ain't you, Illinois?'

'Yes.'

'Didn't hear you.'

'Yes, sir!' shouted the boy in the silent room, tears running down his red cheeks.

'Good. Now that's clear . . .'

Hollis swung the bat in a low fast arc up into the boy's mouth, smashing his teeth and nose and slamming his head against the wooden back of his seat, where he bounced off and mashed his face onto the table gushing blood and dribbling teeth.

Hollis turned around as the girl shrieked in horror and leaned over to help the boy.

'Now, where was I?' he said, pocketing the boy's blood-splattered .22.

Several women screamed, men swore. Another child began crying and a man stood up near the entrance.

'Yes?' frowned Hollis.

'There's no need for violence, sir. Just take our money and leave.'

'And you are?'

'Frank Stone.'

Hollis walked the three tables to face him. He looked to be a businessman.

'Correct me if I'm wrong, Frank, but I appear to be in charge here.'

The man nodded.

'Can't hear you.'

'Yes, you're in charge. I was just—'

'And as the man in charge I get to make the rules.'

'Yes, you do, but I'm a doctor. Can I see to that man?'

'A doctor? A *real* doctor?'

'Yes. If you'll just . . .'

'There you go again, Frank, telling me what to do.'

'I'm sorry. It's just that—'

'Not sorry enough.'

Hollis swung the bat again and smashed him in the face. He slumped back onto his table then rolled onto the floor clutching at his jaw.

As the man writhed in agony, Hollis flicked a broken tooth out of his victim's mound of chicken wings.

'Is there a dentist in the house?' he said.

He wiped the blood from the bat on the man's back.

'Okay, people, show's over. I'm losing my patience. I want all the drivers to stand up and wave their car keys at me. *Now!*'

Several men stood up fumbling their keys.

'Any of you come out with anything other than keys will not live to regret it.'

Ten seconds later there were eight men and two women and one waitress standing. Hollis went to each one in turn, snagged the keys and asked them what car they drove.

As each identified their car he tossed the keys out of the smashed window and forced the person to sit. As he reached the seventh man there was a voice behind him.

'That's far enough, you fuck. Now put the bat down.'

Hollis let out a long sigh and turned round. Standing by the cashdesk was a big bald man in a dirty white apron, holding a double-barrelled shotgun.

Hollis laughed. 'Anyone got any complaints about the food, here's the man to talk to.'

'Cut the shit and drop the bat.'

'Or what? You'll blow half your fucking customers away? That shot'll spread a good six feet before you get me. This lady here, this girl, this baby, they'll all get it. Now you ain't gonna do that, are you?'

The cook squeezed and unsqueezed the barrel of the gun with his left hand. He realized he was dealing with a real psycho, maybe high on drugs. Most people would be terrified of a shotgun, pictures of empty abdomens and missing limbs filling their minds, but this guy was working out trajectories and kill ratios, and he was right: if the cook fired he'd as likely kill or maim a customer as this crazy.

Hollis took two steps towards him. 'You're not going to shoot, face it. You've got too much to lose. Imagine the lawsuits! Like I explained to the young man back there, never pull something you ain't prepared to use.'

Hollis suddenly leaned to his left and grabbed a young blonde girl in a red woollen suit and, holding her in front of him facing the cook, ran the length of the bat under her chin and pulled back hard. The nine-year-old girl didn't even have time to cry out before she was choking, her hands flailing as if trying to sweep air up into her lungs.

'Oh God, no,' said the chef.

'God, right now, right here, ain't the issue. This girl's larynx is.'

The girl's mother grabbed at Hollis's hand but he butted her in the face with the handle of the bat.

'Stay out of this, bitch. You're young enough to drop another. Now you, cook, are you gonna lose that weapon or are you gonna lose customers?'

The cook looked around for help but none came. He had

lost, and in losing knew he had made everything infinitely worse.

'He who hesitates . . .' said Hollis, pulling up on the bat so that the girl's feet left the floor. Her mother shrieked through the hand held to her bloody, smashed nose, her eyes wide enough to pop.

The cook took a step nearer and Hollis hauled the girl another six inches off the floor. Her face was reddening, her feet pedalling.

'What's this girl ever done to hurt you, cook?'

'I . . . I . . .'

'Your move, fry boy.'

The woman on the cash register grabbed the cook's shoulder. 'Phil, you *have* to.'

'Wise words, Phil Fry,' said Hollis, leaning an ear down to the girl's desperate rasping.

A chorus of 'pleases' went round the dining-room and Phil finally relented and, carefully uncocking the shotgun's hammers, lowered it to the floor.

Hollis didn't relinquish his grip on the girl, however. 'Now kick it over here.'

Phil did as ordered and the gun skidded to a halt a yard from Hollis's feet. He slowly lowered the girl to the floor, but kept the bat round her neck.

'I'm getting rather tired of all this hero shit. I'm in charge and there ain't nothing you can do about it. Now, Frying Phil Fuck-up, on your knees.'

There were more gasps and more pleas from around the diner as Glen Campbell asked Susie to tell him where the playground was, but it made no difference. A shaking and resigned Phil got down onto his knees.

Hollis grabbed the girl by the hair and let the bat fall to the floor with a clatter, then picked up the shotgun – it was in good condition, maybe never used before – checked it was loaded then re-cocked both barrels and, dragging the girl by the hair, walked over to the cook.

'The people in the red Blazer. Where'd they go?'

'Don't know. I was out back.'

'You,' he said to the now chalk-faced woman manning the desk. 'Anyone not here who should be?'

'There were two, they went through back.'

'How long ago?'

'Ten, fifteen minutes.'

'You must have seen them, Phil.'

'Yes. Couple. Man, woman, but I didn't know what they were driving.'

'But you didn't say anything, did you, Phil? So where'd they go?'

'Through the back. Didn't see where they went.'

'Anyone else see anything?'

The woman spoke up. 'Man followed them.'

'A man?' Hollis shook his head.

'A man.'

'Age?'

'Twenties. Tall. Like a cop,' said Phil.

Hollis tutted in disgust. 'Like a cop. Wonderful. Now these people in here know who's really responsible for all this: this bitch and Fuck-up Phil here. A fucking *crowd* go through their kitchen and they say nothing. If you'd said—'

'You didn't ask! All you wanted—'

'Shut up, bitch! Did anyone see where this man and the couple went?'

There was no answer, just sniffles and moans and sobbing. And Glen Campbell.

Hollis shook his head. He was torn about what to do next. He had a gun and a shotgun (that was at least eight victims) but there was also a timescale to consider. Fifteen minutes to be made up – twenty if he added in the time he was wasting now – and he needed some insurance. Soon as he left, they'd have the whole state alerted; he wouldn't get within five miles of Ellert before there was a roadblock.

He took the shotgun and pointed it at Phil's face.

'Open your mouth.'

'What?'

'Open up.'

A woman fainted, her partner burbling to God. A waitress fell to her knees, the tray she had been holding all through the terror smashing over the floor. Hollis didn't even blink, such was his focus.

The woman on the cash desk pleaded with him, but he simply pointed the gun at her.

'You volunteering? Phil, get your mouth open. Now.'

Phil opened his quivering mouth and Hollis slotted the cold ends of the barrels between his lips.

'Right, girl,' he said to the nine-year-old cowering by his side. 'Do we shoot Uncle Phil or don't we?'

The girl began crying, staring up at him, red-rimmed wet eyes uncomprehending.

'Your choice, blondie. Do I shoot Phil the Fuck or not?'

People shouted 'No!', encouraging the girl.

'Hey, this ain't no fucking gameshow! Girl's got an important decision to make. Do we shoot Phil?'

She stared at Phil who had turned white and was having

trouble staying upright, urine staining his white trousers, his wide eyes saying everything.

The girl shook her head.

'Can't hear you.'

'No. Don't shoot. Don't shoot him.'

'Okay, but it was your choice, okay?'

'Okay,' she said, forcing a smile of relief.

He slowly pulled the gun out of Phil's mouth, who immediately collapsed and began gagging.

'What's your name?' Hollis said to the girl, a smile slicing his red, burning face.

'Jess. Jessica.'

Hollis stood upright, his voice loud and precise.

'Well, Jessica, you chose not to shoot Phil, so we'll have to shoot this bitch instead.'

He pointed the gun at the woman behind the counter and pulled both triggers and blasted her in the chest. The impact blew her back against the diner wall, where she crashed to the floor, cigarette packs tumbling over her.

'When I want an answer,' he said leaning over the counter, 'I want an answer.'

He then dropped the shotgun and, grabbing the girl around the waist, pulled the guardsman's revolver from his pocket and, holding it to her head, walked to the door.

'I'll be keeping Jessica here as insurance. The longer you take to call the cops, the longer she lives. And remember, if Phil there had told me the truth straight out, none of this might have happened.'

There were screams and sobs and the girl's mother begged incoherently and kicked at the woman trying to console her, and a couple of men shouted for him to leave the girl but he ignored them.

He booted open the door and dragged the struggling, shrieking girl along the exterior of the diner and around to his own car where he shoved her in the driver's door, then hustled her over to the passenger seat, using the young man's revolver as persuasion. Then he reversed out in a shower of gravel, and squealed away along the highway towards Ellert.

Glen Campbell, meanwhile was on his way to Phoenix.

33

'Where are you taking us?' said Cheryl.

She and Stanley were in the back of the agents' Grand Am, their hands cuffed behind their backs.

'To a quiet spot,' said the driver, smiling at his fellow agent.

'Why?'

'So we can make a couple of bangs without upsetting the locals, what d'you think?' said the other one in the seat in front of Stanley.

'You'll be upsetting us,' said Stanley, his arms numb.

'Not part of the equation,' said the driver.

'You could always let us go,' said Cheryl.

The passenger turned round, gun in hand, and pointed it at her. 'And you could always shut your mouth.'

'Siemens order you to do this?' asked Stanley.

They locked eyes.

'I'm OCI too,' added Stanley. 'Out of Fort Worth.'

The driver looked up at his mirror. 'I hate Texas.'

The man with gun turned back and settled in his seat, gun on his lap.

'How about bribery?' said Cheryl.

'What have you got that we can't take after we kill you?'

Stanley shook his head.

They had been in the car five minutes, heading for Ellert, but he doubted they would reach the town limits. They didn't seem to have any way out.

He looked at Cheryl and shrugged his shoulders. 'Sorry.'

'Not your fault.'

'It is. If I hadn't—'

'Shut up, Stanley.'

He leaned his hot head against the cold window. They were doomed.

Cheryl looked around the car. Their doors had child-proof locks so they couldn't be opened from the inside. The front seats did have low head restraints so their captors' heads were vulnerable, but with their hands cuffed behind their backs, neither she nor Stanley could grab at them.

They took a tight bend fast and she was thrown over onto Stanley's lap, her mouth brushing his thigh.

'Sorry,' she said.

'No need,' said Stanley.

'Will you two shut the fuck up!'

Cheryl righted herself. What the hell were they going to do?

She leaned back out of sight of the rearview mirror, then nudged Stanley with her knee. When he looked at her, she nodded her head at the man in front of her and gnashed her teeth.

Stanley didn't understand.

She nodded at him and frowned, but didn't dare to speak.

Charades? he thought. *What a time to . . .* She was nodding at the man in front of Stanley. *What about him?*

She lifted her legs as best she could, nodded at the man's head and made a kicking motion.

Kick him in the head? Even if he could get his legs up high enough, what was the use?

She nodded at the driver and bared her teeth again, then

rubbed her cheek on her shoulder and looked down at her own neck.

She wanted him to . . . and then she'd . . . it was stupid. He shook his head.

She nodded.

'Get ready,' she mouthed, moving into the middle of the back seat.

Oh shit, thought Stanley. If this didn't work they'd be shot in the car. Outside in the open there was always a chance but . . .

She mouthed 'Ready' again.

He reluctantly nodded and squirmed down in the seat until he could pull his knees up to his chest and worm his feet up the back of the seat in front of him. It seemed every muscle in his body was about to snap and the pain made him angry, but the anger made him work all the harder to get his feet into the right position.

Then the agent in front of him looked over.

'What the fuck?'

Perfect. Stanley jabbed him full in the face with his left heel and the man slammed back against his window, his initial howl of pain silenced by the hurtful impact.

The driver immediately slammed on his brakes, swearing louder than his shrieking tyres, as the car slewed off the road and came to a jarring halt against a tree.

Stanley was banged up against the seat in front, the wind knocked out of him, but Cheryl had braced herself and, as the car stopped and the driver was jerked back into his seat by his seatbelt, she hurled herself at him and sank her teeth into his neck and bit hard enough to rupture his flesh.

He batted at her with his hands, squealing like a wounded

animal, but Cheryl bit all the harder, quickly persuading him that struggling was a bad idea.

Stanley, dragging air into his sore lungs, gasped out the next step.

'You . . . driver . . . get out the key to the cuffs . . . or she rips your fucking . . . throat out.'

The man tried to speak but Cheryl growled in his ear and bit harder. She didn't know how long she could hold on because it was only the grip of her teeth that was keeping her upright.

The driver raised his hands in surrender, reached inside his pocket and held up the key.

What now? thought Stanley. 'Toss it over to me,' he ordered, sitting back.

The driver threw it over his head and it landed in Stanley's lap.

Oh shit . . .

Stanley leaned forward and raised his bottom and shook his hips, keeping his right thigh highest. Eventually the key jumped off his lap and landed on the seat. He turned to the window and fumbled blindly behind him until he found the key. As he turned the annoyingly small piece of metal the right way round, he heard the other agent mumbling back to consciousness. Not much time.

He edged his backside forward until his back was to Cheryl and with one hand he located the handcuffs she was holding out to him and then, finding the keyhole with his finger, he edged the key into the slot and, much to his surprise, got it in, turned it and felt the cuff snap open.

Cheryl immediately reached over into the driver's jacket

and pulled out his gun and holding it to his head let go his neck, spitting out blood.

'Fucking aftershave.'

The man fell forward, grabbing at his neck, but she thought he might have another weapon under his seat so she knocked him out with his gun. The other man was coming to, so she grabbed his hair and slammed his head back against the bloodied window, then she sat back and caught her breath, hysterical joy bubbling to the surface.

'Save it,' said Stanley, realizing she was about to whoop. 'Got to get out of here.'

She took the key and undid his handcuffs.

Clambering over the driver, she opened his door, undid his seatbelt and pushed him out onto the snow-covered verge, then climbed out and unlocked the back door and let a cramped Stanley fall onto the ground.

Five minutes later they had dragged the two agents through some trees to a small clearing, where they cuffed the two of them back to back around a fir tree and tossed away the key.

They then headed back to the car with the men's IDs, wallets and Beretta. Opening the car's trunk, they found a pair of OCI LAW jackets and a couple of rifles and, in the glovebox, a map with the route to the lodge marked out.

They checked the car for damage – the front was dented, one light broken – but after some wheel-spinning, it disconnected itself from the tree, and Cheryl drove on to Ellert.

34

The little girl wouldn't shut up. Whining and whimpering, asking for her goddamn momma. Eventually Hollis slapped her across the face.

'One fucking word out of you and you die. One move I don't like, you die. Either way, you won't see your fucking momma again.'

The girl stared at him, her face wet and red, her eyes circles. She nodded dumbly, snot running into her mouth, but not having the nerve to wipe it away.

Hollis smiled at the girl but even at her age she could read a liar and she eased away, trying to shrink into something he wouldn't notice, her mind filled with comforting thoughts of her mother and home.

He had to assume Fulbright and the bitch had been grabbed by OCI people, otherwise there would have been police cars all over the place, but once he spotted them a couple of OCI goons would present no problems. He saw some skidmarks but paid them no heed. There were skids every quarter-mile or so, some of them quite spectacular; this pair had led straight to the base of a damaged tree, but so what? Then something clicked in his mind and he slowed the car, did a three-point turn, and drove back to the skid.

They were in a straight line and fresh – snow threatened but hadn't started falling yet. But why these skidmarks? What was so . . . Then he saw it, on the verge. Blood.

He looked down at the girl. She would have to come with him. He checked over her clothes. Besides her red blouse, jacket and skirt, she wore a narrow plastic belt with Mickey Mouse faces on it. That would do.

Checking there was no other traffic, he told the child to take off the belt and get out. She meekly obeyed, probably too young to take it as a sexual threat. There was still some innocence in the world, then. He'd sort that out soon enough. (When he was this girl's age, his mother was feeding him her stringy teats while she gave him an enema.) He tied the belt round her neck then, wrapping the remainder around his wrist, he walked her like a dog to the splattering of blood, from which he spotted a trail of spots leading into the trees. Interesting. He tugged the girl and she followed him like an automaton.

The blood spots brought him to a clearing where, cuffed to a tree, stood two men in jeans and check shirts, one with his shirt front and collar stained with blood, the other bloody about the head.

'Hey, buddy, are we glad to see . . .' But the man with the scalp wound trailed off as he saw what had come their way.

'Wrong,' said Hollis.

He dragged the girl towards the men, and looked them over like specimens.

'Fulbright and the girl do this?'

'Who are you?' asked the injured man.

Hollis shot him in the head.

'*I'm* asking the questions.' He turned to the other man. 'Now, did they do this to you?'

The man was dragged to his knees by the weight of his dead partner, and all he could do was nod dumbly through his pain as the girl stared at the corpse, unable to comprehend the bloody new world she had suddenly entered.

'Now, I can make this slow, but I'm sure you'd want to spare the kid's feelings, so just answer my questions and you won't have to worry about the democratic process no more.'

'Fuck you.'

Hollis shot him in the knee. The man screamed in agony and vented a stream of breathless obscenities.

Hollis punched him across the mouth with the revolver.

'Not in front of the kid. Now, where were you taking Fulbright and the girl?'

The man didn't answer, his face scrunched up in pain, wordless sounds issuing through broken teeth.

Hollis prodded the bleeding knee. The man shrieked.

'So it's slow you want?'

'To the lodge! To Mr Thiemens,' he lisped, blood spitting with each 's'. 'We thcared them a bit, but all we wath doing wath delivering them.'

'Where is this lodge?'

'Ellert. We had a map. There'th a road up. Ith manned, tho we'd get through no problemth.'

'Any other way up?'

'Cable car. There'th a rethort near the lodge, but we were told to take the road.'

'How long you been here?'

'Ten minuth.'

'What's at the lodge?'

The man's anger broke through his fear and pain. 'I don't know, you cockthucker!'

Hollis pushed the .38's barrel to the man's temple.

'I told you about that mouth of yours.'

By the time he had carried the girl back to the car he was regretting the waste of ammunition. He now only had three bullets left. Sloppy. Damn Fulbright; he and the bitch would fucking *pay* for all of this.

He laid the girl down on the back seat of the car, wiping away the blood and brains that had splashed on her blank face from the second man's head, then changed his mind and instead pulled her out and dragged her by the belt round her throat into the bushes and left her, uninterested in whether he had choked her or not.

He got back into the car and drove off. The child would be a liability in her shocked state; he might as well have been carrying a corpse. Besides, if he caught sight of Fulbright she might get in his way, and he wanted that bastard so bad he didn't want anything to fuck it up. God, he was so close he could feel it in his balls.

35

They had originally planned to drive straight through the roadblock, using stolen OCI identification, but as they waited for Ellert's only traffic light to change they had seen the uniformed policemen on duty. Whether real cops or OCI men, they were checking IDs very carefully and comparing them to something on their clipboards. More than likely it would be photographs of the two of them and, dyed hair or no, even using Eminent Domain would fail to get the pair of them through. Besides, there was the problem of the daily password. Siemens must have been really panicked about their impending arrival; Stanley only wished they could live up to his concern.

So Cheryl had wheeled the car behind the Ellert Experience – a mall made up of shops and a little folk museum: presumably the 'experience' – and, parking in a quiet corner, they considered their limited options.

Through the quickly misting-up windows they could see the road to the lodge running up the mountainside for a couple of miles, police cars stationed every half mile or so, their blue and red roof-lights spinning lazily like Christmas-tree illuminations against the white of the mountainside. From the town, the lodge itself couldn't be seen but their map showed it to be over a ridge to the northwest.

The only other way up was the cable car. It ran from the centre of Ellert for over a mile and a half, rising some two thousand feet over the valley to a wheelhouse on the top of the highest point of the ridge.

As the world became enshrouded in condensation, they got out of the Grand Am and walked to the corner of the minimall, aware that there were policemen everywhere they looked. Ellert could have been home to a goddamned police academy they were so omnipresent. Hugging the wall of a bookshop, they watched the cable cars working.

Stanley reckoned each car carried about twenty passengers and there was a line waiting – a line at least a hundred people long. Counting only four cable cars, that meant, given the agonizing slowness of their ascent and descent, they would be in line for the best part of twenty minutes. That was twenty minutes of standing in the heart of a town thronged with policemen each specifically looking for them, armed with photographs and guns. They couldn't have been more vulnerable if they'd been naked and had WANTED pasted on their foreheads.

What's more, every single person in the line was dressed for skiing and was carrying skis, whereas he and Cheryl were dressed for a trip to the local museum.

'We need to buy gear that blends us in,' said Stanley.

'We'll have to buy cheap,' said Cheryl, feeling for the wallets in her pocket.

Sly's Ski Shack, next to the bookshop, looked promising. It was probably the shabbiest shop in town.

Ten minutes later they emerged, weighed down with large bags containing secondhand quilted red ski jackets, blue ski pants and boots, plus one pair of skis – and twenty-eight dollars change. They walked back to the car, raised its trunk lid for cover and, making sure no one was looking, changed into their ski clothes. Then they trudged their nervous way over to the cable lift.

Ellert was an ugly little place, its plainness relieved only by a covering of snow and a mountainous backdrop that would have made Cleveland look good. The town had no adventurous or even resort-style architecture, just grey boxy buildings, dull shops, dreary motels, a couple of sawmills and a grid street pattern that, running as it was with grey slush, looked like unsuccessful sewer engineering. Even the coloured lights strung up between the streetlamps and skeletal trees conspired to look as if someone had forgotten to take them down from the previous year. People clearly didn't come for the town itself but for the skiing and, unlike Stanley and Cheryl, they came ready equipped. Still, most people they encountered seemed cheery enough and, with music blaring out from various stores, the place had a festive air of sorts. It was apparent that a lot of people were content to look up at the mountain and breathe in the snowflakes that were starting to fall, and think of the ski fun to come, rather than contemplate the rundown dump they were waiting in. Stanley bought their five-dollar cable-car tickets and they joined the line.

An enterprising kid was touting hot chocolate in Styrofoam cups, and they bought one each. It was weak and too sweet, but it was hot and that was what counted.

They tried to blend in with the crowd, which wasn't hard. Everyone seemed to be trying to outdo each other in the brightness department, oranges and yellows and pinks and limes and blues predominating, with absurd patterns and colour combinations running riot like they had been clothed by a bunch of blind tailors using offcuts from a bad Vegas floorshow. Chatter was loud, the air filled with vapour, the mood one of holiday happiness, though they did detect the odd comment complaining about the closed mountain road.

The line continued to move forward and carried on growing, some squealing schoolgirls bringing up the rear, but it was to be ten long minutes before they were within striking distance of boarding the cable car.

Behind them a police siren started up and they jumped and stared at each other until they realized it was heading away out of town. The line collectively craned their necks in the opposite direction and speculated about the cause.

It was only as they reached the entrance to the cable-car wheelhouse that they spotted the two policemen standing to the side of the gate checking IDs as people entered.

Cheryl and Stanley were three places from the front after the next red cable car had filled. Once passengers had disembarked, each car slowly ground its way in a loop round the inside of the station. Its doors were then reopened by the car's attendant and new passengers let on board, and then it would take flight up the mountainside.

Stanley overheard one of the cops say he'd had a radio message about two girls being found dead out on the highway. For some reason this news struck a chord within Stanley, and he looked at Cheryl, but she was staring back down the line, her body language screaming unease.

'Forget it,' he said. 'Go now and you'll have those two goons wondering why we stand in line for twenty minutes then turn and leave at first sight of a cop. We'll have to bluff it.'

Cheryl knew he was being wildly optimistic and fumbled out her stolen OCI card to prove her point. It portrayed a burly male, and Stanley's was no better, the man heavier than him and with curly hair. Stanley didn't know what else to do. At a crime scene, a quick flash of a badge was enough to get on site, but when it was a manhunt like this, detail counted. They had no other means of identification and these two probably had a description of them both anyway. They were screwed.

Their car slowly descended towards them. Tall, with high windows unspoiled by bars, and a small railing around its roof like a luggage rack, it had twin sliding doors on each side and no seats, and took, he now realized, a maximum of sixteen passengers.

The car reached the final tower, juddered its protest, then eased on down the last hundred yards to the wheelhouse. It contained just four people.

They only had a minute now. Stanley anxiously scanned the line behind him but it offered no comfort. Snow was starting to fall quite heavily, though there was little wind, so it was almost vertical. Another time it would have added to the Christmasy feel of the place, but now it was just so much frozen precipitation. The only consolation was that it gave them an excuse to put their hoods up, which helped hide their faces.

The car reached the cable station, its arrival echoing noisily in the plain concrete box. The attendant slid open the doors and people stepped onto terra firma.

Stanley felt in his shirt for the Eminent Domain warrant and wondered if it would work. Probably not; these two cops wouldn't know it from a marriage licence, and would have to call someone senior who would call someone at OCI who would have to verify it, and they'd be back where they started.

He could feel his heart pumping. To be this close to the lodge and maybe some answers, and yet to have two local cops screw it all up . . . There was no point dashing through into the cable car, as they'd simply come after them, and moving away now would attract attention.

One of the cops stood up. He was big and blond and bored and his voluminous fur-trimmed brown uniform jacket made him look like a wrestler. 'Okay, next carful, please.'

The couple in front of Stanley and Cheryl showed their driving licences and were both waved through, then the cops turned their attention to Stanley and Cheryl.

'Need to see ID, lady,' said the blond cop to Cheryl.

She put her hand in her pocket like there was something there. For his part Stanley patted his chest and offered a smile to the other cop – a plainly irritated older man with a ruddy face reddened by more than the cold – but the man refused to accept it and held out his gloved hand.

Suddenly there was another siren and a car roared past. Stanley jumped with fright then, inspired, said: 'They after that pervert?'

'What pervert?' perked up the blond cop.

'The one by that hot-dog place. Flashed my wife but we thought with all the sirens you'd gone after him.'

The two cops looked at each other.

'A flasher?' said the older man. 'Here? What'd he look like?'

Cheryl picked up the story.

'He was big. Twenties. Had tattoos. Wearing a black coat.'

Stanley looked back over the heads of the crowd. 'Well, if they're not after him, who is?'

Stanley waited a moment and, as expected, was rewarded with a girlish shriek, one of many they had had to endure from the back of the line over the last ten minutes, but this one could be turned to their advantage.

'There he is! I think. See, near the back. He must be flashing some girl now.'

The two bored cops didn't need any further encouragement.

'Wait here. We might need you to make a statement,' said the blond cop as he followed his colleague through the crowd.

'How about, "You're a thick hick,"' said Cheryl as she and Stanley walked into the cable-car station and on into the cable car itself.

'Nice move, Fulbright,' she offered.

'You're welcome.'

Once inside they moved to the front of the car and held on to one of several metal poles that rose from floor to ceiling, and prayed the thing would fill up and move before the cops came back and remembered why they were there.

'Can they hold these things up for long?' asked Stanley.

'Don't think so, otherwise all the cars stop. They'll have to set it off soon.'

Through the steamed-up windows they saw the crowd moving onto the platform, a kid in a red hat trying to stop the flow as impatient skiers attempted to make up for lost time.

Then they saw the cops fighting their way back through the crowd, their eyes fixed on the car.

Come on, come on, urged Stanley of the car.

The car had filled up, a mix of young men and women and

some children, all wrapped in coats and jackets and trousers like quilts, their upright skis clattering together like broad swords as they juggled for the best view.

The policemen got onto the platform and remonstrated with the young redcap, but he shrugged at them through the car doors as it set off.

A couple of bumps, a loud creak, and then they felt motion and suddenly they were out into the afternoon and the car was flooded with light, and snow dazzled them on all sides.

Cheryl squeezed Stanley's hand and banged her forehead onto his shoulder.

'This is getting too intense,' she said.

'For you?'

'Yes, even for me,' she had to admit.

He could smell her as he hugged her. It was a nice smell, a mix of sweat and soap, an odour he remembered from some of his sexual encounters in the past. That, and the adrenalin coursing through his veins, were giving him the beginnings of a hard-on. Such were the mysteries of the human body.

The car rose agonizingly slowly, as if it were struggling to find the strength to complete its journey, but Stanley knew that was just his imagination. He checked out their fellow passengers.

There were five men and six women of various ages, together with a couple of young boys, all dressed in bulky clothes and carrying skis like flagless banners. Those who didn't have their hoods up wore hats or ski-masks, and most wore dark glasses or goggles to take in the views (that was something Stanley should have bought in the shop but they didn't have enough cash). Luckily, bright though the surrounding snow-fields were, the sun was clouded out and it was tolerable.

He looked back over the shoulders of the other passengers towards Ellert, the town steadily shrinking as they climbed the mountain, its ugly greyness like a stain on a crumpled eiderdown. And then it suddenly occurred to Stanley why the town was such a dump. Siemens.

Whatever the lodge was there for, the last thing Siemens wanted was to be stuck just outside another Aspen. No doubt he had used his influence over the past years to keep the town from prospering – except, of course, those privileged locals charged with ensuring the town's failure, who would have grown rich from his bribes. There was tourism sure, enough to deflect curiosity and provide some cover, but not enough to present a security risk.

Stanley stared down at the town, sad for all those people deliberately prevented from making the most of their location by that evil fucker. What was it with this guy that he could even stop ordinary people making an honest buck? Stanley turned to Cheryl and, without thinking, hugged her.

Cheryl welcomed his embrace but didn't know why he had done it or, more importantly, why she liked it. Maybe she was just tired and needed a hug. She certainly wasn't about to think it was anything more than that. She wondered about the Helsinki Syndrome, how people taken hostage tend to end up siding with their captors against those trying to rescue them. Maybe she had a touch of that: because it was the two of them against what seemed like everyone else, naturally she would think more of her only ally than she would in other circumstances. Still, he was good-looking and, from what she had seen in the hotel, in good shape all over.

What the hell, if they got out of this she might even make a play for him. She knew he wouldn't say no. Might even be fun, as long as he put a bit of *oomph* into it – she hadn't any time for gentleness – but somehow he struck her as a log fire and fur rugs kind of guy. Boring.

Their eyes met and both looked away, as if embarrassed that there could be anything between the two of them, but they didn't break apart. Stanley only hoped she wasn't able to read his thoughts.

They were halfway up the mountain when, to Stanley's dismay, he saw that a police car had set off from Ellert and was speeding up the winding road. It would be touch and go whether it reached the top before them, but even if it didn't he had little doubt there were already cops or OCI waiting. They would be sitting ducks.

He had just leaned his mouth to Cheryl's ear to whisper this new problem to her, when a voice broke through the gentle murmuring in the car.

'Very fucking touching.'

All conversation stopped.

Stanley and Cheryl looked towards the voice. It had been male, and loud: a voice meant to be heard.

A figure stepped forward, dressed in a bright yellow ski jacket with a tight red knitted ski-mask over his head, which he pulled off to reveal a face redder than the cold-chilled faces around him.

'Hollis!' said Stanley, the shock of seeing the dead man alive actually making his heart skip a beat.

'Correct, Fulbright.' Hollis was pleased to observe how stunned the man was to see him. Now, before he got his brain in gear . . . it had worked before, why not do it again?

He grabbed a young boy of about twelve years of age round the neck and pulled him in front of him and pointed a gun at his head.

'You were dead,' said an appalled Cheryl, unable to accept the man was alive. 'I . . . in the store . . .'

'Yes, bitch, you electrocuted me. I'm going to pay you back, but for now *I'm* doing the talking. Now, listen up, everyone. I ain't got nothing against you people, just this pair here, so do what you're told and the kid won't get hurt.'

The car rode past a supporting tower and everyone shifted – but no one moved their eyes from Hollis.

'What do you want?' said Stanley, letting go his terrified grip of Cheryl and slowly moving in front of her.

'You. Dead. Now.'

Stanley shook his head.

'Oh yes, Fulbright. Open the door.'

Stanley looked through the steamed-up window. Snow-covered rocks drifted past more than two hundred feet below. His heart banged in his chest at the sight.

He could feel Cheryl stirring behind him, but Hollis also noticed her movement.

'If that's a gun, bitch, it better be on the floor in two seconds or I'll blow this kid's brains out!'

The boy began to cry, his mother pleading with Hollis. Hollis was having fun. He had grabbed a bottle of perfume from the two girls he had flagged down just outside Ellert and killed for their skiing gear. He had intended getting his rage up by spraying the Obsession on his face, but as soon as he had spotted Fulbright ahead of him in the line for the car he'd had no need of artificial stimulants; just the sight of that prick and the cunt with him had been enough. It had taken all Hollis's control not to go for them in the line but he wanted Fulbright to pay for his impertinence, and now he had him he was going to squeeze every ounce of pleasure out of it before he killed every witness. Power, that was the key: the power to be better than all the other scuttling little grubs that passed for humans in this world.

Cheryl reached into her jacket as everyone else, except Hollis and Stanley, shied back to the windows, their sudden movement swaying the cable car. She brought into sight the Beretta they had taken from the OCI men.

'That *is* a big one,' said Hollis. 'Now drop it on the floor. And, Fulbright, I told you to open the fucking door.'

Stanley didn't know what to do, but Hollis tightened his arms around the boy's neck. He was crying, his eyes wide, but the increased pressure on his throat cut off his sobs and he began to gasp, his hands scrabbling along Hollis's fat yellow forearm like a piano player on speed.

'Don't hurt my boy. Don't hurt my boy,' pleaded his mother, her anguished face absurd in its green fur halo.

'Shut the fuck up!' Hollis commanded, the woman complying straight away as if she was used to being ordered around.

'Touching, ain't it, parental concern?' said Hollis. 'Now, are you going to open that door or are you going to upset this lady when I ventilate her kid?'

Stanley held his hands out to placate the man, then slowly turned to the door. The young attendant offered no assistance, instead cowering out of the way as if Stanley was radioactive. Stanley quickly figured out how the door's lock worked and, pulling up the metal peg, he flipped back the catch, then slowly slid the door halfway open.

Cold air rushed in like greedy hands, fingers of frozen mountain air scratching at a dozen hot faces. Looking down, Stanley could see the jagged rocks all the more clearly, a deadly mattress covered in a blanket of powdery snow. There would be no chance of survival, not even the vain hope of landing in a snowdrift; it simply wouldn't be deep enough.

Stanley considered going for his own gun, but knew he wouldn't make it before Hollis started shooting – and then he probably wouldn't stop.

'Now, you, woman, drop the fucking gun.'

Cheryl stared defiantly at Hollis, but only received a rasping choke from the boy for her stand. Even if she could get a shot off, the boy would die.

'Okay, okay,' she said.

'Toss it out the door.'

'Okay.' She lifted her arm towards the door, but Stanley caught it and took the gun from her.

'First rule a law officer learns, Hollis – even a fuck-up like me – is never give up your gun.'

Hollis laughed. 'Funny, I was just saying the same thing.'

Stanley cocked the Beretta and pointed it at him.

'Your move, asshole. Shoot the boy, I shoot you.'

Hollis laughed again. This was getting to be even more fun. 'Precisely, you prick, but you ain't gonna have this boy's blood on your whiter than white hands are you?'

'Wrong,' said Stanley.

'Oh yeah, like you'd let me shoot him?'

Stanley brought his other hand up and cupped the gun butt, his aim squarely on Hollis's face.

'Yes,' said Stanley.

There were gasps from everyone in the car. He guessed they were praying he'd just go quietly so their feud could be sorted without any further bloodshed but, whether they knew it or not, he was trying to save them all.

'Even if I jump,' explained Stanley, 'you'll still be killing him and every witness here. We're *all* dead. Better one dies than everyone.'

The boy looked at him, the import of what he was saying sinking in. Urine began coursing down his jeans, steam rising, the smell strong in the confines of the car. His mother now screamed at Stanley as if this was all his fault.

'Not my baby, not my baby! This isn't anything to do with us. Why should we suffer?'

There was muttered agreement.

'Shut up, all of you!' said Cheryl.

They passed another gantry, and there was a collective intake of breath as both men were shaken.

Hollis shook his red, leering face. 'I don't believe you, Fulbright.' He slid the gun round the boy's cheek and forced it into the corner of his mouth.

'Suck it, boy. Suck it like it was a dick.'

The boy began to gag, his mother suddenly speechless.

'Shut up, Hollis,' said Stanley. 'Too many people have died and I don't even know why, but whatever happens it stops here – and if that means this boy dying, then so be it.'

'This isn't fucking *Star Trek*! There's nothing noble here. I want you dead and I'm willing to trade this boy's life for yours.'

'You're wrong, Hollis. The question here is: do *you* want to die?'

Several people began to talk to God, the mother becoming

incoherent with hysteria, a man next to her struggling to stop her grabbing for her son.

Another man on Stanley's right spoke up. 'Look, mister, we don't know nothing about this. Can't you just—?'

'Shut up. I'm trying to save your life – don't you realize that, you dumb shit!'

'Hey, there's no need—'

Cheryl kicked the man in the crotch and he went down.

Hollis nodded approvingly. 'So what now, hero?' he said.

'How far have we got to go?' Stanley asked Cheryl.

She looked round up the mountain. 'About two minutes.'

Stanley nodded at the flashing lights of a police car racing up the mountain road.

'Once we get to the top, Hollis, it's over. There'll be a reception committee. You're going nowhere but, before I shoot you, answer me one thing.'

'You won't shoot.' Hollis was intrigued by Fulbright's stand, but it was fast becoming irritating.

'Like you, Hollis, I've nothing to lose. Neither of us is getting out of this mess once Siemens catches up with us. So, tell me, why did Siemens have you kill all those innocent people?'

'They weren't innocent.'

'So what had they done? Never mind the sheriff and those other poor saps who got blown up in Riva, just tell me why you killed the waitress. What's so fucking dangerous that serving hash gets you killed?'

'I don't know and I don't care.'

'Yes, you do! You've been following orders just like me, but now Siemens'll want you dead. So tell me why the waitress had to die.'

Hollis's darting eyes betrayed his indecision.

'Why did you kill the fucking waitress?' screamed Stanley.

The man's screwing with your head, Kent. Just get it over with. Kill the fuck. Kill the fuck!

'I don't fucking know . . . and I don't fucking care!'

Hollis finally snapped and swung the gun away from the boy and aimed it at Stanley and fired.

Stanley fired back.

Hollis fired again, the gunshots painfully loud in the cold cabin.

People screamed and ducked away, the car swinging wildly.

Stanley fired twice more.

Hollis vented a guttural moan, as if the sound was too painful to risk letting out, then he looked down at the bulky clothing covering his chest. Even through the fat parka, red was beginning to stain the yellow material.

He didn't feel any pain, but breathing was difficult and there was blood, so much blood. He could feel it hot on his chest and running down into his trousers.

Blood. My blood. I'm shot. He shot me! But he should be dead. He's the one should be bleeding, not me.

'But I shot you,' Hollis whined, blinking at the greyness that seemed to be filling the car.

Stanley edged towards him and took the gun from his limp hand.

Hey, you can't do that . . .

'Cold weather requires extra protection,' Stanley said, unzipping his voluminous red parka to reveal yellow LAW letters on a blue background. He slapped them.

'Put two of them on back to front, just in case.'

Hollis's face was visibly draining of colour, his pupils enlarging as his life ebbed away. He couldn't understand what was happening. How could he be dying?

No, not me. No . . .

Stanley grabbed him by the collar and he didn't offer any resistance, just coughed weakly and leaked blood down his chin. Stanley then swung him round to the open door and held him in its gap, his back to the drop.

'You really *don't* know why you were killing those people, do you?'

Hollis's face went blank, dribbling blood its only movement.

Not me, momma. Not me.

'Thought so,' said Stanley and he pushed the barrel of his Beretta into the man's bloody bubbling mouth.

'And it's loaded this time.'

Momma, save me, momma.

'I know this won't look good, but frankly I don't give a damn.'

Momma?

He pulled the trigger and the back of Hollis's head exploded into the cold afternoon air, splattering like polluted rain on the rocks a hundred feet below.

His eyes stilled and Stanley stared into the pupils and saw an emptiness little different from the time he had seen those same eyes close to in the Winnebago. He spat into the slack face, then pushed Hollis back so that he fell out of the car and crashed headfirst onto the unyielding rocks. His broken body began a long tumble down the mountain, his legs and arms windmilling like a broken propellor.

Stanley felt *good.*

The stunned silence in the car was finally broken by screams – and not all from women – and a string of obscenities from Cheryl.

The mother of the boy became even more hysterical as she hugged the weeping child harder than Hollis had ever done.

'Christ, Stanley, don't ever do that again,' said a shaking Cheryl, not knowing what to do as Stanley continued to stare after the receding body of Hollis.

'Won't need to,' he said.

He had no regrets about what he had done but, he realized with sadness, whatever the outcome of their experience, his execution of Hollis had killed a part of his own humanity. Stanley only prayed he would have the time to let it return.

He turned back to the people in the car, all of whom cowered away as they spotted the gun still held in his hand.

'Sorry for what happened and what you saw, but I'm going to have to ask you to suffer some more.'

'Hey man, you shouldn't have—' said a male voice.

'Shut the fuck up,' snapped Cheryl.

'Don't kill us!' said the man she had kicked in the balls, who had shuffled on his knees to the back of the car.

'All of you shut up and no one'll get hurt. Cheryl, check the station. Anyone up there?'

She wiped the condensation off the window at the front of the car and looked up at the platform fifty yards ahead.

'Couple of cops, but that car won't make it.'

Stanley looked to his left. It had skidded off the road. Assholes.

'Okay, people, this is what I want you to do.'

Once he had explained what he required, some nodded, some continued to cower, but all obeyed.

As the cable car ground to a halt in the wheelhouse, Cheryl and Stanley assembled the occupants around them and then they shuffled out as best they could through the car's door and onto the chilly platform, where two cops were standing with their revolvers drawn.

'You two!' shouted Cheryl from within the crowd. She had taken Stanley's gun, while he had kept hers, and she waved it in the air. 'Drop the guns now or people start dying!'

The cops couldn't see Stanley, but the terrified faces of the people in front of them swayed their thinking and first one, then the second, placed their weapons on the cement floor.

'Now everyone get back on the car – you two cops as well!'

Stanley broke free of the crowd and kicked the cops' guns into the crawlspace underneath the cabin, then made them step inside it as the car slowly wound its way around under the big overhead wheel.

When everyone had been herded on, Stanley slammed the door shut and watched with relief as the car dropped under the overhang covering the cables, and out into the daylight.

'Right, so what now?' said Cheryl.

'The lodge.'

They ran through the empty building, their echoing footsteps adding a tattoo to the eerie rhythmic groaning from the cable equipment turning above their heads. Then up the ramp to the entrance, and out into the chill air. There were three cars parked up by the unmanned ticket booth.

'How far is the lodge from here?' asked Cheryl as she checked over the three vehicles: one a brand new Range Rover, another a rusted Dodge pick-up, the third a police Jeep.

Stanley pulled out the map they had taken from the OCI agents.

'Maybe a mile.'

'A mile and a quarter to be precise,' said a voice behind them.

They spun round to see Siemens standing on the upper balcony of the wheelhouse, three LAW uniformed men beside him, all pointing high-powered rifles.

'I have to admire your resourcefulness, Mr Fulbright. I may need to re-evaluate our psych tests, because your results did not indicate this level of intelligence.' He began to descend the steps to the car park, his frame dwarfed by a tailored black fur coat and a fur hat. He looked like a Russian general with money.

'The flyer?' he said. 'Hollis, I presume?'

'Yes.'

'Shame, but I admire your tenacity. You've led us a merry dance.'

He reached Stanley and offered him his hand to shake. Stanley spat at it. Siemens shook his head disdainfully, then turned his gaze on Cheryl.

'Miss Kenney, from what I hear, you are even more of a find. I shall enjoy talking to you. Now, into the Range Rover, if you would be so kind.'

'Make us,' said Cheryl.

'Very well,' he said, still smiling.

He pulled out a small white gun and fired it into Cheryl's face, then turned and fired it at Stanley's hand.

'Always willing to oblige,' he said.

Stanley and Cheryl's worlds went blank so quickly that neither of them felt the icy gravel that rushed up to meet them.

36

Cheryl was the first to come around, her head woozy, her body weak. There was a slight pain in her cheek where she had been shot and she rubbed her face but found no mark.

She looked about her. She was sitting in a straightback tubular steel and canvas chair, Stanley in an identical chair on her left, and they were in a large bare office with a desk in front of them, behind which sat Siemens in a winged black leather chair, his hands on the desk staring at them. The rest of the room was poorly lit but seemed bereft of furniture. She couldn't make out a door.

'Interesting drug, isn't it?' said Siemens leaning forward. He was wearing a light grey suit and black shirt, and looked immaculate.

'Borrowed it from some friends in the CIA. It's frozen and formed into a dart and fired from the gun by compressed air. Penetrates the skin without leaving a trace. Its drawback is that it only works when the air temperature is below freezing, otherwise the bullet melts or you need a gun with a refrigeration pack.'

Stanley was roused by the sound of Siemens talking, and the man welcomed him.

'Agent Fulbright, glad you could join us. I was just explaining—'

'Skip it,' said Stanley, trying to get his eyes to work. Christ, he was tired. 'And I resign.'

'Humour. Good to see there's still a spark after all you've been through.' Siemens stood up and walked around to the front of the desk and perched on its top like a friendly tutor.

'I call this my quiet room. I come here to think. I lead a very complicated life and I need the quiet to help me "get it together" as they say. Now, I'm not vindictive—'

Stanley laughed. 'You're no better than Hollis.'

'I beg to differ. I have a reason for what I do: every action has a purpose. Hollis, on the other hand, was patently insane, a man driven by his own demons, but the evil that controlled and pushed him into a godforsaken world of his mind's own making, that is what I treasured and why I used him. I'm not going to bore you with all the facts, but pertinent details won't go amiss. By the way, would you like a drink?'

Both shook their heads, even though their drugging had given them raging thirsts.

It was Siemens's turn to laugh. 'I'm fully aware of the side-effects of N44, but if you wish to suffer . . . Anyway, you are both going to die, I won't pretend otherwise, and you are going to die in a way you cannot begin to comprehend. Few have experienced this death, yet each was privileged – as you will be. I may even tell you what is to happen . . .'

'Just get on with it,' said Cheryl, 'before you bore us to death.'

Siemens smiled broadly. 'Spunk! I love it. You would have been such an asset to OCI, Cheryl. Shame . . . Now, where was I? Oh yes. While you die I will be on my way back to Seattle to erase the final evidence of File Seventy-Seven. It doesn't matter – it's all up here anyway,' he added, tapping his forehead. 'But just in case you've done something stupid, like tell anyone what little you know . . . Hollis tried to blackmail me but I suspect you have foiled his plan. Even if you haven't, I'll cope. I always do. Without corroboration it's just so much fantasy and, besides, you don't know what happened, because if you did you wouldn't be here, where it all started.'

'It started in Gudgen,' said Stanley, trying to bluff, 'with that UFO in 1977.'

'Yes and no. This place is where it really started, about six months later. *This* is the key.'

'Key to what?' said Cheryl, her head still spinning.

Siemens just smiled.

'What happened on the boat?' said Stanley, trying to keep on an even footing with the man.

'Ah, the boat. We found what had crashed – about sixty feet underwater, quite visible. We hauled it up in a net, and landed it on the deck. It wasn't heavy and it wasn't large, about the size of this desk actually. Egg-shaped, I suppose, though more streamlined. Casing looking like scorched ceramic. We tapped it, listened to it, hit it. Nothing happened. It might as well have been a rock. And then . . .'

He drifted off, his eyes fixed on a point over their heads.

'It *was* a UFO?' said Cheryl, for some reason excited.

'Indeed it was. We still have no idea where from, but it certainly wasn't from here – or possibly even now.'

Stanley was astonished. 'Meaning what?'

'Meaning many theories have been proposed by so-called experts over the years – including other planets, other dimensions, time travel – but the truth is we don't know and probably won't know, as I have no intention of throwing the debate open to any other interested parties.'

'But if it was from . . . somewhere else, surely you have a duty—?'

Siemens burst out laughing, the sound like machine-gun fire in the silence of the room.

'I know what my goddamn duty is, Miss Kenney, and it isn't to share. And when the work is done, well . . .'

'What work? Killing people?' challenged Stanley.

Siemens looked at him contemptuously and turned his attention back to Cheryl.

She realized he favoured her in the conversation, and knew that if they were to learn anything she had better play along with him.

'Why were you on that boat? You weren't with OCI then, were you?'

'Good heavens, no. OCI came afterwards, *because* of what happened. No, I was a high-school drop-out, into beer and broads. Scum, really. I know now it was because I was too bright; I was held back by stupid parents and the backwater schooling I received, and I reacted to the boredom by causing trouble. First chance, I signed on to take the nightwatches on the boat, while the Paalborgs and their hand Ernie boozed it up. Their boat was as much a way of getting away from home as making a living, like a private drinking club. But as soon as we got that thing on board, I changed. I could see everything so much clearer, like curtains being drawn back on a bright morning after a night of rain and wind.'

'Very poetic,' sneered Stanley.

'That's *exactly* what it was, Stanley. Poetry. Beauty. Art. A true revelation, almost divine. It gave me a new faith – and that's when the voices started talking to me, telling me what to do.'

'You went schizo. Hollis would say the same,' said Stanley.

'Shut up!' said Cheryl. 'Let him speak.'

Stanley was surprised at her vehemence. Whose side was she on?

'Well put, Cheryl,' said Siemens. 'I remember distinctly what it wanted me to do, and my questioning it and then . . . well, it letting me decide.'

'The UFO talked to you?'

'Its occupants, yes.'

Stanley shook his head, despite the dizziness this produced. 'You're mad.'

'What did you decide to do?' said Cheryl, intrigued.

'Kill everyone, frankly. And I tried. Got to the fishermen, but the government agents subdued me, knocked me out. When I came to, however, they suddenly did whatever I told them, like they'd been drugged or programmed. It was damn weird. Now I know what happened, but at the time . . . So, we got our story right, got back to shore, covered it all up.'

'What happened to the UFO?'

'It disappeared. Just vaporized and dissolved into a pool on the deck.'

'Convenient,' said Stanley.

'If you've nothing constructive to say—' said Siemens.

'Did you arrange the car crash?' said Stanley, refusing to be swayed from the moral issues by the fantastical element of Siemens's tale.

'For Ernie Boscome? You *have* done your homework. Yes, we'd agreed to pay him a lot of money but he was getting cold feet. He *had* to go. Then I let the people in Washington examine me, test me, operate on me even, then I took charge.'

'You took charge – just like that? How old were you? Eighteen?' said Stanley.

'Yes. It was apparent I was privy to information they weren't, like the precise location of this place. My encounter on the boat helped me home in on what had landed here. Then, having located it for them, they were more than willing to meet my demands.

'I began OCI then. I had my backers in Washington, elected and unelected. A private audience with the man who had communicated with aliens invariably drew a positive response from those who were sympathetic. OCI was originally set up to supervise all the work involved in constructing this lodge in order to study the UFO that had landed deep in the permanent snowfield. But news spread – the Air Force, the CIA, NASA, they all wanted a piece – so OCI's remit was expanded, the story of the UFO literally buried, and I was groomed for the top job, taking over in 1987. With Eminent Domain also in hand, originally requested by OCI as a tool to fight against suspected Iranian terrorists – the hostage crisis was on and everyone was paranoid about bombings and assassinations. Carter was desperate to win a second term, and anything that would help counter the humiliation over the hostages was okayed.'

'So he didn't know it was—'

'To help in uncovering – and covering up – a crashed UFO? Good God, no. Carter was probably the most honest president we've had in forty years, but that didn't make him a good president. This is a man who didn't see the irony of telling *Playboy* magazine that looking at another woman with lustful thoughts was committing adultery; who even said he had seen a UFO. Who'd trust *him* to keep quiet about OCI having one hidden away?'

'So what?'

'So what? You're the president of the world's strongest nation, still knee-deep in the Cold War, beaten in Vietnam by a bunch of pyjama-clad goons, and fighting a rearguard action against the Ayatollah who's humiliating you in the eyes of the world. For the man in charge to then actually admit he thought there might be aliens, who by definition would have to be more technologically advanced than the US war machine, was just plain foolish. No, my people got his advisors to get him to sign Eminent Domain as a secret anti-terrorist measure – and once a secret exists, it has to stay secret.'

'What about other people interested in UFOs?' said Cheryl. 'The Air Force had something going—'

'When the government sets up an investigation to prove something isn't so, that's exactly what it's going to prove. Just look at the Warren Commission. Yes, Project Sigma and NASA wanted a piece of what we had, but not only did we have Eminent Domain on this site but, put crudely, our friends were bigger than their friends.

'As you have found out, part of our work has been the elimination of criminals – and not only is that more important than hunting out kooks who've had their bottoms probed by Martians, it's also a whole lot more serious. Anyone who started getting uppity was leaned on – and leaned on all the way, if necessary.'

'By "leaned on" you mean killed?' said Cheryl.

'I prefer "persuaded". OCI has carte blanche to do virtually anything without question, as long as we're not *seen* to be doing it. Eminent Domain and friends in the right places take care of that.'

'And you had Eminent Domain all this time?'

Siemens sighed as if it was all so obvious he needn't say more, but he did.

'The President's signature is required on hundreds of documents a day – letters, memos, acknowledgements, bills, reports, speeches. So many he can't possibly read them all, so he appoints advisors he can trust to keep things flowing smoothly. But if we've gotten to the advisors . . .

'Look at Reagan. Christ, everyone in the *world* knew the guy wasn't all there, but he kept quiet about it until he'd been out of office six years! Bush was so determined to prove being President wasn't so tough, he did half his work on the back of golf carts. And as for Clinton . . . Getting Eminent Domain renewed each year was easy. A national scandal, really . . .' Siemens seemed pleased.

'Even if it allows you to let Hollis loose?'

'Yes. No one knew about him except a few trusted aides – most, sadly, no longer with us. Including Baxter. He's dead, by the way, as is that veterinarian who took him in. A friend of yours?'

He looked at them both, and it was Cheryl who finally snapped and lunged at him, but her co-ordination was still shot and her frail legs betrayed her, and she collapsed onto the floor.

Stanley fell to his knees and crawled over to help her, and it was as they huddled together that Stanley's own anger broke through.

'Who *are* these people you have killed? Why did Hollis have to kill them – the innocent ones?'

'Isn't that obvious? You've already made the UFO connection. Don't disappoint me.'

'But there is no connection between them, according to Baxter,' said Cheryl. 'Different backgrounds, ages . . .'

'Where were you on 26 June 1977?'

'I don't know!' said Cheryl.

'And *you* won't either, will you, Stanley?'

He refused to be drawn.

'Nobody does. It's just another day – no way of checking that far back on where you were or why or what you were doing. But, using OCI, *I* can. It takes time, has taken years, but eventually I'd find out where you'd been. And you too, Cheryl. Conversely, I could find out who else was in a certain place on that date.'

'So?'

'So every one of those people was in or near the town of Didra on the Oregon border that night.'

'So fucking what? There were hundreds in Gudgen who saw a UFO, too. You didn't have *them* assassinated!'

Siemens shook his head as if they were infants too young to appreciate his teachings. He reached over the desk, pulled open a drawer and tossed a revolver at Cheryl.

It landed in her lap and she stared down at the .38 as if she didn't believe it was real.

'What's the trick?' she asked.

'No trick.' He pulled open his jacket and exposed his black shirt. 'Shoot me.'

'No, no, there's something—'

'Check it,' he said. 'The barrel's clear, cylinder's full, the bullets aren't blanks. See?'

Carefully, as if it was booby-trapped, Cheryl picked up

the gun, looked it over, flipped out the cylinder and extracted one of the bullets and held it up to the light, then put it back in, slapped the cylinder home and pointed it at Siemens.

'Come on. Shoot, girl, shoot,' he urged.

Cheryl felt the trigger behind her finger and took careful aim at his chest.

'Come on. Surely you're not worried about doing it in cold blood? You've killed people getting here, you know *I* murder "innocent" people, and there's no one else here to see. Kill me and you might escape. Even if you don't make it, at least I'll be dead.'

She steadied her aim but still didn't shoot. Something was warning her not to. It was a trick. The gun was rigged, there was someone waiting to shoot her, there must be some catch.

Siemens walked over to her, leant down and slapped her across the face.

'Come on, kill me. Shoot me! Come on, you fucking bitch, shoot me! *Shoot me!*'

Anger welled up inside her and she pointed the gun up at his sneering face, her own face contorted in hatred.

He leaned forward and slipped his lips over the end of the barrel.

'Hoot ee,' he urged. 'Hoot ee ow!'

Cheryl stared up at him, her body shaking. To squeeze the trigger was the one thing she wanted to do more than anything. To blow the fuck's brains out and avenge everyone who had died because of his sick orders: the people she had seen die at the computer store, and Mulligan, Clyde, Baxter, poor old Sam Dinkley . . .

She tensed, all her hatred focused through her finger and the cold curl of metal it held.

'Oot me, itch!' Siemens shouted, his voice filling the room as his eyes filled hers.

She began to squeeze the trigger, waiting for the bang, the blood, the release . . .

'Daddy!' she suddenly shouted, dropping the gun to the floor between her thighs.

'Daddy, daddy, I . . . *no*!'

She tore herself away from Siemens and fell sideways, sobbing, her world filled with unspeakable horror and remorse. *So close, so close.* Her head shook from side to side as she tried to blot out the picture that still filled her mind, drool running in a thick loop to the floor.

Siemens stood up and laughed.

Stanley, however, saw his chance and dropped to the gun and, grabbing it, rammed his head into Siemens's midriff and ran him back to the desk, where both men crashed onto its top.

Stanley immediately rolled himself off, pleased his knees were holding out, and brought the gun up to Siemens's face, cocked and ready to fire.

The man was winded but as soon as he saw the gun poked at his mouth he smiled.

'Do it,' he said.

'No problem,' said Stanley. 'You're no different from Hollis, are you? Just he got his hands dirty while you hid in your office in your designer suit like some chickenshit general.'

'Something like that, Stanley. So go on, do it. Shoot me. Blow my brains all over the fucking room!'

Stanley jabbed the gun at the man's lips but Siemens's smile broadened even further, his eyes wide with amusement.

'Go on, Stanley. Kill me. *Kill me!*'

Stanley began pulling the trigger, desperate to blow the cocksucker's smile to kingdom come, but then his eyes blurred and the man's face took on a strange aspect. Like paint running, his features began to meld and blend. Stanley found he couldn't focus. He blinked, squeezed his eyes shut, then looked again at the leering visage beneath him. *Concentrate, Stanley. Concentrate.*

'Shoot me,' Siemens insisted, grabbing hold of Stanley's hand and jabbing the gun into his cheek. 'Right here. Now.'

Unable to believe what he now saw, Stanley looked back over his shoulder at Cheryl on the floor. She was staring up at him, deep racking breaths shaking her frame, her eyes wide with horror.

He turned back to the desk, his own eyes now as wide as hers.

He looked back at Cheryl again, unable to comprehend what was happening.

Then he stared down at the face under his gun, his hand trembling uncontrollably, his mind unable to form words, let alone contemplate a reaction.

'Cheryl?' he finally managed, his voice as weak as his evaporated resolve.

Siemens punched him in the face, but all Stanley could do was repeat Cheryl's name again.

Siemens then came off the desk and hammered him about the head until he dropped the gun and, stumbling back like a blubbering child, Stanley tripped over Cheryl.

Siemens laughed contemptuously and picked up the .38.

As Cheryl and Stanley clung to each other in appalled disbelief, Siemens pointed the revolver at the two of them.

'*That's* why they had to die, and why Hollis had to do it. Now get up.'

Too dazed to argue, they got to their feet, supporting each other as they did so. Confused though they were – and aware that his gun contained six very real, very deadly bullets – they edged out of the room.

He then walked them down a dim sloping corridor with no other doors leading off it, until they reached a metal door at the end with a large single handle in its centre.

'Open it,' said Siemens.

Both hesitated, despite the gun.

'I swear to you that on the other side of that door is an empty room. No dogs, no pit, no armed men, just an empty room. Now get in.'

Stanley reached for the large handle, pulled it down and pushed the door open.

Beyond was a small room that appeared to have been hacked out of solid rock, and it was empty as promised but for an identical polished metal door on the opposite side ten feet away.

'In!' ordered Siemens.

They both stepped inside and Siemens reached in behind them and grabbed the door handle. Cheryl turned to him, her face streaked with tears.

'What happened?'

'You may find out in the next few minutes, but I doubt it. Let's just call it one of life's great mysteries.'

He pulled the door shut with a metallic clang and walked

away, his steps receding back up the corridor until all they could hear was their own laboured breathing.

Stanley tried the door but it wouldn't budge. They were trapped, unless . . .

They both eyed the other door, opposite. Obviously they were meant to open that, but what lay beyond?

Then they heard Siemens calling in the distance: 'Bet you can't resist trying the other door.'

'What's behind it?' shouted Stanley, his voice hoarse.

'Try it and you'll find out. Human curiosity is so reliably predictable.'

They heard another door slam and then silence reigned.

Suddenly Stanley bent double and groaned at the pain that creased his abdomen, his bowels audibly gurgling.

'You okay?' asked Cheryl, though her attention was on the second door.

'Yes. Just gut . . . oh God. Sorry.' He let go a loud fart but it did the trick.

Unperturbed, Cheryl reached for the untried door handle and gave it a slight push. It moved downward an inch and felt as if it would go the whole way.

'So what do we do?' she asked.

'I don't know. What *happened* in there?'

'I . . . I don't want to talk about it.'

'You could have shot him.'

'And so could you, but you didn't!' She refused to return his gaze.

Stanley straightened up and rubbed his stomach.

'What did you see, Cheryl? You said something about—'

She whirled round and slapped him hard across the face. 'Shut up about it!'

She stared at him, her eyes flinty, tears like diamond steppingstones tracing her red cheeks.'What did *you* see, Stanley? What put the shits up you, big man?'

Her tone was cold and challenging. Stanley felt ashamed to answer, but he did.

'You,' he said quietly.

'What?'

'*You*. I saw you, okay? You were on the table. Not Siemens, but you. You were wearing a short red tartan skirt, white socks . . . a fluffy white sweater, angora maybe, your hair long and blonde. It was shaggy . . . You looked . . . well you looked lovely.'

She was flabbergasted. 'But it was Siemens.'

'I know, I know, but all I could see . . . One second it was him and then . . .' He didn't know what else to say; he knew it was true but that didn't make it sane.

He leaned back against the smooth rock wall, closed his eyes and pictured the scene. 'I saw . . . I had the gun in my hand, in his face. I was going to pull the trigger. I swear to God I was going to blow his face off – and I remember I was so angry that you hadn't done it. I'd already killed Hollis and I thought . . . well, I thought it was your turn. Sorry. And then he changed. Sort of melted – and he was you.'

He looked at Cheryl. She was staring at him, new tears filling her reddened eyes.

'I was that close to pulling the trigger, too,' she said, her voice a monotone. 'One more little squeeze and blam, it would have been done, and then . . . then there was a smell, pot roast. Swear to God I smelled pot roast. *Burned* pot roast. And then I was looking at my father. I couldn't . . . My *father* was sitting looking at me, like I remembered him when mommy died, a big man all broken, like a sick tree, all withered and . . . I took to cooking his meals; he was useless at it and I wanted to help, to make him happy but I was even worse! I always burned it. Either he came in late or I mistimed it or . . . Burned pot roast and daddy's sweet rough face . . . I loved him then more than I've loved anyone since, when there was just the two of us and that big empty house without mommy cooking and mommy cleaning and mommy messing with her hair in the bathroom or hanging out the wash in the yard. Just me and daddy . . . But why should I think of him when I wanted to kill that bastard? Why daddy? Why then?'

Neither had an answer worth the offering so silence returned to the room.

Stanley suddenly took a deep breath, grabbed the door handle she'd just tried and pushed it down and shoved the door open. Both peered into the gloom.

It was a large room, also hewn out of bare rock, almost a cavern. There was some light and, as their eyes grew accustomed to the dimness, they both estimated the room at fifty feet square, with curved walls running up to a height of about twenty-five feet. Their door was in the middle of one end of the room; they could have been looking at a section of tunnel. Dead centre of the room was a small platform, like a rock table or altar. While the room's walls were rough, this rock in the centre looked to have been cut and polished marble-smooth. For all they knew it *could* be marble. It was about the size of a coffin.

'Well?' said Stanley.

Cheryl tried the handle to the door behind them, but it was still unyielding. She shrugged her shoulders. 'We don't have much choice, do we?'

Stanley cautiously led the way in.

The light inside the room was yellowish but, try as they might, they couldn't see any source of illumination, and while the small room they had left threw their shadows into relief on the earth floor, it clearly wasn't the only source of light. The larger room was also warm enough to suggest heating, but again there were no heaters visible. As they were inside the mountain, it should have been much cooler.

They braved another two steps.

'This is what it's all about?' Cheryl asked, hugging herself, though not from the cold.

'What?' said Stanley, his mind finding it hard to focus. Too many damn questions.

'This is why the lodge is like a bunker,' she said looking around. 'I don't know what it looks like outside, but Sam Dinkley's friend said it was ugly. Everything we've seen looks like a . . . like an air-raid shelter rather than somewhere to take a vacation.'

Stanley swung his gaze across the ceiling. 'They built *over* this place, you reckon?'

'No windows; only that door in. It was built to keep this room under wraps – and the whole place was built after the UFO came down. Buried in the snow, he said . . .'

They looked across at the small mesa of polished rock.

'UFO?' said Stanley and shivered, but again it wasn't from the cold. 'Never believed in them.'

Somehow neither of them was now convinced of his scepticism. Without realizing it they had edged together and were touching hips. The sudden contact caused them to look at each other and then, without a word, they hugged,

Cheryl's softness melding into Stanley's wiry frame. Together they edged towards the plinth, until they could see its top.

For some reason Stanley had expected to find it transparent, like a showcase in a museum, but it was just rock – grey and dull.

'I've got to touch it,' said Cheryl, tightening her grip around Stanley's waist.

'I know,' said Stanley, staring into her eyes. 'I know.'

Something was guiding them, or drawing them, and they both knew something was going to happen, but they were equally aware it could be deadly. It was like sliding down ice on a long, winding hill road; the slide was exhilarating and exciting, but just around the next bend there could be a truck pounding its way up the hill.

Stanley edged his hand down to the flat surface that stood barely three feet from the floor, but at the last moment he drew back and tightened his grip on Cheryl.

She took hold of his hand and squeezed it. They looked at each other.

'We have to do this,' she said.

'I know,' he repeated. They stared at each other for a time, each trying to read the other's thoughts, but their minds were filled with too many confused images and memories.

'I love you,' Stanley finally said.

Cheryl smiled, a crack in the mask of doubt she had been wearing the last few hours.

'I know,' she said, and pecked him on the cheek.

He didn't ask her if she reciprocated his feelings; it didn't matter, not then. As long as she knew . . .

Together they lowered their hands to the top of the plinth. Inches from contact, Cheryl said: 'I'm sorry.'

Stanley knew what she meant and merely squeezed her hand the harder, then let their fingers brush the cold surface.

Instantly the room exploded into every conceivable colour, from red to green to blue to gold to purple to orange, the light caressing and probing and touching every surface and every part of their bodies like water. It was on their hands, their faces, in their hair, and was slowly but surely creeping into their clothes. It was neither warm nor cold, pleasant nor uncomfortable; it just *was.*

Soon they were drowning in colour, breathing now an impossibility, movement a distant dream. Both tried to scream but their muscles wouldn't respond, their eyes couldn't close.

Light invaded every pore. It roared down their throats and up their nostrils. They could feel its scything power in their ears. It was under their clothes, under their skin, in their lungs, their hearts, their heads. A million colours, a billion hues, lighting up their very nerves. And through the hurricane palette of colours they saw each other, saw *through* each other, saw their bones, their organs, muscles, arteries, veins, capillaries. They were in light and the light was in them, and then the colours began to brighten and blend until all was a golden dreamy fog and they found themselves floating, their feet off the ground, their bodies weightless, their hearts stilled, as they melted together and became one with the yellow-white aura that filled the room like a nuclear explosion frozen within a billionth of a second of its incomprehensibly terrible ignition.

Then suddenly the all-pervading light vanished, the unparalleled intimacy ceased, and they fell to the floor, their limbs entangled, their minds irredeemably ravaged, as impossible darkness stole over them like the infinite blackness of space.

37

Siemens boarded the unmarked Bell 222 helicopter on the pad behind the lodge and ordered the pilot to fly to Seattle, where he would wipe his files and his problems would be over.

Yes, there would be a fuss about Hollis in the cable car, but his men were already in charge (and, once the body had been retrieved, the letter he had been blackmailing him with would be destroyed). And, yes, he would also have to dispose of the bodies of Fulbright and Kenney when they were removed from the chamber, but so what? He'd sent more than two dozen people into that room over the years, and the result had always been death or insanity followed by suicide, and he'd managed to get rid of their bodies one way or another.

He himself could survive in the room but chose not to enter it any more. Whatever lay within the melted rock was uncontactable; its secrets would have to remain unfathomed for all time. Perhaps he would be better off ridding himself of its liability altogether. After all, the entire edifice of his plan was built on the simple proposition that *he* was in charge. It was very unlikely, he knew now, that he would succumb to illness, but there was always the possibility of accidents. Worse, what if he was so badly injured that his enemies in government could move in on him while he was indisposed?

So he opened his trusty IBM laptop. The lodge was wired

to self-destruct, explosives having been placed within its structure so that it would collapse in on itself, hundreds of tons of reinforced concrete falling onto the chamber. And now, of course, it could also destroy the bodies of that troublesome pair – and, with them and Hollis gone, his files wiped, the lodge destroyed, he would be *completely* secure. The work Hollis had been doing might be interrupted, but Siemens would source another sociopath and use him in the same way.

And who would investigate the explosion? The sheriff? Well, as all Ellert officials were so corrupted he could have ordered them to rename their ugly little town 'CUNT' and no one would have objected, there was no problem there. Oregon? Easy – he had the place sewn up. Washington, DC? The lodge was his, he would not be a suspect, in fact he would be allowed to conduct his own investigation, and there would be enough people keen to keep their own and OCI's involvement quiet. (The hidden cameras in the lodge's guest rooms had long been a valuable source of blackmail material.) No, he would be able to handle the flak, especially if he could assure them that no one had been killed – and, apart from the by now late Stanley Fulbright and Cheryl Kenney, the building was deserted.

There were also the two missing agents he had sent to intercept Fulbright and Kenney, but when their remains were found, who'd care?

He patched his laptop through to the lodge computer and overrode the system's numerous objections, assuring it three times that the destruct sequence was indeed required. Just as he thought the computer had developed a sense of self-preservation, it complied and let him have his way.

The lodge was primed to explode in ninety minutes.

He snapped the laptop shut. Ninety minutes and everything would be back to normal. It was a shame so many of his best clothes would be destroyed. His shoes, too, and the shirts and ties, but these sacrifices sometimes have to be made.

38

Consciousness came to Cheryl and Stanley at the same time and in the same way.

A long dream of timeless drifting in warming, motherly blackness, like being wrapped up tight in bed on a cold night, was ended by an approaching yellow light which grew until it became the crescent of a comet's tail that slowly encircled them, the head and tail growing tighter but with the power of a life-saving tourniquet rather than the deathgrip of a noose. Then it began to touch their bare flesh with the gentle caress of a caring parent, a friendly reassuring presence promising safety. And then they opened their eyes and the yellow was gone, but its spirit was still there with them in the bare chamber, invisible but constant, like a true love that can be trusted at all times.

Stanley saw Cheryl lying next to him naked and, looking down, found he too had been stripped. He sat up, surprised his mind was clear. He vaguely remembered the maelstrom of colour that had enveloped every inch of their bodies but, far from feeling as if they had been trapped in a tornado – an event that would have had the power to rip their clothes off as theirs had been (he could see the shredded fabric several yards away from them) – he felt as if he had just woken from a long, fever-induced sleep and his body had been recharged and reinvigorated. He felt great. *Alive.*

Drugs. Siemens must have drugged them. How or why,

Stanley didn't know or care. All he knew was that they had *both* passed out and here they were, buck naked. Then, looking across at the motionless Cheryl, an even worse thought occurred to him: he wondered if she might have been raped.

He stood up and for a brief moment was pleased that, for him at least, there were no apparent repercussions. No headache, no swimming vision, no unresponsive limbs. He leaned down to Cheryl, whom he found looking up at him.

'What happened?' she asked.

'You're asking *me?*' He helped her to her feet.

Stanley was slightly abashed to be naked in front of her, but she didn't seem to have noticed. She walked over to their clothes and inspected the tattered remains.

'Either you're one hell of a lover or something else happened here.'

'How do you feel?' he asked.

She walked back to him, her body moving in all the right places but as if in slow motion. 'Good. Very good. Surprising.'

She ran her hands over her forearms, her breasts, her midriff. She felt marvellous. She squatted down, then leapt up immediately without any ill effects to her thighs and calves or her sense of balance. She felt *great.*

Stanley, slightly taken aback by this sudden outburst of athleticism – to say nothing of the reverberations it set up on her chest – turned back to the low altar in the middle of the room. It looked unchanged.

'And all because we touched that?' he said.

'Which we won't be touching again. Come on.'

They walked the perimeter of the chamber, satisfying

themselves there were no other ways out, then entered the small anteroom and tried the handle on the outer door.

'It won't move,' said Stanley, the cords taut in his neck as he tried to force it down.

'Here, two might be better.'

For some reason Stanley didn't argue. Given her size, she could probably exert a similar pressure, therefore his efforts would literally be doubled. But, obvious as that was, her suggestion made *incredible* sense, as if he *knew* it would work – as if all it took was for them to work *together*.

They both leaned down on the handle, but there was no movement. Both drew breath, then pushed down again and this time, just as they were about to give up, the handle suddenly jerked down and the door clicked open.

'Told you,' she said.

'Indeed you did. After you, madam.'

Cheryl edged past him, her warm backside brushing his balls. He made no objection, though his penis began to raise its head. He wondered if their flippancy, and his arousal, were justified, given their circumstances, but for some reason that didn't bother him. Something indefinable had changed within him; something *positive* had happened – as mad as that might seem – and he was right to feel good about it; he just wished he knew what it was.

They worked their way up the corridor, their bare feet flip-flopping on the cold stone floor, the light from the chamber to their rear casting their shadows ahead of them like scarecrows on stilts trying to keep them away from Siemens's crop of secrets. At the head of the corridor they stopped. They had come to a solid wall. On the right was Siemens's 'quiet room', on the left another door, with no other way in or out of the corridor apparent. They entered the quiet room and looked it over.

It was empty except for the two seats they had sat in previously, Siemens's leather chair, and the desk which had one wide thin drawer. Inside this they found the contents of their now-shredded pockets, including their stolen OCI IDs and Baxter's Eminent Domain warrant. Stanley picked up all three and followed Cheryl across the corridor into the other room.

Opening the door they found themselves in what looked like a hotel bedroom, a king-size plum-coloured bed dominating one wall, a telephone and console of switches set into the wall to the right of its quilted headboard. Set into the opposite wall were a number of small video screens ranged at head height in two rows of five, and a small desk-cum-shelf of buttons underneath. Otherwise the room was empty apart from an open door leading to a small bathroom containing a toilet and shower.

Cheryl sat on the bed and examined the array of switches on the small inset console. Each was marked with its function. She pressed a button marked CLOSET and a door slid open to the left of the bank of video monitors. Stanley dropped the OCI cards and Eminent Domain wallet onto the bed, then took a look.

It was a walk-in closet big enough to pass for a small boutique! Rack after rack of designer-label suits, jackets and trousers ran the length of the long thin room. Beneath were a couple of hundred pairs of shoes and tiered shelves containing innumerable shirts and socks and underwear.

Cheryl also walked inside and ran her hands over the shoulders of the suits racked at head height. She pulled one out at random. It was a Ralph van Lauren.

'Never been worn, I bet. The guy has a fetish for clothes,' she said.

'Among other things,' said Stanley, eyeing a collection of chains and collars that hung on a rack.

She picked up a shirt – Van Deusen – from the dozens that were stacked in the open shelves that periodically broke up the run of suits. She turned it over.

'Still got the pins in.'

She picked up another three. Same story.

Stanley walked past her to a display of socks, literally hundreds of pairs all hanging on a metal tree. He picked up a pair still held together by a Collins nametag.

'The man *collects* clothes,' said Stanley. 'I wonder if the government knows about this?'

'Probably not. It doesn't seem to know about anything else!'

She looked at Stanley. He was still naked. Well, they certainly had an answer for that: an entire shopful of brand new clothes. They would certainly be stylish fugitives. She let her eyes roam over Stanley's body. His shoulders, his well-defined chest with its matting of hair, his tight stomach, his generous penis and balls, his lengthy thighs. A girl could get to . . .

He caught her looking at him and he put his hands on his hips and stared back, drinking his own fill of her large breasts, her cute little stomach, the thin thatch of blonde pubic hair like an afterthought, the long shapely—

Both stopped staring.

'There's something . . .' he said.

She nodded, ignoring the slow role of his penis as it continued to engorge.

'What is it?' he said. 'I mean you're gorgeous and everything but . . .'

What was it? she thought. Yes, he was attractive and yes she had grown to like him, but there was something about his body. She had seen it before, in the guesthouse and in the hotel. So why . . . ? Suddenly she turned him round and examined his back. They were gone; the bruises had disappeared!

She turned him round and examined his forearms, his stomach, his head. Where Hollis had shot him and caused a four-inch-long scar across his forehead, there wasn't even a mark. No scab, no rupture of the flesh, nothing.

She looked down at herself. There had been a bruise on her breast where Hollis had grabbed her before the car crash: now gone. There had been marks on her thigh: vanished.

She turned around in a slow circle.

'No bruises,' she said. 'No bruises, no cuts, not even a scratch.'

Stanley checked her over. 'You're right. You had a nasty scratch across your right shoulder. It's gone. And that cut on your arm.' He ran his fingers over the skin. It was perfectly smooth, not a hint that it had been breached.

They suddenly pulled apart and Cheryl leaned against the racks of suits while Stanley stood, his hands crossed over his crotch, trying to hide his semi hard-on.

Cheryl nodded at his discomfiture. 'Don't worry about that. It's flattering. But this . . . it's that room, isn't it?'

Stanley nodded. 'Whatever happened in there not only had the power to shred our clothes but also to heal our wounds.'

'God,' she said.

'Maybe,' said Stanley, deliberately misinterpreting her oath. He felt very queasy. Something had been done to his body, and he was living inside it. Like a woman feeling violated after a rape, he felt unclean in his own skin. Someone, or something, had interfered with the natural healing processes of his body and speeded them up or cancelled them out or . . . or what? *What was going on?*

He suddenly bolted past Cheryl and ran to the bathroom. He knelt over the toilet and tried to retch but his body wouldn't respond and soon he found himself in the bizarre predicament of wanting to throw up – something he had always detested – while his stomach remained absolutely unruffled.

He sat back on the cold tiled floor and looked up at Cheryl as she leaned against the door jamb, her crossed arms scooping up her breasts so that her nipples pointed at him like accusing fingers.

'Finished?' she challenged.

He stood up, and smiled weakly. 'Yes.' His stomach had never felt so serene; it was a place of resolute calmness, untroubled by his situation.

'You'd better look at this, then,' said Cheryl.

She led him into the bedroom and pointed at the video monitors. There were ten colour screens, though the dull decor of the lodge rendered their pictures grey. Each offered a slowly panning shot of various rooms in the same building.

'No people, anywhere,' she said.

She walked to the small desk and punched some keys at random. The shots changed, some to different angles, others to new locations, some of them becoming less distinct.

'There's not a soul in this building.'

She kept punching buttons, and more bedrooms were revealed.

'Why so many cameras in bedrooms?' said Stanley.

'Blackmail, of course! He gets people up here, supplies hookers, gets videos – and they're his. God knows how many senators and congressmen and others he's got control of – and no wonder he's so well funded.'

Stanley didn't know what to say.

'And look at this.' She pointed at a digital counter under a plastic shield beneath the lip of the desk, red numbers counting down.

'What is it?'

She eyed the number. 'It says "Eighteen: twenty-four . . . twenty-three . . . twenty-two . . ." but I don't see a microwave oven or a video recorder on rewind.'

'So it's the countdown on . . . ?' He grabbed for the shield but it held firm. He started to worry.

'Oh, come on, no. You don't think . . . ?' he said.

'Building owned by secret murderous government agency is empty, we're supposed to be dead, numbers counting down in the private room of the guy in charge, who tried to kill us . . . What am I?'

'We're not playing *Jeopardy*.'

'Oh no?'

'Eighteen minutes?'

'Seventeen minutes, fifty-three seconds.'

'And counting.'

They dashed for the closet and hauled on clothes as fast as they could, both going for Calvin Klein underpants and vests, Guess jeans and a flurry of famous label shirts, sweaters and large black leather coats, thick socks and hiking boots. They then scrambled back to the bed.

'Fourteen minutes, eleven seconds,' announced Cheryl. 'There's a rack of watches; find one with a stopwatch.'

As soon as he had snapped the Rolex onto his wrist, he set its counter running.

'Okay, we've got fourteen minutes before—'

'Right, but how are we going to get out?'

A very good question. Not only did they not have any idea of the lodge's layout but, more importantly, they didn't even know a way out of the *room* they were in.

'Be logical,' said Cheryl, slowly casting her eyes around. 'We know there's no way out of the chamber, no way out of the corridor. That leaves here and his quiet room. If it's quiet he won't want disturbing, so he would control the only door. That leaves here . . .'

'Fine, but where?'

They ran to opposite sides of the room and worked their fingers along the grey walls, rapping with their knuckles, but it was clear the room was carved out of solid rock. They met after completing one sweep of it.

'That leaves the bathroom . . . no room in there for a door, period. So, it's the closet,' said Cheryl.

They raced into the closet and began tearing clothes off racks and piling them on the floor as they worked their way down its twenty feet length.

'Here!' shouted Stanley.

He had tried to pull out a tray of boxer shorts, and found instead that the entire unit had swung out from the wall behind.

'We make a good team, Fulbright,' said Cheryl, barging

past him and leading the way up the spiral staircase, then stopping and running back into the bedroom, where she snatched up and pocketed the OCI IDs and Eminent Domain. *Getting sloppy*, she thought.

They entered a large lounge through a mirrored door behind a bar. It looked like a refugee from a *Crime Story* re-run: the room full of twisted chrome furniture and African art, with wide splashes of dirty reds and browns on the furniture, the throw rugs, the wall hangings. Neither was in any doubt that every item was an original. Dashing across to a door which they pushed open, they ran through into a corridor.

'Left or right?' said Stanley.

'Up,' said Cheryl pointing to the slight rise on the left.

They clattered up the dimly lit passage until they reached three other doors. The one to the left gave on to a kitchen with no exits; the door in front was a dining-room with, again, no other exit; the third was a thirty-seat private cinema, through which they hurried to a door marked EXIT, and on into another large lounge decorated exactly as the first. However, this one had several smaller rooms ranged around its outer edge.

The first was an armoury, its unsmashable, glass-fronted cabinets sneering at their attempts to break through to the tempting selection of revolvers and shotguns on display.

The second and third comprised a cloakroom and a bathroom, both bare.

The fourth was a video-monitor room, which merely repeated some of the screen images they had already seen in Siemens's room.

'How long?' asked Cheryl.

'Nine minutes.'

'Why is this place like a rabbit warren?'

'And no windows? The views outside must be spectacular.'

'Secret is as secret does,' Cheryl said.

They re-crossed the main room to a door leading onto a large airy passage, a skylight letting in blue sky some twenty feet above their heads. To their left was a large frosted-glass door and, beyond it, white and blue.

They rushed over to the door, but it had no handle and no locks. It was clearly electronically operated, probably from the video room, but they couldn't risk the time it would cost them in checking to see if they could identify the right switch.

There was one final door which led – the saints be praised – to a garage, three cars deep, in which sat two identical brown Jeep Grand Cherokees. The floor rose slightly to two large metal doors. Stanley found a control and slammed the green OPEN button. Nothing happened. He banged it again and again, cursing its lack of cooperation.

'Get in a Jeep. We'll drive out,' said Cheryl.

Stanley pulled open the driver's door nearest to him and climbed in. No keys. Cheryl saw his lack of success and ran round to the second car. Pulling open the driver's door, she found keys in the ignition.

'How long have we got?' she shouted, beckoning him over.

'Seven minutes, going on six.'

They climbed in, she switched on the engine, gunned it in first, and let the Jeep fly at the metal doors.

The Jeep slammed into the doors as if they were made of concrete, hurling them both into the dashboard. Stanley banged his nose and it began bleeding.

'Hang on this time!' Cheryl said needlessly as she reversed up, slotted into first, and floored the accelerator.

It took three more jarring impacts, each like the frustrated batterings of a rhinoceros against the bars of its enclosure, before the metal doors succumbed to their onslaught and they exited into daylight and snow.

The doors dragged for several screeching yards, throwing sparks into the afternoon, but then they got caught on the concrete wall that bordered the steep drive leading down to the garage, and the Jeep finally rode over them. Cheryl slewed the car to the left, barely keeping control, onto a road freshly laden with snow.

'Time?' she shouted above the protests of the engine as she missed a gear.

'Four minutes.'

'All we can do,' she said, letting the wheel spin, 'is get as far away as possible.'

The road in front hadn't seen a vehicle in the last hour or more. Cheryl caught a glimpse of the lodge as they drove down the hill, and Stanley turned round to look at it through the misted rear window.

It was only visible as a large slab interrupting the skyline of the mountain's jagged raw edges; and the wrecked entrance to the garage and the glass-fronted door nearby were the only evidence of human habitation. Whatever this place had been built for, it sure as hell wasn't to take advantage of the potential views.

'Your nose,' Cheryl said, glancing over at Stanley.

'What about it?' he said feeling his nostrils.

'It's not bleeding.'

She was right. There was blood on his top lip, and on the

back of his hand where he had wiped his nose, but that was all to be seen. It also didn't hurt him.

'This is weird,' he offered lamely.

Cheryl did not dispute his summation. 'How long now?'

'Three minutes. Getting on for two.'

They crested a short rise and Cheryl slammed on the brakes. The Jeep careered to a reluctant stop, facing sideways against the road, its hood grazing an insubstantial guardrail that offered little practical help against a drop of several hundred feet.

'Look at that!' she shouted, already backing up the Jeep, its tyres zithering on the crusty surface.

They could see the upper cable-car station below them at the other end of a long loop of road. The cable cars were still moving, but what drew their attention was the cluster of vehicles around the wheelhouse. There were three police cars, all with lights flashing, three brown cars so obviously Federal issue they should have had GOVERNMENT painted on their doors, plus a couple of others probably belonging to OCI. A state-trooper Jeep was also grinding a careful path up the mountain road, no doubt to join the party.

Stanley grasped the dashboard in front of him and dug his nails into the plastic, trying to concentrate. 'We've got two minutes. If this place blows, they're all going to come up that way.'

'So we can't drive down it, because we'll get stopped.'

'But we still want to get down to Ellert.'

'That only leaves skiing, or the cable car.'

'It *is* working, but it's also swarming with cops. So,' he looked at his watch. 'With *ninety-five* seconds to go, what do we do?'

Cheryl answered by flooring the accelerator. As the Jeep snaked on down the road, she had to fight the wheel every inch of the way, tyres digging into drifted snow and slush, spray flying like defiant spit.

As they reached the final stretch before the wheelhouse, she eased down and let the Jeep drift into the parking lot, where she rolled it to the furthest edge away from the main entrance. There was one cop on the door and he looked at them with interest, but made no move towards them.

'Right,' said Cheryl. 'Act normal.'

Stanley gave her a look, then stepped out.

The state-trooper Jeep that had been climbing the hill pulled in behind their own and two cops got out, both bundled up against the weather.

'Hi, how's it going?' said one to Stanley.

'Under control,' he said, Cheryl nudging him to get out his OCI identification, which he flashed briefly. 'We've just been ordered down here to see what's what.'

The two troopers walked past them, unimpressed, but while they might have little time for these OCI people, at least they believed they *were* OCI.

The troopers stopped and talked to the cop on the door, who looked over at Stanley and Cheryl, laughing at something one of the troopers said, then stepped aside and let the men in.

'How long?' said Cheryl.

'Seconds,' he said.

'Open the back of the Jeep, and pretend to be getting some gear out. We're not dressed for snow; that's probably why they were laughing.'

He nodded and joined her at the rear of the Jeep, where

she opened the door and leaned into the rear compartment.

He held his watch out in front of her and she saw it reach fourteen minutes – then carry on adding seconds: one, two, three . . .

'Maybe we were wrong,' she offered.

'Well if we were, we're in big big shit.'

He nodded through the Jeep's side window at two men in suits who were now talking to the cop on the door, who in turn was pointing at them.

'I think we're—'

There was a sudden rumble that they could feel in their guts, then under their feet, and then the Jeep began to vibrate. Then there was a muffled explosion and they turned to look back up the road. Nothing.

Then there was a loud *crack* and flames shot thirty feet in the air, and debris began to rain over them and the wheelhouse, most of it snow and ice, but rocks too.

They dived for cover under the Jeep and listened to the thud-thud-thudding on the ground around them, and the tinny thwack of stone on metal and the occasional muted *ssssh* as a windshield or window crazed. Then they could hear swearing and shouting and, as the ground continued rumbling beneath them as if it contained the world's highest subway, they pushed themselves outwards to see several men running to their cars and skidding their way out of the parking lot.

Looking back up to the lodge, all they could see was a horizontal plume of grey smoke drifting towards them across the white mountainside like a lazy serpent, but there were no accompanying flames and, mercifully, no more explosions.

They walked to the doors of their Jeep and were about to

get in – at least they would look as if they were as curious as the panicking policemen around them – when one cursing sergeant stormed up to them flashing his badge.

'Wilkinson, Ellert PD, I'm commandeering this vehicle. Goddamn Raskin's taken the unit.'

Stanley and Cheryl stared at one another, unable to believe their luck.

'You got a problem with that, boy?' said the red-faced sergeant, the remains of his obviously spilt coffee still steaming down his beige shirt front.

'No, no. Take it, take it,' insisted Stanley.

They jumped out and let him get in and drive off, then stood watching as, one by one, every car in the lot was driven up the hill, every one of them using their flashers and sirens despite the fact that there was no other traffic. And soon they were alone; just the pair of them, with an empty parking lot and the cable-car wheelhouse slowly grinding away nearby.

They were about to dash inside – a cable car was swaying its way up the last hundred feet – when Stanley held his hand up.

'Bound to be someone still in there. They can't all have gone.'

He peered through the half-open door and, sure enough, could spot three policemen: two facing away from them in the entrance hall, one waiting for the cable car to arrive.

Stanley leaned back against the building's icy wall. 'Damn! Three of them. All armed. No way we're going to bluff it out.'

'We could try.'

Stanley edged back to check out the cops again: two local and one state trooper. He turned back to Cheryl, a sour smile on his face.

'The two local cops, they're the ones saw us get on the car earlier. They'll shoot us on sight.'

'So what do we do? We've got to get down, and this is the only way.'

Stanley walked to the edge of the entrance platform and gazed up at the roof. 'Let's see what's up there.'

Cheryl followed him as he darted across the front of the wheelhouse to the staircase at the side, which Siemens had used to come down and apprehend them. Then, careful not to make any noise – the stairs were metal – they worked their way up onto the top of the building.

It had a steeply sloping roof that rose in a four-sided pyramid fifteen feet high, but there was a small perimeter walkway that ran to the front of the building, and Stanley led the way. Snow had packed hard into this narrow space, but they managed to clamber round the right side of the roof, clinging on to the sloping tiles whenever they felt themselves beginning to slip.

Finally they were at the open side of the wheelhouse, the cable car disappearing into the void beneath them in order to disgorge its passengers, if any. There was a guardrail set into the two-feet-high parapet that edged the roof, then a steeply sloping concrete overhang above the twin cables, giving a drop of ten feet to reach the roof of an approaching cable car, with a drop of a hundred feet beyond that to the rocks below.

'Well, what now?' said Cheryl, disappointed that there was no obvious answer.

'No idea. Just wanted to see if there was.'

They heard the car clanking its way inside, then slowing down as someone disembarked. Then the sound of loud but indistinct voices and the clatter of feet inside the empty building, as the car began grinding its way around the massive wheel beneath their feet.

Then they heard more voices, a door slamming open, and running footsteps in the car park, a door sliding shut, then the cable car beginning to move off.

Cheryl started to edge past Stanley and work her way round the roof – her hands were freezing and she wanted off it as fast as possible – but a large clump of snow that had seemed welded to the roof and parapet broke loose and, with a surprised yelp, she fell face-first onto the roof's sloping surface, her boots making sudden contact with thin air – and she began sliding feet-first between Stanley's legs.

As he grabbed for her, he lost his own footing and fell with her, his right leg catching on a support of the guardrail, so that he slid down the roof and slammed his balls into the support rail. Too shocked by the sudden pain to yell, he let go his tenuous hold on Cheryl's hand and could only watch in horror as she continued to slide from under him and out over the steep slope of the overhanging roof.

She grabbed his ankle and got a grip with both her hands, her own legs dangling in mid-air over a ten-storey drop.

'Oh God, Stanley, I'm slipping. Help me, help me!'

Ignoring the pain in his groin, Stanley tried to lean over to snag one of her hands, but couldn't reach far enough.

The building beneath began to rumble, and little rills of snow cascaded down the roof and onto the overhang around Cheryl's upper body, like soil sprinkled at a funeral.

'I'm slipping!' she hissed, but she might as well have been grasping at the snowflakes around her, such was the inevitability of her fingers betraying her need for purchase.

One of her hands slid further, and she twisted outwards so that she was facing into the valley, the sky-wide vista mocking their desperate struggle.

The cable car continued to rumble underneath, its overhead trolley emerging into sight as the bright red cabin beneath it slowly swung out into the open.

'Cheryl, jump! Don't argue. Just jump onto the car!'

She looked back up at him.

'You'll make it. Trust me. Go! *Now!*'

She turned, looked down, and let go.

The sudden release of her weight from his leg caused him to whip back and slap into the steep roof with his face.

Oh God. Oh God. Did she make it? He hunched up his shoulders as if they could block his ears to the inevitable scream – but there was nothing. A fall like that and she'd be dead in a couple of seconds, probably no time even for a scream. *Oh God in heaven no, not Cheryl, not like that, not after all this . . .*

39

He braved a look back over his shoulder, saw something on the cable-car roof thirty yards out into the valley, and rolled himself onto his back, one foot pressing against the support rail to give him balance.

She'd made it! She was on top of the car, hugging the trellised metal of its stanchion, her legs hanging over the right side. It was a precarious position, but if she could keep her grip she might make it.

He then heard a shout.

'Hey you, what d'you—? Stop or I'll fire!'

What?

Stanley pushed himself up onto the wheelhouse roof, rolled carefully to one side until he was kneeling in the walkway, then he crabbed his way back round two sides of it to the metal staircase. As he clattered down he heard a shot, then another.

Jesus Christ, the lunatic was firing at her!

He dashed across the parking lot to the entrance, aware of voices shouting at him from the road leading up to the lodge. Storming through the door, he charged down the ramp leading to the cable-car platform. The cop heard him and turned, but was too slow.

With a scream born of anger, Stanley hurled himself at the fawn-shrouded figure, and hit him full-square. The man landed with a loud exhalation of breath, his eyes closing as his gun launched itself into space in the wake of the cable car.

Stanley got up off him immediately and, checking the man's uniform, realized he had knocked out the Ellert sheriff.

'You crazy bastard!' he screamed. 'What were you doing?'

He looked out into the bright afternoon – a too white window onto a too real world – and saw Cheryl still clinging perilously to the cable car's trolley stanchion, but with an added problem in the form of the state trooper inside the cabin reaching out of its open door to grab at her legs. The sheriff must have come up in the car and ordered the man to go down to the town.

But what the hell was he trying to do? Even if he got hold of her legs, he couldn't pull her into the car. The best he could hope for was to pull her off and drop her into the valley below.

Stanley shouted once, but realized the wheelhouse would only eat his words, so he looked round for what else he could do. If the sheriff hadn't lost his gun, Stanley might have tried shooting the trooper in the cable car, but at this distance – sixty yards minimum – he was just as likely to hit Cheryl.

He heard shouting from outside. *Damn!* The two local cops must be coming back. What could he do?

Stanley made to run to the entrance, hoping to jump one of them, grab his gun . . . then stopped and looked upwards.

'No, don't be stupid,' he heard himself saying. 'You couldn't be thinking that, surely? You're not that stupid.'

He then looked to his left. There was a ladder leading up to a small, empty control-room, and running from the top of the ladder was a catwalk that led round the front of the wheelhouse and out over the cables.

No, no. You're mad.

Then a voice told him he wasn't. Of all the options it was the only logical one, so he should take it. 'Do it,' the voice urged, 'for both your sakes.' It was his voice; he knew it was his own voice, but the words . . .

He hauled up the sheriff by his collar and stripped him of his sheepskin jacket, then he hurried over to the ladder and climbed up it. Just inside the door of the control room, a fetid little box smelling of coffee and farts, Stanley found a can of grease which he poured over the back of the sheriff's jacket in heavy cloying globs. He then ran pellmell along the catwalk until he was directly over the cable.

The cops outside were within seconds of bursting in, and would shoot first and ask questions later, particularly when they found their sheriff laid out cold. Stanley had no alternative.

Looking about him he spotted a small piece of discarded grey electrical flex about four feet long which he threaded up through one jacket arm and out through the other. Madness!

No, it was a calculated risk. The alternatives were death or capture, for him and for Cheryl; but this way there was the hope that he might be able to save them both.

He edged his way down until he was beside the cable itself, his feet resting precariously on a very thin ledge. The cable was now on a level with his eyes. Wrapping one end of the electrical flex around the fingers and palm of his right hand, he tossed the jacket-covered flex over the cable and, as the two ends became balanced, he launched himself into space with a yell of terror, grabbing desperately for the other sleeve of the jacket. If he missed he would fall to his death.

But he did catch it and, for the brief second that the grease failed to lubricate the cable, he was able to steady himself and hitch his left hand up so that he could wrap the other end of the flex around his left wrist. And then the thirty-degree drop, combined with the lack of friction provided by the grease, proved irresistible – and he began his slide down the cable.

He saw the snowy cliff give way to a slope of rock-strewn scree at least a hundred feet below him, the eddies of swirling snowflakes looking like shoals of tiny silver fish over an ocean abyss. The wind then caught him and began to buffet him, the insanity of his act suddenly becoming all too apparent.

As he slid down the cable with his speed increasing steadily, the car – originally three hundred yards further down the hillside – came closer and closer. Stanley kicked his legs to help moderate the progress of his makeshift sling, but this had little or no effect. At least the jacket seemed to be holding together, but there was not much Stanley could do except go where gravity took him.

To his horror, his momentum continued to increase, the wind whipping through his clothes, flaring his open coat outwards like the Batcape. God alone knew what anyone watching would make of his appearance – or his insane action, come to that.

He tried to assess, through blurred eyes, exactly where the cable car was positioned, but all he could see now was white. His arms were beginning to hurt and his fingers were numb, except at the joints where hot pain stabbed him with the suggestion that he loosen his grip. If he hadn't wrapped the flex around his fingers he would probably have already given in to this pain, regardless of the deadly consequences. But how much longer could he last? Or the sheriff's jacket, for that matter? It was beginning to fray and smoke – it might soon burn up and plunge him to his death.

He passed right over a group of men – policemen, mountain rescuers – who were hauling a black bag on a stretcher across the mountainside towards an ambulance standing on the road to his left. None of them even noticed him.

Squinting down the cable, he realized that the moving car was only seconds away, and he himself had no means of stopping. Unable even to move his hands or arms, he might as well be a bunch of clothes on a coathanger for all the power he had to alter his course. He was now on the point of colliding with the vehicle – or, worse, hitting Cheryl and knocking her to her death.

Then he spotted her lying on top of the cable car, one of her legs dangling over its side, and her face set in agony as she tried to kick away from a hand that reached up out of the open door and held her ankle. At that moment she looked up and saw Stanley and screamed, just as he finally reached the car.

Lifting his feet at the last moment to buffer himself against the stanchion, Stanley let go of his makeshift sling and crashed into the metal support, the impact forcing the breath out of him, and rocking the car below violently. Then he fell back onto his bottom, his curses tumbling about him as he scrabbled for a handhold.

Cheryl was unable to help him, her own grip tenuous and

now made worse by the car's sudden jerking movement. There was a terrible creaking sound and for a moment both were convinced the cable car was about to plummet to the rocks below, but then the yawing slowed and it continued on its way as if unperturbed.

Stanley crabbed back over the roof until he could grab the stanchion and pull himself upright, with his arm threaded through the metal latticework.

'Jesus Christ!' was all he could say as he watched the sheriff's coat drop off the cable and spin down into the emptiness that surrounded them.

Cheryl found renewed strength in Stanley's arrival and, rolling onto her back, hooked her own arm round the stanchion and dragged her foot free of the trooper's grasp. They lay back breathing deeply.

Shots suddenly rang out again, a piece of roof metal taking flight next to Cheryl's hip. Then another by her knee. Stanley looked back up the length of the cable to the wheelhouse, and saw puffs of smoke from the black hole of its entrance. The cops were firing at them.

'You fuckers! You crazy fuckers!' screamed Cheryl.

Two more shots rang out, and there was a dull thud to the rear of the car and the cabin swayed. Stanley looked back up the hill to see more smoke, and they felt another strange thud.

He grabbed Cheryl's shoulder and drew her head towards him.

'I think they shot the window out. This car'll have safety glass we can kick in now. We could get inside.'

'What about the trooper?'

'He'll be on the floor, scared of getting shot!'

There was another shot from up the hill, but this time there was no impact, not even the whistle of a passing bullet. Either they were too far away – being halfway down the valley now – or the wind had deflected the bullet's trajectory.

On his belly, Stanley edged himself along the centre of the cable car's roof. Reaching its rear, he snaked his shoulders over the thin rail running around its edge and forced his head and shoulders out into space. The drop must have been three hundred feet by now, the rocks giving way to white swathes of snowdrifts that covered God-knows-what – but whatever did lie underneath, any fall was bound to break every bone in their bodies.

He peered down at the cable window, trying not to think of the height – or of the slow swinging of the car as the wind caressed it. He noticed that the glass was frosted, and not due to the low temperature, for a bullet hole was clearly visible. That meant the window was now vulnerable. Without wanting to waste another minute – the trooper would realize sooner rather than later that he was no longer in danger of being shot by his own side – Stanley grabbed the roof rail, curling his painful fingers around its cold tubular steel, then carefully swung his body around until his legs were hanging into space.

The window reached to waist height. If his momentum was strong enough, and the window gave at his first kick, he would be able to crash into the car and surprise the cop. However, if it didn't, he would either fall into space, or the trooper would shoot him in the gut. He braced his feet to either side of the window, took a deep gulp of freezing air and kicked off, bringing his legs together so as to hit the window heel-first.

There was a dreadful split second when the window simply seemed to bend inwards, as if made of plastic, then its resistance dissipated, and a glass blizzard enveloped him as he let go his grip on the rail and lunged his body forwards.

His feet found a firm surface and he hurled himself blindly forward into the car, knocking the startled cop back to the floor and head-butting him. Then, getting to his knees, Stanley checked the trooper was properly out of it, and called back up to Cheryl.

'It's okay. You can get down now.'

It proved easier and simpler than either expected, Cheryl tentatively lowering herself over the back of the car for Stanley to grab her round the waist and pull her in.

They hugged each other, their deep breathing filling the car with a thin fog until they woke up to their new predicament: they were only three minutes from Ellert, and no doubt dozens of armed police were ready to re-enact the end of *Bonnie and Clyde.*

Stanley looked down at the unconscious trooper, a thin smear of blood over his brow. 'That's five years in itself,' he commented.

'If Siemens ever lets it come to trial.'

They gazed down at the town and saw that the cable-car station was surrounded by a twinkling field of blue and red lights.

'Looks like a convention,' said Stanley.

'And *we're* the entertainment.'

'What are we going to do? Jump before we get there?'

Cheryl shook her head. 'That's a fifty-feet drop. If they don't shoot us in mid-air, we'll be shot later on the ground.'

'Looks like the game's up.'

'No, it isn't,' said Cheryl. 'There might just be a way.'

Three minutes later the cable car edged into the lower wheelhouse where it stopped, creaking slowly back and forth. The assembled cops, guns down, shuffled amid tendrils of nervous vapour as they waited to see what had been delivered to them.

A state trooper captain, swathed in a dark leather jacket and carrying his cocked .38, stepped forward and shouted: 'I want to see your weapons tossed out the door. Now!'

No response – and the windows of the car were all steamed up so no one could see inside.

'Toss your weapons out or we'll open fire!' shouted the captain, his face sheened with sweat despite the chill.

His pronouncement was echoed by a general clatter of bolts being slammed back and safeties being released.

'No you won't!' shouted Cheryl. 'Not while I've got one of your boys hostage! Now step back or I'll blow his fucking brains out!'

The captain lowered his gun, then leaned back towards one of his men, who confirmed that there had been a trooper on the car. The captain shook his head and raised his arms to waist height, waving everyone back a couple of steps.

'Kill that cable motor!' he shouted and seconds later the cable stopped moving, the giant wheel above him stilled and the motor slowly whined down into silence.

There was a shuffling of feet then the wheelhouse became silent again, save for the odd groan from the cable over their heads as the car settled.

Cheryl appeared in the door of the car to find a couple of dozen guns pointed at her head and a similar number of edgy cops staring her down. She pulled the trooper into sight, holding the barrel of his revolver in his mouth.

'Doesn't matter how fast or accurate any of you boys are, this asshole dies if I die. Now, which of you wants to go tell his wife and kids you pulled the trigger?'

'Look, lady, whoever you are,' said the captain. 'You're not going anywhere and you know it.'

She thrust the gun into the man's mouth far enough to make him gag, his hand flapping ineffectively at his side. 'What's happening here is you are getting all these assholes out of here and then you and me are gonna talk.'

The captain shook his head.

'Hey, I just blew up a dozen people on the mountain. You think one more cop makes any fucking difference?' She introduced a higher pitch into her voice, hoping it sounded like hysteria. 'This man will *die* in ten seconds if your men aren't out of here. You'll shoot me then, but you try and live with the knowledge it was you made me blow his fucking brains out. And just think, boys, one of you poor suckers will have to shovel up the mess and put it in a bag and hose down this floor. Good memory, eh? Get your Polaroid cameras out for that one. So, ten seconds. This is *not* open to discussion. One, two, three, four . . .'

The captain stared at Cheryl as she counted, trying to read her, but all he saw was ruthless determination, a succeed-at-all-costs desperation. He tried to calm his anger and temper his fast-growing hatred by concentrating on treating the situation with calculated professionalism.

'Six, seven . . .'

'Okay, okay! Everyone out!'

Christ, that was close, thought Cheryl.

There were protests, even a couple of promises that some hotshots could take her down, but he barked his order again and, slowly, the policemen dispersed.

'Okay, lady,' said the captain, as the last man left the wheelhouse. 'Let's talk.' He still had his .38 pointed at her head.

Cheryl moved out of the car and onto the platform.

'It couldn't be simpler. I want that chopper out there. You stop the pilot taking off, me and this trooper here walk over there, get in, I fly us off.'

'No way, lady. No way. You ain't—'

She pulled the gun out of the man's mouth and pointed it at the captain. 'You die, and I still have him.'

'Shoot me, I shoot you,' he said.

'Well, we'll get them to engrave "At least I shot the bitch" on your headstone then. Some comfort, huh? How old are you? Forty? You're only halfway through your life. Maybe five years from a pension? Why throw it away?'

'It's my job.'

'Then you're in the wrong business. I'm going out that door with him, and you're going to let me.'

'Sorry, lady. No.'

Cheryl hooked her arm around her hostage's neck and pointed the gun at the sheriff's face.

She nodded at the ring on his left hand. 'What's your wife's name?'

The captain paused, then answered: 'Elaine.'

'Love her?'

'Yes.'

'Kids?'

'Three.'

'Tell me their names – and by the time you say the last one you'll be dead.'

'You don't mean . . .'

'Say goodbye to your children. Their names. Say them!'

'Jody-Anne. Kevin. Cin . . . Cin . . .'

He dropped the gun.

'Good. Believe me, Captain, nothing's worth dying for. Do what I say and no one will get killed.'

'I'll get you for this.'

'You'll try. Right, I want you to turn round and put on your own cuffs.'

'I haven't—'

She jabbed the gun at him. 'Was it Cindy or Cynthia?'

He pulled out his handcuffs from his back trouser pocket and slipped one end onto his left wrist.

'Now, turn round and cuff your other wrist behind your back.'

He put his hands behind his back and fumbled the other cuff onto his right wrist.

'Good. Now come and stand behind me, facing away. Do anything and I'll blow his head off.'

The captain did as requested, visibly shaken by her threats despite his bravado, and slowly they walked to the wheelhouse door, the trooper in front, Cheryl in the middle, the captain walking backwards bringing up the rear. They emerged into late afternoon sun, shadows long on the ground.

'Order everyone back, and the chopper to wait. Now!'

'I want everyone to make a path to the chopper. Tell Charlie to keep it on the ground.'

After a long pause, the crowd of policemen and stupid

onlookers parted and they began a slow trudge through the slush in a hundred yard semicircle around a fence to the open area where the black chopper sat, its spinning rotors whipping up snow into a blinding froth.

'Where are you going?' said the captain, embarrassed in front of his men, but trying to maintain some grip on the situation.

'Like I'm going to log a flight plan. Ten minutes I'll be out of the state and it won't be your problem.'

'That'll mean the FBI.'

'Ooh, I'm quaking in my boots. Now shut up and get these assholes out of the way.'

The three ran the gauntlet of hatred and swearing, the impotence of the policemen doubling their intimidatory looks, their body language a dictionary of threats. There were Ellert cops, county cops, Oregon state troopers, men in suits and even a couple of LAW jackets. The phrase 'The whole shooting match' occurred to Cheryl and she forced the all-too-appropriate thought away.

Several cops tried to block their way but one look at the face of the hostage and the gun in his mouth persuaded them that while being held up to ridicule by a mere woman called for a macho stance, reality dictated compliance – at least for the time being.

There were those, however, who though they seemed the most intimidatory, would suddenly cower away as if confronted by a gang rather than a single female. For them the afternoon was to become a confused jumble of conflicting emotions and absurdity.

About halfway to the chopper, and concerned at the slowness of their progress, Cheryl shouted: 'Imagine you were this man? Would you want people getting in my way? Think about it, assholes.'

It seemed to do the trick, though the level of personal abuse rose proportionately.

In the distance a siren could be heard, but Cheryl was focused. She knew that sooner or later someone would have the brains to check out the wheelhouse and look in the cable car and find the unconscious trooper dressed in Stanley's clothes. If he was then to come around, or one of the men was to recognize him, the game would be up and she would be left holding a gun to the head of her own accomplice and, frankly, not one person would give a damn if she shot him or not. Chances were that the two of them would end up shot so many times the medical examiner would probably give up counting the holes.

Stanley could see the helicopter was within reach, but so often things had been so close only for them to lose out that he doubted they'd make it. Cheryl's plan was simple and seemed to be working, but if anyone recognized him . . . In the distance he could see a police car making its way down the mountain, lights flashing, siren blaring. If it contained the two deputies they had evaded in Ellert before they went up to the lodge, they would be doomed.

He began to speed up, hoping his keenness to escape would be seen as the act of a terrified man desperate to obey his captor. Every time he spotted a state trooper's uniform he would turn his head away or look at the floor, anxious that they wouldn't read his nameplate and be unable to match it to his face.

The icy whirlwind caused by the helicopter's spinning blades suddenly scratched across his eyes and he had to duck down to keep from being blinded. *Damn, if Cheryl's eyes caught the blast . . .*

Cheryl anticipated the downdraught – years of flying choppers had made it a sixth sense – and she turned her head just enough to keep the black and white police McDonnel Douglas 500 in view without having snow shotgunned into her eyes.

Above the roar of the engine she shouted for the captain to order the pilot out.

The captain then yelled at a cop near him and the man ran off through the policemen and across the open area surrounding the helicopter. He pulled open the pilot's door and, after a lot of frantic gesticulation, the pilot clambered out as the chopper engine wound down. He trotted after the cop into the crowd.

They were standing just outside the circle of the rotors. Cheryl dug her elbow into the captain's back.

'On your knees!'

He obeyed, not sure what he expected to happen.

Cheryl turned round and, with the gun still pointed at the stooping Stanley's head, she walked backwards to the helicopter. Positioning herself beside him she held the gun to his head at arm's length, then fumbled behind her and pulled open the 500's unlocked door and glanced up inside. No passengers. Good.

She worked her way up into the seat, the gun held at Stanley's head on a level with her waist, then grabbed him by the hair and made him climb in backwards onto her lap.

The captain turned to look at her, then stood up and motioned one of his men to undo his handcuffs, shouting that the key was in his breast pocket, but the frightened young cop dropped the key and lost it in the snow.

Stanley worked his way into the passenger seat, Cheryl slammed the door and began winding up the engine.

There was a commotion by the wheelhouse and several policemen began barging their way through the crowd that had now obliterated the path to the helicopter.

The captain was swearing at the cop who had dropped the key, pushing him onto his backside with his foot, then kicking at the snow and slush as he tried to find it himself.

Cheryl had almost reached take-off revolutions when she saw the crowd part and the trooper from the cable car, dressed in Stanley's clothes and sporting a dramatic smear of blood down one side of his face, stumble towards the captain, who was kneeling facing the helicopter and shouting at anyone who could hear him above its roar to pick up the key he had finally located.

An older policeman dashed forward and picked up the key. Pulling the captain to his feet, he undid one cuff.

The second his hand was free, the captain grabbed the holstered revolver from the cop who had freed him and pointed it at Cheryl's face. She in turn shook her head, her gun on her lap pointing at Stanley's midriff.

The captain was about to run towards her, his head stooped for safety under the screaming rotors, when there was an outburst of concerted shouting and four policemen dashed towards him, one of them helping the limping trooper.

Cheryl pushed forward on the collective pitch lever, and began to lift off.

The captain had a mimed conversation with the policemen – like a game of charades on speed – then grabbed the trooper and shook him. The man nodded, his bloodied face showing his dazed state.

The captain immediately turned and ran back towards the helicopter as Cheryl lifted off, leaping onto the chopper's runner and grabbed for the handle of Cheryl's door.

Ten feet off the ground, his face screwed up against the freezing bombardment from the rotors, he succeeded in getting the door open.

Above the roar of the engine and against the tornado of snow that was quickly dispersing the crowd, he shouted: '*Land! Land or I shoot!*'

Cheryl stared at him, managing to keep the chopper just off the ground. For some reason she knew he wouldn't shoot – and it had nothing to do with his self-preservation.

'What was her name?' she shouted. 'Cindy?'

Whether he heard her or not, he certainly read her lips, and then his face drained of what little colour the howling wind had left him, tears formed in his eyes, and the gun fell from his hand onto the ground below.

Cheryl felt sorry for him, and deliberately dipped the chopper before she pushed him off the runner and he fell back onto the ground.

Immediately he was surrounded by helpers, as Cheryl took the helicopter up and forward over the town until, out of firing range, she circled back and headed northwest along the line of the mountains, keeping her height no more than two hundred feet above the tree tops to evade any requests for radar tracking that might be made by the maddened law officers in Ellert.

On the ground Captain Mondino ignored the pain in his

twisted ankle as men helped him hobble blindly to a nearby police cruiser. All he could see was his youngest daughter, Cindy, a beautiful three-year-old bearing with unnatural bravery the burden of cystic fibrosis, and himself standing over her bed pointing a gun at her head as she wheezily slept, debating whether an end to her suffering was preferable to his own when he would be charged with her murder.

He wept, and those about him sympathized because already his ankle was visibly swelling, but *he* knew why he hadn't shot the fugitive – and it had nothing to do with protecting his men from a crashing chopper.

No, when he had leapt onto the runner all he could see was his humiliation and his very public errors of judgement, and he had wanted revenge: to blow the bitch and her conniving associate out of the sky, regardless of the cost. What he wasn't prepared to do, however, was to kill his own daughter.

So he wept as his confused mind tortured him all the more for his failings.

40

Cheryl pushed the McDonnel Douglas 500 to its limit, her efforts focused on keeping it steady despite the headwinds that threw snow past the windows. Their destination was Seattle, their last hope of catching Siemens.

'Baxter said Siemens's agency was in the Fothergill Building,' explained Stanley without enthusiasm. 'So if he's gone to get rid of any last evidence, we might still get to him, especially if he thinks we're dead.'

'And then what?'

'Don't know. Doubt we'll be there in time to stop him wiping his records, so . . .'

'Exactly. So . . . ?'

'That was smart, what you did to get us the chopper,' he finally said.

'Nothing to what you did on that cable. Took some guts.'

He shook his head. 'No, it was logical. I don't know what happened back in that chamber but things are different now. Do you feel it?'

'I *know* it. When that captain jumped on the chopper, I *knew* when he looked me in the eye that he wouldn't shoot. It's . . . I never felt better in my life, I know people aren't going to hurt me, or you, and I'm sure that what we're doing is right. Righteous even.'

'Even if it means . . . ?'

She glanced at his anxious face. 'You know it's so. Only problem is if we can't.'

Stanley nodded and looked out of his window. The snow was changing to sleet, and he supposed as they got nearer to the coast it would become rain. His memories of Seattle always involved rain; he only hoped they wouldn't also become tainted by blood. If he lived to have memories, that is.

Cheryl turned to look at Stanley. 'Thanks anyway,' she said.

'What for?'

'The cable car. However logical, it was still brave.'

'It wasn't brave; it was just the only option. I could have stayed there and got shot or arrested, or I could have tried to get down by the road – and then got shot or arrested. So it was the best-odds option.'

'And you figured that out?'

'Look,' he said, 'let's be honest about this. Whatever was in that room, it's in *us* now, isn't it?'

Cheryl didn't want to think about that.

'No bruises, no cuts, so at the very least it healed us,' Stanley expanded on his theory. 'But I feel better than I have done since, well, since I was a teenager. Full of life – and no way should we feel that good, not after what we've been through. Before we went in there we felt like we could have slept for a week. Now I don't want to sleep. I want to move, to be up and doing something. I feel so *alive*.'

Cheryl finally allowed her mind to accept what she had been suspecting.

'The things we did, especially you sliding down that cable like fucking Batman . . . No offence, but the you I've known the last couple of days, you wouldn't have done that.'

'No offence taken – and you're right. I'd have hummed and hawed until it would have been too late to do anything, and then I would have just cursed myself for being a coward. But something *made* me.'

'And it's the something we're worried about. All that UFO shit, I didn't really believe it. All this could have been Siemens sitting on a meteorite that was solid diamond, working out some way to market the damn thing. But it isn't. Siemens knew there was something in that thing in the chamber. Something that was still alive. And now it's in us.'

Stanley took a deep breath. 'So why put us in there? Unless he thought we would die . . .'

'. . . which means he's probably put other people in that room who *have* died.'

'Makes a sick sense. So why aren't we dead?'

'Maybe it's slow.'

'No, it's not that. And I'll tell you something else. I think the same thing happened to Siemens when he was on that boat in '77. They didn't just speak to him.'

It was not a comforting thought.

Cheryl wheeled the chopper down through a gap in the trees, found a highway and headed north.

An hour later Stanley spotted the Fothergill Building, black against a threatening steel-grey sky, and Cheryl landed on the roof next to a white Bell 222. It was the same helicopter they had seen fly over Ellert when they were waiting to board the cable car. Siemens *was* here.

She pushed open her door and jumped onto the roof. Then, bent double, she ran over to the other helicopter.

She opened the pilot's door and leaned in, unclipping a Remington 870 pump-action shotgun from a rack between the front seats and, using its butt, smashed the control panel – then ran past Stanley to the roof exit.

Pausing outside the door, she said, 'Assume someone flew him here. That leaves at least one man spare – and he won't be in with Siemens if Siemens is wiping files.'

'You mean—?'

'Yeah,' she said, priming the shotgun. 'Violence.'

'You're enjoying this.'

'Only if we win.'

She took hold of the doorhandle, then pulled it open and aimed the shotgun down the stairwell. Nothing. Just a dozen steps leading down to a bend.

She whispered to Stanley, 'All they've seen so far is a police chopper. They're not going to shoot, but they may well have their weapons drawn. Be ready.'

Stanley checked the gun he had liberated from the trooper in the cable car. Three bullets – again! Just their luck if they found *four* men. Before he could point this out, Cheryl was gone, dashing down the steps two at a time and thudding against the bottom wall, the gun at her waist pointing down the next flight. God, why did she have to act like Sigourney fucking Weaver everywhere they went?

He ran down and joined her. He edged close to her – he could smell her sweat – and asked what they should do.

She nodded at the door with a large 28 painted on it, and he reached for its handle.

'One, two, three,' they counted together. He pulled it open and she stepped into the gap, the shotgun raised.

A wall, an empty passage.

She led the way down its short length to the door at the end and peered round. A man was sitting at a reception desk, his back to her, watching a football game on a TV and supping a can of Pepsi.

She pulled her head back and nodded.

'Twenty feet, dead ahead. Back to us. Got to knock him out before he warns Siemens.'

Luckily the corridor leading to the reception area was carpeted, so her approach would be quiet. Taking a deep breath, she stepped out and began to run, Stanley following. As she reached the man she clubbed his head, using the shotgun like a baseball bat, and he fell like a stone.

She then leaned over the desk and pulled open the top drawer and found a floorplan; Siemens's office was clearly marked in the opposite corner of the building.

'He's up there,' she said, matching up a nearby room marked Accounts with the same room indicated on the map.

They set off together, jogging past the elevators and down the long corridor to the other end of the building.

Siemens's office lay behind a secretary's desk, and its door was closed. Stanley put up his hand and walked over to the door and listened with his ear to the dark wood.

From inside the room he could just hear blips and clicks and the familiar tip-tap-tapping of a computer keyboard being used. He nodded and reached for the doorknob, twisted it, then pushed the door open and the two of them burst in.

Siemens was standing behind a desk in front of a huge panoramic window revealing the Seattle skyline at twilight. He looked up at his intruders, his face betraying his astonishment at their presence. Regardless of the weapons trained on him, he reached down and pulled a silver .38 out of his top drawer and aimed it at Stanley who was slowly walking towards him, his own revolver pointed at Siemens's head. Cheryl walked to the middle of the room, her shotgun trained on Siemens's stomach.

'Put it down, you fuck,' she said.

'Persistent, I'll give you that, but no, I won't put—'

Siemens had almost finished wiping all relevant files on his word processor – as an added security measure he had previously spread the files across several menus, and was now having trouble remembering all their locations and all the relevant passwords. Only his laptop carried all the codes as a prompt, and even these he had to access through other passwords. And then these two fuck-ups had turned up. He honestly thought they'd be dead, but his shock was short-lived as the danger they represented became apparent: if he couldn't rid himself of them, everything else could be lost. However messy, they had to die, and if that had to happen here in his office, he'd worry about cleaning up afterwards – and, knowing they couldn't shoot him, whatever their intentions, he had them. *He had them.*

He cocked the .38 and aimed it at Stanley, fully intending to blow him away, then he'd take careful aim and take care of . . .

Oh God no! No, not now, not here . . .

It was a stand-off. Cheryl and Stanley had their guns pointed at Siemens, he had his wavering between the two of them. Cheryl could now see her father but, fight the image as much as she could, the illogicality of it couldn't break through her natural horror.

For his part, Stanley saw Cheryl, an image of romantic

loveliness, and though he trained the gun upon her his finger was limp.

As for Siemens, he had two targets but both were identical twins, two people he loved more than any others in the world and who he could never hurt. Nonetheless – in the same way Cheryl and Stanley struggled to fight the mad images before them – he tried to reason out his own delusion, speaking aloud.

'The aliens don't have physical bodies; they exist as, well, spirits, ghosts. I've never seen them, so I don't know, but they're so far advanced they don't need bodies. But they do need somewhere to live. We're perfect hosts. They're up here, in our heads. Symbiosis. We provide a haven, and in return they keep that haven as safe as possible. They fight any and all infections we might pick up, from colds to cancer to HIV, and if we're injured the healing process is accelerated. To all intents and purposes we remain in showroom condition for the whole of our natural lives which, thanks to their work, will probably stretch to a hundred and twenty, a hundred and thirty years. And unless we're murdered or involved in a major accident, we'll survive. Get sliced in half in a car wreck, not a lot they can do. Cut your hand, break a leg, no problem. But they've got a couple of other tricks up their sleeve to make sure we keep ourselves out of danger.'

'And this is one of them?' said Stanley.

'Yes. Threaten them directly and something up here kicks in with the person doing the threatening, so they get to see the image of the one person they would never harm. And, however illogical it might be to see your best friend or partner or long-dead parent, your brain just sees a reason not to proceed, and you stop. Brilliant really.'

'So what I'm seeing now,' said Cheryl talking to her father, 'is the last person I would hurt?'

Stanley nodded agreement.

Cheryl's father and Cheryl smiled back at them. 'Pretty freaky, eh? And pretty goddamn useful.'

'And that police captain in Ellert will have seen his daughter,' said Cheryl. 'No wonder he jumped.'

'And what about all those people you had Hollis kill?'

'Same as us. Why do you think I used Hollis? Soon as his victims' defences came up, the man saw the thing he loved the most in his entire life: his mother. And he'd *murdered* his mother. You should read the reports on his head: Hollis was one fucked-up asshole. His mother spent twenty years teaching him *on a daily basis* that love was pain, and he followed that through by torturing her to death – subjecting her to unbelievable agonies – to prove how much he loved her. Every time one of my targets changed into Hollis's mother, he loved them to death again. Only a mind as screwed up as Hollis's would murder the one thing he loved above all else, again and again and again.'

'But why?'

Siemens sat on the edge of his desk and looked at the pair of himselves. It was weird explaining to yourself in stereo why you did what you do, but the longer he talked, the more chance he thought there might be of breaking down this alien defence mechanism. After all, wounds might heal quicker, but holes in heads couldn't be plugged – and all it would need would be two little squeezes.

'It's taken me a while to fit it together but the dreams . . . What crashed offshore at Gudgen was a mothership. And the other UFOs – they were lifeboats. Only the one in Ellert came down in one piece and remained intact. One hit the ocean, God knows where. Another hit a cliff face in Canada and exploded, watched only by some caribou. The third exploded over a town called Didra, and about three hundred people who saw it suddenly became host to three hundred aliens – and have been their hosts ever since. That in itself could have been dealt with – quarantine the town, develop a cover, remove the infected individuals – but unfortunately the explosion took place over the highway about a mile and a half south of the town, at a time when it was packed with tourists *leaving* the Annual Didra Woodcarving Contest. Virtually everyone who was affected that night lived somewhere else – and there's a surprising number of people who'll travel a long way to see wood being carved – which is why we've had such problems tracking them down.

'None of them know it, of course, but some of their doctors must have thought something's mighty odd with cancers suddenly clearing up, prostates shrinking, bad gums coming good, ulcers healing . . . Three hundred people in perfect health, and all of them careful to avoid anything that might endanger them. Skydivers who have grounded themselves, drunk drivers who don't drink anymore, junkies who kicked their habits. And think of wives who no longer get beaten, guys who don't get bullied or picked on by their boss. Anyone threatens them, this defence mechanism jumps into the fray, and whoever's threatening them backs off. They don't know why; they just do. Consequently we have three hundred very safe, very healthy, very ordinary people all going about their business, their whole existences dictated by the need for that thing in their head to survive. And, as long as they do survive, *my* friends up here are kept at bay.'

'What do you mean?' said Stanley.

'Prison ship. The big UFO that landed off Gudgen was carrying rejects and bad cases, and when it developed a malfunction the guards took off in their lifeboats, convinced that when the ship hit, it would be destroyed – and all the fuck-ups in it. 'Cept it didn't. It was programmed to, but not before we'd got it up out of the water, and those still alive in it had found me. And *they* have their own agenda for survival.'

'So why kill these other people? You break out of prison, you don't go round killing all the guards?' said Cheryl.

'You do if their existence is what stops you carrying out your crime. Imagine you'd planned the perfect robbery, but the guards you had in prison knew about it. Get rid of them and there's no witnesses, and no one to stop you.'

'But they're not planning a robbery, are they?'

'Oh yes, they are. About five billion of them in fact.'

'*Five billion?*' said Cheryl. 'Oh God . . . you mean . . . you mean the population of the earth?'

'Yes. Every last one.'

'And it's only the things in *our* heads and those in the heads of the people from Didra stopping you?' said Stanley.

Siemens nodded and tapped more keys on his laptop.

'Stop that!' ordered Stanley to the false Cheryl.

'Or what?' He touched a couple more keys, and smiled as more evidence vanished forever.

Cheryl edged towards her father. 'So what happens when you've eliminated all of . . .'

'Say it. Don't be ashamed.'

'All of *us*.'

'Then my friends can set to work.'

'Doing what?'

'Establishing their own eminent domain here on earth. And, incidentally, justifying all the anti-alien paranoia. Ironic really.'

'How will they take over?'

'I have friends in high places. They will be persuaded to do . . . things. Pretty soon this country will be in a position to fuck up the world – and everything in it.'

'But the good and the bad things which are now up *here*,' Stanley pointed at his head. 'They all need *us* to survive.'

'No, they don't. *Your* friends just need somewhere safe to live while they guard *my* friends. As long as just one of your friends lives, my friends are kept at bay, but when all are eliminated they can do as they wish.'

'*Our* friends are that powerful?'

'No, *my* friends are that weak. For every one in your head there are dozens in mine, but without restraint they can grow and multiply and take host in other bodies and spread and—'

'Which bodies?'

'Those friends of mine who are in a position to further their search for eminent domain.'

'How?'

'By destroying humanity.'

'*How?*'

'These questions are so tiresome.' He tapped more keys. 'Any way they choose. Disease, famine, warfare – nuclear or biological – any means will serve. And once they have achieved dominance, then they will be free to wander the big nothing they have created.'

'In you?'

Siemens didn't answer; *couldn't* answer: they wouldn't let him consider his eventual fate, only offer him the future they desired.

'But what happens when *you* die?'

'They'll be free. Remember, they have no physical existence and are trapped in my head only as long as their guards exist in your heads, and in all those other heads out there.'

Cheryl found it difficult to grasp the enormity of what Siemens was telling them, then she remembered something:

'You thought we'd die in that room, didn't you? Even before you set off the explosion.'

'Yes,' he said frowning. 'I'd sent others in there. They all died, one way or another.'

'Who?'

'My people.'

Stanley spoke up. 'By your people you mean loyal OCI people: your killers?'

'Yes. Who else could I trust once they came out of the chamber? Unfortunately, most of them didn't. And those that did were insane. Our alien friends in the chamber don't take kindly to *my* kind of people, but they obviously *love* you two.'

But why? Stanley asked himself. He was a killer twice over and Cheryl too had tried killing Hollis. Either they had survived because they were fundamentally good, or the aliens were using Cheryl and himself to get to Siemens. (The cynic in him favoured the latter; after all, Siemens had said they were playing host to guards whose prisoners the bastard was carrying in *his* head.)

Just then there was a knock and the office door opened,

and Stanley and Cheryl glanced over to see a man in blue jeans and red sweatshirt holding several sheets of drawings. 'Hey, Karel, you never said . . . Oh shit,' said the man.

'Come in, Jeff. Come in!' said Siemens. 'You might just have saved the day.'

'Run!' shouted Stanley, but Jeff Beam, SB&H's creative director, was hesitating, and Stanley knew it was too late.

'Come in and walk over here. Now!' said Siemens.

'Look, what's going on? These two trying to rob you?'

'Could say something like that. Just get over here, Jeff.'

The guy slowly walked around the edge of the room, keeping as far as possible from Cheryl and Stanley, who kept their guns trained on Siemens.

Beam spotted Stanley's uniform. 'You . . . you a cop?'

'Yes, so do what I say and stop where you are.'

'You stop, Jeff, and you're dead,' said Siemens. 'They're not what they seem. You ever seen cops wearing Cat boots?'

Beam looked at their feet, then hurried over to Siemens.

'Good. Now look at this,' Siemens said, pointing at the screen of his computer.

Beam looked down at it, screwed up his face as if he couldn't read it, then leaned closer. 'It's—'

Too late. Siemens had him round the throat, the gun to his head, his face ablaze with joy. 'Now it's a different ballgame. You two drop your weapons – or I drop him.'

Cheryl looked at Stanley. They didn't have any choice, but they still had one advantage. Siemens wouldn't shoot them; *couldn't* shoot them.

Stanley let the gun roll from his hand and then fall to the floor. Cheryl slowly bent down and leaned the shotgun against the chair on her right.

'That's better. Now Jeff and I are going out that door, and you are going to stay here.'

'That's assuming we let you.'

Siemens laughed. He could see Cheryl and Stanley again, now that his anger was focused on Beam. 'But you two are the *good* guys. You're not about to let this poor innocent creative director die, are you?'

'Why not? Just be another on your list,' said Stanley. 'Only difference is *you'd* be pulling the trigger this time, not Hollis.'

Siemens considered this. Given the way they'd survived Hollis's murderous pursuit, perhaps Stanley wasn't lying and, now they had their alien baggage, maybe . . . No, of course not. They couldn't let him kill Beam. It wasn't in them, or in their benign benefactors. Logic would dictate that the safest option for them would be to let him out of the room at any cost.

'No, you won't. *You're* not murderers, leastways not from choice. You won't do anything.'

Cheryl's mind was racing, all the choices set out before her like a game of chess, with every possible combination of the next five moves laid out clearly. She was able to pick out the consequences of all actions and see the safest – and whatever happened, it all led to the same conclusion: Siemens would kill this guy.

With Beam dead there was still the possibility Siemens could cover his tracks and come out of this mess intact (after all, he'd kept working on that computer; there must be data still to be erased). Leave Beam alive and he'd be a witness against him, so whether it was in here or in the corridor or in the lobby, the creative director was going to die. Logic thus dictated that, given that Beam was expendable, the most important thing to do was retain contact with Siemens until an opportunity presented itself to neutralize him.

She looked over at Stanley, and he looked back. They couldn't read each other's minds but both knew instinctively they had reached the same conclusion.

Stanley turned to the creative director, the man's wide eyes scanning the room as if a SWAT team were about to make a miraculous appearance.

'I'm sorry, Mr Beam, but your boss is going to kill you whatever happens. We're not letting him leave.'

'But I don't know—'

Siemens increased his pressure on the man's neck.

'You logical bastards! Is it any wonder I want you all fucking dead?'

He walked round to the side of his desk, his back to the window overlooking the rainy Seattle dusk.

Cheryl advanced towards him, blocking his exit.

'I'll shoot him!' shouted Siemens.

'Yes, you will,' said Cheryl. 'But then what? Back to square one, except that shot'll be heard by security. And soon you'll have the whole Seattle Police Department up here. Your chopper's out of action; so's the pilot. You sure your friends in your head could take out a couple of dozen men at once? Christ, the way cops shoot themselves, they might get you by accident! So let's just be realistic. You let—'

Stanley had been judging the distance to Siemens. He knew he couldn't attack the man – he might as well start laying into Cheryl – but he could focus on the hostage. What he needed was to get the man away from Siemens. If he could then shield him, Beam would be safe: Siemens couldn't shoot Stanley.

There was a chair to his left and front. It would give him the lift he needed to get over the desk.

A small voice tried to dissuade him from his action. Logic had already dictated that Beam was expendable because Siemens would kill him anyway, but Stanley wasn't going to surrender just yet. Too many innocents – human and alien – had died already. *He* was going to make a difference.

As Siemens talked to Cheryl, Stanley jumped up onto the chair, got the rebound he wanted from its springs, and launched himself headlong across the wide table, his arms open. He grabbed Beam round the waist and used his momentum to wrench him from the startled Siemens's grasp and pull him away and on towards the window.

Too late he realized his mistake, and with a sickening *whuump* he and Beam crashed full force into the deep window. There was a long second as the window reverberated, their reflected images bending to breaking point, but it held and, instead of plummeting thirty storeys, they bounced back and fell to the floor, stunned, the glass continuing to vibrate like a bell.

Siemens had been knocked over, but quickly regained his feet. As he stood up he grabbed for his gun on the desk, but Cheryl ran around to him.

Siemens smiled and turned his gun towards Beam's head, taking aim past her.

'Pointless,' he said. 'Brave but pointless.'

Cheryl forced herself onto the gun, feeling its barrel press into her sternum. She looked into her father's face and ordered him to pull the trigger. 'Shoot *me*. Now.'

Their eyes locked, hers on her father, Siemens's on his

own image. He wanted to fire, to show them his true power, but he couldn't shoot himself – that would be suicide.

Instead he backed away from her, grabbed his laptop computer, and trotted across the room and out into the corridor.

Letting out a long breath, Cheryl turned to the two other men. Stanley was beginning to rise, but Beam had a large egg forming on his forehead, and could do little but sit back against the wall and try and focus through his pain.

Cheryl shook him by the collar; the man was actually going cross-eyed. 'Where will he have gone? Has he got a car?'

'He . . . yes . . . limo. Downstairs.'

'Basement or out front?'

'Basement. Level 5.'

'How would he get there?'

'Elevator. Private. He's got the only key.'

'Right, let's go.'

'What's going on?' Beam said, his eyes wide and unblinking.

She picked up the shotgun. 'You're creative, you'll think of something, but I guarantee you won't guess the truth.'

Stanley picked up his .38. 'That's for sure.'

As they ran out of the room Beam reached up for the telephone, but something short-circuited in his brain and instead he slumped back, unconscious.

They charged out of the office and ran full-speed down the long empty corridor to the elevators, the numerous advertisements framed on the wall failing to attract their attention.

At reception they found two main elevators with a smaller single-door elevator in the centre. Stanley banged all the call buttons and was rewarded with two *up* arrows from the large elevators, but no response at all from the middle one. He guessed it would be locked off.

'He's gone into the basement,' said Cheryl, thinking it through. 'He has to get out of the elevator, into the car, start it up, drive up four levels, key the exit gate, drive up onto the street. He's got only a couple of minutes on us and I doubt his private elevator is express, so if we can get out the front to the parking exit—'

'We may just be in time for him to run us over!'

'We could always shoot out his tyres.'

'Would you shoot out your dad's tyres?'

'This is ridiculous! What *are* we going to do?'

'Follow him and hope?'

'Great plan.'

'Don't blame me. Blame the little boogers up here.' He tapped his temple.

'He took his laptop with him, so there must still be evidence in it,' said Cheryl.

'Not just *in* it, or he could have shot it up and killed it. He needs it to key into a workstation or a mainframe. Get that laptop and we may still have ourselves some evidence.'

After much nervous shuffling, frantic button stabbing and cursing, the left elevator finally arrived and they piled in, Cheryl jabbing the G button until her fingernail broke.

The ride down seemed interminable, both of them only grateful that it was Sunday and the building was empty, so the elevator didn't have to call at any other floors.

'Security?' asked Stanley as they dropped past tenth.

Cheryl held up her shotgun. 'You'd have to be pretty stupid to argue with this for only three dollars an hour.'

'But then you'd have to be pretty stupid to even work for three bucks an hour . . .'

The elevator halted smoothly, the doors slid open and they stepped out into an empty grey marbled foyer. Ahead of them were the front doors to the building, locked no doubt and to the right stood a wide security desk. It was unmanned.

'Maybe they're off eating.'

Cheryl had a sudden terrible thought and leaned back inside the elevator. Oh shit. She stepped back out.

'There's a camera in there.' She looked down at her shotgun, then at Stanley's .38.

'Oh hell,' muttered Stanley.

'Oh hell, yes!' shouted a triumphant voice from his right. Stanley spun around to see a blue uniform topped by long hair and a scuzzy cap standing thirty feet away, his gun held at arm's length and pointing at their chests.

'Lady, don't even twitch!' It was a voice to their left now.

Carefully turning their heads they saw a middle-aged man in a tighter version of the other guard's uniform, a huge .44 Magnum waving uneasily at them.

'We haven't got time for this,' muttered Stanley.

'Well, let your boogers do the talking.'

She stepped out into the foyer, turned to face the middle-aged guard, and held her shotgun over her head. 'Well shoot me, you fucker. Right between my eyes.'

Seconds later the man had lowered his gun and was mumbling something about Janis into his chest.

'Hey, Bob, Bob, what's happening?' shouted the other guard, his bravado evaporating.

Stanley started to walk towards him.

The younger guard was suddenly frightened, despite having his gun and a hat with SECURITY written on it.

'What's happening,' said Stanley, 'is you're about to shit your pants.'

'Hey, get back. What do you . . . ? Come on, man, I don't wanna have to . . . Oh God, come on . . .'

Stanley had reached him and held out his hand.

'You don't want to shoot me, do you?'

The man – little more than a teenager really, acne betraying his youth – started to cry, his face a study in puzzlement and fear. 'What you doing here, dad?'

'Saving the world, apparently,' said Stanley, swapping his depleted .38 for the kid's revolver.

Cheryl called over to him. She had taken the other man's hefty .44.

'Come on, Stanley. Time's wasting.'

They ran towards the main doors, skidding to a halt as they reached their huge glass obstruction.

Cheryl grabbed for the bar and pushed, then pulled, then tried the other door.

They both turned to look back at the guards.

'Any of you two got the key?' Stanley shouted.

The two weeping men, one leaning against the wall, face buried in his hands, the older man on his knees talking to the cap he was rotating in his hands, offered no response.

'Shit!' said Stanley.

'Stand back. No time for finessing.'

Taking three steps back, Cheryl slid the barrel on the pump, then fired at the right-hand door.

Blam! Instantly a hole appeared, in the middle of a field of white, and then the entire door dissolved with a loud *siiish* onto the tiled steps outside.

'Not exactly subtle,' said Stanley, as they stepped through the door and carefully crunched their way over the debris and out into the rain-soaked evening.

'But strangely effective. Which way's north?'

Stanley led the way to the right, running across a wide mezzanine, then down a long sweep of lawn to the sidewalk. Several people had stopped to watch their progress, one couple ducking out of the way. Stanley didn't want anyone trying to stop them, so he made sure everyone could see his gun.

They rounded the end of the building, rain lashing their faces, and came to the ramp leading down to the underground car park, but Stanley didn't stop there. He ran straight out into the two-lane road and was instantly illuminated by headlights.

'*Stanley!*' screamed Cheryl, only just managing to skid to a halt herself.

He froze, unable to decide whether to run on or dash back.

Cheryl dropped to one knee and drew up the shotgun, intent on blasting the car, but the overhead lighting gave her a glimpse of the driver – and when she saw her father her finger stilled.

Stanley tried to pull up his .38 but he too caught a glimpse of Siemens – in the image of Cheryl – and knew he couldn't shoot the woman he loved. By then it was too late to get out of the way.

Siemens gunned the Lincoln and aimed for the brightly lit figure static in his beams. He had guessed they would follow, but not that they would manage it so fast. Still, he could end it once and for . . .

Then he saw himself standing there, and hiked the wheel to the right. The car slammed against the ramp's wall, then careened back and up the ramp, where it took off and flew into the street and grounded amid a shower of sparks, before roaring off.

Stanley felt the side of the car brush his knees, but it otherwise missed him and he could only stare after it in astonishment as it sped away. But then he could see their only chance disappearing, when they had been *so* close, and with a howl of outrage he turned and ran after the speeding vehicle.

Cheryl started to run after Stanley, stuffing the heavy pistol into her pants waistband as she tried to catch up with him, but the man was powered by anger and was quickly outpacing her, though how he hoped to catch up with a speeding car she didn't know. She suddenly heard car horns and realized that she herself was in the middle of the road, so she slowed and crossed over to the other sidewalk. Then, as the Lincoln receded into the distance with Stanley racing after it, she came to a halt. What the hell could she do?

She wondered about going back up to Siemens's office and seeing if he really had wiped his computer, but already she could hear police sirens responding to their recent fracas in the lobby and, love her or not, the security guys would recognize her – and, with her and Stanley's fingerprints all over the computer store and poor old Clyde Hetherington's surgery, they would already be FBI targets.

She edged back into an apartment-building doorway as red and blue lights strobed the street and a siren scream announced the arrival of cops. Luckily they hadn't yet spotted the stretch Lincoln being pursued by a madman with a shotgun, but that too would only be a matter of time. Cheryl needed to think of a way of helping Stanley.

She started to walk briskly, hugging the buildings and nipping across sidestreets as she came to them. Traffic was heavier than she would have expected for a Sunday evening, and she noticed that the main drag was grinding to a halt. There was a chance Siemens might be caught up in it, and if he was, then Stanley would have a chance. She began jogging, and soon spotted the cause of the jam.

There was a carnival in full swing in a park, the illuminated rides lighting up the lowering afternoon. As she watched several hundred people thronging about the attractions and stalls, the raucous sound of laughter and over-amplified music was gradually drowned out by a white ghost slowly descending from the heavens, its rotors whipping the air into a chilly maelstrom that rummaged through the crowd's clothing and bit into any face brave enough to stare up at it. Now, if only she could use that . . .

She felt the handle of the gun in her waistband. No, too risky. There'd be cops – she could already see them on crowd control – and she couldn't guarantee to look them *all* in the face, and with the lights and the noise and the wind . . . And then she remembered. She had something more powerful than any handgun: more powerful than *any* weapon.

She began pushing her way through the crowd to the improvised landing pad with its giant H painted on the grass.

41

For the first time that he could remember, Stanley was pleased that the traffic was snarled up. He had just run past a carnival, and it looked like the cars either trying to leave or enter the park were causing the problem. Both that and what seemed to be an accident on an expressway that shot over the street a couple of hundred yards ahead. There were several police-car and ambulance lights flashing over to the right, with vehicles moving very slowly and backing up the ramps.

And then he saw the Lincoln, stranded in fender-to-fender traffic a hundred yards ahead. Despite being out of breath, he found his second wind and ran, hunched down, towards the limo between the rows of stalled vehicles. The trouble was: what could he do when he caught up with Siemens? Walk up to the car and pump all he could into it?

Objection number one, it was bulletproof, guaranteed. Number two, therefore, he wouldn't get Siemens anyway. Number three, any cop within earshot would see what was happening and be on the scene before he could finish. And then all Siemens would need to do was get out of the car, change into goddamn Cheryl, and Stanley would drop his gun and beg forgiveness; then Siemens would order in the cops and he'd be hauled off God knows where. But, to add to all these there was a number four.

Because he *knew* Siemens was driving the limousine, he

didn't believe he would actually manage to shoot at him anyway, blacked-out windows notwithstanding.

Slowing, Stanley slipped the shotgun up under his armpit and proceeded between the two lines of traffic. The persistent rain bathed his face and hair, and he had to wipe his brow a couple of times to stop drops running into his eyes. That his clothes were getting soaked mattered not a jot, but the gathering dark, despite the streetlighting, was beginning to make colours indistinct and playing tricks with his eyesight – and he had enough optical illusions to cope with already.

Stanley ducked down behind a VW Rabbit and edged along the passenger's side. If Siemens caught sight of him, he'd only have to step out of the car and it would be over.

The next car was a Rolls Royce, of all things: a black convertible. He crouched down and crossed behind it, hugging its curves until he was level with the driver's door. Then there came a tap on the window and an electric hum louder than the idling engine.

'What the hell do you think you're doing?' said a voice.

Stanley looked up and blinked rain out of his eyes. A black guy in a grey suit – probably a lawyer – was giving him a look he must have learned from one of his meaner clients. Stanley shortcircuited their discussion by sliding out the shotgun and tapping the man's immaculate paintwork.

'Rain's getting in your car, sir.'

'So it is,' said the guy, his face suddenly assuming the aspect of a client who had just been handed a five-year stretch.

The window wound up and Stanley continued his advance on the Lincoln but, just as he reached the front of the Rolls

Royce, the traffic started to move again. *Shit!* And the brake lights of the Lincoln suddenly went out as it crept away from him. As it gave a sudden spurt, and headed for a gap in the inside lane, Stanley threw caution to the wind and, running after it, hurled himself onto the trunk, grabbing the boomerang-shaped antenna and hauling his feet up onto the wide fender. Then he pulled the shotgun over his head and latched it round the antenna so that it wouldn't slide off.

Just as he was pondering the value of this move, the Lincoln suddenly veered left, roared through a car-long hole left by a stalled Toyota, and mounted the kerb, scattering pedestrians as Siemens righted the car and began to use the sidewalk as a third lane.

Stanley had little alternative but to hold on for dear life. As long as Siemens didn't catch sight of him in his mirror he would be safe, except, of course, that he would still be subject to centrifugal force: already the car was weaving from side to side and, to Stanley's horror, his left leg slipped and began dragging on the sidewalk.

As she reached the edge of the crowd and found the first of several policemen holding back the ring of people from the descending helicopter, Cheryl remembered something Stanley had said: something about the flash of an ID being enough to get people onto a crime scene. She decided it was worth a try here with these cops.

She pulled out her OCI card – the one belonging to a Harley Bennet – and collared a cop.

'Bennet, OCI. Who's in charge here?' she shouted into his ear.

The cop barely had time to take in the red initials on the card's grey background before she put it away.

He pointed across the circle to a man wearing a yellow rain slicker and a police cap covered in plastic to protect it from the rain.

'Sergeant Ramirez! What's it about?'

But Cheryl had already gone, working her way around the edge of the crowd like a seasoned busker begging for cash.

After a minute or so she reached Sergeant Ramirez and again flashed her ID.

'Bennet, OCI. I need some help!' she shouted above the roar from the helicopter. It was seconds away from landing.

'Bit busy now, ma'am. Can't it wait?'

She shook her head. 'Pursuing a fugitive! Need assistance!'

He perked up at her explanation – it was obviously a damn sight more interesting than crowd control. He scanned the rain-soaked cheering mob that surrounded the landing area.

'Who? Where?'

'I need the chopper! Need your help getting it!'

He pointed up at the approaching whirlwind. 'Coast Guard! Not my jurisdiction! You'll have to ask them!'

His words were all but stolen by the wind and roar.

'I know, I know!' she yelled. 'But I can't get to them without your help!'

The wheels of the white Sikorsky S-61 Sea King touched down and its bulbous body settled like a brooding goose.

'What about a police chopper?'

'Already on the job!' she screamed, her throat beginning to hurt with the effort.

'I didn't hear!'

'How could you?' she screamed pointing at the helicopter.

He smiled and nodded.

As soon as the Sea King was secured, the sergeant waved her to stay, then trotted over to the door that was sliding open in its side, and waited as a man climbed out. Unfortunately he was dressed as a sea hawk. At the sight of him, the gathered crowd let out a yell that could be heard even above the helicopter's motor, and as the man-bird started to trot around the chopper, the downdraught steadily stripping him of his white feathers, the sergeant clambered up into the machine.

Cheryl took her chance and ran across the open circle, stooping low even though she knew the blades were ten feet above her head, and jumped aboard.

The sergeant turned as she bumped into him. Above the roar of the engines, he shouted at her to get off, even as a Coast Guard lieutenant was yelling at him to also get off.

Cheryl didn't want to waste any more time so she pulled out the Eminent Domain warrant they had picked up in the lodge and she handed it to the sergeant.

'Know what this is?' she yelled.

He turned it over in his hands and nodded slowly.

'Yeah. Never seen one, though!'

'Well, now you have, and if you know what it is you'd better tell the pilot I want his chopper!'

He seemed about to protest but Cheryl pushed up to him, ignoring the lieutenant. 'That gives me the right to commandeer this chopper, and that's just what I'm doing!'

The lieutenant piped up. 'I don't know what either of you want, but *I* want you off—'

The sergeant knew OCI had a lot more clout than the US

Coast Guard – and a much better chance of fucking up his career – so he chose sides and waved the Eminent Domain in the lieutenant's face. 'Know what this is?'

The lieutenant read the title, took the wallet, looked it over, his face showing that he didn't know it from a daily newspaper.

'Show it to your pilot. See if he does!'

'When you've gotten off—'

Cheryl pulled her revolver. 'Show it to your fucking pilot before I get your superiors to show you early fucking retirement!'

Her voice was about to give up and she was worried that, despite the gun, she wouldn't sound convincing. However, the lieutenant seemed impressed and he clambered forward to talk to the pilot.

Cheryl immediately slipped the gun back into her waistband. 'Sorry!' she shouted to the sergeant.

'Know how you feel!' he yelled back, smiling.

The lieutenant came back and waved Cheryl up to the flightdeck, his face betraying his humiliation.

The pilot had removed his helmet – it had BRICKHOUSE stencilled on it – and was waving the Eminent Domain wallet. Although the engine was slowing, the noise was still loud enough to necessitate shouting.

'I know what this is but I can't obey it without authorization!'

'Who from?'

'A commander or higher! Get that, you got yourself a taxi!'

She pulled the gun again. 'I'm in a hurry. Get up!'

The lieutenant backed away, but when he saw the pilot look at him, he reached up to grab the gun. Cheryl swung the gun round and hit him full in the face, and he fell like a stone.

'What the fuck—' said the pilot, reaching for a revolver strapped to his seat.

Cheryl looked him straight in the eye. 'Time to go!'

The pilot's face paled and sudden inexplicable fear crept into it.

'What's happening?' shouted the co-pilot.

'*You*, get off this chopper!' shouted Cheryl.

She waved the gun at him. His helmet said SPARTACUS.

'Hijack? You're joking!'

'Whatever you want to call it, just fucking move!'

The co-pilot looked to his pilot, who nodded dumbly, and the two of them began to clamber out of their seats.

Cheryl suddenly felt a gun in her back.

'Don't know who the fuck you are, lady, but no way even Eminent Domain means you get to whack people about!'

Cheryl slowly turned to face him, then thrust her face at the sergeant. 'Then you'd better shoot me, 'cos I ain't getting off this fucking bird!'

Sergeant Ramirez stared at her, his face set hard, then it began to change. Doubt spread across it like a strain, and his hand began to waver.

'Oh God . . .' he managed before spinning round and throwing up through the open hatchway onto a policeman standing guard.

Cheryl turned just in time to stop the pilot hitting her with his helmet, and in seconds he too had shrunk back, his mind reeling at what he saw.

'Take your buddy out of here! Now!'

Muttering dumb agreement, he pushed his co-pilot ahead

of him and, at Cheryl's urging, both they and Sergeant Ramirez jumped out onto the grass. Cheryl reached over and pulled the hatch home then, aware that she had only seconds' grace, she hurried along the deck, stepped over the recumbent lieutenant, and climbed up into the cockpit where she quickly settled herself into the pilot's seat.

She knew the layout of a Sea King – she'd chatted to pilots and reps at trade shows – but it was still daunting, like being dropped behind the wheel of a Mack when all you've been used to is Pintos and Novas. But the fundamentals were the same and, more importantly, it would give her a real edge over Siemens – if she could find him.

Even as she increased rotation, winding the chopper up to take-off speed, there was hammering at the doors and policemen ran round to the front and pointed their revolvers up at her. She shook her head at them, knowing full well they wouldn't dare shoot while she had the Sea King going in the middle of a crowd.

Giving them and the sergeant, who had just run into view, a quick parting wave, she pushed down on the collective pitch lever and let the helicopter rise. It was a heavy bitch to handle, but she was up to the task.

Thirty feet straight up, she flicked on its searchlight, blinding all those looking up at her and effectively neutralizing any opposition. She then rose a further thirty feet to be sure she was clear of the fairground equipment, then carefully eased the machine forward, letting it clatter slowly across the crowd and out towards the street.

Trees loomed into view and she pulled the helicopter up to a hundred and fifty feet, the crowd below her thinning as they sought shelter from the driving wind and the storm of garbage that whistled madly around the site. Then she slowly turned the Sea King around and set off over the street, the evening gloom raped by its piercing blue-white light that carved a circle four lanes wide on the road beneath her. All she hoped was that the traffic had jammed up enough for her to locate the Lincoln. What she would do then she didn't know, but she'd think of something.

The Lincoln speeded up, pedestrians of all ages screaming as it thundered along the sidewalk, mailboxes, newspaper stands, garbage bins smashed aside. Twice Siemens clipped streetlights, and twice the car juddered and Stanley almost lost his grip.

The car reached an intersection and slewed to a halt. Then, just as Stanley was renewing his tenuous hold, the limousine carefully wove its way through the traffic, shunting smaller fry aside and scraping past buses and trucks. Stanley's trailing feet kept clipping the road, and he realized that sooner or later his flailing legs would come into contact with something more unyielding than evening air, and then it would be over.

He hunched up over the antenna, planting his feet squarely on the rain-slicked fender, but, in adjusting his position, he lost the shotgun which fell off and disappeared under the wheels of a bus. *Shit!*

It was obvious now that Siemens could see him in his mirror and was trying to shake him off, but at least he wouldn't try to shoot him. It was little consolation.

The car veered in and out of traffic until it slammed up broadside against a refrigerated meat truck, then accelerated, dragging its way along the full length of the truck before breaking for a freeway on-ramp. The traffic was backed up and moving slowly, but Siemens ignored it and roared up the inside, the right side of the car shaved in a shower of sparks by the retaining wall.

He reached the freeway and found that, by staying on the shoulder, he could enjoy an uninterrupted journey. He knew Stanley was hanging onto the trunk, and Siemens would have liked nothing better than to blow him away by firing through the back window, but knew that he couldn't. However, if the passenger chose tc lose his grip and fall off, that was another matter.

Cheryl couldn't see the Lincoln. The street was jammed, looking more like a parking lot than an arterial roadway. *Damn, damn, damn!*

She slowed and hovered over an intersection, the down-draught from the chopper scattering every loose object within fifty yards. Pedestrians sheltered in doorways, and drivers who poked their heads out of their windows immediately retracted them as the icy blast hit them full-face.

She slowly rotated the Sea King through three hundred and sixty degrees as she surveyed each stretch of road that led away from the crossing. Nothing, not a—

Suddenly, over to her right, she saw sparks. Maybe welding? . . . but they were moving. What causes sparks and moves?

She feathered the pedals to point the Sea King towards the sparks, then zoomed forwards.

*

Siemens didn't hesitate to crash through the flares and wooden barriers erected near the collision site, policemen waving frantically at him to stop, then diving for cover as he roared ahead. Having left behind the overturned pick-up and the remains of a Peugeot, the freeway proved to be relatively clear, as only one lane of traffic was being allowed past the accident.

Foot down, Siemens began to slowly steer from one side of the four-lane road to the other, side-stepping other vehicles. It was vital he eliminate Fulbright, the girl, and now Beam, too. To do that he needed to regroup and call in his best agents.

He grabbed for the mobile phone but his urgent need to avoid a Mercury pulling a U-Haul trailer made him drop it, and he knew he wouldn't be able to retrieve it from the footwell without stopping – and he wasn't stopping until that cunt on his trunk had eaten asphalt.

As for Stanley, he had no option but to hang on. And then he felt the antenna shift.

Cheryl peered ahead through the gloom. The freeway lighting rendered everything bland and repetitive, but she thought she saw a big car scything past a wreck. A police car, its lights flashing, set off after it but something blocked its path and it had to stop, sliding sideways across the only free lane.

She dropped down lower, thirty feet from the freeway, aware that she was too low, but desperate to find the Lincoln. If the car she had spotted wasn't it, she would have to wheel back and start at the beginning, which was a virtual guarantee that she would never find the limousine. And she wondered where Stanley had got to.

There it was! The Lincoln! And what the hell? Stanley? Stanley! Clinging to its back, hunched over the U-shaped antenna like a hood ornament with a bad sense of direction.

She had thought she would either try and land in front of the Lincoln, or maybe slap its roof or windshield with the Sea King's landing gear – anything to force Siemens to halt. Cornered, they might not be able to kill him, but they sure as hell could try turning him over to the authorities – and with testimony from that guy in his agency they might just buy enough time for their other accusations to be checked out. It was a mighty big might, but it was all they had. But now, with Stanley stranded on the car, her plan was irrelevant.

She flew over the Lincoln, the searchlight picking out every detail, not least Stanley's terrified face as he looked up at her passing, his hair and clothes chopped into a fury by the helicopter. What the hell was she supposed to do now?

She looked up – *bridge!* – and forced the Sea King up and over its span, the engine above roaring its compliance, then came down again just in front of the limousine, flying sideways. What the hell could she do except watch the bastard? The chopper handled like a pig and it was taking all her strength just to get it to respond. No way would she be able to do anything else. And with bridges, and God knows what else, looming up out of the dark ahead, she couldn't get much lower than she was. She might as well be watching the O. J. Simpson chase on TV for all the good she could do.

Then she felt hot breath on her neck and something digging into her side.

'Land this fucking bird!' demanded the lieutenant. 'And land it *now*!'

Stanley's hands were growing numb. The cold rain was dashing his face and body and drumming its way through every layer of his clothing, but most importantly he was losing the feeling – and with it the grip – in his fingers.

Blinking away the rain, he tried to see if there was anything else he could hold onto, but the Lincoln offered no other handholds. Goddamned drag co-efficients. And then he felt the antenna jolt to the left: it was working itself loose.

'I can't land now!' bellowed Cheryl over the roar in the helicopter. 'Got work to do!'

The lieutenant shouted back. 'Land it or I shoot!'

'And we both die?'

'If need be!'

Stupid little fuck.

'Okay, okay, but I need help. Get in the other seat, give me some guidance!'

The lieutenant edged past her, his gun stuck painfully in her side as he climbed round her, but as he crouched to ease himself over into the co-pilot's seat, their eyes met – and he was hers.

'You're going to do what I say, aren't you?' she shouted.

The look on his face!

'Put the gun down, now!'

After a long pause, during which Cheryl didn't dare break eye contact and was therefore flying blind, he finally broke.

'Yes, ma,' he said, his eyes as wide as a child's come Christmas morning.

'Stay in your seat, put on the helmet, hook up the mike. And then put mine on for me!'

He obeyed, albeit in slow motion, but he obeyed nonetheless, his eyes showing a pitiful combination of terror and compliance, like she was threatening to torch his favourite toy. *Weird shit, weird shit.*

A minute later they were in communication, he sitting staring at her like she was a ghost. Thankfully his confusion overrode his panic, and he answered her questions as if sitting an oral examination.

'What's your name?' she asked into her helmet microphone, making sure that she looked over at him whenever she could.

'Darren. You know that . . . ma.'

'Sorry, Darren. Bet you didn't know your ma could fly choppers.'

'No, I . . .' His mind couldn't work it out, so he just went with the flow. Ma knew best.

'Never mind, Darren. Just do what I say and everything'll be okay. Now, you see that limo down there, with the guy on the trunk?'

'Oh yeah,' he said, peering down at the car haloed by the helicopter's blue-white searchlight.

'I need to get that guy off – save him. He's very brave but very foolish. I want you to get a horse-collar winched down to him.'

'We haven't got one.'

'*What?* A fucking Coast Guard chopper, you ain't got a breeches buoy?'

'No need for cussing, ma. We were out lifting gear off a beached cargo ship before we picked the mascot up at the Kingdome.'

'Okay, okay, I'm sorry . . . son.'

She overshot the limousine and slowed the helicopter, and was rewarded by the sight of the Lincoln sliding into view a hundred feet beneath her, a fool stuck to its behind.

'So what have we got?' she shouted.

'Cargo hook!'

Fuck. 'It'll have to do! Get back there and winch it down.'

'While we're moving?'

'Trust me!'

He did as he was told, like the obedient boy he had plainly always been, and she felt the cold air blast through the helicopter as he pulled open the side door.

She peered over her shoulder at him, again fixing his eyes with her own, lasering him with her otherness. He had donned his helmet; his nickname was DARE DEVIL. As if.

'Winch it down to him! I'll worry about the flying!'

He seemed to hesitate, as if distance marred his vision.

'Do your duty, Darren!'

He nodded, and seemed to stiffen as if coming to attention but, squatting as he was by the open door with the wind whipping across his face, the practical requirements of the task at hand took precedence, and he hooked on his safety harness – much to Cheryl's relief – then swung the boom out, started the electric winch and, slowly but surely, the heavy hook disappeared from sight and down into the blazing white, rain-slashed night below.

Satisfied the lieutenant would do as ordered, she turned her full attention back to flying the Sea King. And just in time. Another bridge came into view and she forced the Sea King up and over it, the searchlight momentarily losing its quarry and instead strobing four lanes of traffic, the light bleaching all colour and turning them into four lanes of bland wheeled boxes. Then she lowered the helicopter as much as she dared, her eyes straining to see if there were any further looming obstructions.

It seemed clear in front and for the time being, despite their speed approaching sixty knots, she was able to concentrate on the task at hand: saving Stanley. She only hoped he could grab the cable so she could pull him clear.

Siemens couldn't understand why his world had turned white but then, peering up through the windshield, he caught sight of the helicopter hovering a hundred feet above him like a bloated white vulture, its rotors swirling eddies of raindrops through the blinding beam like a million streaks of lightning. It was keeping pace with him. Who the hell could that be? It looked too big to be a police chopper. Then he caught a glimpse of white and the wording: COAST GUARD. *Coast Guard? What the—?*

He felt the car starting to swerve and he addressed his attention to the road ahead. Traffic was building up again, so he was forced to stay in lane rather than having the whole freeway to move across. He didn't know where he was going, and he didn't know what to do about Fulbright, and then he realized who must be in the helicopter.

He banged the steering-wheel with his fist. The girl – Kenney! She was a helicopter pilot. It must be her, chasing after her idiot boyfriend.

He thumbed the window button and let it whine down, then pulled the .38 out of his waistband and leaned out and looked up at the Sea King. He could barely spot the craft in the hurricane it was generating, let alone see the pilot and he couldn't be *absolutely* sure it was her – so there would be no problem shooting.

The lieutenant ducked back inside the helicopter, shrieking.

'He's shooting at us, ma! He's shooting! Handgun!'

Cheryl looked back at him, caught his eye.

'Do what you can. Do your job. Make me proud!'

The guy almost saluted!

He edged back to the door, peered over the drop. 'Nearly there. You need to drop back five feet.'

Five feet? She'd be lucky to park this brute within five hundred yards of a target. It was like driving a bus without brakes. She was already terrified of banking it; instead she had to slow and hover and rotate the craft at every turn. She wasn't sure of the width of the rotors, or how high she was above the landing gear – it was a whole different world, like jumping from the Cessna to a DC3! Nonetheless she managed to slow slightly, as requested.

'Too far. Move forward. The cable's about ten feet above him. Keep her steady. I'll lower it some more.'

Cheryl was just about to do as asked when another bridge came out of nowhere.

'Hang on!' she shouted, whipping the Sea King up into the air. It juddered in protest at her sudden movement, the rotors clacking louder, but she got it up and over and then down again. But she misjudged their speed and height, and the wildly swinging hook clipped Stanley's head.

What the hell? Something smashed into the back of Stanley's head and his blurred vision fogged even more. He heard more gunshots. *I'm shot! I've been shot!?*

He lifted his head up and saw something swinging wildly about. *Oh God.*

He ducked down, hugging the ever-more-shaking antenna, and felt a scrape across his shoulders. *They're trying to knock me off the fucking car!*

Then the helicopter above rose slightly, pulling the large hook and its heavy collar with it, and the wire swung in a long lazy arc around the front of the car until it smashed into the windshield and the car began to snake wildly.

Whatever they're trying to do, thought Stanley, clinging on for dear life, his head pounding, *the crazy bastards aren't getting it right*. The antenna shifted, the boomerang flapping.

'You hit the windshield!' screamed the lieutenant.

Fuck, fuck, fuck!

Cheryl wrestled with the controls and the helicopter rose twenty feet. She had to think this through. Maybe if she just followed—

There was a weird noise from above – a wrong sound, like peas rattling in a can – then a shriek in her earphones.

'*He's hit us! He's hit us!*'

It was true. For the third time in a week Cheryl felt an aircraft dying in her hands, the controls starting to shake as if they were losing their grip. The fucker's shot a Sea King with a revolver! It wasn't right. It shouldn't happen.

Smoke plumed outside the right window, the engine making a strange noise like it was bleeding.

'We're hit!' shouted the lieutenant. 'We're going down!'

Not fucking yet, we ain't. Not without Stanley.

'Read me into the car again!'

'But you've got to land, ma! We're burning!'

Smoke swirled into the cabin making him cough, then just as quickly was sucked out again.

Cheryl spun to look at him, his face streaming with tears from the smoke. 'Do as your ma says!'

He looked stricken with remorse, as if he'd just been chastized for wetting his bed.

'Sorry, sorry!'

'Okay . . . now read me in. We got a man to save.'

He leaned out of the door, pulling his microphone closer to his mouth. 'Go forward . . . ten feet, eight . . . two. Got it. Now down. Down ten feet. Steady, steady . . .'

Cheryl was fighting a losing battle. The Sea King was sick and just wanted to lie down until it got better, but it still had work to do. *Come on, baby. Come on.*

Stanley saw the cable swinging wildly above him, the hook at its end as lethal as an executioner's axe. He wondered what was happening, then his befuddled mind cleared long enough for him to realize that if Siemens was shooting at the chopper, then the chopper was the man's enemy and that the hook and cable were a lifeline rather than something designed to knock him off his precarious perch.

But suddenly the helicopter lifted, the cable jerked out of view and he was alone again on the back of the speeding limousine.

Siemens was straining to see through the car windshield, half of it turned to crystal by the impact from the helicopter line. His only hope would be to get off the freeway or into a tunnel, somewhere the helicopter couldn't follow. Even if it then landed, he'd be able to deal with the pilot one way or another. He started to look for an off-ramp.

'Fucking bridges!' screamed Cheryl as she begged the chopper to give her its all. It complied with obvious reluctance, and then obeyed her command for it to drop too easily for her liking. The bitch was losing lift.

She scanned the instruments, but what she could feel through the controls and what she could see through the windshield told her all she needed to know. That and the yelling from the lieutenant.

'Careful, careful, it's swinging. It's swinging!'

A sudden gust of wind caught her unaware and the helicopter shifted. She corrected the movement almost immediately but not soon enough for the unplanned change in altitude not to be transmitted down the cable.

As if it had been waiting for this very moment, it whipped up twenty feet in the air then dived for the car like a snake striking at prey.

The heavy hook smashed into the car trunk between

Stanley's legs, denting the metalwork, forcing the suspension down and the car to veer, then it was up again seeking new targets.

Stanley looked up, and through windstung eyes saw the cable head whirl in a J-shaped loop then drop straight for his head. He had no alternative. Even if they were doing sixty miles an hour, he would have to let go. It was either that or be smashed to a pulp.

'Out of control! *Out of control!*' screamed the lieutenant.

'What? The chopper? The cable? The car? What?' shrieked Cheryl back.

Siemens was fighting the wheel. Something had hit the back of the car and he thought a tyre might be deflating. He had emergency inflaters, but at this speed he could still lose it.

No, the voice said. *Stay, wait, see . . .*

Stanley hugged the antenna as the hook scythed by his head and smashed into the back window of the Lincoln and showered him in a flurry of glass.

He waited for it to smash back at him, but nothing happened. He looked up over his arms. It was jammed. He could see it rising and falling as if it had its head caught in a trap, but the angle and size of the window and the shape of the hook meant it couldn't be pulled out vertically. He also guessed that the car was bombproof and would have an internal safety cage that wouldn't give up without a fight. The helicopter had caught the limousine.

'It's stuck!' shouted the lieutenant to Cheryl.

'The cable?'

'In the car's back window. Won't come loose.'

Cheryl spat sweat off her top lip. Shit. She could pull it free but what that would do to the Lincoln and to Stanley she dreaded to think. All she could hope was to match the car's speed, give the cable some slack and hope it worked itself loose. Things couldn't get worse.

Then she saw the bridge and the electricity pylons half a mile ahead.

Stanley looked through the smashed rear window and saw, to the right of the windshield, the road ahead of the limousine. A bridge. The helicopter was going to have to rise, and take the car with it – and he couldn't hope to hang on during that kind of journey. As it was, his hands were dead; he couldn't feel if he was holding on or not. And what if the hook slipped free?

There was a four-lane bridge and beyond that, about forty feet higher, electricity cables straddling the gap between two giant pylons. She'd have to get higher than all of them to be sure, and at their speed she had about twenty seconds to do it.

'Still stuck!'

She dropped the helicopter fifteen feet, pulled it up, aware that at any second the controls could give up the ghost and drop the machine like the dead weight it was sure to become in fifteen seconds if she didn't do something.

'No go!' shouted the lieutenant as he watched the line tauten yet remain steadfastly locked into the car.

Could she fly *under* the bridge? In this house? *Gimme a break.* But how about *between* the bridge and the pylons? She wasn't sure of her top and bottom, and if she was dragging a car it could clip the bridge, and she'd plough into the freeway on the other side just as surely as if the chopper had been tethered to the structure. No, she needed to get up, and get up high, and get the fuck up there *now*!

She prayed Stanley would do something, because if he didn't he was road meat.

She increased engine power and demanded that God become her co-pilot.

Stanley felt the antenna jolt, then the boomerang twisted to the left. It was about to snap. His only hope was to grab the hook: whatever happened, that was going to stay connected to the helicopter even if the car wasn't – and adrenalin, terror and that logical inner voice told him he had no other option.

He kicked himself up onto the trunk and grabbed the inside of the windowframe with his right hand, ignoring the pain as the shattered glass dug its rounded edges into his fingers. Then he hauled one dead leg, then the other, onto the trunk, heaved himself round the antenna, praying it wouldn't break off, and put his other hand into the window, his foot onto the antenna. It jerked, as if about to snap, but held long enough for him to reach for the cable that slapped in circles above him. Above the hook itself, and out of the car, was a collar of metal six inches in diameter. This was his target. Now or never.

He grabbed the cable above the collar with both hands, frightened that he couldn't actually feel anything in his fingers. Then the antenna finally snapped and he had only his hands to save himself, his feet sliding on the slick trunk as if it was coated in ice. Luckily the cable slackened momentarily and he was able to haul himself up, the muscles in his arms suddenly alert to his efforts, giving him enough power to drape his legs round the collar so that it acted as a seat. Then, wrapping himself round the cable like it was a long-lost lover, its cold thinness failing to reassure his terrified mind, he closed his eyes and prayed and cursed in equal measure.

'Stanley! Stanley! *Stanley!*' cried Cheryl.

She had no option; she knew that. She hauled the helicopter into the sky, aware of the two-ton weight on the end of the line and the Sea King's stubborn refusal to carry it. It was lame and it was damned if it was going to work.

She pushed on the controls, hearing herself begging the chopper to lift, hearing the lieutenant telling her he loved her, sensing the motor above her choking on its own vomit.

Suddenly they were rising.

'Car! Car!' The lieutenant whooped. 'Got it! We're lifting it!'

It was a start.

But the bridge was closer. So close she could see the

vehicles on it, and pedestrians – some stopping to stare. Oh Christ, they were on a level with her, and the car was a good forty feet below.

Every muscle in Cheryl's body transmitted its desperate demand to the helicopter. *Please, please, please, give me the power I need.*

The helicopter responded, sluggish and protesting though it had been, then with a sudden roar it accepted its payload and soared up and up and up. But the bridge was coming ever nearer – only a matter of seconds now – and even though she was looking down on them, she could read the horror in the faces of the people on its span.

Stanley clung on for dear life, the cold and rain and wind and downdraught conspiring to blow him from his perch, but he refused to succumb. He forced open one eye, and saw the car beneath him dangling above the freeway like a shark that had given up the fight, its engine racing, its hood scraping sparks into the night. He shut his eyes again.

'Come on, come on, come on, baby!' howled Cheryl as the Sea King rose. *Get me up there. Get me up where there's no goddamn bridges and no goddamn wires.*

'Okay, okay,' the lieutenant was saying over and over. 'Okay, okay, looks like . . . *fuck!*'

Cheryl could feel there was something wrong. The helicopter suddenly screamed a protest as it hunched down on its tail and showed her a view of the grey-black sky above. *Oh God, no*, they were going to topple backwards.

Then, just as suddenly as it had been jerked back, the helicopter was free and they were catapulted forward, and the electric cables were there, stretched before the Sea King like a tripwire ready to bring her down to earth.

Siemens hadn't belted himself in, so when the hook had latched itself onto the car through the rear window he had been able to turn and see what had happened – and realize what the result could be. He had swerved the car from side to side in an attempt to dislodge the hook before he had caught sight of Stanley climbing over the trunk of the car and reaching up for the cable.

He managed to slam on the brakes at the precise instant that the rear end of the Lincoln left the ground, but before he could brace himself, and he was flung into the windshield and found himself winded in the footwell, gravity his enemy.

And there, on his back, all he could do was look up through the car at the blinding searchlight of the helicopter as it tore through the gaping hole in the tinted glass of the rear window. He was airborne.

He grabbed at the steering wheel, the effort pulling muscles all over his back, but he ignored the pain. They would soon heal. Then he reached for the back of the passenger seat to pull himself up and, with a howl of agony, grabbed a handful of plush black leather. He twisted his head to look over his shoulder and down through the windshield and saw his death.

He didn't have time to scream but something in his head did.

*

The Lincoln clipped the edge of the bridge, people scattering out of its path. The impact sliced the hook through the limousine's roof and it came free, whipping wildly into the night as the car began to cartwheel across the bridge, the first three lanes clear, the fourth occupied by a semi hauling a bulldozer. The Lincoln's rear hit the bulldozer, flipping it higher into the air where it shot out over the freeway and rolled end over end in the air until its hood ploughed into the rear of a Texaco tanker, the car's unstoppable disintegration immediately accelerated by eight thousand gallons of fuel igniting and erupting into the night.

The freeway behind the tanker was empty – vehicles witnessing the tussle between the limousine and the Coast Guard helicopter having kept their distance – and the tanker was in the inside lane so the brunt of the explosion was borne by empty freeway on its right and by a couple of cars on the other carriageway, both of which were bowled over by the blast but, luckily, saved from the rain of flaming fuel which instead shot up into the air and over to the right, turning a junkyard of wrecked automobiles into the Fourth of July.

Unfortunately, the sheet of flame that plumed skywards engulfed the lower end of the cable, and blew hot breath into the helicopter and over its occupants.

Cheryl, quite simply, lost it. The helicopter had done its damnedest, but the fireball soldered controls and melted control panels. As the ship bucked the firestorm, the lieutenant was thrown across the cabin, his clothes smoking, his helmet now only saying RE D.

Cheryl had no option but to wheel the helicopter away from the fire and find open ground.

Stanley meanwhile watched the limousine hurtle through the night and bury itself in the tanker and, knowing what would happen, hugged the swinging cable all the tighter, shielding his eyes and holding his breath.

The heat of hell engulfed him and he felt his exposed skin blistering and his clothes begin to flame, the world a deadly yellow-white even behind his closed eyelids.

Cheryl caught sight of water glinting to the west through the raging heat haze that licked the sky in front of her. Ditching was the best chance – the *only* chance.

The lieutenant righted himself, patting at his smouldering clothes. He edged over to the open door, aware that the helicopter was now in a low spin, a sure sign of control damage. He peered outside, the fire to the chopper's rear slowly wheeling into sight again. He looked down the cable. Something smoked at its end, a grey whisper trailing a circle in the light from the searchlight.

'He's on the line!' he shouted before giving in to a coughing jag.

What?

'The man . . . he's on the cable . . . on the cable!'

Cheryl was simultaneously ecstatic and also terrified: the poor bastard would be a kebab. *His* only chance would be water, too.

She let the chopper descend as fast as she could, but the motor above sounded its last warning and she paid attention, concentrating instead on holding the juddering Sea King level and heading for the water.

As it loomed closer, a dark sheet rippled yellow by the reflected flames from the freeway, Cheryl sent up a silent prayer.

Stanley, be alive, she urged, *and see what I'm doing.*

She reached the water – it looked like a lake and not the bay – and she wheeled the helicopter round in as narrow a circle as the dying machine would sustain.

Stanley was in agony, a million hot pokers stabbing his whole body. His hands felt as if they had been melted, his face scalded off. He was dizzy, inordinately tired. Letting go would be so . . .

He dared to open his eyes and he saw water. He needed no second urging. Begging for its cold embrace and uncaring how high up he might be, he let go, the skin on his right forearm peeling as it unfused itself from the hot cable.

He tumbled backwards in a long lazy somersault until he hit the water forty feet below, its cold instantly slamming him awake as it injected itself into every burn, making him scream in agony and swallow an icy breathful.

He thrashed himself to the surface and saw the helicopter whipping up a frenzy around him as it hovered, its search-light beam an almost solid entity in the darkness, like an acrylic stand holding up a model, then it began to falter, its tail dipping, the engine stuttering. The pilot regained control momentarily and immediately headed towards the shore some fifty yards away. Stanley began to swim towards it.

Cheryl didn't want to wreck the helicopter, or kill the lieutenant. Both had saved her, and Stanley, and helped deal with Siemens, even if nothing had gone according to plan. They were friends therefore and, like Stanley, she wanted to save them.

'Brace yourself!' she yelled, her arms feeling as if they were about to be wrenched out of their sockets as she argued with the dying controls.

Suddenly her foot hit the floor. The tail-rotor control had

gone, and the chopper was beginning to spin. *Now*, she had to get it down now!

The water's edge came temptingly closer, but it kept veering out of sight as the helicopter spun faster and faster. Come on, *come on* . . .

Then they were over land, water only visible half of the time. She eased the helicopter down, wary of its landing gear catching on something and flipping it over. She felt the wheels make tentative contact, but they kept sliding. *Fuck it, Cheryl. Dunk it. Just dunk the bitch. Now!*

With a bone-jarring thump it landed, the wheels digging channels in the earth, the fuselage twisting and straining as the tail tried to keep revolving but – Praise be to Sikorsky! – the chopper held together and, most importantly, stayed upright. She killed the motor, tossed off her helmet and tumbled down into the cabin.

The lieutenant was by the door, dazed. He had been flash-burned, but nothing serious: no more than bad sunburn and a wait for new eyebrows. She knelt down to him, her heart pounding, her face showing tears and a smile and relief and terror. With a shaking hand, she cupped his chin.

'You did good, lieutenant. You did good. Just promise me one thing?'

'What?' He was barely with her.

'Tell them anything you want, but *don't* tell them who you thought was flying her.'

'Thought? But—'

'Hey, is your ma supposed to fly Sea Kings? Tell them anything, but don't tell them you saw your ma, okay?'

'Okay.'

'Good. Thanks for your help.'

He smiled, then fainted.

Cheryl jumped out of the cabin onto soggy earth, then turning, kissed her hand and slapped the helicopter's steaming rump. 'Atta baby. You done good, too!'

The helicopter rotors continued to slowly revolve above her like a giant's waving hand, the engine smoking.

She hurried back the way she had flown and, running into the cold water without a break in her stride, began to shout for Stanley.

She was thigh deep before she spotted him, and he noticed her as he frantically splashed his way to shore. She grabbed him under the arms and hauled him upright.

'S'okay, Stanley! You can stand now. It's not deep.'

He stopped and stood up.

'Oh,' was all he could say.

She looked him over as best she could in the semi-darkness offered by the chopper's searchlight which still blazed into the ground five feet beneath its belly. He was burned, but she suspected it wouldn't turn out to be serious. In fact, something told her, it could well turn out to be nothing at all, given a little time.

'Come on. We're still not out of the woods yet,' she said.

'Siemens dead?' Stanley gasped.

'Yeah, even the shit he had in his head couldn't put that fucker back together again.'

They heard a siren way off and she realized their part of the world had finally turned silent as the helicopter's motor stilled.

'Come on. They'll be here soon.'

'Maybe . . . maybe we should just surrender,' Stanley said. 'Tell them . . . tell them . . .' He couldn't finish.

'Tell them we just creamed the head of OCI? You might as well kill the President and say it was just a prank. Come on, Batman, we've got some more flying to do.'

She tugged him out of the water and they half trotted, half limped their way around its perimeter for a quarter of a mile, lights from emergency vehicles dotting the horizon in most directions.

Finally they reached a fence and, after a struggle, Cheryl succeeded in boosting Stanley over it, even if he did tumble onto his backside on the other side. She then climbed after him over the eight-feet-high fence, and they found themselves in the parking lot of a refinery, where a dozen or more cars sat unguarded.

Five minutes later they were in a Ford Contour heading south, the guard on the gate still trying to work out how his wife could have been parked at the refinery when he knew for sure she was at her sister's over the bay in Vancouver.

They drove in silence, their only reactions being mutual panic whenever police cars screamed past them in one direction or another.

'I'm so tired,' Stanley finally announced, stating the obvious as he slumped on the front seat.

'Get some sleep. I'll drive us.'

'Where? You're as tired as I am, and we're wanted by every cop in the country. We need to lay low, get back into shape . . .' He coughed up phlegm that tasted of ashes. 'And we need to split up.'

'Split up? How do you work—?'

Although tired enough to welcome an offer of euthanasia, his mind had gone through all the possibilities and, as seemed to happen more and more often since their encounter with the 'lifeboat' in the ski lodge, the best option was as blindingly clear as if presented on a multiple-choice question paper with the answers already filled in.

'They're looking for a man and a woman. Separate, and we've halved the odds of being spotted.'

'But what are we—?'

'We split up. Recuperate. Then in a week or so we meet up somewhere safe and quiet, see what our next move should be.'

'No, we've come this far, we should—'

'No, Cheryl. Find a quiet spot, hotwire me a car, then you keep going south – and I'll go east.'

She slowed the car. 'This is wrong, Stanley. We're a team. We've got to stick together, see what we can . . .'

'No arguments. We don't know what we're going to do or who we can turn to. We need space – time to think, sleep, breathe . . . You know it makes sense.' He tapped her temple. 'Don't you?'

She refused to acknowledge his last point but, by the time she was able to think of a suitable comeback, he had fallen asleep. She only wished she could join him.

WARM

She who has never loved has never lived.

JOHN GAY

42

Cheryl had done as Stanley wanted. She'd hotwired him a Hyundai Lantra and agreed to his terms: they were to meet a week later, at noon, in Didra, the town where the other 'lifeboat' had exploded and the aliens had invaded the onlookers. She was to get hold of a local *Yellow Pages* and the first diner she found listed was where they would get back together.

She had watched him drive off, tears in her eyes, convinced she would never see him again. Not because he would desert her – they had too much in common now for her to believe that – but because those bastards at OCI might catch up with him – or her.

She hopped back into the Contour and headed south.

She drove for two hours until she found a small motel off the highway near Kelso where she pulled in and paid for a couple of nights, using cash she'd found stuffed behind her stolen OCI card.

In the room she ran a bath, then soaked in it for over an hour, topping it up as it cooled until the tub couldn't hold any more water. Then she got out, dried herself down and got into bed. All the time her mind had been a blank. She had wanted to think over her options, to work out the events of that day – and the days before – in order to understand what had happened and what she had to do, but her mind refused to cooperate. All it wanted was peace and quiet, and so she stared at the faucets on the bath and counted the drips, and then lay back and watched the intermittent sweep of headlights from the highway cross the ceiling.

Once in bed, she had again stared up at the ceiling, this time letting its beige colour flood her senses until she was swimming in cream, her whole body suffused by a sea of off-white – and then sleep claimed her and her body began to repair itself.

She slept for two days and two nights, finally being woken by a gentle tapping at the door. Still fogged by her deep slumber, she had answered it to find the motel owner asking if she was all right. She explained to the concerned old man that she had the flu and offered to pay for another night, but he said there was no hurry and did she need a doctor? She declined his offer and went back to bed.

Nice man.

Thursday she had settled up. Then, like a newly released prisoner suddenly aware of all the wonders the outside world had to offer – bright fall colours, cool refreshing air, beautiful mountain views – she drove into the nearest town, dumped the car and caught a bus to Portland.

The next couple of days passed without incident. She found herself simply enjoying the feeling of being alive, as she slowly made her way from Portland to The Dalles, Hermiston, Walla Walla and Lewiston. She knew her newfound peace of mind was partly a reaction to the events of the week before, but also a desire to make the most of what could be her last taste of freedom if anyone was to catch up with her.

It wasn't until the Friday that she realized she hadn't even thought of booze, and on the odd occasion when sex had sprung to mind it was invariably accompanied by an image of Stanley and his naked body.

On the Saturday she had found a park bench in Clarkson and, despite the steady tumble of rain, had settled in for an hour of people-watching.

There was a man exercising his dog: he old and frail, the dog young and hearty and eager to please his slowcoach of an owner. There were kids playing tag football, though invariably finding mud to slip and slide in. There was a brace of mothers with their strollers, a cop taking photographs of birds, and what was a blatantly clandestine meeting between a man and a woman, their prearranged 'accidental' encounter leading to a shared lunch of nuts and fruit on a nearby bench. Ordinary people doing ordinary things and not worrying about anything else. At one time she would have thought it deadly dull and hied off to the nearest bar in search of booze or a boner, but today . . . today was different.

Today was a day she might well have missed because she would have been dead, unloved and unwept over. But she was alive and, what's more, the man who had helped keep her alive loved her; had actually risked his life for her. The men she had previously known wouldn't have done that: Christ, they'd probably have trampled her in the rush to leave!

She watched a young couple – kids really – hugging under a tree, the girl short and looking up to her boyfriend, the both of them deep in conversation about nothing in particular. How often had she had nothing conversations that meant so much? Never – that's how often. For all her fucking and speeding and flying, she'd be lucky to end up like the old man, with only some dumb dog for a friend. Then, to her amazement – and horror – she found herself eager to see what the babies in the strollers looked like. *Time to go, Cheryl!*

So she'd upped and marched through the rain to a coffee shop and ordered their biggest cappuccino: it was almost as good as sex, a lot safer, and someone else cleaned up the mess.

And that night, instead of going on the prowl – it was Saturday after all – she'd stayed in and watched TV. Whatever it was she had, she had it bad.

Sunday had dawned and she had hitched a lift on a Peterbilt hauling lumber, safe in the knowledge that if the guy tried anything on, he'd soon be whimpering his apologies.

Arriving in Didra a little after eleven, she found a phonebook and checked out the diners. Forty minutes later, she was supping good coffee at a dive called Alvin's A-Okay and looking out of the window at the main drag, half convinced she would never see Stanley again.

By 12:11 she was entirely convinced, and called over the waitress for the check but changed her mind. *Another half hour, 12:45 tops, then I'm out of here.*

Jesus, I'm turning into a schoolgirl!

At 12:30 two men came in, one young, one old, their faces shielded by black baseball caps. They looked suspicious. The rain had long stopped but these two were acting like they didn't want to—

Stanley doffed his cap and smiled at her. She leapt up and ran over to him and hugged him, then immediately parted when she realized she didn't know who the other guy was.

He could have been a cop, OCI. *It could all be a trap! They'd coerced Stanley into—*

She stepped back suddenly and braved a look at the other man.

It was Sam Dinkley!

Unable to believe her eyes, she let them lead her blubbering back to her table, where they ordered up coffee and doughnuts. Promising to reveal all once the food had been delivered, Stanley simply held her hands tightly on the plastic tablecloth, while an embarrassed Dinkley busied himself with the view outside.

Two minutes later and, alone with coffee and what looked like the daily ration of doughnuts for the entire Didra Police Department, Stanley told her what had happened once they had parted.

'After I left you I drove east for about forty miles then had to stop. Pulled the car off the highway behind some trees and slept there for a day or so. Then drove on a couple of miles, found a motel and flaked out some more. The burns were already healing – and that without any ointment or dressings – and another day and a half's rest saw me back to normal.'

It was true. Cheryl pulled his face this way and that. Not a mark. Incredible.

'I tell you, it's the strangest feeling. It's like . . . like refilling a lighter. The flame gets lower and lower until you need to top it up with gas, then it's ready to work, but you forgot you'd adjusted the flame to compensate for the lack of fuel, so the first time you use it again it goes *whoosh* right up into your face. That's how I feel, like I spent all my life *forcing* the flame to rise but now I feel so . . . so great. Bursting.

Better than I've ever done. Anyway, cured, fixed, whatever the hell it is, I started to make phone calls.

'I used a couple of people I knew in OCI to get in direct touch with the guy who replaced Siemens. All I said was: "Mr Drexill, this is Stanley Fulbright, Agent A512. I've resigned. Watch your post." Then I put the phone down, untraced, and went into a stationery store, bought a pad and pens, and sat down and wrote down absolutely everything that happened from the moment I got the call from Baxter to catch the chopper out to Riva – up to Siemens being killed.

'I'm afraid to say I used real names, including yours and Sam's. I knew he'd know them anyway, but I also hoped it would convince him of my sincerity.

'I gave him the full works: Hollis, Siemens, Baxter, File Seventy-Seven, the UFO, that room, everything. Ran to eighteen pages. Then I signed it and added a PS. Said I'd photocopied it three times and sent the copies to three addresses with strict instructions that, in the event of my not contacting these people once a week for the foreseeable future, my statement was to be handed over to whoever they felt was best qualified to deal with its contents. Got that idea from Hollis – at least the fucker was good for one thing.

'Then I rang the library at Gudgen to find out about—'

'Don't apologize again. It's getting tiresome,' said Dinkley. 'Ever since he called me up on the phone he's been saying he's sorry for getting me into this mess.'

'But Hollis must have got to you,' said Cheryl.

'Oh, he did. And I think he came real close to seeing me off, but at the last minute his need to get after you two got the better of him, and he let me be. I think Deputy Knox calling by might also have had something to do with it. But I knew what he wanted to do, and he knew I knew. Tell you honest, first time I ever shit my pants. The look in that guy's eyes . . .'

'Anyway,' continued Stanley. 'They thought I was pulling some prank, and then they put Sam on the line. I could have wept. I told him most of what had happened and the old fool believed me.'

'Hey, less of the old,' said Dinkley.

'Not least because he'd seen the stuff on TV about you and the chopper,' said Stanley.

'Bet there were some TV people cursing they didn't get *that* on film!' laughed Dinkley. 'All I saw was the wreckage and the story from some coastguard who was in the chopper.'

'Did he mention his mother?' asked Cheryl.

'No? Why would he?'

Cheryl gave Stanley a look and he smiled, understanding exactly what she meant. He continued his story.

'I called this Drexill up again yesterday morning, asked him if we had a deal. He tried to keep me on the line, so I hung up. They can get a trace in twelve seconds sometimes. I thought I was going to have to leave it – not come today, and hope you could look out for yourself. For all I knew, I was being tailed and they were just waiting till they could get the two of us together.'

'And?'

Stanley laughed. 'I was!'

'What?' She looked round, expecting to see a dozen cops with guns drawn.

Stanley clasped her shaking hand. 'It's okay. It's settled. It's over.'

'But if they were tailing you . . .'

'OCI people had been watching Sam since they knew Hollis had been in Gudgen – and they followed him to my motel. Last night about eleven they stormed my room, dragged Sam out to a van, and this guy Drexill, the new head of OCI, he sits me down in a chair, pulls a bead on me with his gun and sends everyone else out the door. Then he takes out my letter and sets it down on his lap.'

Stanley paused, thinking back to the night before. He had come close to dying more than once over the last couple of weeks but that was the single instance when he believed his time had truly come. Just him, a gun, and a man who had everything to gain by his death and nothing to lose – and who was every bit as sane as himself.

Drexill had spoken with a quiet Southern accent that perfectly suited his appearance: tall, handsome yet somehow forgettable, like a shirt model in a Sears catalogue. He could have been a farmer or a schoolteacher. Unfortunately, he was the successor to a man who had sanctioned the murder of hundreds of people.

Finally, as Stanley was finding himself sheathed in sweat, the man had nodded down at the letter.

'These, sir, are the ravings of a madman and not worth the paper they're printed on.'

He had then proceeded to rip the letter up and put it in the fireplace – all the time keeping his gun on Stanley – then set the pieces alight. Only when the last shred had burned up did he sit back down and put his .38 away.

'Don't want any incriminating evidence, do we?' he said. Then he had pulled out a CD-ROM and held it out for Stanley to inspect.

'We were going through all the mess Siemens had left and we found he'd ordered all the damaged computer gear from the store in Clinger to be trashed. I ordered everything broken open – there had to be some reason you stopped by there in the middle of running away from Siemens, and it weren't no Microsoft sale – and we found this CD jammed in a drive. Drive was broken, CD was intact. Took it back to Fort Worth and got what we could printed out. Seems all that gibberish you were talking about was based on fact. So I had them retrace your moves – and Siemens's – from the moment you landed in Riva, and your story mostly checks out.

'Despite what they did to the town, someone remembers you arriving, and your leaving in a police Jeep with a man answering Hollis's description. Got agents in the Solardome confirm you were in the Winnebago all night, that you escaped the chopper crash and stole the Winnebago – and that at no time had Baxter or Hollis left the RV. Got plenty of witnesses from the hotel – even got confirmation of your nude walk to the clothes store. The computer store gave us more trouble but we did find people – hushed up by Siemens but willing to talk now – who saw Hollis enter the store armed and shooting. Someone also saw him leaving on a police bike. Got eyewitness reports of your stealing that Cessna, and a cop on a bike chasing you before killing another cop. As for Baxter, we don't know where he is but he's undoubtedly – and unfortunately – dead. Siemens had an op squad we're now checking out, to see if *they* got rid of his body. Clinger PD got an anonymous call about a break-in at a vet's, and found the vet, Hetherington, dead. They also found a lot of fingerprints belonging to you and a woman called Cheryl Kenney, and also Baxter. There was no Baxter, as I said, but there was an X-ray of the thigh of a male who'd had a hip replacement operation, and on the X-ray was a shot of a transmitter – an OCI transmitter.

'We also checked out the remains of the lodge, but it's damaged beyond fixing.

'But we've got a lot of people who are willing to talk now we have the evidence Siemens was using against them. We're offering amnesty if they tell us all they know. Siemens's back pages don't make pretty reading, and it reflects on us all in OCI, and on other agencies that had dealings with him, that he wasn't stopped sooner. I can tell you now, there's going to be a few senators, congressmen and other higher-ups taking very early retirement or announcing sudden illnesses over the next few weeks. Serve the bastards right.

'They also ran an autopsy on Hollis – we got to the body just before Siemens's people were going to cremate it. Proves he *was* Handry, and that Siemens *did* fix his execution. That's going to be kept *very* quiet. OCI does good work – *you* did good work before all this blew up – and we don't want to screw that for the sake of one bad apple.'

'One bad *apple*?' spluttered Stanley.

Drexill ignored his reaction. 'Hollis also had a letter on him, addressed to *People* magazine, explaining why someone should check out a certain package that had been delivered. Seems he had been blackmailing Siemens. Just like you, Mr Fulbright, have been blackmailing me. So, given all that you know that you shouldn't know, and my knowing stuff about you and that "lifeboat" that no one else should know, give me one good reason why I don't just blow your head off here and now.'

'Who did you see?' said Stanley, staring at the man.

'Pardon?'

'You know what I mean. Who did you see when you pointed the gun at me before?'

'I saw my brother, Mr Fulbright. He was called Michael, and he died a year ago of a heart attack. He was sixty-one, good man, four kids. He looked after me when our parents divorced. From age seven until I left college he was there for me, a brother, a father, a friend. Best goddamn person I ever knew, bar none. I miss him, miss him like hell . . .

'And I tell you this, Fulbright, if I *hadn't* seen him I would have killed you – and your friend outside – and I would have tracked down Miss Kenney and I would have killed her too. Siemens might have overstepped the mark, but we're talking national security here. Covering up his fuck-ups is vital, otherwise the whole shitpile comes tumbling down. Corrupt and rotten as it is, it's the best we've got, and the alternative is unthinkable because whatever it is it ain't the democratic paradise the bleeding hearts think it should or would be. We're too far down the road for the machine to be turned off. Understand? There are people at all levels on all sides involved here. They may not have known about this alien shit, but they knew about the other criminal killings. If that came out, *no one* would survive, because no one would believe anyone any more. It would be Watergate, Iran-Contra, Whitewater all rolled up into one stinking bundle to the power ten. And with Eminent Domain being used by Siemens through *five* presidencies, all the good that has been done over the last couple of decades would be tainted – and some of that stuff is good and righteous and cost a lot to get done, and we can't afford for it to come undone. It's been revoked, incidentally.'

'What?'

'Eminent Domain. No one's got it now, not even me.' Then he said, matter-of-factly, 'Besides, Siemens may have been out of control, but he might still have been right. What guarantees do I have that you and the others like you aren't hatching some plan up here, right now?' He tapped his head. 'You and your little buddies from God-knows-where.'

'None,' Stanley had to admit. 'But after nineteen years don't you think "we" would have "hatched" something by now, even if only to defend ourselves from Siemens?'

'Depends how long you take to hatch.'

They continued to stare at each other, until finally Drexill's stern face cracked a little and he got up and went to the door.

'You, Mr Fulbright, died in that gas-tanker explosion on the freeway last Sunday. We don't know who was flying the Sikorsky. Inquiries continue. "Black male in his fifties" is the best description we have. Tragically, I now learn, Miss Kenney died in that other helicopter crash in the Solardome.'

He opened the door and waved for his men to release Sam Dinkley.

'And that's it?' said Stanley, genuinely angry. 'So many people dead, and it gets covered up like it never happened?'

'Like *what* ever happened?'

'But so many people . . .'

'You must have seen those sci-fi movies where the aliens crashland their UFO, and the government chases them all over the place trying to catch them just so's they can get them on an operating table and cut them up? And there's always some friendly human trying to help them escape?'

'Yeah.'

'*They're true!* And right now, I'm the only friendly human around. Take it or leave it.'

'I'll take it.'

'Good choice. And, Fulbright?'

'Yes?'

'You'd better be the *good* guys.'

And with that he stepped aside to let Sam Dinkley enter, then walked out and slammed the door behind him.

'And you believe him?' said Cheryl, her heart racing.

'Yes. We no longer officially exist. But, as you can see, we do. The good news is Sam has contacts and for a price they can get us false IDs – drivers' licences, social security numbers, whatever – so we can change our names and, if we steer clear of Clinger and avoid getting our fingerprints taken for any reason, we should be okay.'

'And you believe they won't be following us?'

'Why should they?'

'Because we've got fucking aliens in us!'

Sam Dinkley laughed and looked around the diner nervously. 'Hang on, Cheryl. They didn't quite hear that up in Canada.'

She looked shamefaced and peered at the turned heads.

Stanley nodded at the mound of doughnuts and explained to the onlookers within hearing: 'Sugar rush. Gets her sometimes.'

People turned away. *Tourists.*

'Hey, I ain't joking, Stanley,' she hissed. 'We're freaks.'

'But you don't feel that way, do you?'

This she had to agree with. The last few days, try as she

might to worry herself with the knowledge that she was home to an alien entity, she couldn't get worked up about it. If it had been threadworms or lice or a cancer, then her flesh would have crawled, but this simply didn't have the same effect. In fact it made no difference. Perhaps that was part of their deal: keep you healthy, endow you with self-defence skills they don't teach in China, and then give you what? *Acceptance?* Maybe it *was* like cancer after all, that calm people find when they've gone through all other emotions: with death inevitable they accept their fate and become relaxed, serene. Well, she didn't feel serene, but she sure as hell felt good.

Stanley was still thinking about why he believed Drexill would keep his word about leaving the two of them alone.

'I got the impression Drexill felt he owed our "guests" something after all the killings,' he said. 'A peace offering maybe. I don't know . . . just be grateful. And *relax*.'

'Oh, I am grateful,' Cheryl said, sitting back. 'I feel fine. Like a motel.'

Stanley knew she was kidding, and the two of them laughed.

'How much is this ID going to cost?'

'Ah, well, that's the bad news. Two thousand dollars.'

'Two grand?'

'Each.'

'I haven't got two *hundred* left – and I doubt they'll be letting me have my Corvette back to trade in.'

'Hardly. And all my stuff's gone,' said Stanley glumly.

'You'd think they could have given us something.'

'They gave you your lives,' said Dinkley. 'Don't know how much they're worth, but I'd say it was a damn sight more than any 'Vette or one-bed apartment.'

'Wise words from a man with one lung who still smokes,' said Stanley supping his coffee and watching as Sam played with his empty briar.

'So how do we get the cash?' said Cheryl.

'Sam's got it all figured.'

'Yeah. The *Oracle* needs to move with the times, get all its back issues on microfiche or disk. Stanley here knows about computers—'

'I'm a computer operator, not an expert.'

'Can I finish? I'll pay Stanley to sort it out, and he can pay me back out of his wages – say a hundred a week.'

'Pay back a hundred a week?'

'No, that's his wages.'

Cheryl stared at him. 'You cheeky—'

'Plus he gets free board up to the Pacific View. It'll soon be off-season and Harriet owes me a favour or two, not least the free write-ups she gets in our tourist specials.'

'Well, that's Stanley taken care of. What about me?'

'The free room offer stands for you too. As for a job, we'll probably be able to fix something up. Six months we'll be fair and square, and you can get on with your lives.'

'*Six months?*' said Cheryl. 'That's so . . .'

'After what we've been through,' pointed out Stanley, 'it'll be a vacation. Besides, I've got a feeling our little friends inside will be more than happy if we stick to the quiet life.'

She held his hand and stared at him. 'A quiet *long* life.'

'You won't get bored?' he said. *Lovely eyes*, he thought.

'With what?' she said, then reached over and kissed him full on the lips, a show of affection that quickly became an intimate kiss that drew *tuts* and *whoops* from their fellow diners in equal measure.

Dinkley eventually coughed them apart. 'Hey, enough of the tonsil hockey.'

Cheryl and Stanley looked sheepish – and flushed – but continued to eye each other. Finally Cheryl spoke up.

'I know what you'd see if you tried to kill me. I think I can guess what I'd see now if I tried to kill *you*.'

Stanley offered her a tableknife. 'Want to prove it?'

'Oh, there are much nicer ways of proving it.'

Stanley looked at her, then leaned over to Dinkley. 'How long a drive is it back to Gudgen?'

'Fast or slow?' he asked.

Cheryl tapped her forehead. 'I bet, no matter what we want, it turns out to be a real slow and careful drive.'

'I am convinced that UFOs exist – because I have seen one. It was big, it was very bright, it changed colours, and it was about the size of the moon. We watched it for about ten minutes but none of us could figure out what it was.'

JIMMY CARTER, *former US President*

All Pan Books are available at your local bookshop or newsagent, or can be ordered direct from the publisher. Indicate the number of copies required and fill in the form below.

Send to: Macmillan General Books C.S.
Book Service By Post
PO Box 29, Douglas I-O-M
IM99 1BQ

or phone: 01624 675137, quoting title, author and credit card number.

or fax: 01624 670923, quoting title, author, and credit card number.

or Internet: http://www.bookpost.co.uk

Please enclose a remittance* to the value of the cover price plus 75 pence per book for post and packing. Overseas customers please allow £1.00 per copy for post and packing.

*Payment may be made in sterling by UK personal cheque, Eurocheque, postal order, sterling draft or international money order, made payable to Book Service By Post.

Alternatively by Access/Visa/MasterCard

Card No. | | | | | | | | | | | | | | | | |

Expiry Date | | | | | | | | | | | | | | | | |

Signature ____________________

Applicable only in the UK and BFPO addresses.

While every effort is made to keep prices low, it is sometimes necessary to increase prices at short notice. Pan Books reserve the right to show on covers and charge new retail prices which may differ from those advertised in the text or elsewhere.

NAME AND ADDRESS IN BLOCK CAPITAL LETTERS PLEASE

Name ____________________

Address ____________________

____

____

____

8/95

Please allow 28 days for delivery.
Please tick box if you do not wish to receive any additional information. ☐